# THE STIEHL ASSASSIN

# THE FALL OF
# SHANNARA

# TERRY
# BROOKS

## THE STIEHL ASSASSIN

orbit

www.orbitbooks.net

ORBIT

First published in Great Britain in 2019 by Orbit

1 3 5 7 9 10 8 6 4 2

A CIP catalogue record for this book
is available from the British Library.

HB ISBN 978-0-356-51024-8
C format 978-0-356-51022-4

Printed and bound in Great Britain by
Clays Ltd, Elcograf S.p.A.

Papers used by Orbit are from well-managed forests
and other responsible sources.

Orbit
An imprint of
Little, Brown Book Group
Carmelite House
50 Victoria Embankment
London EC4Y 0DZ

An Hachette UK Company
www.hachette.co.uk

www.orbitbooks.net

*Hunter Brooks Alba,*
*As Grandsons Go, He's Got The Right Stuff.*

# I

A WINTER TABLEAU, STARK AND COMPELLING.
Not a hundred yards from the west gates of the fortress walls of Paranor, a small clearing is revealed within the giant old growth, barely visible through the curtain of new snowfall. An earlier snow leaves the clearing and the surrounding forest in a foot-deep covering of white. Darkness no longer shrouds the world, as the night has diminished and the first glimmerings of dawn have surfaced on the distant horizon.

All is silent in the forest; birds and animals alike have gone still.

All is sleep-claimed and frozen in place; there is an unnatural feeling to the air as Tavo Kaynin staggers forward, thrown off balance by the force of his thrust.

He has slipped from hiding, crept up on his sister from behind, bearing in his hand the legendary blade known as the Stiehl, and has driven it through her back. The killing blow is the culmination of a journey he has pursued since he decided that she betrayed him through abandonment and neglect and therefore must die. The satisfaction he feels when he strikes her down is immense, a release of pent-up frustration and rage that has haunted him for weeks. Here, at last, is an end to it. Here, at last, is the revenge he has been seeking.

Yet even as he revels in his success, he experiences an unexpected *sense of loss. His sister is the last of his family, the last connection to anything from his old life, and a sudden welling-up of doubt and deep mistrust of his own feelings infuses him. By killing her, he brings about a desperately needed resolution to his madness. Or does he? What has he truly done?*

*A split second later, his feelings are scattered to the winds blowing softly around him.*

*Something is wrong, he realizes.*

*His weapon and arm have both passed completely through her body, have found no substance but only empty air. He staggers off balance now as a result, his momentum unhindered by his anticipated encounter with flesh and blood—by a solidity he should have found from driving his knife into her body. Instead, she is no longer even in evidence—she has vanished entirely—and he realizes instantly that he is mistaken about everything.*

*"Stand where you are!" Drisker Arc hisses as he wheels toward Tavo.*

*Tavo tries to regain his feet and flee, but the Druid is already on top of him, his hands fastening about his arm, wrenching it so violently that the Stiehl drops into the snow and disappears. At the same time, he sees that his sister stands to the other side of the Druid, unharmed and watching in shock.*

*He has been tricked.*

*He responds instinctively, lashing out at the Druid and his sister and their two companions—the Blade and the Elven prince—summoning the magic of his wishsong. But his voice is stilled before any sound can gather sufficient force to save him. He manages but one small croak before the Druid has hold of his throat and has closed off his windpipe. Air wheezes from his lungs, but it is not nearly enough to do more than produce a truncated gasp. He thrashes and squirms in his captor's grip, but he cannot break free.*

*Everything begins to go black.*

*"Dar Leah!" the Druid calls out sharply, and the Blade is there instantly. "Take him from me."*

*Tavo is gripped immediately by new hands and pulled down into the snow. A blade presses up against his throat, the sharp edge cut-*

ting into his skin. *The implication is clear. If he moves, he will die. He sees how matters stand, and while a fresh wave of rage and frustration surges through him, he knows better than to test that blade. He goes limp in those strong hands and hopes that Clizia will save him.*

Drisker has placed himself in front of Tarsha, and the Elven prince has moved up beside him. Together, they present a wall of defense against whatever Clizia Porse might choose to do. *It seems to Tavo that she will choose to do nothing but will instead disappear back into the night. Why shouldn't she? Tavo would, if their places were reversed. He has failed her completely. He has disobeyed her instructions to kill the Druid first and Tarsha after, and as a result he has been defeated entirely. The Druid witch is a demanding mistress and she will see him as both an ineffective and an unnecessary ally. She will not risk herself further.*

*His head sinks in despair.*

*Moments pass, and nothing happens.* She is already gone, *he thinks. The clearing has turned silent with fresh expectation, the snowfall growing heavier and the dawn's light fading back into deepest gray as a result. Breath from those gathered about him clouds the air in white puffs, and a small shifting of bodies provides the only evidence that all is not frozen solid.*

"Nothing," Brecon Elessedil whispers finally.

Drisker Arc contradicts him at once. "She is here."

*The truth is quick to show itself as the words leave his lips. A massive wind arises out of nowhere, surging through the little clearing, emerging from the woods with rage and purpose, whipping against the poised figures with such violence that they stagger back several steps in response to the battering, ducking their heads protectively. The darkness deepens and the howling of the sudden wind reaches an ear-shattering crescendo.*

She comes for me, *Tavo thinks, elated.*

*But the blade still presses up against his neck, and his magic still will not respond to his efforts to summon it, so his own attempts to free himself fail as the hands of his captor tighten further.*

*Shadows gather and close around him, and the Druid makes ward-*

ing gestures that summon blue lines of magic to pulse and shimmer against the dark. The little company huddles watchfully in the teeth of the wind, keeping one another and Tavo close, letting no one come at them unexpectedly.

Then finally the Elf brings out his talismanic stones, and light flashes out into the woods. Drisker comes to his feet, prepared to lash out, but the Elfstones find nothing of Clizia close by, their brightness ending not two dozen feet into the gloom. An instant later the wind dies, the shadows disappear, and the world returns to what it was in the early-dawn light.

"She's gone," Brecon announces.

"For now, yes," the Druid agrees. "She has hidden herself to prevent us from finding her. This magic is ancient and strong enough even to thwart the Elfstones. Very rare."

They all rise, the Blade dragging Tavo up with him. They all stand together to look off into the forest, making sure they are not mistaken. But the silence of the forest is deep and unbroken; Clizia Porse has fled.

"What was that about?" the Blade asks.

Tavo Kaynin is wondering the same thing.

"Whatever it was, it failed," the Elf offers, kicking snow from his boots.

Next to them, Tavo is aware that Tarsha is looking over at him, and he cannot bring himself to meet her gaze. He is unable to face what he knows he will see in her eyes. Enraged as he is by his failure to kill her, he is also unexpectedly ashamed that he even thought to try. A new consciousness is seeping through him—one that is making him question everything he believed was true. Fluken is nowhere to be found, his voice stilled. All his advice now seems empty and self-serving. If Fluken were truly a friend, he would be there to help Tavo. He would be standing by Tavo as he has repeatedly claimed he would. But Fluken does not live up to his promises. He flees with the witch, a faithless liar.

"She did not fail," Drisker says suddenly, breaking the silence. He is nudging the snow in front of him with his boot. "She did exactly what she intended to."

He kneels down and musses the snow about with his gloved hand for a moment, then looks up. "She regained the Stiehl."

• • •

Once they had allowed his words to sink in and come to terms with the implications, they discussed briefly what to do next. There were choices aplenty—all of them worthy, but many contradictory.

"We should find her and put an end to her," Brecon Elessedil declared. "She cannot have gotten far, and we have the means of tracking her down. She is too dangerous to be allowed to survive. Look how much trouble she has made already. She trapped Drisker in Paranor and left him to die. She stole the Stiehl and gave it to Tarsha's brother so that he would kill her. And she seeks far more than that, unless I am misguided."

"You are not," Drisker replied with a deep sigh. "She seeks to rebuild the Druid order in her own image, with herself as Ard Rhys. She will use whatever means she can to achieve this, and we know now that she had some sort of alliance with the Skaar that was meant to further her plans. But she is not our primary concern, as dangerous as she clearly is. Our primary concern is with the coming war between the Skaar and the people of the Four Lands. We already know what the Skaar are capable of doing, and their behavior suggests they are here to find a home for their people at the very least, and perhaps to subjugate the entire Four Lands at the worst. Do I have it right, Dar Leah? You seem to know the most about this."

Dar hesitated. He knew considerably more than they did thanks to his conversations with Ajin d'Amphere—more than any of them could have guessed. Mostly, he had kept what he knew about her—and what she had revealed in their unexpected meeting after Paranor's return—to himself. During their journey to save the Keep and its Druids, he had revealed to Drisker the details of his two brief encounters with Ajin d'Amphere, both of which took place before he even knew who she was. While Drisker was locked away, they had encountered each other a third time, and on that occasion she had revealed both her identity and the purpose of the Skaar invasion. Most of this, he had imparted to Brecon Elessedil. But even then he could not be certain how much she revealed was the truth and how much was not. He thought he understood something more of her motivations, and if he was right they confirmed what Drisker had always suspected. But even after both Brecon and he had come face-to-face with the Skaar princess in Arborlon—following her bold attempt to persuade the prince's father to ally the Elven nation to the Skaar in an effort to hold off the Federation—he had held back the more personal nature of Ajin's interest in him. He kept thinking it was either a whim or an attempt at subterfuge; he found it hard to believe that she was truly as interested in him as she professed.

Of one thing, he *was* certain. Where Ajin d'Amphere was concerned, you could never be certain of anything—and he was not convinced he knew all that much about her even now.

He shook his head. "She said the Skaar came here to establish a new homeland. Yet my senses say—and I think Brecon will agree—that she loves to play games and seems intent on pitting each Race in the Four Lands against the others. She was in some way allied with Clizia, which allowed her to gain entrance into Paranor and slaughter the Druids. When Clizia banished Paranor from the land, she then sought an alliance with the Elves. But I'm still not sure what she really wants."

*Except perhaps where I am concerned. And can I believe even that is real?*

Tarsha stepped forward. "I know you have much more important things to consider, but I have my brother back, and for that, Drisker, I will always be grateful. You saved my life when he would have taken it, and you found a way to subdue him. Maybe this will give me a chance to help Tavo."

The Druid shook his head dismissively. "I merely responded when my senses warned me. I knew what he was about."

He paused. "Or did I?"

He turned to Tavo, hunched over and shivering to one side of the Blade. "Dar," he said. "Find wood and build us a fire. We are freezing out here, and there is no reason to fear any further attacks from Clizia just now. Brecon, perhaps you can help."

He did not make it sound like anything more than a request, but there was an emphasis to his words that sent both men moving away and into the trees in search of deadwood. "Tarsha, come close," he told her.

Dar Leah gave Tavo Kaynin over to Drisker and departed the clearing with Brecon on his heels, wondering what was about to happen.

Drisker waited for Tarsha to approach, beckoning her closer when she hesitated. He forced Tavo to his knees, then placed both big hands on the girl's shoulders. "We have a decision to make, and we must not make it lightly. I think you know that your brother is still a danger to both himself and us. And I think you know that his problems are not going to go away without a good bit of healing, and I don't know that we have time to give it to him."

"I have time," she said at once.

"Not so. You cannot be with him as he is, and we cannot spare the time he needs. Nor can he be left where Clizia can find him again—especially now that she has the Stiehl back. It would be kinder and quicker to put an end to your brother right now."

He saw the startled look in her eyes and put a finger to her lips. "Say nothing yet. Only hear me out. I said it might be quicker and kinder, but it is not what we are going to do. We are going to keep him with us, and we are going to give you a chance to help him. But you must agree that you and he will remain with us, that you will come with us and do what is needed to help the Four Lands and her people, and that you will pledge to fulfill your promise to serve as my student for the agreed-upon time. We, in turn, will see to it that Tavo gets as much help as we can manage to give him."

She took a deep breath and exhaled slowly. "Perhaps we should take him to the Stors for care."

"Perhaps, but they do not treat emotional and psychological dysfunction. They treat physical ailments and injuries and have no expertise in treating mental disorders. Besides, he is entirely too dangerous to be around anyone save you and me. You know that, don't you?"

She nodded. "He is too dangerous for me, too," she whispered. "How can I ask you to keep him with us?"

"You don't have to. I am offering." He took his hands away and straightened. "A few adjustments will be necessary to make this work.

I will do so, but I need you to leave me for now. Go into the woods with Dar and Brecon and keep them company. I want you all to stay away until I call you."

She glanced over quickly at Tavo, who was looking at her now with a gaze that said he was both beaten and defeated. "You won't—"

"Tarsha," he said, interrupting her quickly. "I mean him no harm. He has been ill-used since setting out to find you. Yes, he has killed men and destroyed property, but he has suffered abuse that no one survives unscathed. He has been a damaged creature for many years, if what I have been given to understand is true, so he responds in the only way his mind will allow him to. He cannot reason as you and I can. He cannot see the difference between right and wrong. Not yet. But he can be made to see. He can be made to come to terms with how his mind works."

She brushed back loose strands of her white-blond hair where the wind had blown them across her face. "I wish that for him. I wish he could be made to understand."

"Then go, Tarsha. Leave me to do what I must to begin his healing, and come back only when you are summoned. Will you do that?"

She was already turning away. "That and much more, if it will help my brother. Thank you, Drisker, for all you are doing for him. But I will not hold you to more than that. I will not blame you if you fail."

She walked from the clearing and into the shadows of the trees beyond, fading into the mist.

*But I will blame myself,* Drisker thought, keeping the words to himself.

# 2

DRISKER ARC WAS NOT AT ALL SURE HE WAS MAKing the right decision, but having settled on it, he was determined to follow through. He moved back over to Tavo Kaynin, who had slumped to the ground, head lowered, shoulders hunched. He knelt next to Tarsha's brother and lifted his head by his chin so that their eyes met.

"You know what I should do with you, don't you?" he asked softly.

Tavo nodded, his gaze averted.

"Look at me!" Drisker demanded.

He waited until the other did, letting Tavo see the cold fury that burned in his eyes.

"But that isn't what's going to happen, Tavo. You are going to live because your sister loves you—and because she has pleaded for your life. She thinks you are a good man somewhere deep inside, and that, with time and effort, you can rid yourself of the creature you have become. I am more doubtful, but I think Tarsha deserves the chance she seeks. So no one is going to hurt you."

He paused. "On the other hand, you are not going to be allowed to hurt anyone else. So what shall we do with you? We must keep you with us, but we must watch you constantly. We will allow you to be a

part of our company and share in our efforts to save the Four Lands—
not that you care about any of this just now, but you will."

"She . . . left me," Tavo croaked weakly, his voice carrying no more
than a glimmer of the strength it had possessed earlier. "She abandoned me."

Drisker bent close. "If you mean Tarsha, you are mistaken. She left
to find help for you, and she succeeded. *I* am that help. If you mean
that poisonous witch Clizia Porse, you are correct. She cast you away
the moment you became useless to her. You have been her tool all
along. She crafted you into a killing weapon using the dark magic of
that blade, and sent you to kill your sister for reasons . . ."

He paused. Tavo was shaking his head in disagreement. "She . . .
told me to . . . kill you. You were the one . . . she wanted dead. I disobeyed. I wanted . . . to kill Tarsha . . . not you. That's . . . what I
meant."

Drisker nodded slowly. There was hope yet, if Tavo was seeing
that much clearly. "Now you know, then, what you were worth to her.
She would never have helped you unless it served her own interests.
But your sister? Tarsha would help you in any way she could. She
believes in you. Are you worth believing in?"

Tavo shook his head once more. "I . . . don't think so."

"Are you willing to help her prove you wrong?"

A nod, but no further words.

"Then this is what is going to happen. I am going to restore your
voice, but you are not going to be able to use your magic again without my permission. You will have to prove yourself in order for that
permission to be granted—and that may not happen for a long time.
You will be one of us, but you will be given no weapons. You will
travel where we decide and do only what we tell you to do. If you try
to run away, you will be returned. If you try to hurt any of us, you
can expect to be punished. No exceptions. You will talk with Tarsha
when she asks you to, and if she chooses to speak to you about what
happened when you were sent to your uncle, you will answer. And
you will listen to what she says. You will be her patient and she will
try to heal you."

Tavo's eyes were blank, and his expression was vacant. It was difficult for Drisker to tell if he understood what he was being told or not. But he did not harbor a great deal of hope that Tavo, once he was feeling stronger, would remain this docile.

Drisker pulled him up so that their faces were only inches apart. "If I find that you are deceiving me—even in the smallest of matters— the kindness I am extending you will end. You can imagine the rest. Do we have an understanding?"

A nod.

"Say the words. Make the promise."

"I . . . understand."

Drisker studied his face carefully, and then set him back on the ground. "If you are lying to me, I will kill you."

He pulled from his pocket a long strand of polished wire and began to burnish it with his fingers, whispering words and chanting softly as he did so. The wire began to glow with a soft bluish light, and heat began to radiate from its surface. Magic filled the air—a pungent smell that caused Tavo to shrink back and squeeze his eyes closed in response. The Druid ignored him, working the wire, smoothing and polishing it until it shone a brilliant silver and small markings began to appear.

"Come alive, precious thing," he whispered. And the wire began to writhe and twist in his fingers.

He worked it for almost an hour—a slow and arduous effort that left him sweating within his robes. But he did not desist or slacken, keeping a steady pace. To Tavo, he gave no thought, unworried that he might bolt or attack him or otherwise misbehave; he had seen it in Tavo's eyes when he had warned him. For now, there would be no foolish acts.

The time crept by, but Tarsha and the others stayed away as he had directed, leaving him alone with his work. The fine wire—part of a string drawn from a metal created centuries ago and housed in the Druid archives—continued to gain strength and brilliance, lengthening now as well as softening, steadily becoming close to a living presence. The day was advancing, but a wintry gloom persisted and the air did not warm. All around him lay the snowfall, a white covering over limbs and trunks, over ground and brush, soft and feathery. The forest was still. No animals asserted their presence, and no birds flew or sang.

The world felt hushed and waiting, invisible eyes watching.

When he had finished working the wire to his satisfaction, it had become less round and more flat. The runes he had summoned earlier had become deeply etched on both sides and still glowed with silvery light. He wound it twice about itself, then turned to Tavo.

"Lean forward," he ordered.

The young man did, with no hesitation or reluctance, either too beaten down to resist or perhaps sensing in some way that the Druid meant to help him, after all. Drisker placed the doubled length of metal about Tavo's neck and pressed with his fingers to seal the ends together. Magic flared briefly as the bonding was achieved, and then it was done.

Drisker sat back and nodded approvingly. "Sit up straight and look at me."

Tavo did so—his eyes focused now, his gaze clear. He started to reach for the band about his neck, but Drisker stopped him with a word.

"No."

Tavo drew back his hands instantly, waiting on the Druid. "The collar remains on, Tavo," Drisker said. "It is an inhibitor. It will prevent you from attempting to use your voice to summon the wishsong's magic. If you violate that prohibition, the pain you will experience will be an excruciating reminder to not try again. That said, you now have your voice back and can speak in a normal way."

Drisker rose, leaving him where he was, and summoned the others with a quick call. When he glanced back at Tavo, the young man was still sitting where Drisker had left him.

"Get up," Drisker ordered. "There's nothing wrong with you now. Say something. Let's see if I am right about your voice."

"I can feel the difference. My voice is fine."

Drisker was already turning away. Easy to fix his voice, but his mind was another thing entirely.

•  •  •

Tarsha had walked from the clearing in a state of uncertainty, leaving her brother behind with Drisker Arc. It was difficult to do so, imagining what sorts of things the Druid might have planned once she was out of sight. She was aware that Drisker did not think it a good idea to keep her brother around, even given her insistence that she must do something to help him. She was also aware that all three men would have preferred Tavo out of the picture completely. (She could not bring herself to use the word *dead*.) None of them liked or trusted her brother, and she could hardly blame them for it. Nevertheless, he *was* her brother and the only family she had left. And she couldn't help seeing him as the older brother she'd looked up to in their early years, before the wishsong had begun to manifest in either of them.

But she trusted Drisker, and if he said no harm would come to Tavo while she was gone, she would take him at his word.

She took her time finding Dar and Brecon, slowing noticeably as a new realization dawned on her—one unrelated to her concerns about her brother. It had been days since she had given any thought to Parlindru and her strange predictions of Tarsha's future. The seer had made a strong impression on her, coming and going as she did without anyone seeing her. She was a calming presence, and her words were burned deep into Tarsha's memory—especially those three predictions about the future.

But it was this one that returned to her now: *Three times shall you die, but each death shall see you rise anew.*

Was this not what had just happened? Tavo had come to kill her and he had thought his efforts successful until he discovered that Drisker had tricked him, moving Tarsha aside while leaving a clear image for her brother to attack. In essence, she *had* died and risen anew. If not in the literal sense, then surely in the abstract.

Oddly, this didn't trouble her any more than did the prediction that she would love three times but only one would last. She had given little thought to any of Parlindru's predictions because, after all, what good would it do? If the predictions were to come true, they were inevitable events and all she could do was await their coming. Perhaps her love for Tavo was one of three. Perhaps her deep affection for Drisker was a second. The third remained a mystery, but not a troubling one. She did pause to think what it meant that she might die twice more and rise each time, but she still thought it best to let this be. Better to let go of what you could not control and worry about what you could.

Stealing through the forest shadows, she picked up her pace and quickly found her companions, arms full of firewood as they continued to gather fuel for their fire. She was reminded again of how cold she was, and she hoped Drisker would summon them back soon so they could get warm. The day was brightening further now, the gloom pushed back a bit even within the heavy old growth, so a bit of the chill had gone out of the air.

She told Dar and Brecon what Drisker had asked of them and why, and after a quick exchange of glances, both set down their wood and stood with her as they waited for the Druid's summons.

"So he thinks to keep your brother with us?" Brecon asked after a moment, the disbelief in his voice evident.

Tarsha nodded. "He is committed to it. I suggested it might be best if he leaves Tavo with me and goes on with the rest of you, but I think he worries that Tavo would be too much for me—even though he says the reason has more to do with Clizia Porse."

"It might be some of each," Dar said. He was rubbing his arms to generate some warmth within his heavy cloak. "Or even something we haven't thought about. He is a Druid, remember, even now. And Druids are all the same in that they dissemble and conceal as a matter of course. His reasons are his own, and he will keep them that way."

"But what can he do if he keeps Tavo with us?" Brecon asked, stamping his feet, his breath clouding the air. "How will he protect you, Tarsha, when he must reason with a twisted mind?"

She winced inwardly at those last words but kept her expression neutral. The Elven prince was simply expressing a concern for her safety, not making a judgment. "I don't know," she admitted. "But he seemed to have something specific in mind."

Brecon made a disgruntled sound. "Doesn't he always?"

Dar Leah shook his head slowly. "Not always. And perhaps not so much now as before he went into Paranor. He does not seem quite the same man to me as he was before being trapped inside."

"I sense that, too," Tarsha said. "I know it might be odd, but it feels to me as if he has been softened by whatever happened to him in there. His edges seem blunted, his temper and his darkness less severe."

"But he is more intense, too. More focused on his commitment to the Druid order. Before, he walked away from the Druids, gave up his position as Ard Rhys, and retired to Emberen without once looking back. If not for the Skaar invasion, he would still be in self-imposed exile. But now I sense a renewed purpose in him, a determination to embrace his role as Druid once more. When there is time, I want to ask him what exactly he endured in exile and how he finally managed to bring Paranor back into the Four Lands."

"It could not have been a simple thing," Tarsha agreed quickly. "He must have gone through some sort of catharsis to bring about the Keep's return. When he first came to me while I was with Clizia and not yet aware of what she intended for me, he was distraught and despairing of his future. He did not seem to know what to do to escape his fate. There was a sadness to him then that is now gone. Something happened to him in Paranor, and I think it was more than finding a way to get free."

They stood silently for a time, trying various ways to stay warm, thinking over the mystery of Drisker and Paranor's emergence from limbo. Tarsha believed that the Druid was clearly a stronger person now, and that whatever was to happen to him, it would not include running away once again to Emberen. That part of his life was over.

She hoped that this new commitment she sensed in him included a renewed dedication to teaching her how to use her magic. He had reminded her that she was still his student, and still beholden to serve him for the time she had promised, so she had reason to hope her lessons would continue even in the face of all else that was happening.

"You should return to Arborlon, Brec," Dar said suddenly. "None of this is your problem. You've done your part by using the Elfstones to get us this far. You don't owe us anything more."

Brecon nodded. "You could make that argument. But maybe I do owe something to the Elves and to myself when it comes to Ajin d'Amphere and the Skaar. They aren't going to vanish on their own, and we both know that the Four Lands remain in danger as a result. I'm not my father. I'm not interested in sitting back in the safe haven of Arborlon while the rest of the Four Lands falls to pieces."

"No one is suggesting that you should," the Blade assured him quickly. "But your mother is going to wonder what has become of you, and sooner or later your father is going to find out the Elfstones are missing and know who took them. You could put all that right by leaving now and going home."

"What, and abandon my duties as a protector of Tarsha Kaynin?" He feigned indignation. "I think not! She may need me to carry her to safety again before things are fully settled."

For a second, Tarsha was furious at the idea she needed looking after in any way at all, but then she realized she had heard something unexpected in the Elf's voice. He wasn't complaining. He was expressing an unexpected interest in her—one that hinted of attraction. Within the covering of her cloak's cowl, she blushed in spite of herself.

"You are rather good at spiriting beautiful maidens from danger," Dar Leah acknowledged with a laugh. "Maybe that's your real calling. You seem up to the task."

"Enough already," Tarsha interjected, frowning at them. "I am already in Brecon's debt and do not think to impose further. I can look after myself."

After that, the conversation died away. Tarsha was still getting used to the idea that the Elven prince might find her attractive when Drisker's call reached them. *Foolishness,* she thought. *Attraction has no place in my life.* Joining the other two in picking up the fallen firewood, she hurried back through the forest to see what had become of her brother.

# 3

SHEA OHMSFORD WAS SWIFTLY COMING TO TERMS
with how hard it was going to be to rescue Tindall from Assidian Deep. It was somewhere after midnight, but he could
not be certain of how much. He had been maneuvering his way
through the sewage ducts of the prison for what felt like hours. Inside
those metal tunnels, it was impossible to tell if it was day or night.

It was a prison all its own.

Shea was not happy about his role—and less so once Rocan Arneas had advised him of what he was going to have to do even to
reach the cell where Tindall was imprisoned. Assidian Deep was a
dark, monstrous tomb, a Federation disposal system for those who
had transgressed in the worst of ways or fallen so far out of favor with
those in power that there was no coming back. Entering it under any
circumstances was bad, but entering it through the sewage ducts was
almost unbearable.

Still, Shea had reached the nineteenth floor, where Tindall was
supposedly held, before real trouble surfaced.

He had just removed an iron grate that barred his way down the
duct he needed to follow when he heard something approaching. It
was a mechanical sound—a whisking, whirring, scraping sound—so
it wasn't difficult to guess that it was a scrubber. Rocan had said that

they would all be shut down for the night. But given the way every-thing connected with this endeavor had gone so far, Shea was not surprised to discover that someone had apparently forgotten to hit the off switch on at least one of the things. He hesitated a moment, debating whether to go back. Perhaps if he retreated down the ladder to the next level, the scrubber would turn around and go back the other way. But as he needed to be in this very tunnel to find Tindall, he'd then be left following behind a live scrubber, and that idea cer-tainly held little appeal.

If it even was a scrubber. Maybe there was something else wander-ing about in here. Maybe he was mistaken about it being a scrubber.

But he wasn't.

The machine slipped into view: a horrific assemblage of append-ages ending in scrapers and wheels churning with gears that drove the metal beast inexorably forward. Shea knew at once that there was no getting past something that filled the duct system as completely as this did. Those arms moved up and down against the walls and ceiling and its squat body rolled flat against the floor, metal brushes working hard to loosen debris and waste.

Shea backed away quickly. His better judgment told him to get down the ladder as fast as he could and wait for the scrubber to turn around. Or even to go back to Rocan and attempt a different ap-proach, if that's what it came to.

Then an unexpected idea occurred to him, and he looked down at the substance he still held in his hand: the leather wrapping with the corrosive clay. What would happen if those damp, grimy wheels rolled over a clump of this?

He flattened a wad and stuck it on the floor directly in the path of the scrubber. Then he hastily spat on the clay and ducked down the ladder as the substance flared and dissolved into a puddle of acid. He didn't want to be in the vicinity when the scrubber encountered the acid. That is, if it didn't eat through the stone floor of the tunnel first. But there were not a lot of options left.

There he hung, waiting breathlessly. He did not have to wait long. After only a few seconds, gears and wheels lost their rhythm and began to clunk and grind with a clear indication of damage. Cautiously, Shea climbed back up to where he could peek over the edge of the duct and look down its length. The scrubber was now a mostly inert mass of half-dissolved metal. It was jerking in distress, and some of the undissolved appendages on top were still moving, but slowly the substance was doing its work.

Yet would it be enough?

Shea watched for an anxious moment, but then the acid must have penetrated to the mechanical heart of the beast, for it stopped shuddering and went still. Its undercarriage had dissolved enough to leave a boy-sized gap between its back and the tunnel roof. Still, forcing himself over its humped top and through that deadly tangle of frozen limbs—all while avoiding the acid that continued to eat away at its undercarriage—was one of the hardest things he had ever done.

There was a moment when it shifted beneath him, one of its outstretched arms brushing his cheek, and he was certain it would come to life again and shred him. But then he was up and over, and fleeing down the tunnel, hoping he had seen the last of the scrubbers for this lifetime.

His progress now was much quicker and surer; no further obstacles impeded his way, and nothing emerged from the gloom to challenge him. Partway along, he found the nineteenth-floor access hatch just where Rocan's map had said it would be: a six-rung steel ladder embedded in the rock leading up to it. If there were to be problems, this was where he was likely to find them—right on the other side of that hatch. He climbed the ladder carefully, trying to muffle his movements, and when he reached the trapdoor he gave it a gentle nudge. It resisted his efforts momentarily and then gave way. Keeping tight hold of the circular handle at the top of the door, he raised it all the way, climbed another step, poked his head out, and looked around.

A long corridor of rough stone stretched away in both directions, disappearing into gloom. The walls were unbroken barriers save where heavy metal doors were embedded in metal frames, their surfaces dusty and old and worn, smooth except for a small metal slide that served as a peephole for viewing whoever was locked within. More than that, Shea couldn't tell from where he was. His directions showed Tindall's cell marked with an X and the number 1935 written next to it. If he assumed 19 was the floor, then he should be looking for cell 35.

But in which direction should he go—left or right? He shook his head in disgust, a mouse measuring its chances of avoiding the cat once it left its bolt-hole.

He hesitated a moment longer, wanting to be sure of what he was doing, and then levered himself through the trapdoor and into the gloom-filled corridor above. Keeping tight hold of the handle, he gently lowered the door back into place.

And immediately heard the sound of something coming.

Panic set in, worse than with the scrubber. At least that would have been a hasty death. If he were caught here, he would live out the rest of his days behind one of these metal doors: a slow, agonizing, *living* death. There was nowhere to go, nowhere to hide. He instinctively turned away from the sounds approaching and went up the hall the other way. He kept his footfalls light and smooth, forcing himself to remember that any noise at all would give him away. He glanced at the numbers on the cell doors as he went: 19 . . . 20 . . . 21 . . . Okay, right direction, then. But what good would that do him if he was found and trapped out here?

*A hiding place! I need a hiding place!*

As if in answer to his plea, one appeared. A cell door on his left stood slightly ajar. Without even stopping to consider whether this was a good idea or not, he slipped inside and closed the door so that it almost latched. Then he backed himself against the door to one side so that anyone looking through the peephole slider wouldn't be able to see him.

The sounds drew closer.

*Scrape. Scrape. Scrape.*

Somehow the scraping made things even worse. Whatever was out there was not walking as a human would. The sounds were irregular, a dragging of metal on stone. He closed his eyes in dismay.

Why had he ever let himself get into this? What was he thinking to come into this forbidden place—this tomb from which no one ever returned?

He started making bargains with himself. If he got out of this, he would extricate himself from Rocan Arneas's clutches once and for all. He would turn his back on Arishaig and flee. He would not even think about the credits he was losing. He would forget the promises of a bright future. He would never do something this stupid again.

*Scrape. Scrape. Scrape.*

Then the scraping stopped. Right outside his door. The peephole slider opened to permit whatever was outside a view into the cell. Shea pressed up against the wall and closed his eyes. Then opened them as he heard the door nudge open slightly, a few inches, no more.

A long pause. Intense silence settled over everything. Shea tried not to breathe.

Then the slider abruptly closed, the door was pulled shut, and the lock engaged.

Shea felt his heart stop. He was trapped.

For an instant, he panicked—remembering his thoughts of a living death while out in the corridor. He tried the door, but it would not open; there was no give at all. He had no way to contact Rocan from up here. There was no one save Rocan who knew he was here, and no one who could help him now. He had let this happen by making a bad choice and now he was . . .

He caught himself. What was he thinking? A wave of disgust swept through him. He was supposed to be smarter than this. Of course he could get out. He had let himself panic for no reason!

He reached into his pocket and pulled out the corrosive clay. Between the unexpected grate and the live scrubber, he had already used more than he was supposed to, but there might still be enough left to free himself from this cell and Tindall from his after. A small amount on each lock should do the trick, while leaving enough for Tindall's window bars. He could still do what he had set out to do.

He opened the leather and measured what remained of his store of clay. Enough, he decided. He placed a wad of the clay where the lock secured to the door, spit on it, and jumped back. Immediately the metal began to steam and foam and finally just melt away, and the door was open. He held it in place a moment, listening for sounds of the scraping creature, then opened the door and peered out.

No one in sight.

He felt a fresh urgency to reach Tindall and get them both free before anything further happened. He stepped through the cell door and pulled it closed again, then quickly made his way down the hall toward cell 1935. When he found it, not all that far ahead, he pressed himself flat against the door and listened. Hearing nothing, he looked up and down the corridor, peering into the cavernous gloom, afraid he would draw the attention of that creature once again.

He slid back the peephole cover and peered inside. The gloom was marginally lightened by a wash of gray light that spilled through a barred window on the back wall. It illuminated almost nothing, and Shea could not even tell if the cell was occupied.

Another glance to be sure no one was coming, and then he pressed his mouth against the opening. "Tindall? Are you in there?" he whispered.

Nothing. He waited a moment.

A sharper whisper now: "Tindall! Answer me!"

A rustling this time—someone moving about. A voice, cracked and ragged, answered. "Who's there? What do you want?"

"I'm a friend of Rocan's."

"Rocan's here?"

"Not right here, but yes. He sent me. I'm going to get you out!"

A long pause, and then an eye appeared at the peephole. Shea backed away, startled at first, then held his ground so that the other could see him clearly.

"You're just a boy! You can't get me out. Go find Rocan!"

"Look, Rocan sent me because—"

"Go get him! Do what I told you!"

The old man was practically shouting at him. Shea backed away and looked up and down the hallway once more, certain that someone must have heard. But apparently no one had, because no one appeared.

He exhaled sharply. He'd had enough of this spiky oldster. He moved back up to the peephole, close enough that he and Tindall were eye-to-eye.

"What's wrong with you?" he hissed, pressing his mouth right up against the grate. "Keep your voice down! There's something patrolling the halls out here, and I don't want it coming after me!"

Tindall grinned, a crooked twist of his mouth through a thicket of beard that hadn't seen a trim in some time. "Oh, that's old Steel Toe. He's just a keeper of the cells, not a guard. Heard him scraping along, did you? He lost his foot and most of a leg a while back when he worked the crystal mines. Had to replace it all with metal. Cost him his job and brought him here to find work. He's almost deaf, too."

Shea didn't care if Steel Toe could hear him or not. Someone else might. "Stand away from the door. I'm going to open it and get you out."

He waited while Tindall moved back, then stuck a wad of the clay on the lock and spit on it. Once again, the clay hissed and steamed and bubbled, and the lock's fastenings melted away. Quick as a cat, the boy pulled the door open.

Tindall stood in the middle of his cell, watching him. He was old and bent, all in rags with a huge bristle of gray beard that hung down to his chest. His face was weathered and lined with age, but his eyes had a sharp, predatory look. He was clapping his hands softly as the boy entered as if pleased by something.

"That's my invention!" he crowed, pointing to the ruined lock. "I developed that substance. Gets through anything, doesn't it? Smart of you to bring it, although I'll warrant that was more Rocan's doing than yours. How old are you, anyway?"

Shea glared at him. "How old are *you*?"

The sharp eyes blinked. "Point taken. So what do we do now? This whole building is locked down from cellar to rooftop."

Shea pulled the cell door closed behind him and walked over to the barred window. The last of the clay went to removing its four bars, then, without asking, he went over to Tindall and ripped a piece of fabric from the tattered rags of the old man's clothing.

"Hey!" Tindall protested, but Shea just glared him into silence. He hung the cloth out the window, then turned back to the single piece of furniture in the room—a narrow-slatted bed—and sat down.

"Now," he icily informed Tindall, "we wait."

Although Tindall repeatedly asked for more details, Shea did not bother to reply beyond assuring the man they were following Rocan's instructions. After all, he didn't really know any details; all he knew was how he got from the gates of Assidian Deep up to the old man's cell, and he didn't feel like talking about that.

None of this discouraged Tindall—even after being rebuffed— from striking out on his own narrative journey.

"Been here almost two months. Picked up by that Federation oaf Zakonis—who got lucky, I might add, 'cause normally he couldn't find his way out of a closet—and he brought me here for interrogation. Did a few unpleasant things to parts of me, but nothing that won't heal in time—except for that one finger, maybe. Anyway, he wanted to know where Rocan was, and I couldn't tell him because fortunately I didn't know for sure—not that I would have told him if I did. Or maybe I did tell him where he lived. Yep, I did give that one up. Anyway, we danced about for a time, but then he lost interest and just left me locked up here."

He sighed. "Spent years in service to the Federation, you know. And this is how they repay me. Helped them develop all sorts of useful devices for their military—some of which really should belong to the public. Handheld communicators, for one. Not fully developed yet, but close enough. Everyone could have one of those. But, no, they want it all for themselves, to keep it for the soldiers, and the common man be damned. That's how they think in this dictatorial government. Used to be a more open, democratic bunch, the Coalition Council, but that went away a while back. Ketter Vause likes it just how it is these days—him in charge and everyone else scrambling for a seat at his feet. Dangerous way to live, though. One day, some of those sitting at his feet will work around to his back and it will be all over for our Prime Minister."

He shrugged. "But I suppose they'll just select another snake to feed on the chickens. Isn't that how it always happens? You go from bad to worse and nothing changes? Doesn't matter to me, though. I'm old and my time in this hellish world is almost done."

Shea rolled his eyes. Why did old people feel it was necessary to talk all the time?

"Don't say much, do you?" Tindall asked suddenly.

The boy shook his head. "I don't have that much to say."

"Neither do I, but I say it anyway." He laughed at his own humor. "Enlighten me—what's going on out there in the world? A few rumors leak through these walls, so I know there's been some sort of invasion. What do you know about that?"

Shea shrugged. "I hear it's an army of magic users. They can make themselves disappear in battle. I guess they destroyed Paranor."

"Ohhh, Ketter Vause won't like that one bit! He'll send that army of his out there to smash them. Magic users or not, he's going to want to make them disappear *permanently*. Is Rocan involved in all this?"

Shea shook his head. Let Rocan tell Tindall if they ever got out of here. He was tired of talking, tired of this cell, tired of waiting, and tired of Tindall. He glanced at the door, checking to be sure it was still closed. He wished he knew how much longer Rocan was going to keep them waiting. He wished he knew something about how Rocan planned to get them out of Assidian Deep. It would be morning before long.

"How long did it take you to build Annabelle?" he asked impulsively.

Tindall looked startled and took what appeared to be a menacing step toward Shea. "How do you know about Annabelle? Has Rocan been talking out of school? Telling you things he ought not to be telling? You forget all of it. None of it is your concern, *boy!*"

Shea gave him a look. "Whether it is or not, *old man,* I've seen your machine and Rocan *has* told me a few things about it. So it's way too late for you to be acting as if it's some sort of state secret."

"That machine is special!" the old man sputtered. "It has the capability to change everything. It might even change—"

"I know, I know." Shea cut him short. "It might even change the world."

"Well, it might. Annabelle can work miracles, and I'm the only one who knows how to make her operate. I built her, I tested her, I gave her life. She's one of a kind, and no one thought for a minute I could build something so perfect!"

"Good for you, but don't break your arm patting yourself on the back. If we don't get out of here, you won't get a chance to do anything with good old Annabelle."

Tindall for once was silent, apparently unwilling to comment more on either his marvelous machine or the possibility of Rocan keeping his promise to rescue them. Shea found himself wondering why Rocan hadn't told him what was going to happen after he reached Tindall's cell. What if something went wrong?

But not much later, he heard a decided scraping sound below Tindall's cell window and jumped up in alarm, leaning out to see what was happening. And there was Seelah, attached to the wall about six feet below, staring up at him with her golden eyes bright and shining. For a moment the boy couldn't believe what he was seeing. She seemed to be gripping the rugged stone with claws extending from hands and feet, looking as if this was something she did all the time. Maybe she couldn't come inside Assidian Deep's iron cells, but apparently there was nothing stopping her from climbing the prison's outer walls.

"Seelah," he whispered, his tone one of gratitude more than of disbelief.

The shape-shifter rewarded him with that beautiful smile—the one that radiated affection and intense longing, the one that melted his heart as if it were formed of soft butter. She came up the wall swiftly, stopped just below him, and reached up with one hand, the claws disappearing in favor of fingers and a palm that caressed his cheek like satin.

"I don't believe you're here," he said softly, reveling in her touch.

He looked for a harness or a rope on her back, but she carried nothing. "Do you plan to carry us down?"

She nodded and held up one finger. *One at a time.* "Tindall, get over here," he ordered.

In the distance, the sky was beginning to lighten. Morning was coming on fast. They didn't want to be caught on the wall when the sun crested and brightened the city.

Tindall was at his side, looking anxious. "Climb through," the boy told him. "Slide down onto her back and hook your arms around her neck. She'll carry you down. I'll keep hold of you until you're in place."

The old man didn't say a word. He moved to where Shea was offering his coupled hands and stepped into them. Shea boosted him up so he could climb out, holding on tightly as he did so. Tindall weighed more than seemed possible for such a frail old thing, but the boy kept careful hold of him until he was settled in place.

Without turning around, Seelah scooted down the wall much faster than Shea had expected—now and then slowing to allow her passenger to adjust his position or hold on her. It took them no more than five minutes to reach the ground. When Tindall stepped off her back, there was Rocan, emerging from the shadows to embrace him.

A moment later Seelah was coming back up the wall for Shea when the alarm sounded, horns blaring from the Deep's high tower, a wailing death knell for anyone who transgressed.

And Shea Ohmsford knew who that someone was.

# 4

IN THE FOOTHILLS LEADING INTO THE DRAGON'S TEETH above the north banks of the Mermidon, Ajin d'Amphere stood at the forefront of her soldiers and awaited her father's coming. There were perhaps two hundred members of her command standing with her, eager and excited—and with totally mistaken expectations. It was their belief that the king had arrived to join forces against the massive Federation army poised just on the other side of the river. It was their belief that his arrival was a cause for celebration.

And for them, perhaps, it would be. But not for her.

Kol'Dre was at her side, resolute and unmoving, standing with her now as he had stood with her for almost ten years against every conceivable threat she had faced—her comrade-in-arms, her most trusted adviser, and her closest friend. Kol was not fooled like the others, but not yet persuaded that matters would take the turn she was convinced they must. He knew her father well, but not as well as she did. In her mind, there was no doubt what was going to happen. Her father's character, his temperament, his insistence on obedience and compliance from all of his subjects—but particularly from her— did not leave any room for ambiguity.

Facing them were dozens of newly arrived Skaar soldiers, all of them looking fresh and clean and ready to act. Ajin's command was worn ragged by the struggles of the past few weeks. They had fought several hard battles, and they carried the marks and the memories of each. Their newly arrived fellows had come directly from home and not yet wielded a single weapon or faced a single enemy.

That would change soon enough, she thought darkly.

Unless she could find a way to prevent it from happening in the way she feared it would.

Overhead and behind the newly arrived command, the Skaar fleet hovered above the trees of the surrounding forests, poised to strike or stand down, as per her father's orders. She had seen the command ship lower earthward, bearing the soldiers who stood before her, and she knew her father would be with them. He had sent them ahead to clear a path, and he was timing his appearance for maximum impact on his daughter and the soldiers she had brought with her. Drama, theatrics, and awe were the tools Cor d'Amphere employed as king of the Skaar, and his methods were familiar to her. He never made an appearance without at least one at his command—and preferably all three.

She had intended that her father's arrival should come at the pinnacle of her confrontation with the Federation and its Prime Minister, Ketter Vause. But fighting a battle was not part of the plan—unless she was certain the Skaar would win. Instead, she wanted to intimidate the Federation and enter into negotiations that would allow both sides to save face and the Skaar to pursue their continued struggle for survival. With their homeland turning to a frozen waste and their people facing certain starvation, they needed a new country in which to make a life. The Four Lands offered that homeland, and the Northland with its tribes of Gnomes and Trolls would serve. It might not be the end of their occupation of this new continent, but it would certainly be a manageable start.

But her father's mind had been poisoned toward her, and her advice on everything regarding the Four Lands would likely not be heeded.

Still, she must try to persuade him. She must try to turn aside his anger and mistaken belief regarding her actions, and be made to see

that a battle at this time and place could not end well. An odd thing
for a Skaar princess to advocate, but she understood the nature of the
enemy they were facing and the power that it wielded better than he,
and she recognized the dangers it posed to the Skaar. It was one thing
to be confident—and quite another to be foolish. Her father was not
the soldier she was, and lacked her ability to command in the field.
He lacked her experience, as well, and led the Skaar army only by
virtue of being the king of its people. She, on the other hand, led because she had proven herself to her soldiers, over and over again—by
setting an example, by leading them from the front, by showing them
how battles could be won against any force. But she could not tell him
this. She could not be so bold and expect to walk away.

Not even in private. And in public, before so many men and
women of his Skaar . . .

"He comes," Kol'Dre whispered suddenly.

Before them, there was movement within the ranks of the newly
arrived—a shifting of bodies and a scattering of cheers and shouts.
Ajin watched the soldiers part, and then her father strode into view.

Cor d'Amphere was not a particularly impressive man, let alone
king, but he exuded confidence and certainty in his position as he
came toward her, head held high, eyes fixed on his daughter. She met
his gaze with her own and held it, refusing to back away or bow or
do anything but stand there and await whatever he had planned for
her. All around her, soldiers were bowing in recognition of his office
and his power, including Kol—but then Kol always did know when
it was advisable to bow and when not to. She should have shown deference, as well, but her stubborn refusal to be intimidated kept her
from doing so.

Besides, whatever was going to happen would not be changed by
a bow or a posture of supplication or anything else. She held herself
frozen in place.

The cost was quickly apparent. Her father came up to her and,
without a word, struck her across the face with the palm of his hand
with enough force to send her staggering backward. But she kept on
her feet, the sting of the blow kindling anger toward her father of
which she did not think herself capable. Gasps and a few muttered

oaths rose from the men and women behind her—her soldiers, who loved her; her comrades, who believed in her and would follow her anywhere. She ignored them. This was between her father and herself.

Slowly she straightened and came back to stand before him. "Was that really necessary?" she asked.

"I thought so," he answered. Anger equal to her own burned in his eyes. "You crossed a line, daughter—a line that no one has the right to cross."

"I crossed no line. I came to the Four Lands and I swept through the Trolls who opposed us, and took Paranor in spite of the vaunted Druid magic. I wiped out their order. Then I faced down the Federation and destroyed its advance force when it came against us—"

"And thereby brought the bulk of the Federation army down on our heads, it appears!" he interrupted, shouting her down.

Silence fell over those collected, everyone waiting to see what would happen next. Father and daughter were both possessed of strong personalities. Once they had shared a closeness, true, but that was before his second marriage and before she developed a true following and reputation of her own. Now, she was aware, she was becoming a bigger threat to him by the day.

Ajin recognized the extent of the danger she was facing in her father's scowl and clenched fists. Nothing would be gained if she alienated him completely. She had to stop things from progressing further.

She dropped to one knee and bowed her head. "I have failed to protect the Keep and its treasures. I have risked too much to bring the enemy to meet us. I am at fault, and I accept all blame. I offer no excuses."

Her father glared at her a moment longer and then nodded. "Your apology is accepted. And I am glad that you recognize your mistakes. I trust you see why you cannot overstep the limits I set for you. You cannot make decisions like the ones you have made here without consulting with me first."

"Father," she said quietly, still on her knees. "In my defense, I did attempt to reach you with messages several times—particularly regarding my feeling that negotiating with the Federation might lead to an agreement that would keep them at bay. I may have misjudged, but I did try to consult you first. Another prevented me from doing so."

Her father nodded, unsmiling. "You tread on dangerous ground, Ajin. Be careful what you say next."

She took his warning to heart. "Sten'Or arranged to have the messages intercepted so that they would not reach you. I am not even sure what brought you here today. I had asked for you to come, but he told me when I questioned him that you would never receive that message."

"So my arrival is a surprise?" No change in expression or tone of voice, but a hint of something else. "Is that what you are telling me?"

She nodded. "May I rise?"

He gestured permission and she rose, standing as close as she had before, hoping his anger had lessened. But shards of it lingered still in his eyes as he studied her. "And where is Sten'Or?"

"Locked away. I could no longer trust him to be honest with me once I found out he was tampering with my messages to you."

"We will see. Have him brought to me. Now."

Ajin turned to Kol'Dre, who departed immediately to fetch their prisoner. Moments later, he returned, guiding the now unfettered and clearly unrepentant Skaar commander with a hand clasped firmly on his arm. Sten'Or was already talking as he came up to stand next to Ajin.

"She works to undermine your authority and your position as king, my lord," he said at once. "She plots against you and the queen. She sees herself as more the commander of your army than you are, and exceeds her authority well beyond what you permitted her. I want her removed from command and myself reinstated."

Cor d'Amphere nodded. "Did you tamper with her messages to me?"

"No, my lord. Not a one."

"Did someone else?"

A pause this time. "I could not say for certain. I was here, with my soldiers, when those messages came to you."

"Except, Sten'Or, they didn't come to me. They came to someone else. Do you have any thoughts as to whom they might have reached, if not me? They were addressed to me, I presume. So who do you think would dare to intercept them?"

Sten'Or kept his composure, shaking his head in a perplexed way. "I cannot imagine such a thing."

"And if I told you that not only can I imagine it, but I know for certain who dared? What would you say to that?"

The Skaar commander looked away quickly and then back again. "I would say they should be punished. You are king, my lord. No one should transgress against you." He gave Ajin a baleful look to indicate she was not above such punishment.

"Well, then. Let's deal with the matter in a direct way. Ajin, will you kindly step a few paces over toward your confidant?"

He gave a nod toward Kol'Dre. Ajin did as she was told, wondering what was happening. Her father waited until he was satisfied with where she was standing, and then he stepped forward to face Sten'Or directly. "Kneel, Commander, and receive my reward for your service to the crown."

Sten'Or hesitated, and then knelt as ordered, eyes on the king. "Bow your head, Sten'Or."

As the Skaar commander did so, Cor d'Amphere nodded to a man standing off to one side whom, until now, Ajin had barely noticed. The man was a giant, all muscle and bulk. He was carrying a huge battle-ax, and at the king's nod he came forward swiftly, the ax already rising. In a single fluid motion, he swung the blade through Sten'Or's neck, severing his head from his shoulders. It was done so swiftly and silently that the victim was dispatched before he even knew what was happening. He died without a sound, his head rolling a few feet before coming to a stop, his body slumping to the ground in a lifeless heap. Fresh gasps rose from the soldiers who watched it happen. But Ajin never moved, her eyes fixed on her father as he strolled forward and kicked the dead man with casual indifference.

"This man was a traitor to the crown and a pretender to the throne. He paid the price for his treachery, and now he is to be forgotten by all. His name will never be spoken again." The king beckoned to his guards. "Take the remains and dispose of them."

Then he walked over and stood very close to Ajin, his voice dropping to a barely audible whisper. "He lied, Ajin, which I am pleased to be able to acknowledge you did not. It does not pay to lie to me, because I know the truth far better than my enemies or my friends or my family think."

He paused and bent closer still, his words meant only for her. "I found out about the messages awhile back. I knew the truth, but concluded that the truth was best not revealed. Do you understand what I am saying? You are not to speak further about this business to anyone. I will do what needs doing myself."

He waited for her response, so she nodded her understanding. "What action will you take?" she ventured. "You know that my mother, were she still queen, would never . . ."

His hand seized her shoulder in a crushing grip. "My private affairs do not concern you!" he snapped. "You have problems enough of your own, don't you think? Now stand back and attend me."

She moved to put a few additional feet between them. It occurred to her briefly that he was within easy striking distance. It would have taken her no time at all to draw any of the blades she carried and kill him on the spot. She could not be certain of the reaction of the soldiers surrounding her, but it might be worth finding out. His soldiers might kill her, but they might also accede to her claim to the throne and choose to support her. She was popular, after all. In many respects, she was one of them—raised and trained among them, a comrade-in-arms who had fought beside them and never once asked not to be first into battle.

But killing her father, even as much as she despised him for his treatment of her mother, was not something she thought she could live with.

"Let it be known," Cor d'Amphere declared in an exaggerated voice intended to reach everyone, "that my daughter has exceeded her authority in bringing the advance force of the Skaar army into a confrontation with a potential enemy. She did this without permission and in a reckless manner. But I have forgiven her, and she has regained my favor and retains her rank as a full commander."

He paused meaningfully. "But let it also be known that when I am disobeyed, there must be punishment—even if you are the daughter of a king. So I am relieving Ajin d'Amphere, princess of the Skaar people, of her command of the advance force and ordering her back to Skaarsland where she will be confined to quarters to await my return."

The echo of his voice died out abruptly in the ensuing silence. Ajin stared at him in disbelief. "You cannot do this to me," she hissed.

He cocked an eyebrow, and the lines on his face tightened. "I just did. Be grateful I did not do worse. An airship with crew and guards will be provided for your return. Go gather your things and prepare yourself for departure." He held up his hand in warning, cutting off whatever argument she was about to make with a sharp word of warning. "No, Ajin! Do not even think to argue further with me, now or later. The matter is settled. Now go!"

She stood there amid her soldiers, disgraced and dismissed by her father, an object lesson in what it meant to displease the king. Whether you were a commoner or a king's child, your fate was decided. She had done so much for him in her short life, given so much to show him how valuable and worthy she was of his—well, not his love perhaps, because that would be asking too much, but at least his respect.

And now it was all being cast aside in a way that would leave her diminished in the eyes of her people.

Now she wished she had killed him. She hated him in that moment with such passion, she would have given anything for the chance to strike him down. Nothing that might have happened to her for such an act could possibly be worse than this. His disrespect for her had burned a hole through her heart.

Kol'Dre stepped forward, coming over to stand next to her. "I will see that the princess is safely escorted home, my lord," he said.

But Cor d'Amphere shook his head. "You will remain here with me, Penetrator. You are too valuable a resource to be sent home. You know much about this country and its peoples that I do not. I will need that information, and you are the one to give it to me. Say your goodbyes."

He turned away, walking back into the ranks of his soldiers, giving orders to them to deploy and prepare to engage in battle. His back was to her. He was not even bothering to look her way. She thought again that she could draw her blade, reach him in three quick steps, and hurt him the way he had hurt her. She had not thought him worth all that much anyway, since he had banished her mother in favor of the *pretender.* She almost gave in to the urge. But Kol'Dre must have read her mind, so quickly did he step in front of her, blocking her way.

"No, Ajin," he said softly. "That is not the way."

And so her chance was lost, and she was cast out.

In the aftermath of her humiliation, Kol'Dre accompanied her to where she could gather her things in preparation for the journey home. Neither said anything until they were inside her tent and alone. She turned to face him then, fighting against the tears that threatened to break through.

"That was unforgivable!" she shouted, suddenly not caring if she was heard or not.

"It was expected," Kol corrected. "Your father likes to make examples of those who cross him. In his mind, your failure to seek his permission before you invaded Paranor and destroyed the Druids was a disobedience of the worst sort. Made worse, I might add, by the fact that you are his daughter. He could forgive the rest, but not that. You understand, don't you, Ajin, that he could not let that pass? Even if you had consulted him on everything else. Even if he did know the truth about Sten'Or. To ignore your transgression—real or perceived—would be to show weakness to his soldiers, and he could never stand to let that happen. Especially when you are already so popular."

"I don't want to hear excuses, Kol," she replied, sitting on her bedding and shaking her head in dismay, the weight of her punishment threatening to break her. "He could have settled on something besides sending me home! I fought for him when I could have stayed put in the north and simply waited for him to do his own fighting. I found a way to breach the walls of Paranor and I seized it for him.

I destroyed the Druids for him. Everything I did was for *him*—to help him keep his promise to our people that he would find them a new home. And he throws me over because I exposed his scheming bitch-wife—that conniving *pretender* to the throne that rightfully belongs to my mother. He chooses to protect her even after she betrays him by trying to get to me. He knows this, and still he hides the truth!"

Kol sat next to her, nodding. "But he hides it for another reason, as well. He hides it because to reveal what she has done would expose him to ridicule. The Skaar people might even go so far as to think him a fool. He cannot abide that, so he pushes the matter aside—at least for now. He might choose to exact retribution at a later date."

She made an exasperated sound. "I will be the one to exact retribution long before he thinks to act. If I am to be sent home, I will have my chance. And what better way to spend my time?"

Kol'Dre gave her a look. "You might want to consider the possibility that your father has already thought of this. How fitting if his treacherous wife died at the hand of his troublesome daughter?"

Ajin shook her head dismissively. "He will do nothing. He has no intention of causing her harm while she remains young and eager to provide him with male heirs. I am simply another obstacle standing in his way—just like my mother."

"There is another consideration, Ajin, one you might want to remember. He is afraid of you. Deep down, where he hides his darkest secrets, he sees what you have become in the eyes of his soldiers. He sees how they revere you. How short a step is it to go from princess to queen? He worries that you have become more popular than he is, and what that would mean for his future as king. Given enough of an excuse to do so, the Skaar might find a reason to throw him over and make you their new ruler."

She shook her head slowly. "If he thinks I would embrace that future, then he doesn't know me at all. I have never sought the throne. I have never given it a thought. I am content to be what I am—a commander of soldiers, an expert on the field of battle. I want nothing of what he has."

"But he cannot be sure of that, can he?"

She considered a moment. "I suppose not. So much the worse for him, then. Such thinking exposes him as weak and cowardly, susceptible to fears that have no basis in fact."

"It has ever been thus in the history of the world. Rulers rule because they hold power, and their one fear is that someone will take that power from them and reduce them to nothing. Your father is no different. His biggest failing lies in not recognizing loyalty when he sees it—especially in his own daughter. He should be grateful for all you have done and encourage you to continue your good work. I despair of what will happen here once you are gone. I do not think him the equal of Ketter Vause when it comes to negotiations."

"Perhaps he believes that in battle, with the whole of the Skaar army behind him, he will crush the Federation and take the head of its Prime Minister as a souvenir with or without me."

"But a battle of that sort would be costly to the Skaar, as well, and there are other forces waiting in the wings that he would then have to contend with. Far better if he can find a common ground with the Federation and form an alliance that will benefit both sides."

Ajin rose, grabbing for her weapons and few personal belongings, which she stuffed into a large pack that she then slung across her shoulder. "You must do what you can to see this happens, Kol. I may not be with you in the flesh, but I will be with you in spirit. You are the cleverer of us, and if there is a way to turn my father's mind toward the accommodation you so rightfully point out must happen, it will be up to you to find it. I will go back to our homeland because I must, but I will look for a way to return, as well. Somehow, I will find that way and seize it. It is here with you and the army that I belong, and I will not let my father sentence me to exile so easily."

She embraced him, pulling him against her. She saw the shock in his eyes and laughed. "Haven't held a woman close for a while? Miss the feel of that exquisite softness?" She pushed him away dismissively. "You are my best friend, my confidant, and my loyal Penetrator. Never forget that. We belong together."

She knew he would like hearing those words—imagining them a

declaration of something that quite possibly meant much more. But in her mind—as he considered again the deeper hopes he harbored for them—she saw the chiseled features and effortless movements of Darcon Leah and found herself flushed and wanting.

"Ajin," Kol said, interrupting her momentary lapse, "I will work to find a way, too. Perhaps a chance will come to persuade your father to bring you back. Perhaps his anger toward you will diminish, and he will come to see again how much he depends on you."

She nodded wordlessly, the flush fading, the memories of the Blade retreating into her mind as her current circumstances again pressed in on her. She adjusted the pack once more, smiled her most winning smile, and walked from the tent without another word, back into the bustling camp and the airship waiting with its crew and guards to convey her home.

# 5

FROZEN IN PLACE FOR WHAT SEEMED LIKE ENDLESS moments, Shea tried to decide what to do. He could not imagine how anyone had found them out; there was no chance that anyone could have seen them inside the prison. Maybe the broken-down scrubber had been discovered.

Whatever the case, the horns were still wailing.

Seelah was climbing rapidly toward the open window of the prison cell, but how safe was it for the two of them to get back down with the brilliant dawn light now bathing the walls they must descend? If anyone working as a guard was paying even the slightest bit of attention, there was no way they could descend unseen. Perhaps he was expecting too much. Tindall was now safely down, and that was the job Shea had been sent to do.

On the other hand, he didn't much care for his chances if he stayed where he was. What did it matter now if he was seen, with alarms sounding all about him?

Then he heard the sound of voices in the hallway somewhere down the corridor outside the cell, and a scuffling of feet accompanying a clanging of iron doors opening and closing. His decision made, he climbed through the window instantly and hung there in the frame, waiting for Seelah to reach him.

His throat tightened as the sounds drew nearer. *Hurry! Hurry!*

She was there within seconds, offering him her back. "There are guards coming!" he warned breathlessly.

She motioned for him to climb on and he did so swiftly, fastening his arms and legs about her lithe, strong body. Almost before he was in place, she was off at an even faster pace than she had set during Tindall's escape, propelling herself backward down the rugged stone, claws gripping and scrabbling as they descended—so quickly that Shea closed his eyes so as not to become dizzy. The voices and noises of the men in the hallway disappeared behind them, and the wind became a rough-woven blanket that whipped about him and muffled all sounds. He felt himself dropping as if stripped of support. Clinging to his rescuer with a frantic intensity—her steely cat muscles rippling beneath him, her limbs moving in synchronized rhythm, an inhuman engine of terrible force—he still seemed to be tumbling away, the two of them bereft of any real support.

*Not so fast,* he wanted to scream. *Slow down!* But he was afraid to say anything that might distract her.

Then abruptly they were on the ground and Rocan was peeling him off Seelah's back, trying desperately not to laugh.

"You should see your face!" he exclaimed after extracting Shea and setting him back on his feet. "You look like you just witnessed your own death!"

Shea grimaced. "That's not so far from the truth. And it's not funny!"

He stood there shaking, rubbing his arms and legs to make the tremors stop and to regain some feeling in limbs gone numb with the effort of clinging to his rescuer. It took him a moment to regain his composure, then he remembered to turn to Seelah and give her a smile and a few quick words of thanks. The shape-shifter, her beautiful features beaming at him, returned the smile twofold.

"Come away," Rocan urged the boy and the old man. "We've gotten you both safely out of the cell, but we're not free of trouble yet. We can't linger."

He bundled them off toward the gates they had come through,

providing each with a heavy cloak to guard against recognition, shoo-
ing them along with words of encouragement, glancing back over his
shoulder anxiously. Shea found himself wondering how they were
going to get through the gates. While there had been no problem getting inside Assidian Deep, thanks to Rocan bribing one of the watch,
there was no reason to assume they would have help getting out.

And he was right. As they neared the gates, he saw three guards
standing in their path with the opening behind them tightly sealed.
In spite of everything they had accomplished thus far, they were still
trapped.

He glanced around for Seelah, but she was nowhere to be seen.

Abruptly, Rocan made a sharp right turn, steering them away
from the gates and the men. Shea waited for someone to try to stop
them or to call out, but none of the men made any effort. They just
stood there watching.

"Why aren't they coming after us?" the boy asked Rocan in a
hushed voice. "Don't they know who we are?"

Rocan smiled. "Maybe they do, and maybe they don't. But they
don't care. If we leave them alone and don't try to get through their
post, they have no interest in us. If anyone asks later, they can say
they saw us but did as they were ordered and stayed put. After all,
how could we possibly get out of here if all the gates were closed and
guarded?"

He paused and smiled. "Enough credits will buy you anything,
so long as what's asked doesn't inconvenience those who are bought.
Men like those three just need to be able to say they did what they
were told and the fault, whatever its nature, must lie elsewhere. Remember, this isn't exactly the sort of job that anyone who holds it
feels much attached to."

Shea wasn't sure he understood this rationale, but he was willing
to accept it if it got them out of there. But that *if* remained a matter of
concern. All they seemed to be doing now was following the wall of
the prison to where they would find yet another closed gate with yet
another contingent of guards.

Instead, though, they reached a set of stables with horses and feed, positioned back in the shadows of an overhang jutting from the north wall. Wagons and carriages in service to the men who worked the prison were parked off to one side, some of them dusty and worn, only one or two still in good working order. Here, the wall dropped lower to allow for a smaller set of gates where only a single man stood, rigid and unmoving as they approached. As they drew closer, Shea realized the guard was armored from head to foot, holding a halberd in one hand, butt resting on the ground.

When they reached the man, Rocan went right up to him and put a friendly hand on his shoulder. "All right with you if we leave through these gates, my friend? It won't get you in trouble, will it?"

The man said nothing.

Rocan nodded. "Silence is a sign of acquiescence, I believe." He glanced back at Shea and Tindall. "Come along. These service gates will provide us with the exit we seek."

"What's wrong with him?" Shea asked as Rocan unbarred the smaller gates and pushed one of the two doors ajar. "Is he dead or something?"

The Rover shrugged. "He's just the shell of the man he once was. He hasn't been the same since he suffered a real out-of-body experience sometime last night. You know, like those astral projection followers believe happens to you once you get far enough into your own self. Never bought into it myself, but some do. Maybe this fellow was one of them."

Shea realized, giving the motionless man another glance, what he was looking at. "He isn't in there, is he? That armor is empty."

Tindall gave a low chuckle. "Nothing gets by you, boy, does it?"

Shea felt like telling the old coot that if he called him "boy" one more time, he was going to flatten him. But by then they were on the other side of the wall and Rocan was pulling the door of the service gate closed behind him. There, Seelah was waiting with a carriage, holding the lead rope on a pair of horses as they stamped and shifted about impatiently.

Rocan ushered Shea and Tindall inside, then climbed into the driver's seat. The boy looked, but he couldn't tell what had happened to Seelah. "Hold on. The ride may get a bit bumpy before we get to where we're going. Hah! Get on there!"

His yell sent the pair in the traces charging ahead, and the carriage and its occupants were off.

Assidian Deep was left behind after only a few minutes. They were traveling swiftly over whatever avenue of passage the Rover had settled on, and Shea found that even by looking out the windows of the carriage he could not tell where they were, let alone where they might be going. Seated across from him, Tindall bounced and squirmed as the wheels passed down a series of rutted and heavily pocked surfaces, groaning and grumbling the entire time as if escaping the prison wasn't worth the cost.

Shea ignored him. Served him right for being such a grump. Maybe all the jouncing and discomfort would shake the bad disposition and lack of gratitude out of him.

The ride went on for a long time—an endless time, it seemed—leaving the boy wishing they had simply settled on walking to wherever it was they were going. On the other hand, he had gotten his wish for Tindall to stop griping. The old man was collapsed on the carriage seat and had somehow managed to fall asleep.

Several times, Shea peered out the windows to see what was happening. Not once did he notice anything troubling. No one was behaving as if an alarm had sounded or anything at all was wrong with the new day. It was as if they had moved into a different time and place entirely. The buildings and the people they charged through barely gave them a glance, save in the few instances when they were almost run down. Apparently what happened in Assidian Deep was not something that any of them cared about.

More than once, memories of what had transpired during the night intruded on Shea's thoughts—dark images, like the whisperings of the ducts and the cleaners and the man Tindall called Steel Toe. But each time he was quick to tamp them down. Thinking on the nightmare of last night was not something he wanted to do even now that he was safely away from it.

Although he did pause long enough to remind himself never to let Rocan Arneas talk him into anything like that again.

When the carriage finally drew to a halt and Shea climbed down from inside, he knew at once where he was. It was the warehouse Rocan had brought him to that first night after they had escaped from Federation commander Zakonis and his men to find a new safe haven. It was in here that Annabelle was housed, high up on the second level in a room roughly the size of a small village.

Tindall stumbled out of the carriage behind him, rubbing his eyes and looking around. "Ah, home again!" he announced. "Now we'll see!"

He did not bother to reveal what, exactly, they would see, but Shea didn't ask because he didn't care. He walked over to Rocan instead, who was tethering the horses in place. "What happens now?"

The Rover gestured toward the entry doors. "We go inside, of course."

Shea glanced at the horses and carriage. "Seelah will see to those," Rocan said. "She borrowed them yesterday and now feels an obligation to return them. It won't take long. You and Tindall could both use a bath and some rest. It's been a long night. Come along."

He released the locks on the entry doors and they went inside, leaving the horses and carriage tethered outside. "Won't someone steal them?" Shea asked, glancing back as the doors closed behind them.

"Not likely. This district is dangerous, as you know from personal experience, but nowhere near as dangerous as Seelah."

Rocan and the boy walked side by side down the hallways to the stairs leading up, with Tindall trailing along behind, back to grumbling about one thing or another.

"So even though she wasn't able to go inside Assidian Deep, she could climb its walls without it affecting her?" Shea asked. "It is only the iron of the prison that weakens her and makes her sick? You planned for her to come get us all along? But couldn't Tindall have gotten out that way without me going in? Couldn't Seelah have placed the compound on the bars from outside the cell—or given him the substance to do it himself—and then simply pulled him through the window once it was open?"

Rocan glanced over. "Full of questions this morning, aren't you? Well, I like a young man who doesn't just accept events and wants to know the reasons behind them. So ask yourself this—how in command of himself, physically and emotionally, do you think Tindall is? How does he seem to you?"

"A few oars shy of a full boat," Shea answered at once. "And I am already sick of him griping about everything. Is he always like this?"

"Pretty much. But he gets away with it because he is so smart. There's no one else like him; no one even comes close. His ability to create and build is astounding, Shea. It hasn't always brought him happiness or wealth, but it gives him immense satisfaction to solve problems other men and women would simply consider unsolvable. His mind works differently than any other mind I've encountered. He looks at something from inside his head, takes a road no one else would have even thought of taking, and comes up with a way to make the impossible possible."

"Like with Annabelle?"

The Rover shrugged. "Not exactly. But if you want to know about Annabelle, you'll have to ask Tindall." He shook his head. "No one else can tell the story like it demands to be told."

Shea nodded. "I'd like to hear that story if he can stop calling me 'boy' for five minutes and stop grumbling about everything."

The Rover nodded. "Well, you'll have your chance. I'm going out for a while. We need to leave this city. And with Annabelle, if we want to keep her."

And with a smile and a wave to Tindall, he was out the door and gone.

Left alone with the old man, Shea decided to wash up first before talking to Tindall about Annabelle or anything else. He was feeling grungy and rank from crawling through the sewer ducts of Assidian Deep, and he wasn't sure when he would get a chance to clean up again if Rocan planned on leaving soon. So he made his way over to the small washroom that the Rover had indicated earlier, entered, and closed the door behind him.

Soon enough, he had steaming water in the tub and was soaking himself in a half-catatonic state, letting the warmth ease the aches in his muscles and erase the stench of sewage from his body. When he was finished he washed his clothes in the bathwater, then hung them on a series of pipes, hoping they would dry before it was time to leave. Lacking another outfit, he wrapped up in the cloak Rocan had given him and went back out to find Tindall.

The old man was sitting on a bench, looking up at Annabelle in a speculative way, leaning forward with his elbows on his knees and his hands clasped.

"She's something, isn't she?" he said to the boy without looking over.

"I guess so." Shea sat down next to him.

"Took me ten years to build her." The other's tone suggested he was mostly talking to himself. "Ten years of trial and error, of fighting off interference from officials who thought they knew better than I did how it ought to be done, of working not just openly but in secret, of scrounging for credits and equipment and supplies and all the rest. It wasn't easy, I can tell you."

"Doesn't sound it."

"Mostly, in this world, when you come up with an idea for an invention, you go through a few stages. There's the stage where you question yourself because the idea's still too new and seems too preposterous. Then there's the stage where you come to believe fully and completely, and commit yourself body and soul to the proving of it— only no one else believes in it. Then there's the stage where, even if everyone comes to believe and gets behind the idea, you find that the execution will be more difficult than you had thought possible. Things don't work the way you hoped they would. The parts don't hold up to the strain or don't serve their purpose. The credits dry up. Testing fails over and over. Patience grows short and time becomes an issue."

He paused, turning to look at Shea. "But the worst stage is the one when you finally complete your work and realize that those you thought supported you are only interested in doing so because they want control over what you have invented. They want it for their own private, selfish reasons and have no intention of seeing it used for the betterment of Mankind. That one is the worst stage—the most depressing and despicable."

"The Federation wants your machine for themselves?"

"Oh, yes. But not because they want to use it for the peaceful purposes for which it was intended. That would be bad, but tolerable. No, what they want is to employ it as a weapon. They want to use it as a hammer against everyone who crosses them. Because if no one else has anything like it, they can't compete. Meaning they are forced into a state of dependence on the possessor's willingness to share."

Shea nodded. "There's not much chance of that happening with the Federation these days, is there?"

"Not much at all," Tindall agreed.

They were quiet for a bit as Shea took a few moments to think through what the scientist had just said. Then he asked, "Does Annabelle really work now? Can she do what you built her to do?"

"What? Change the weather?" Tindall nodded slowly. "She can do that and more. She can actually *make* weather, in some instances." He looked over again. "You know, in the Old World, before the Great Wars, they had machines that could impact the weather, so this isn't a new idea. Those machines could affect the movement of the winds and clouds, could make it rain or be dry, could make it snow or . . ."

He trailed off. "All that technology was lost. All that science disappeared with those who understood it, or was simply cast aside by those that survived but were afraid of what would happen were it brought back. Poisons, weapons, plague, and all the other dreadful end-days advancements—no one wanted that back. So they turned to magic instead, and only in the last hundred years or so have they started looking at science again for their answers. Mostly here, in the Federation, where magic is considered untrustworthy, and new ways of advancing civilization—or, more accurately, advancing the interests of those in power—are being sought. Elves, Dwarves, Druids, they prefer to keep things just as they are. The Elves have always used magic; it's the backbone of their culture. The others, they just don't like change. But magic is dangerous, too. More so, maybe."

Shea thought about it. "Not that many can use magic," he said finally.

"Fewer still can use it well. It's too dangerous, too dependent on the intent of the users. It doesn't always work the way you want it to. It doesn't always perform as you expect. Science is more reliable. It always has been. Machines and mechanical devices of all sorts will always work the way you expect once you get the science right. The margin for error shrinks to almost nothing. A machine does exactly what you built it for. It doesn't just go off on a lark."

Shea frowned. "But that's not so, is it? Doesn't science sometimes prove unpredictable, too? And not just in a random way. And even if you use it for a good cause to begin with, sometimes it can be used for a bad one, too. Or the other way around. A machine is just like magic. It depends on the user's intent."

Tindall gave him a long look. "Well said. You're right, of course." He gave the boy a smile. "There's more to you than meets the eye, Shea. That was a well-stated argument. But I would argue in response that you always know and understand a machine's function. And anyone can learn to operate a machine. But none of that's true with magic. Not everyone can use magic. Only some can use it, which creates a privileged class, and even the most talented can't always be sure of the result. It is a mercurial, quixotic form of power, and the Druids mostly keep it for themselves for just that reason. Plus, there is no safety net with magic. That's why it will never be available for use by the common man."

Shea shifted a bit on the seat. "But doesn't that mean that there are fewer chances for things to go wrong? If fewer people can use magic, then fewer bad things are likely to happen. Machines, though, can be operated by anyone. And if anybody can use a machine, then the possibility of it being used for evil increases."

Tindall sighed. "And then there's the argument about what constitutes good or evil usage. A very subjective standard, at best—one that gets broken down and put back together in new ways all the time." He paused, rubbing his hands as if to rid himself of the thought. "But I still think it is wrong for power to be placed in the hands of just a few, like the way the Druids control magic."

"You might not have to worry about it anymore," Shea said. "I heard the Druids were wiped out by those invaders."

The old man nodded slowly. "I heard that, too. Another of those rumors that creeps into prison cells to entertain the occupants. I heard that one from a guard, who heard it from a cousin, who heard it from whomever. But is it true? It doesn't seem possible, given the power of Paranor and its occupants and all those many safeguards employed against anyone breaching the walls."

Shea worked his bare foot across the rough flooring. "Well, you know what they say. Nothing can ever keep you safe from everything. There's always something that can get you, even if you have magic."

Tindall did not reply, returning to his contemplation of Annabelle. Shea found himself wondering what the old man would do now that he was an escaped prisoner hunted by the Federation. He was in his twilight years and not in great shape. If the Federation wanted him back, they would not find it all that difficult. So Tindall would have to leave the Southland and move to another corner of the Four Lands. Probably, he would have to go into hiding. And what would he do then? To invent things, you needed credits and someone to provide for you while you worked. Even Shea knew that much.

Perhaps Tindall and Rocan could join forces; they both seemed to share similar values when it came to the welfare of the Four Lands. And they shared a history. Rocan appeared to be well enough off. And he probably had a large Rover family somewhere to help back him up if the Federation went on hunting for him—which they would, wouldn't they?

Shea shook his head, finding the whole business too convoluted, then excused himself to go dress. Pulling on his mostly dry clothing, he considered their discussion anew. None of the answers to the questions he had asked mattered all that much—not to him. What mattered was how he could detach himself from both men and return to Varfleet before things had a chance to get any worse.

He went back out and sat down again with the old man, mulling things over for a time without coming to any definitive conclusion as to how he should handle his departure. He didn't want to leave without saying why, or leave Tindall alone while Rocan was gone. And he didn't want to take the coward's way out by slipping away unnoticed and without explaining himself. He didn't like what impression that would leave in the minds of those he abandoned. He might not amount to much, but he was better than that.

"Did you hear something?" Tindall asked suddenly.

Shea shook his head, still lost in thought. Moments later the door to the chamber flew open and a dozen Federation soldiers surged into the room, weapons drawn.

And Commander Zakonis followed them in, a smile on his face.

# 6

CLIZIA PORSE WAS SEVERAL MILES AWAY BY THE time Drisker Arc had finished collaring Tavo Kaynin, already taking steps to cut her losses. Letting Tavo go was the easiest choice she had ever made. He was reckless, undependable, and mentally unsound, offering her no real assurance that he would ever be able to do anything she asked of him. The evidence had been provided this very morning by his failure to kill Drisker as she had ordered, instead giving in to his uncontrollable obsession with killing his sister.

And he had even failed to do that, somehow revealing himself enough for the Druid to trick him and take him captive.

Fine, then. Let the fool have him. He would cause Drisker more trouble than Clizia could ever think to create, and distract him from the things he needed to be doing. She had recovered the Stiehl, and that was all that mattered. At least this most dangerous of all weapons would never fail her.

Admittedly, she was stung by the extent of what she had failed to accomplish over the past few weeks, especially where Drisker Arc was concerned. Her conspiracy with the Skaar had succeeded in drawing the Druid into the Keep, and there she had imprisoned him by dispatching Paranor into a limbo existence, effectively ending any threat he might present. With the Black Elfstone in her possession, she controlled when, if ever, the Druid's Keep and its reluctant prisoner might be returned to the Four Lands.

Or so she had imagined. Because, as it happened, she did not have possession of the Black Elfstone after all. Had she only thought she had taken it from his unconscious body? Or was something else at play? Whatever the case, all her efforts had gone for naught. Drisker had managed somehow to extricate himself without her help and return Paranor to the Four Lands. He had undone everything she had accomplished, and placed her alliance with the Skaar princess in serious jeopardy. She was now a fugitive from Drisker and his companions herself, and likely no longer welcome much of anywhere in the Four Lands, including the encampment of the beleaguered Skaar.

And yet there was still hope.

There was always hope.

Her hard, sharp features tightened as she felt her disappointment shift to rage, her eyes aglow with the dark magic she longed to release against this man who had defied her. She was sitting in her small two-man airship, grounded and in hiding near the mouth of the Kennon Pass, on the far side of the Dragon's Teeth. She had flown there directly following her escape from Drisker, the Stiehl successfully retrieved, but her path forward was a puzzle awaiting a solution. She needed direction, not simply a vague, long-term goal of resurrecting the fallen Druid order with herself as Ard Rhys. That would come with time, but not without better planning for what must happen first. It had been clear before Drisker's return what was needed, but now she must reassess.

It was cold within the unheated shell of her small craft, but it was pointless to fly any farther without a specific destination. She might have disembarked and made camp for the night, built herself a fire and gotten some sleep, but she was too angry and unsettled to allow herself any rest without knowing what lay ahead.

Drisker would come searching for her; that much was certain. He would have already tried, but she had magic, too. And hers would have kept her hidden long enough for her to get this far. But there was a cost for using magic to deflect the power of the Seeking Stones, and she could not afford to use it freely. Her mind and body were already wearied and aching from the effort this time. Soon, Drisker would try using the Elfstones again. Now that he knew the extent of her treachery, he would not be satisfied with anything less than tracking her down and eliminating her. Her part in the destruction of the entire Druid order was something he would take personally, even given his exile. He was that kind of man. Cross him where friendships and commitment to a cause were concerned—even one as hopeless as preserving the old Druid order—and he would not rest until things were put right. It would be the same with her.

So she must find a way to protect herself better, and that meant finding an ally who would stand with her against Drisker.

She thought back to the fleet of airships that had drawn her attention the previous night. Airships from the north, where no airships were to be found—especially not in those numbers. Not in the tribal lands of the Trolls, those bestial, primitive creatures. Given their size, most of them must have been transports for soldiers and supplies. So if they did not come from the Four Lands—as she was certain they did not—then it was logical to assume they might be Skaar vessels.

Which meant the Skaar king had arrived ahead of schedule.

She had wondered about Ajin d'Amphere's ability to control her father's movements. Her Penetrator, the man known to Clizia as Kassen, had seemed confident that Ajin's father would allow her the freedom she required to gain a beachhead in the Four Lands before the larger army would follow, but Clizia had not been so sure. It felt more likely to her that Cor d'Amphere would be like most rulers—distrustful of allowing too much power or control to fall into the hands of others. Cor d'Amphere had not sounded to her like a particularly complacent ruler, not even where his daughter was concerned.

Now, it seemed, she had been right. The arrival of those airships might signal the king's impatience with Ajin's progress. Unless, of course, his daughter had summoned her father early.

In either case, it was to the Skaar that Clizia must offer her services. That alliance was stronger than any she was likely to secure with any of the other governments of the Four Lands, and likely the best she could hope to find right now. She had harbored hopes for an alliance after her visit to the Elves, but it seemed that her efforts to charm Gerrendren Elessedil had failed. And she could no longer afford to wait on the Elven king, in any event. Not with Drisker Arc hunting for her.

She powered up the two-man and engaged the thrusters. The small craft lifted off, rising from its place of hiding and heading for the Mermidon and the Skaar encampment. Clizia flew until the forefront of a vast storm forced her into hiding. Then, when it finally passed a little before dawn, she continued on, flying close to the mountains as she made her way downriver, keeping within their shadow as the sky lightened on the horizon ahead. She would need to get close enough to the encampment to walk in and confront the princess, and she did not want to be spotted before then. It was a bold decision to face down Ajin d'Amphere with her failures, but she thought she had the means to win her over and regain her confidence.

And now, perhaps, if she was right in her reading of the meaning of those airships, win her father over, as well.

The morning was about two hours advanced when she reached her destination. Ahead, the Mermidon's surface shimmered bright silver with the emergence of the new day, and streams of sunlight pierced the forest canopy on both sides of the river. But then she glanced farther on and saw that things were not at all what she was expecting. Immediately she slowed her little craft to fully take in what she was seeing.

The skies on both sides of the Mermidon, for as far as the eye could see, were filled with warships. Their huge dark shapes were clearly outlined against the eastern horizon—shapes that she presumed to be Skaar warships to the north, and what she knew for certain to be Federation warships to the south, facing off against each other with the river between. Most were transports or battleships, huge and dominant, but they were flanked by dozens of smaller vessels, as well.

Clizia surveyed the massed ships, her mind whirling. To a casual glance, it looked like battle was imminent. But if the Skaar warships were indeed the vessels she had seen flying overhead two nights ago, this standoff had been under way for at least a day. So what were they waiting for? What would be the spark that fired this tinder? She certainly didn't want to find *herself* the cause. Frowning, she landed in a patch of open rolling grasslands that formed a part of the foothills fronting the giant Dragon's Teeth. Entering the Skaar encampment to see the princess and her father might require a bit more subtlety than she had anticipated.

She powered down her airship and sat back in her pilot box, considering her options. Act now and go in or sit back and wait to see what might happen?

*Act now* won out.

On their return, Dar and Brecon built a fire in the clearing where they had left Drisker and Tavo Kaynin. Tarsha stood off to one side, and no one said much of anything until the task was accomplished. Then all of them crowded close to the flames to warm themselves while Drisker explained what he had done to Tavo.

"We'll take him with us." He glanced around, meeting the eyes of each in turn, making a silent assessment. "I know this is cause for some concern, but I think the inhibiting magic of the collar he now wears will serve as a preventive measure against any misbehavior. Tavo understands what will happen if he disobeys me, and he is grateful that we are giving him another chance and letting him remain with his sister."

He glanced at the young man, drew his attention, and cocked one eyebrow questioningly. Tavo nodded his agreement slowly. It looked to be a wooden gesture, but then everything about him was stilted and awkward at present. Drisker knew he would need Tarsha's time and patience to help change that, but for now it was enough.

"So we are a company for now?" Dar Leah asked him—more a statement of fact than a question. "But where do we go next?"

Drisker glanced over his shoulder toward the dark bulk of Paranor. "We cannot remain here. Nothing will be settled by hiding behind these walls. The Keep is restored, and I am returned; that is all that matters where Paranor is concerned. But we have to decide which of several more difficult problems we will resolve first. Tarsha is committed to helping her brother, but she will also be accompanying us." He looked over at her. "And make no mistake, you have a part to play, Tarsha. An important part."

Tarsha looked startled. "But I am only a . . ."

Drisker held up one hand to cut her off. "Leave it for now. I will speak alone with you later. For now, simply accept that I know whereof I speak."

The girl went quiet, her eyes shifting to her brother. Tavo was looking at her with a mix of curiosity and confusion, and she gave him a small smile. His response was a subtle shift of expression that caused her to drop the smile quickly.

"But we have to do something about Clizia," Drisker continued. "We have to find her before she can cause any more trouble. We also have to do something about the Skaar. We can't let them continue to threaten the Four Lands."

"Well, I can see us doing something about Clizia," Brecon Elessedil said. "After all, we should be able to track her anywhere with the Elfstones. She might have evaded their searching capabilities once, but she can't hide from us forever. And now there are four of us to deal with whatever defenses she might have."

"Numbers aren't the best measure of success where Clizia is concerned," Drisker said. "In any case, I don't think going after Clizia is our best choice."

The others stared at him. "Well, then, what is?" Dar asked.

A shrug. "I'm not sure yet. But I think we might need some help finding out."

"And where will we find this help, Drisker?" Tarsha spoke for the first time since the fire had been lit. She was rosy-cheeked by now, likely warm clear through. "You have an idea, don't you?"

Drisker nodded. "But it will require that we travel. All of us. We cannot risk splitting up our company while Clizia is out there. For now, we will have to stick together. At least until my question about our future is answered."

"But who will provide the answer?" Dar persisted.

Drisker's smile was dark and full of menace. "The dead will."

On the north bank of the Mermidon, well above the Skaar defenses and main camp, Clizia Porse decided to take a chance. If she abandoned her two-man where she was, it would take her hours to reach the heart of the encampment and the princess. Hours, as well, to find out what exactly was going on. But if she flew in from the west and north at low altitude, she could conceivably get much closer without anyone spotting her. Or even paying attention to her if they did, since hers was such a small craft and of obviously no threat to anyone by itself.

She took a final look downriver and confirmed that there was still no movement by the warships massed to either side of the Mermidon.

Satisfied, she powered up her small airship and flew inland to allow for an approach from behind the Skaar lines. She stayed low against the foothills and in the shadow of the Dragon's Teeth, just as she had on her earlier approach. If she were judging the situation correctly, the Skaar had formed a defensive line inland from the river, on heights that backed up against the mountains but jutted out enough that the princess could maneuver her soldiers easily from behind their defenses. Clizia could spy out some of those troops and see movement from behind their barriers. But it was the main camp that drew her attention, for it was there the activity was heaviest.

She changed her approach so that she came down farther back than where she had previously intended, closer to the rear lines of the Skaar and close to where the Skaar warships were moored. The shadows cast by those of the giant vessels that were aloft blackened the earth and draped her in darkness as she passed beneath. She found a clearing within a copse of fir into which her vessel fit perfectly, and the surrounding ring of trees would provide the perfect cover for all but a thorough inspection. She scanned all about as she climbed out, but saw nothing of a Skaar watch.

Of course, the Skaar could make themselves invisible, so she could be mistaken. But she would find that out soon enough.

She moved toward the encampment, summoning her magic as she did so in case she needed a defense. But no one approached her as she slipped through the trees, skirting the open summit of the hills to draw ever closer to her destination. Already, she could hear a murmur of voices mixed with a few cheers. Ahead, the trees closed up again, providing her with fresh cover. Good enough.

She had reached their perimeter when a Skaar soldier stepped into view, materializing right next to her.

"Stay where you are."

She had learned their language while communicating with Kassen, and therefore understood the order. She waited patiently until a second member of the watch appeared to her other side. As they flanked her, she took on the posture and look of a confused old woman.

"Don't hurt me," she begged.

"Who are you?" the second one asked. "What are you doing here?"

She shook her head, looking down at her feet. "I meant no harm. I was just gathering berries for my family. They have so little to eat. We live right over there."

She pointed, and when they turned to look she used a confusion spell she had gathered at her fingertips to cause them to doubt what they had seen. When they looked back, she was gone and both were already wondering if she had ever been there. There was no point in taking chances on how they might respond to a simple request to be escorted in. Better to safeguard against the possibility that she might now be viewed as an enemy. Better to remain invisible.

Then she was into the trees, ducking from sight and dropping to one knee to see what retaliation might be coming. But no one appeared and no attack was launched against her. She waited patiently for a few moments longer, wanting to be sure, then rose and continued on. No one else had seen her. It was a two-man watch, sufficient for a rear guard when the enemy was clearly in front of them. She wondered what had brought the Federation army to confront the Skaar, and quickly decided it must have been because of what had happened at Paranor. If Ketter Vause believed the Skaar enough of a threat, he would want to put an end to them as quickly as he could. He might have decided to do so here. Or he might have learned of the larger force entering the Four Lands and come to stop them before they got any farther.

Whatever the case, a battle seemed imminent, and she wanted to be well clear before any fighting began.

She reached a rise and a break in the trees that gave her an over-view of the main sections of the encampment, where soldiers were scurrying about and supplies and weapons were being brought up from the transports. She took note of the fact that the numbers of men and women were far superior to what Ajin d'Amphere had brought with her as an advance force. Enough so that there was very little doubt about what had happened.

Cor d'Amphere, her father, had come early to provide her with a larger force, and would now be in command.

Which meant that Clizia needed to change her plans.

# 7

SHEA OHMSFORD HAD BEEN CONVINCED THE WORST had passed now that he was free from the crushing grip of Assidian Deep with the aged scientist Tindall safely in hand, and back on familiar ground inside the massive warehouse where Rocan had hidden Annabelle, but that was merely wishful thinking. As Zakonis and his Federation soldiers broke through the door and entered the room, it was clear that his future was looking as bleak as ever.

Shea backed away instinctively, already searching for an exit. But he had given no real thought to escape routes or flight, and he had no idea if there even was a way out other than the way he had come in. There were places to hide—supplies and equipment were piled everywhere—but there was no time to reach them. Already, the Federation soldiers were spreading out around the room, surrounding Shea and Tindall—hemming them in, backing them up, so that they were pressed up against the base of Annabelle with nowhere to run.

Zakonis seemed pleased. "Got you back again, Tindall," he said, grinning. Shea grimaced as he noted the deep claw marks on the commander's face—a painful reminder of his encounter with Seelah. "And a bit of street trash as a bonus. Now all we need is your partner in crime. Where is Rocan anyway?"

Tindall gave him a scowl but said nothing.

"He's gone to Varfleet," Shea said impulsively.

"And left you here to fend for yourselves?" Zakonis shook his head. "Not true, boy. We're going to be quite close over the days ahead, and starting off with a lie is a big mistake. Back to Assidian Deep for the two of you, with special lodgings and tender, loving care. You thought you got away from me, but you overlooked something."

He walked over to Tindall, seized him by his ear, and brought him to his knees. Tears of pain ran down the old man's weathered cheeks as the Federation commander used a knife to carve a shallow X into the back of his neck. Shea watched in horror, wanting to help but knowing he could do nothing.

"There you are," Zakonis crowed, rubbing blood around the cut with his thumb. "Know what's in there, old man?" He bent down close, holding Tindall's eyes with his own. "You should. You invented it. A tracker. We inserted it when we brought you into Assidian Deep at the beginning of your stay. Did it while you slept. You never knew. Thought maybe, somehow, you might wander off in spite of our hospitality. But this little beauty sends a signal that we can follow right to wherever you might choose to run."

He shoved Tindall all the way to the floor and stepped away. "A good idea, as it turns out."

He glanced over at Shea. "Seems like you're more involved in all this than Rocan claimed, boy. Quite a lot more. You're going to tell me all about it once we get back to the Deep. You and this old fool are going to tell me everything I want to know."

Shea shuddered. He knew what would happen to him, especially after what he had done to free Tindall. The old man was safe enough—the Federation needed his expertise and skills to help supply the Federation army. But Shea was just a street boy, of no use to anyone—an irritation that could be discarded with the rest of Assidian Deep's refuse once he had revealed what he knew.

He could not pretend he was anything less than terrified. There was no scenario in which he was going to escape a second time. He had to fight down the urge to bolt—even knowing it would be futile—because what was there left for him otherwise? But he held his ground, fought back against the overwhelming urge to give in to his fear, and simply stood there, saying nothing.

Off to one side, Tindall climbed back to his feet. "I won't help you," he announced in a ragged voice.

Zakonis glanced over. "Won't you? I wouldn't bet on that. I think, within a few days, you'll *beg* me to let you help. Now sit back down on that bench. You, boy," he added, gesturing to Shea. "You get over there and sit with him. And no moving around, either of you. We'll all just wait for your friend to return."

He walked over to the open door and carefully closed it once more. "There we are, everything as it was."

The boy and the old man sat together in silence, staring off into space. Shea wondered if there was any chance Rocan would realize what had happened before he walked into the trap. He wondered if somehow the Rover would find a way to free them, despite the odds. Rocan was smart and clever, and he seemed to have a sixth sense for knowing when things were amiss. But it was asking a lot to expect him to intuit that his safehold for Annabelle had been compromised and his implacable Federation nemesis was awaiting his return.

He wondered if there was a way he could warn the Rover. The Federation soldiers were scattered about the room, all facing the entry, while Zakonis stood off to one side, studying Annabelle, hands on his hips. The soldiers all carried flash rips, their commander a sidearm. Too many weapons for Rocan to evade them all. Too many enemies for him to overcome. He had to be alerted before he walked through the doorway.

"What is this thing?" Zakonis asked suddenly, gesturing at Annabelle. "What does it do?"

Tindall glanced over, then shrugged. "It cools or heats the room as needed, depending on the weather. Just makes it more comfortable in here."

Zakonis frowned. "Rather large for something like that, isn't it?"

The old man grunted. "It's a large room."

The commander stared at him balefully for a moment, then he looked away and was silent again.

Shea went back to thinking of ways he might warn Rocan, but nothing reasonable came to mind save leaping up and shouting as the door began to open, and that would be the final nail in his coffin. No, he needed to give a silent warning to the Rover before he entered the room, and Shea had no idea how he could manage that.

Beside him, Tindall edged a bit closer. "Sorry about this, boy," he said softly.

Shea grimaced. "Will you please stop calling me 'boy'?"

"I should have realized they tagged me in the prison," he continued, as if he had not heard Shea speak. "I never even thought about the possibility. I was too busy being angry."

Shea sighed. "I probably wouldn't have thought about it, either, if it were me."

"Hey! Old man! You and the boy quiet down. No talking!" Zakonis was glaring at them. "If you're thinking about warning your friend, I promise you'll feel the kiss of a flash rip the moment you try it."

Shea and Tindall were quiet for a time, glancing at each other and then at Zakonis. But the Federation commander was paying no attention to them. Instead, he was staring at Annabelle, studying her with a focused intensity as if determination alone could unlock her secrets. Shea, still looking for a way to escape, wondered if he could lure Zakonis close enough that he could jump him and seize his weapon. *Sure,* he chided himself. *That would work. Then you would only have a dozen of his fellows to deal with.*

A few minutes passed, then Tindall made a small movement to catch Shea's attention. When he glanced over questioningly, the old man cocked his head toward the back of the room.

Shea looked where he was indicating and saw nothing.

The old man saw his confusion and mouthed a single word.

*Seelah.*

This time when he looked, Shea caught a flash of movement within the stacks of supplies and materials. He had forgotten all about Seelah. He had assumed she was off with Rocan or just off alone somewhere, the way she so often was. But the movement was unmistakable. She was back there.

He looked again. He didn't see anything this time. But a second later, one of four Federation soldiers who had stationed themselves at the back of the room disappeared.

Moments later, a second was gone, snatched away with such swiftness there was almost nothing to indicate he had ever been there at all.

A fierce joy swept through the boy. If Seelah was here, they had a chance. The changeling was a force of nature, and even a dozen soldiers might not be enough to overcome her. Shea decided he would do what he could to help.

"If you agree to let me go," he said to Zakonis, "I will tell you something useful about the old man."

Tindall gave him a surprised look, but Shea ignored him. "I know a few things about him that you might be interested in."

Zakonis didn't bother to look at him, apparently mesmerized by Annabelle. "You're in no position to bargain with me. A few days in the Deep, and you'll tell me everything anyway."

Off to one side, a third soldier disappeared—then, an instant later, the fourth as well.

"Rocan isn't coming back," Shea continued, in his efforts to draw the Federation commander's attention. "But I know where he is."

This time, Zakonis did turn. "You don't know anything."

Shea shrugged. "Have it your way. But you're wasting time waiting for him."

"I'm not letting you go, no matter what you tell me."

"But if I tell you where he can be found . . ."

A fifth man was gone. Suddenly one of the soldiers said, "Where's Huett? Huett?"

The other soldiers joined in, calling for companions who were no longer visible, and a sense of panic crept in when there were no answers. Zakonis turned, an angry look on his face.

A sixth soldier disappeared, right in front of the others, and seconds later the core lights that lit the cavernous room went out, leaving everything shrouded in hazy shadow. A swath of dead gray daylight still revealed Annabelle and her surroundings through the skylight, but the walls and corners of the chamber were almost buried in gloom.

Sounds suddenly erupted from everywhere at once, and the remaining Federation soldiers lost what composure remained and began firing their flash rips in wild bursts. And what had moments earlier been a calm silence evolved quickly into chaos. Shea grabbed Tindall by the shoulders and pulled him to the floor, holding him there forcibly.

The old man struggled to get free. "Let go of me!"

"Stay still!" Shea hissed in his ear. "You'll get shot!"

Flash rips continued to crisscross the room with fiery ropes and loud explosions, but other than destroying equipment and supplies, they seemed to be doing nothing useful. Another soldier disappeared and one more was shot by one of his companions. Zakonis was screaming at his men in fury, trying to restore order, but they were not listening.

Then, abruptly, the firing of flash rips ended, and everything went silent once more. Smoke and the smell of char hung on the air, filling the chamber with haze and stench, giving it a demon-like, surreal look. Zakonis was still standing, wheeling this way and that, searching for movement and calling for his men. None answered. Realizing he was alone, he turned toward Shea and Tindall, raising his weapon. "On your feet! Now!"

A second later he lay prostrate on the floor, his weapon lost, a slender foot pressing down on his back with such force that, even though he struggled mightily, he could not move.

Shea released his grip on Tindall and allowed him to get to his knees. The old man stayed there, staring at the apparition that pinned the Federation commander in place.

"Seelah," he marveled aloud.

Shea, grinning from ear to ear, couldn't even manage that much.

They bound and gagged Zakonis, relieving him of his weapons and throwing him into a corner where they could keep watch on him. Seelah had killed the rest—or they had killed one another—so there was no one else to threaten them. Nevertheless, Shea went back down to the first level of the building to make sure no one was lurking at the doors. But Zakonis had apparently believed strongly enough in himself and his men not to bring further backup, and Shea returned to Tindall confident that—for some time, at least—no one else would be coming.

Seelah, satisfied that they were safe enough, allowed Tindall to go back to gazing at his precious machine and curled up with Shea on the bench, nuzzling him with a sustained and deliberate passion. The boy wasn't all that unhappy to have an incredibly exotic and alluring young woman fawning over him—whatever her species happened to be—even if all the attention she was lavishing on him did make him feel more than a little embarrassed. Soon enough, he kept telling himself, she would tire of this game and move on to something else.

Which, in fact, she eventually did. But it took her an uncomfortably long time.

The morning hours passed, and Rocan failed to return. Midday came and went, and as the afternoon hours lengthened, Shea became increasingly worried that something might have happened to him. If something had, it was difficult to say what Tindall and he might do— together or separately—about the future. He wondered if he should send Seelah out looking for him, and even went so far as to suggest it. But the changeling merely smiled and licked his face.

Zakonis, slouched in the corner, bloody-faced and seething, was studying him with undisguised hatred as he worked at loosening the ropes that bound him. But Shea had learned a few tricks over the years, and one of them was how to tie ropes that, when worked against, simply drew tighter. After a time, the Federation Commander stopped struggling and leaned back against the packing crates in baleful silence. Probably, the boy thought, making his plans for what he would do to him once free again.

It was getting close to twilight when Rocan finally returned. He entered cautiously, edging the door to the chamber open with a blade tip and looking inside until he spied Shea sitting with Tindall, and Zakonis bound and gagged to one side. A grin split his smooth features, and he came all the way in with a hearty laugh.

"Commander Zakonis! What a pleasant surprise. I did not expect to have the pleasure of your company again so soon. But you look so uncomfortable! Don't tell me an old man and a boy put you in this position? Not that I wouldn't put it past them to manage it, of course."

Zakonis glared at him threateningly but could do nothing more.

"Where's Seelah?" the Rover asked Shea.

Seelah had disappeared an hour or so back and had not chosen to reappear since, not even upon Rocan's return, so the boy simply shrugged. Then he noticed the pair of men who had followed the Rover in. They were clothed in rough leathers decorated with colorful scarves and sashes, with various types of blades stuffed into belts, and sheaths strapped about shoulders and waists. It didn't require guesswork to conclude they were Rovers.

Rocan noticed him looking. "Cousins," he explained. "Come to help us with our transportation problems. Some others will be here within the hour with an airship. I thought to lease a suitable vessel from within the city, but there are few within the Federation I'd trust. Family, on the other hand, is a different matter. In Rover life, we embrace and honor our kin; we do not betray one another for any reason. We would not survive for long as a people if we did. Having all of the Races in all of the Four Lands suspicious and mistrustful of our people at best, and antagonistic toward them at worst, serves to provide an important lesson."

He sat down beside Tindall and put his arm around the old man. "Of course, there are always exceptions. Some few deserve our trust and loyalty and love for what they have done for us, and for what they have risked. This man is one, Shea Ohmsford." He squeezed the old man's shoulders and looked at the boy. "You are another."

Shea shook his head, thinking of his plans for going home.

"You risked yourself to save him when I asked it of you. This is what I saw in you in Varfleet. Courage, fortitude, determination, and self-confidence. Now I am asking you to stay with us a little longer, while we attempt to accomplish something wonderful. I am asking you to join us in helping Tindall use Annabelle to aid the Four Lands—to help Annabelle provide something that was once only a dream. Will you come with us?"

Shea looked at his feet, already wavering in his determination to leave. He thought again about returning to Varfleet. Returning to the life he knew before he fell under Rocan's spell and came to Arishaig. Returning to the security and familiarity of his former life, where living hand-to-mouth meant forfeiting the possibility of garnering a small fortune but also meant being able to steer clear of places like Assidian Deep and men like Zakonis.

He was stalling, and he knew it. But he could not make himself give an answer. He was torn between his choices once again.

Then, in the midst of his confusion, he heard clearly for the first time the last thing Rocan had said. *Will you come with us?*

He looked up questioningly. "Come with you where?"

The Rover grinned. "I thought you would never ask."

It was another two hours before the promised transport arrived. By then, the last of the sunlight was fading into the west and the eastern shadows were beginning to overlap the city. Rocan had sent one of his cousins to keep watch on the warehouse roof, but the transport announced itself in a much grander way than he could ever have managed. Sliding silently out of skies gone dark and cloudy, it cast its vast shadow over Annabelle's warehouse so thoroughly that any view through the skylight was blocked out completely. Everyone was looking skyward in shock when Sartren, Rocan's cousin on the roof, came flying down the stairs, breathlessly heralding the airship's arrival, bringing all of them charging up onto the roof for a closer look.

What Shea found was beyond anything he had ever imagined—an airship of such size and scope that it dwarfed even the huge warehouses beneath it. The huge vessel had the appearance of a giant predator—frightening in its blackness, and massive beyond belief. Its prow was curved and blunted to form an ironclad ram, while its stern had been shaved flat and slanted inward to join with the long, deep curve of the keel. Four towering masts rose into the night like giant trees, spars and crosstrees extending like limbs to form a vast forest that secured the light sheaths that fed the giant parse tubes filled with diapson crystals to power the ship. The largest vessels Shea had ever seen hung yards of sheeting to form just half a dozen or so sails. But this airship easily hung twice that.

Shea Ohmsford stood staring in disbelief. The wind blew wildly across the rooftop, scattering his long hair into ragged strands, and he could imagine himself sailing aboard the vessel above him, standing on its decks, looking out over new worlds and wonderful vistas. Even without thinking about it, he slipped off his headband and let his hair flow out, loving the feel, letting his imagination soar. He would not be traveling so far this time, but one day he might. And maybe sooner than later.

"Nothing like her," Sartren offered, clapping a hand on the boy's shoulder as he came up beside him.

Shea shook his head. "Nothing," he agreed. He had not known until now that a vessel of this size could even exist. The excitement and wonder that coursed through left him breathless, and he found himself grinning like a fool.

"Family-built, family-owned, family-sailed," Sartren continued, as if unaware of his besotted look. "She's ours and she's ours alone. Bit of a reach, letting Rocan have a go with her, but he's an insistent sort, and by the end of the voting, he'd gotten his way."

"What's she called?" Shea asked.

"*Behemoth*. It means something like 'larger than you can imagine' or 'much bigger than life.' Something like that. Rovers didn't name her. We built her, but left the naming to a seer. The seer gave her that name, maybe two years ago."

"But you kept it?" Shea brushed away the hair that had blown into his eyes and squinted in the poor light.

Sartren leaned close. "You don't go against the word of a seer, lad. You don't ever risk that."

Then he was gone, and Shea was left alone again, staring upward at the *Behemoth*. She was a fixed point beneath banks of clouds that rolled across the sky with ponderous determination, the stars appearing and fading in the wash. He had not thought he would go with Rocan tonight; he had been ready to leave him and Tindall and their wild schemes and go home. But you could never tell in this world

how fate would change your life, and so it was here. What he had believed to be true yesterday was now as lost as the day itself.

Off to one side, the skylight was sliding open, cranked back by
pulleys and winches, the motors that powered them purring softly
as they engaged. The banks of lights that illuminated the interior had
been kindled once more, and chains were snaking downward from
the *Behemoth* to secure and lift Annabelle away.

By morning they would be gone, and Shea would go with them.

"Where do you want to go most?" Rocan had asked him earlier,
when the boy had pressed him on his intentions.

And he had answered, "I want to go home."

"Then that is where you will go, Shea Ohmsford. That is just where
you will go."

For the Rover had decided that while it was not safe to remain in
Arishaig, it was safe enough to find a hiding place in the Borderlands
and in Varfleet specifically. There, they would be able to go to ground
more easily. There, they would be able to better conceal themselves
from Federation eyes. And there, they had a safehold that not even
Zakonis, with his nose for sniffing out those he sought, would be
likely to uncover. Not that he could find them in any case, now that
Rocan had extracted the tracker from the back of Tindall's neck. That
particular trick was no longer up the commander's proverbial sleeve.

So. Home to Varfleet. Exactly where Shea had wanted to go, and
now he was to be taken there. The conditions might not be as he had
anticipated, and he was not yet free of the strings that bound him to
Rocan and Tindall and the wild plans they were bent on pursuing.
But just at the moment, he was content to go along for the ride and
see where he ended up.

He was still a fifteen-year-old boy, and adventure was a lure he
could not easily dismiss.

# 8

NOT TOO FAR NORTH FROM THE BANKS OF THE Mermidon, an expanded two-man was making its way along the slopes of the Dragon's Teeth. Having decided on a destination, Drisker Arc was quick to usher everyone on board the craft Dar Leah, Brecon Elessedil, and Tarsha Kaynin had flown to Paranor. He was adding himself and Tarsha's brother to their number, but all were able to squeeze in by removing some of the supplies and equipment, which hopefully would still leave them with what they needed to complete their journey.

He was slow to reveal where they were going, although Dar had guessed at the truth before the Druid finally came around to admitting it. By then, they were well under way.

"It has been years since any Druid has made this journey, but I think we must go to the Valley of Shale and the shores of the Hadeshorn, to summon the spirits of the dead," he told them. "If we are successful, the shades of my Druid predecessors will reveal what is needed."

They had lifted off by midday and flown south to the mountains before turning east. It was at that point that Dar, familiar with the Druid history and aware of their previous visits to the Hadeshorn, suspected that Drisker was going to attempt a communication. After all, Drisker had made it plain enough he did not know what he should do next, and a meeting with one of the Druid shades made sense. Sort of, because the shades did not always speak clearly enough for the meaning of their words to be understood—or even always speak the truth. Such a meeting, therefore, was always a bit of a gamble on the part of the supplicant.

"I cannot promise I will be able to get the answers I am looking for," Drisker continued, ruefully. "Shades dissemble and riddle, but I might be able to extract enough information to determine how we should best direct our efforts and what means might be used to try to solve our problems."

No one had much to say to that. Except for Dar himself, no one had any experience with the Hadeshorn or the Druid practice of communicating with the dead. And for the moment, no one seemed to want to know more about how this was done.

So they traveled in silence along the rugged cliff walls, oblivious to what was taking place just on the other side as they passed east, their attention focused on preparing for what lay ahead and the attendant difficulties they were facing. Tarsha was wrapped up in her efforts to help Tavo, and Dar could tell by the furtive looks she gave her brother as they sat across from each other that she was debating about how to proceed. The Blade sat in the front seat of the craft with Brecon, who was piloting, helping with the navigation—both of them listening to Drisker as he periodically offered directions from the bench he occupied just behind them.

The day itself was heavily overcast, not much warmer than the previous night, and the snow was still in evidence on the ground below them, with drifts cradled in the rocks of the higher peaks. It was an unmistakable reminder of the weather that was coming. Winter in the Four Lands was bitter—especially in the far north—and the months it dominated were snow-filled and cold. South of the Mermidon, it held less sway, the snows more scarce and the cold of nightfall milder and quicker to warm with sunrise. In the time he had been in residence, Dar had never cared for winters at Paranor—although the Keep itself stayed warm enough. Venturing forth always required bundling up, for the winds blew the cold down out of the Northland with a steady persistence. As a boy, he had become accustomed to the mild temperatures of the Highlands, and the colder winters of the mountains surrounding Paranor always reminded him of what he was missing.

It was nearing sunset when they ascended through a gap in the peaks where the Dragon's Teeth swung north again to form the eastern wall of Paranor's enclosure. As they rose to clear the rocks, the snows began anew, flurries swirling about them in small bursts. The wind was colder than before at this elevation, and all five passengers wrapped their cloaks tighter. It helped a little, Dar decided, but not much. He hunched lower into his seat and prepared to wait out the crossing.

They completed it within the hour, navigating the jutting outcroppings and ragged splits in the huge peaks, watching the sun descend to the west through gaps that periodically permitted a viewing. No one was saying anything at this point. The wind was blowing with such sound and fury, it was not even reasonable to try. Dar spent what energy he could muster watching the land ahead, trying to catch a glimpse of their destination.

He failed to do so, as the land on the far side of the Dragon's Teeth was overcast with mist and low-hanging clouds. Silvery rays of a hazy sunset pierced the gloom here and there, pinpointing distant bits and pieces of the terrain below, but did little to reveal the sweep of the land itself. What Dar could make out was limited to glimpses of the mountains where they rose above the brume in patches of rock facing and steep cliffs, and now and again the faraway ribbon of the Mermidon as it snaked its way east in a dark churning of white-capped waters.

Eventually, once they were through the mountains and safely on the southern side, Drisker ordered them to bring the craft down into the foothills and find an open meadow in which to land. Brecon did so with ease, bringing them as close as possible to where they would climb into the Valley of Shale. The valley itself remained hidden, the land misted and monochromatic here, too—its features a blend that lacked color and depth, so that nothing much stood out from anything else.

Once they had landed and disembarked from their craft, Drisker called them over. "From here, we walk. We are no more than a couple of hours away, but once at the Hadeshorn, we must wait until just before dawn to attempt contact with the dead. An hour from sunrise is the optimal time to begin summoning them, and then we will have no more than the time it takes for the sun to crest the horizon to make our entreaties. Are you all willing to come with me?"

All but Tavo spoke in the affirmative, but even he gave an uncertain nod. Dar looked at Drisker. "Will the airship be safe if we leave it unguarded? Are we far enough away from civilization that no one will stumble on it? Maybe I should stay behind to keep watch."

The Druid shook his head. "This is wild, remote country. No one will find our ship here. I think it would be better if we stayed together. Once we reach the Valley of Shale, however, I must approach the Hadeshorn alone. You will wait for me on the slopes above, safely out of the way. It would be too dangerous for you to come close to the waters of the lake, and the shades of the Druids will be more likely to respond to me if I am alone."

"I don't understand," Tarsha said. "If we are not allowed to come out of hiding, why are we coming at all?"

"Because it will be safer if we do not separate. Under our present circumstances, there is safety in numbers. Nevertheless, I want you to stay hidden from whoever appears."

"Who is it you will summon?" Dar asked him.

He shook his head. "Allanon, perhaps. I must wait and see how I feel when the time comes. But at the end of the day—or in this case, the beginning—I must settle for whoever chooses to show themselves."

"What if no one comes?"

"Then we will find another way to choose our path." He turned to look toward the higher reaches of the mountains behind them. "There's a storm coming, and it looks to be a bad one. We had better get started."

Aboard what she now thought of as her prison ship, Ajin d'Amphere looked up from ruminating about her father's unfair treatment to notice the darkening skies to the northwest above the Dragon's Teeth.

She was on her way back to Skaarsland and confinement, unable to stop imagining what it would be like for however many months it took her father to return. She was in the company of four guards and a small crew of two. *Four guards.* Her father was taking no chances; he had even had her relieved of her weapons. His final words still echoed in her head. She was going to learn to do what she was told. She was going to learn that her father's rules must be obeyed.

As if that could ever happen.

She watched the banks of storm clouds roll across the peaks, keeping pace with her airship as it flew east along the wall of the mountains. The plan was to fly to the end of the chain before turning north onto the Rabb Plains and continuing to where the Charnals met the Upper Anar, eventually reaching the Tiderace, which they would cross to arrive two weeks later in Skaarsland.

She had not followed that route coming to the Four Lands, but it was the route her captors had selected. Her thoughts traveled back to her arrival at the beachhead where, with her advance force behind her, she would march south to the Mermidon and the beginning of the conquest of the tribal nations and the destruction of the Druids. She had not been given explicit permission to undertake any of this beyond making an incursion inland. But how could her father fail to recognize the importance of what she had accomplished? How could he not understand the value of it? She had given him so much more than a foothold in this, their intended new country. She had given him the means to negotiate for the right to stay and bring their people with them.

And now what would he do? Her father was strong and difficult and implacable. He would ruin it all. He lacked her instincts and battle intelligence. He lacked her charisma. He had relied on her for so long, and now he was throwing all that away in the very dangerous belief that he could do just as well, as long as he had an army behind him.

Maybe Kol'Dre would be able to convince him otherwise, to persuade him that he was making a grave mistake and should bring Ajin back again. Maybe—but somehow she doubted it. He was too stubborn and proud. Too overconfident in his leadership abilities. Too suspicious of her.

She looked at the men around her, none of whom were looking back. They were uncomfortable with this assignment. Perhaps they even thought it a mistake for the same reasons she did. They did not fear her, though they knew she was dangerous even weaponless. Nor should they. She was not about to fight her way free and strike off on her own. If she did, what would she do? Where would she go? What mattered most would be found back where she had come from, and she clearly could not go there.

She wondered how she was going to get through this.

Of one thing she was certain. She was going to have to be very careful once she reached Skaarsland. The *pretender* would be waiting for her, and not with open arms but with unsheathed blades. She would try to have Ajin killed just as quickly as she could manage it. She would make it look like an accident, but would kill her just the same. She would know her efforts to undermine both her husband and Ajin herself had been discovered, and she would seek to solidify whatever power remained to her. Ajin's mother would be in danger, too, and would need protecting. The new queen, the *pretender*, was ambitious and jealous of her place at the king's side, and she would do whatever she felt she must to eliminate competition.

"Something to drink, Princess?" Jor'Alt asked, leaning close.

He offered her a waterskin, waiting for her response. She nodded without answering and took the skin. Unloosening the stopper, she drank deeply and almost gagged. Alcohol of some sort. She had wrongly assumed the contents of the skin, and the sharp bite of this concoction had surprised her. Even so, she welcomed it. She swallowed, then drank some more. Somehow the liquor seemed appropriate for the situation.

She finished and handed it back. "Thank you."

Jor'Alt nodded. "I'm sorry about this," he said quietly.

She understood, and put a hand on his arm. "It isn't something I would ever blame you or any of my soldiers for," she said. "I brought it on myself."

"If I could, I would return you to your father immediately." He was looking back to where they had come from. "Standing with us is your destiny. You should be leading us."

"My father would disagree."

"Your father would be wrong."

He was bold to speak like this in front of the king's daughter, but they knew each other slightly and Ajin was never the sort to run to her father with tales, even when he still listened to her. What happened between soldiers was never to leave their ranks, and she was one of them. They knew she would keep silent.

She smiled at him. "Maybe he will see it that way in time, and you will be able to bring me back."

His rough soldier's face creased with his smile. "But for now, we can at least visit."

They did so, recalling days past and events survived. The other guards in the craft glanced over every now and then but did not presume to add anything to the conversation. For them, it was best to leave things as they were and go about their business, even if that business required virtually nothing of them but to sit silently and wait for the flight home to be complete. None of them would be coming back to the Four Lands right away, after all. The flight was too long and their numbers too few to bother about. They would stay with their friends and families and do what they could there.

For their loved ones. For Skaarsland.

Ajin was thinking about what she would find on her return besides the *pretender* and her schemes. There was always hope. By the time she returned, the weather might have changed. It might have gotten better. The winter might have lessened in its fury, and the wasted, barren fields and their withered crops might have begun a slow regeneration. The cold might have lost its bitterness; the sun might have returned to bring back warmth and light. The sicknesses that had woken in the wake of Skaarsland's endless winter might have at last been overcome and the health of her people might have improved.

But she doubted it. There was no reason for any of this to happen. She would find what she had left, only worse. She would rediscover the hopelessness and despair she remembered all too well.

She glanced ahead. She could see the Rabb grasslands many miles away to the east, mist-shrouded and empty, stretching out from the end of the Dragon's Teeth. The mountains themselves were wrapped in gloom, their lower reaches nearly invisible. Farther up, snow layered the mountainsides. Paranor would have been on the other side, before she had breached its walls and Druid magic had cast it into whatever far-flung place it now inhabited.

She wondered suddenly, unexpectedly, about Darcon Leah.

The journey progressed, and night had long since fallen when the first of the heavy winds struck the aircraft, knocking it momentarily askew. Ajin hunkered lower in her seat, wondering if they shouldn't put down. It would be foolish to fly any farther in this weather.

But that's what it seemed they were doing.

She felt a spike of fear. In spite of her misgivings and even a question or two directed at the pilot about the wisdom of continuing on, they were staying aloft.

Then abruptly the diapson crystals gave out and they were falling into a roiling kettle of fog that left her feeling as if they might tumble away forever.

It took Drisker's little company about two hours to complete the climb to the hidden entrance into the Valley of Shale—a narrow split in the rocks that a climber unfamiliar with the terrain would have avoided as a matter of course. Dar was surprised when the Druid brought a magic-induced light to his fingertips to chase back the darkness and beckoned them to come through, thinking there must surely be an entrance to the valley that was larger and more recognizable than this dangerous-looking fissure. But once they had navigated the hundred feet or so of claustrophobic walls that threatened to close overhead at every turn, he found himself outside once more and standing on slopes leading downward into what was clearly identifiable as a valley.

Here the skies were clear, and moon- and starlight lit the entire valley. Moving forward a few steps, he found he could see far below—through horizontal banks of mist and heavy shadows—to a dark and brooding stretch of water as flat and depthless as hard-packed earth. The Hadeshorn, he realized. The surface of its waters did not shimmer or shift in the slightest. It was impossible to see what waited within, or even to imagine there was a depth to it. All around, on the shores and the slopes of the valley, black shards of obsidian lay jagged and shining, and it was as if the storm had somehow been pushed aside.

The valley was a striking sight—so many different shapes and terrains, dark and flat here while shining brightly there, jagged and smooth, rough and slick. Dar took it all in quickly and was still trying to make it fit in his mind when Drisker beckoned them to sit.

"Wait here for me. Do not come farther into the valley for any reason. Do not think to come to my aid should you see me in apparent distress. There is nothing you can do for me once I go down to her shores. You would only risk your own lives, and it would be for nothing. Stay put until I return to you."

Then he turned away from them and walked toward the dark sprawl of the Hadeshorn and did not look back.

They watched him go in silence, saw him descend to the shoreline and stop there to stare out across the lake's strange waters. He did not move again. He was wrapped in his cloak and hood now, a solitary figure standing black and unmoving, as if he were himself a shade come out of the netherworld. As time passed, the mists that had hung above the lake earlier in thin strips began to tighten and descend toward the earth. It did not take long for them to begin to enclose the Druid, to wrap about him as if to hold him fast. Dar and his companions were forced to peer more closely just to catch a glimpse of him.

And then he was gone entirely.

Hours passed and the night drifted away. They could not see the moon or stars and had to rely on their instincts to advise them on how close the sunrise actually was. It was taking what felt like an abnormally long time. Dar grew steadily more restless with each passing hour, not sure at first why this should be so, then realizing that he was worrying about their transport. If anything happened to the airship, they would be forced to walk out of these mountains to whatever town or city lay closest, and that could take days.

The feeling that he needed to leave here was pressing down on him. He could not explain it, but he felt it necessary to make sure their source of transportation was still all right.

Finally, he turned to the others. "I'm going back to check on the airship. You can meet me back there when Drisker returns."

Looks were exchanged. "I'll come with you," Brecon said.

"No," the Blade replied quickly, knowing this would leave Tarsha alone with her brother. "I'll be all right."

"I'll go with you instead," Tarsha said suddenly, climbing to her feet. "It will be safer if two of us go."

Dar started to object, then saw the wisdom in her offer. This would separate her from Tavo without her appearing to desert him. He gave her brother a quick glance to judge his reaction, but Tavo seemed caught up in the drama that was taking place on the shores of the Hadeshorn and barely glanced over.

"Come, then," Dar agreed, nodding to Brecon to be sure he understood. "We'll try to return before dawn."

Brecon nodded back in acknowledgment but said nothing in reply.

Dar and Tarsha climbed back up the slopes and, fashioning a makeshift torch of a length of wood and dry grasses to light their way, passed through the split that had brought them into the valley, proceeding at a steady pace. The walk back down would be much quicker than the walk up and require less of them to complete it, so both were eager. Dar wasn't especially tired, even though the day had been stressful and it had been awhile since he had slept; he was practiced at staying awake for several days when it was needed. Tarsha, however, was not. She had not slept at all since the previous night, and even then her rest had been fitful. Still, she showed no signs of faltering as they went, so after a while he stopped worrying.

"Thank you for letting me come," she said at one point.

"I should be thanking you for finding a way to keep me from worrying about leaving you alone with your brother."

"I would have been fine, I think. He seems a different person since Drisker talked to him."

"Maybe. But I prefer to be a bit more certain before we test your theory. The danger is still there."

"Fair enough. Anyway, the cold is starting to get to me. I think I might find something warmer back in the airship."

They walked on for about an hour, speaking only occasionally—casual conversation about nothing in particular save when they began speculating about how Drisker's encounter with the shades of the dead was likely to go. Neither felt all that confident in what he might learn—because of both the source of the information and the complexity of the problems. Asking for direction in a situation with so many attendant difficulties was problematic at best and dangerous at worst. Dar didn't like it, but he could not make himself go against the Druid's wishes—especially when he had nothing better to offer.

By the time they had reached the more exposed slopes of the lower Dragon's Teeth and started down, the wind began to whip across them with new ferocity. Their torch had long since extinguished, and the light was pale and washed out. Rain started falling, quickly turning to snow. In the distance, the clouds were black and roiling, and what little remained of the sky with its stars and moon quickly disappeared. Blackness rolled in like a giant carpet, blanketing everything. The storm quickly worsened, and thunder crashed with huge, earth-shaking booms while streaks of lightning split the darkness.

Dar and Tarsha walked with their heads and shoulders bent, eyes on the path ahead, for it became increasingly difficult for them to find their way. Before long, their concentration was given over entirely to the movement of their feet.

"He still won't talk to me," Tarsha said suddenly, a deep sadness in her voice. "Not a word."

The Blade didn't have to ask who she was talking about. "He will. Give him time. He's still getting used to the idea that maybe you were his friend all along and not his betrayer."

"I can't tell what he thinks. I can't tell anything. He might just be waiting to try to kill me again and thinks words are a waste of time. He might be so ashamed of himself he doesn't know how to talk to me anymore. But I don't see how I can be of any help if we don't communicate."

"It's only been one day, Tarsha," Dar reminded her. "You can't expect too much in one day."

"No. But I was hoping for *something*." She gave a long sigh. "It's just been so hard knowing he's blamed me for everything that's happened to him. I can't imagine what he's gone through. Think how it must make him feel to know he killed our parents and all those people while hunting for me. And I'm worried that if he tries to use the magic again, it will destroy him. Can that collar stop him?"

Dar shrugged. "You'll have to trust Drisker on that one. But I don't think he would take any chances with your brother."

"I'm going to make him talk to me tomorrow, no matter how much he tries to avoid it."

"You're a determined young lady. I'm certain you'll get the job done."

The storm was howling so loudly by now that, when they stopped talking, Dar realized they had been yelling at each other in order to be heard. The roar of the wind and slap of the wet snow on their bodies filled the void left by their silence. The temperature was dropping, and the cold was harsh against his exposed face. He was having trouble seeing. If things got worse, they would have to take shelter wherever they could find it.

If there was any to be found, he amended. Glancing about, he could only see open hillsides with scrub and clusters of sparse trees.

Then he heard a strange noise—a high whine that cut in and out abruptly. It was coming from the west, somewhere deep within the storm. When he looked, he saw flashes of light that looked almost like sparks, erratic and of differing intensity.

As he slowed to stare at the source, he knew instinctively that someone was in trouble.

He followed the light's progress as it lurched in and out of low-hanging clouds and banks of heavy mist. Through the curtain of snow that was falling, it had the look of something not quite real.

Tarsha came up beside him, bending close to be heard. "Is that an airship?"

He nodded wordlessly. An airship, fighting to stay aloft.

But seconds later, it was falling out of the sky.

# 9

DRISKER ARC WALKED SLOWLY AND CAUTIOUSLY into the Valley of Shale over acres of razor-sharp obsidian, placing his feet carefully as he proceeded on the loose and slippery shards. A fall on such terrain could result in serious damage; the sharp edges were easily capable of slicing through clothing and skin. All around him, the trailers of mist he had spied from the valley's rim were moving, even in the absence of any wind. Lowering toward the valley floor while lengthening and joining, they were steadily forming a solid mass of brume that would hide the lake and eventually himself, as well, from those he had left behind.

He did not look back at his companions to measure their reaction. He had told them what they must do, and he had to take it on faith that they would obey him. He was thinking ahead to what would take place once sunrise arrived on the shores of the Hadeshorn. He knew from his readings of the Druid Histories what the past had produced, but he had no way of knowing if the past would be repeated here. There had been no reason to even think about it until now. No Druid had come for a visit with the dead since the time of Aphenglow Elessedil.

It was a sobering realization. He would be the first in all that time, and he was not sure how he should prepare himself. He remem-

bered, from Walker Boh's writings, that there might be no real way
to prepare—that expectations were a fool's game and only served to
leave you twisting in the winds of fate. The dead came to the living
when and if they chose. The dead told you what they wished to and
did so in quixotic and devious ways. What you might learn was always determined by how well you read their voices. What you might
learn was frequently buried beneath or within the words, and sometimes from what was not spoken at all.

Intuiting what was true and what was not was of absolute necessity. So he must listen carefully and take nothing for granted. He must
look behind what he was told for hidden meanings. He must be wary
of false assumptions and misinterpretations.

He must also not think of the four who remained on the rim, even
though his tendency was to worry about them. Especially Tarsha and
Tavo. He had done his best to provide them with a chance to put the
past behind them. He had placed the inhibiting collar about Tavo's
neck to prevent him from using his magic. He had extracted Tavo's
promise to listen to his sister's words when they talked and to remember that she had been his greatest champion and, to a large extent, was the reason he was still alive.

It was difficult to say how much of this would work out. Success
would have to be measured incrementally, and it would take time
for the results to reveal themselves. Tarsha would understand this.
She was wise beyond her years, a young girl who took a measured
approach to everything. But Tavo was much less reliable—impulsive
and sometimes uncontrollable, possessed of an erratic and explosive
temper. Both had the magic of the wishsong, but Tarsha knew how to
manage it. It was hard to know if that would ever be true of Tavo. Any
hope for change felt futile. It seemed impossible that Tavo could ever
learn to tame himself sufficiently that using his magic would become
a positive experience.

The Druid reached the edge of the Hadeshorn and took up a
position on the near shore to wait. He was aware of the fog closing
about, and on glancing back up in the direction from which he had
come, he saw that the upper slopes had disappeared entirely. In point

of fact, the fog was so thick by now he could barely make out the shoreline to either side, and the farther shores and the center of the lake had become invisible.

While he waited, he contemplated what he might expect from Clizia Porse as she continued to set about founding a new Druid order with herself at its center. Many possibilities suggested themselves. Paranor had returned to the Four Lands, and she might well try to get inside. She might also seek alliances with some or all of the Races in an effort to gain support for her efforts to rebuild the Druid order. She might renew her alliance with the Skaar. The trick was to outmaneuver her in the interim by finding ways to scuttle her efforts permanently.

And that meant finding a way to stay alive.

The sliver of light that lined the western rim of the valley in silver indicated dawn's approach. Drisker straightened and faced out across the lake. It was time.

Arms stretched wide as if to gather the Hadeshorn to him, he called in the Druid language for a response from those who dwelled within. Almost instantly the waters began to heave, forming white-capped waves and churning with wild abandon. Bursts of spray caught by winds that hadn't been there moments before were blown up, leaving his face and clothing damp. As the waters continued to roil with dissatisfaction and anger—his reading of their response to his intrusion unmistakable—voices called out from the lake's depths. Moaning and howling by turns, they rose skyward to fill the deep silence of the valley. Their pleadings could not be understood, but Drisker moved his arms in a beckoning gesture, seeking to form a connection with one of the Druid shades so that he would have a chance of gaining answers to his questions.

Then the lake's waters split apart, and the dead began to rise. Hundreds, then thousands of smallish white forms surged into the broad beam of a light that emanated from down within the dark—figures that resembled the faceless dead of men, women, and children from all the Races, come forth in a brief, wild burst of freedom. They flung themselves skyward, climbing as if to find new life. But there would be no life given to the dead from this summoning. Their momentary joy was ephemeral and misguided, and it would not survive his departure.

Even so, he could not help reveling in their exultation as he watched them dance on the air. But they were not who he sought, so he kept his gaze directed toward the mist-free center of the lake where the waters had gone oddly still. It was here that a Druid would appear. This was where Drisker must keep watch for his shade.

The cacophony of sounds made by the rising dead drowned out everything but the hissing of the spray they left in their wake and the crashing of the waves as they surged against the shores. Gone was any connection to what Drisker had known before coming down to the lake. Gone was any sense of the world beyond. He had invoked a summoning, and now he was bound to it as surely as if he had been wrapped in chains.

"Allanon!" he called, his voice booming out, rough and demanding.

But it was not Allanon who appeared.

The waters at the lake's exact center—still as glass within the maelstrom swirling all around them as the spirits of the dead continued to fill the skies—birthed a cloaked and hooded figure much smaller in stature. Dark and unknowable from where Drisker waited, the figure stood upon the waters of the Hadeshorn and regarded its summoner from within the shadow of its robes.

Then it started toward him, and he could not deny the cold and empty feeling that settled upon him. Who was this dark wraith? Who was this frightening creature that could make him feel so threatened?

The shade moved steadily closer, giving no hint as to its identity, showing no interest in all the turmoil taking place about it, but only watching Drisker. The Druid breathed deeply. This was not what he had expected, and he already sensed that what followed was not going to go the way he had anticipated—even though he had tried not to look ahead.

A dozen feet away, still standing on the waters of the lake, the figure stopped and slowly pulled back its hood to reveal its face.

It was all Drisker could do to keep from gasping in shock.

* * *

Ajin d'Amphere closed her eyes against the rushing of the wind and the cursing of the pilot, and she braced herself as best she could, unable to do more than pray to the Skaar gods that some sort of miracle would save them.

It would be, for most of them, a futile hope.

The drop seemed to last forever, in no way helped by the spinning of their craft, the rush of the air in their ears as they gained speed, or the mix of thunder and lightning that had begun moments before. She curled herself into a ball, realizing she would probably not survive this. The end of her life, out in a foreign wilderness, far from home, in the company of men she barely knew and their prisoner to boot—she could hardly believe it was happening.

And then they slammed into the earth in a hammer stroke that threw her sideways into a world of pain and darkness.

She did not know how long she was unconscious. Her guess, when she woke, was that it had been no more than a few minutes. Fuzzy-headed and throbbing with pain, she took a moment to regain her senses before she looked around. The rain from earlier had turned to snow, and the first beginnings of white patches were visible from where she lay. She tried to move, and quickly stopped herself as the pain ratcheted up. Pieces of the airship lay all about her, most of it barely identifiable. The vessel had blown apart on impact, leaving the men with her scattered all over the place—some of them likewise in pieces. The darkness blanketed everything, but glimmerings of fire-light from bits of the aircraft that were burning allowed her to see a little of what had happened.

They had come down on a rocky hillside, but had avoided landing on any of the larger boulders—a miracle. Even so, the front of the airship had plowed directly into a rocky outcrop, leaving it so badly crumpled that nothing recognizable remained, including the pilot and his crewman. Of the others, one was folded into himself in a position that told her at once he was dead. Then she saw a second man—or half of him—split in two by a large piece of planking from their craft, which had eviscerated him midsection.

She closed her eyes momentarily and then looked down at herself. The clothing on one side of her body was soaked with blood—her own or someone else's, she couldn't say—but it was enough to tell her that the injury was serious if it was hers. Her legs were numb, as well, and she decided that maybe she shouldn't try moving them just yet. Otherwise, everything seemed to be intact, protected to some small extent perhaps by the heavy greatcoat she had chosen.

Then she noticed the length of mast stretched across the lower part of her legs, just visible in the heavy darkness, and she realized why her legs were numb. She tried moving them, but she was pinned fast against a mix of timbers and earth.

She levered herself into a sitting position and stared at the heavy mast. So she was alive, but what were her chances of staying that way if she couldn't free herself?

Not so good, she thought. Not good at all.

Then a ragged figure staggered into view. Jor'Alt, bloodied and limping, and she felt a surge of hope. He appeared out of the blackness, saw her sitting there looking at him, and stopped. There was a moment of hesitation, then she saw his features tighten. "Princess?"

She couldn't help a smile. "Thanks be to whatever gods there are that you're all right! Are there any others besides you?"

He didn't reply right away, but instead squatted down about ten feet from her. "Dead, all of them. All killed by the impact of the landing. At least, that is what I will tell them when they find me." He hesitated again. "Princess, I am very sorry about how this is going to turn out."

*An odd way to put it.* She tried to make sense of his words. Then suddenly she could and went cold with the realization that followed. "I'm not going to survive, either, am I?"

He shook his head no. "Only me. I killed Ta'Wentz a few moments ago. He was already almost dead, so you could argue that I simply put him out of his misery. That leaves only you, and you will be dead, too."

He brought out his ballach—a Skaar weapon with a wickedly curved short blade.

She couldn't believe it. "Why are you doing this? I thought we were friends."

"Fate determines all our destinies, Princess; it always has. I can't leave you alive. My family back home will die on the day you return. The queen has promised me that this will happen if I fail. I am sorry, but I must protect my family."

She sat up straighter, moving her arms behind her back to brace herself. "You could spare my life and still find a way to save them, Jor'Alt. The queen does not give orders to anyone. My father is still king!"

"Your father is so besotted with his wife that he gives her freedom to do as she wants. You know this from what she has done to you. I was told you would be sent back. I was told to kill you. I will do what is necessary to save my family."

He fingered his ballach's fat blade. "If you do not struggle, I will make it quick."

She nodded. "I will try to do the same for you, Jor'Alt."

The throwing knife she had hidden in her clothing behind her back was already in her hand. She had been searched, of course, but there were places where a man was not likely to look so carefully. Her arm whipped out with all the force she could muster, the weight and strength of her upper body and her depth of experience with weapons behind the throw, and the entire length of the blade buried itself in Jor'Alt's exposed throat. His windpipe severed, his spinal column crushed, he dropped to his knees, choking and gasping, as his hands went to his throat. With a supreme effort, he pulled the throwing knife free, and a fountain of blood gushed forth.

He died quickly.

She watched him collapse and savored the deep sense of relief that flooded through her. But it lasted only a moment as her rage at the *pretender* replaced it, and she howled like a wolf to the darkened skies.

Darcon Leah and Tarsha Kaynin had started in the direction of the airship the moment it became apparent that it was going to crash. They went quickly, but not so as to endanger themselves in this night of darkness and falling snow and in this unfamiliar terrain. They were still some distance off when an explosion of earth and rocks and snow flew into the air, and the sound reverberated and momentarily eclipsed the howl of the wind. Keeping their eyes fixed on the approximate location of the crash site, they pushed on against a crosswind threatening to knock them off their feet.

It was hard going, and they didn't speak to each other as they struggled forward. No words were needed—not yet. Dar was already wondering who had been flying the airship and if anyone inside could possibly have survived. He did not think it would be dangerous to approach; the passengers and crew of the vessel were likely in no condition, even if some were still alive, to present a threat.

And if any were alive and could be saved . . .

A howl split the night, raw and bloodcurdling, momentarily bringing them up short before they surged ahead once more, doubling their pace. Ahead, they could see the dark bulk of the wreck, timbers and planking smoking, and ruined shards of shattered diapson crystals still sparking. They were right on top of the airship before they saw a figure wave to them from the midst of the wreckage.

When they got close enough for their torches to cast light over the wreckage, they saw that the survivor's legs were pinned beneath a heavy piece of mast that had broken off in the crash.

Then abruptly Dar realized who he was looking at, and he found himself completely dumbstruck.

"Darcon Leah," Ajin d'Amphere greeted him. Then she began to laugh. "We just cannot help finding ways back to each other, can we?"

"Apparently not," he said as he knelt next to her. Of all the people he might have expected to find here, she was the very last. Although he was beginning to wonder what sort of capricious fate kept throwing them back together. How was it possible that she could be *here*?

"Are you badly hurt?" Tarsha was kneeling beside the Skaar princess, as well, her face alight with concern.

Dar quickly reached over and moved her back. "Not too close, Tarsha," he warned. "This is Ajin d'Amphere, princess of the Skaar. She was the leader of the advance force that wiped out the Druids, and was directly responsible for sending Paranor and Drisker into limbo. She is *not* a friend."

Ajin shook her head. "You wound me with such harsh words, Dar-con. After all, I saved your life not so long ago and you, in turn, saved mine. We have a strong link, you and I." She shifted her gaze between them. "Besides, I hardly think either of you need worry about me any-more. Not after what I've endured. If you free me from the wreckage, I will tell you all about it. It will probably make you happy to hear."

Dar gave a dismissive grunt. "We'll see. First, let's find out if we can free you to relate your woes."

He motioned Tarsha away, moved over to one end of the timber that trapped Ajin's legs, and bent to lift it. He couldn't. He was unable to move it even an inch. He tried repeatedly, but the weight of the mast defeated him.

"I need an ax," he muttered.

Ajin shook her head. "Everything was scattered on impact, along with all of those aboard—me included—save that one." She pointed at a crumpled man, who was sprawled to one side, his throat torn open, the blood still welling up. "He tried to kill me."

"You must be used to that." Dar walked over and looked down at the man. "Isn't he one of yours?"

"So I thought. A mistake on my part, it appears. But then, I have made quite a few lately. Can you not find a way to free me?"

"If I can get help, maybe . . ."

"I don't think we should wait for that," Tarsha said suddenly. "Look at her left side."

Dar did, and immediately saw that the dark patch he had mis-taken for her clothing was blood. He brushed the snowflakes from his face to clear his vision and knelt down again. "How bad do you think it is, Princess?"

"Ajin," she corrected him. "We agreed." Although to Dar's way of thinking, they hadn't agreed to anything. "I don't know," she contin-ued. "It doesn't hurt much, but the bleeding hasn't stopped."

Dar bent close.

"It's my legs I'm worried about," she added.

"I think we need to free her, and it's probably a job best left to me," Tarsha said, touching his shoulder.

He rose and turned to her. "You'll use the wishsong?"

She nodded. "Can I try?"

He nodded wordlessly, and she moved to stand directly over the broken mast piece where it pinned Ajin in place. The princess looked up at her doubtfully. "Will this hurt?"

Tarsha ignored her, closed her eyes, and began to hum, and Dar could tell she was summoning her magic. It was always impossible to tell how things might turn out—especially where the wishsong was concerned—but Tarsha's face was calm as her humming shifted into a chant that lacked recognizable words but contained sharp, high-pitched sounds that caused Ajin to cover her ears.

Bits of smoke began to rise from the mast directly between Ajin's legs, smoking and then glowing bright red. The Skaar princess, to her credit, did not panic. She held herself perfectly still as Tarsha worked. Until, abruptly, the heavy piece of wood broke apart at the juncture where the magic had been working, and Ajin was free.

Tarsha staggered back a step, looking worn and shaky. Dar quickly guided her into a sitting position and pulled her cloak tight about her slender form. "Well done, Tarsha. The princess owes you a debt of gratitude."

"Which I intend to repay." Ajin tried getting to her feet, found her legs wouldn't hold her, and quickly sat back again. "Not quite ready to stand up yet, I guess. Was that magic, Tarsha?" she asked. "Are you a Druid?"

"She's a Druid's apprentice," Dar answered for her. "And the Druid is not too far away from us. Just stay where you are."

Those last words were an order. Ajin faced him defiantly for a moment, then shrugged. "It's not as if there is anywhere for me to go, Darcon. Even if I could stand. Even," she added playfully, "if you were to decide to come with me."

Dar positioned himself between the two women and wrapped his long arms about his knees. "It's very cold out here. We need a fire to warm up. And Tarsha needs to rest." He paused. "Any chance your soldiers will be out looking for you in this weather?"

Ajin gave him a rueful smile. "Not a chance. Not in this weather or any other. I was being sent home in disgrace when my airship crashed."

"Sounds interesting. I'll gather some wood for that fire, then. Afterward, why don't you tell me everything that's happened to bring you back into my life yet again? Didn't you offer to do as much?"

She gave him a nod. "The offer stands."

"Will you behave if I turn my back for a minute?"

"My word of honor. I'll sit right here."

"Good." Dar got to his feet and moved off into the darkness without looking back.

# 10

ON THE SHORES OF THE HADESHORN, WITH THE wind whipping about him in a series of shrieks and howls and the dead dancing on the air in a frenzy that matched the wildness of the world about them, Drisker Arc stared past sound and fury, past blackness and mist, and saw the past.

It was before his time by several centuries. It was a legend that stretched back for centuries before even that. It was for many the reason that magic was distrusted and the Druids reviled. Memories are strong when they are fed relentlessly, and the memories of the shade he faced now had long since taken on a life of their own. He had read the stories in the Druid Histories during his time as Ard Rhys—had read them late into the night because he could not make himself leave them once he had started.

Tales recorded by the Druids.

Tales of vast upheaval and turmoil.

All of them centered, in one way or another, on *her*.

She was an Ohmsford, stolen as a child from her parents and separated from her brother by a creature of dark magic known as the Morgawr. Taken by him to be made over into his likeness, she was turned into an assassin of such deadly capabilities that she was known and feared everywhere. Later, she traveled to a far distant country called Parkasia, tracking Walker Boh and the brother she had lost and unwittingly found again, her travels leading to discoveries and revelations that eventually had brought her back to face the Morgawr with her brother at her side.

Then, in the years that followed, she had become, through extraordinary circumstances, Ard Rhys of the Druids of Paranor—and then been cast out and imprisoned in the Forbidding through the treachery of a band of the very Druids she was given to lead. She had been subjected to unspeakable tortures at the hands of the Straken Lord, the demon who led the unfortunates walled away in the time of Faerie. Driven nearly to madness and most certainly to desperation beyond anyone's imagining, she had weathered it all and been saved by her nephew, who had come for her when no one else could have and brought her back into the Four Lands.

Yet it did not end there. How could it, given the extraordinary nature of her life? Realizing she would never be accepted by either her Druids or the people of the Four Lands, she had chosen to enter into the service of Mother Tanequil, the root-bound half of the talismanic tree that had given her the means by which she was able to escape the Forbidding. Taken into the service of her savior, she had become a spirit and made forever free of her old life.

It was all written down in the Histories for the Druids to read. Drisker wondered now, as he often had in the past, how many had bothered to do so.

But the writings were not yet finished. Her life, after all, was not over. A final chapter remained. In an attempt to save the Four Lands from the emergence of the Straken Lord and his demons upon the passing of the Ellcrys, one of two twins—Ohmsford descendants in the time of the High Druid Aphenglow Elessedil—had gone to the tanequil and bargained for her release from her spirit form so she could return to the Four Lands as a flesh-and-blood creature that would stand against the invader's dark leader. And when it was done, her hatred for the Straken Lord burned as strongly as the fires of the sun. In the end, she brought him down. But when a new Ellcrys was born, almost simultaneously, the magic of the Forbidding had swept up the escaped demons like leaves to return them to their prison—

and taken her with them. There was to be no return to the tanequil, no transformation back into her spirit form, no allowance for her saving. She was a demon creature herself by then, and the magic made no distinctions.

*Grianne Ohmsford.*

*Shades!*

Drisker shook his head in disbelief. Still in the form in which she had been released from the tanequil, still as dark and terrible as she had been when swept once more into the Forbidding, she had somehow come back through the avenues of the dead to emerge from the Hadeshorn in response to his summoning.

There could only be one explanation for this. Grianne Ohmsford must be one of the dead. She had died during her imprisonment in the Forbidding and been given her release as a Druid shade to take up residence in the dark of the netherworld.

They faced each other in silence for a long time, saying nothing, each studying the other. *Do not think of her as Grianne Ohmsford,* he warned himself. *Think of her only as the Ilse Witch.*

–So this is who now stands in my shoes as Ard Rhys of Paranor. You, Drisker Arc–

"I am all that is left. The other Druids have been killed."

–You don't look strong enough to carry the load. You seem a reluctant bearer at best–

"I am that, but I will do what is needed."

–You left your office and abandoned your responsibilities once before, Drisker Arc. Who is to say you will not do so again–

Drisker took a deep breath. He did not care for the way this conversation had started out, and he was worried that the Ilse Witch had already decided not to give him any answers at all. If she even could. Yet this was something he now believed was possible.

"I was trapped in Paranor when another with the Druid magic sent both the Keep and myself into limbo. To gain my freedom and return the Druid's Keep and its archived magic, I was required to acknowledge my duty to my position as Ard Rhys and endure a testing to be sure I would not fail again."

The shade gestured dismissively, the waters behind her boiled with fresh fury, and the shades of the dead circling overhead shrank back in response. Drisker tried to think how to turn things more his way, how to gain sufficient favor with this creature that she might be willing to speak further with him.

But then she surprised him.

–What questions do you have for me? Speak them now–

The words were spoken with such loathing that for a second Drisker did not respond. When he did, he went on the offensive. "Are you able to speak with me as would another Druid shade? Are you come to the netherworld to be an equal to the others? Or am I wasting my time?"

Her aged face twisted in fury, and in that instant he believed himself a dead man—even though he knew that shades could not directly harm the living or interfere with their lives. The force of her glare, her withering gaze, and the cruel twist of lips suggested she found him of minimal worth, and she would leave him where he stood, yearning for what she would never give him.

–You think me one of the dead. You think me a shade, a ghost woman come from the netherworld to serve up evasive and treacherous answers to questions you have about your future. You know nothing–

"Tell me then," he urged.

For a long moment, she said nothing. She stared at him as if taking his measure, judging the worth of doing as he asked.

–I will speak one more time. Be careful of your response when I am finished. I am not one of the dead. I am not yet come to greet you as a Druid shade. I live still. I live within the Forbidding, leader of the unfortunate creatures trapped there, imprisoned as they are, but with greater magic than they possess and stronger ambitions than they could imagine–

A pause. "So how do you come through their avenues of passage if you are not yet one of the dead?" he asked.

–I do this because I *can*, Drisker Arc. I am barred from this world in my flesh-and-blood form, but not as a spirit able to navigate the paths of the dead. My power allows me to bend the rules. So when I read your thoughts and saw your indecision, I knew you would come here for your answers as Druids have done since the beginning of their time. Are you satisfied now?–

"I am pleased. Who better to address my problem than one who has a foot in two worlds? If you will hear my questions, I will pay close attention to your answers."

A long, low laugh emanated from the creature before him.

–Oh, I am certain of that. You will listen closely if for no better reason than to determine if I am playing false with you, if I am leading you astray, if I seek to undo you completely through misplaced trust. But you do not need to worry, Drisker. I am not a shade, and I have no desire to trick you in any way. On the contrary, I wish to give the exact information you require. Every last piece of it. You need only ask–

But with the Ilse Witch, you could never be sure. The stories about her made that clear enough. And so he saw at once what she had failed to add. "But there are conditions?"

The hunch of her aged shoulders revealed the truth. –There is one. It is this. I do not come out of pity for your plight or any foolish need to do something helpful to an order that in the end betrayed me. I seek one thing and one thing only–

She lifted her face out of the shadow of her cowl, and the expression on her ancient visage was something resembling hope.

–I seek to strike a bargain. If you agree, you will have your answers. If you do not, I will be gone back to whence I came and you will not see me again. Which do you choose?–

At the crash site where Dar had left them, Ajin d'Amphere and Tarsha Kaynin sat facing each other in the near-total darkness, saying nothing.

"You're not exactly suited for this sort of experience, are you?" Ajin asked finally. "Kind of young."

Tarsha gave her a dark look. "You're not that much older than I am. Why would I not be as well suited as you?"

The Skaar princess shrugged. "I've had a tougher life than you. I've been fighting beside my father's soldiers since I was fifteen. I've seen things that would curdle your blood. At a guess, I would say you've never been more than fifty miles from home before."

Ajin was taunting her, Tarsha thought in surprise. Trying to draw her into an argument, but why? Then she remembered Ajin's comments about Dar Leah, and the way she had looked at him, and realized the truth. The Skaar princess fancied herself in love with Dar and wondered about Tarsha's relationship with the Blade.

Tarsha almost laughed. It was so ridiculous that she paused, reconsidering, only to return to the idea immediately. She wasn't mistaken: Ajin was trying to find out if Tarsha was competition.

As if the Blade were a prize Tarsha would have any interest in at all. Brecon Elessedil, maybe. But the Blade was too dark and complicated for her to think of him as anything but a friend.

"You know nothing of me," she said instead to Ajin. "My brother was driven mad by the magic you saw me wield. He was sent to live with my uncle, who abused him in ways that would curdle *your* blood. He killed my uncle, came home and killed my parents, and on the way to find me killed over twenty more people. And then he tried to kill me. Twice! The second attempt occurred only a day ago. So don't try to lecture me about how pampered my life has been. At least you're a princess. I don't even have that. I'm a nobody."

Ajin was silent for a moment, then she smiled. "You're one tough nobody, if a nobody is all you are. And I doubt very much it is. In any event, I apologize."

She held out her hand and Tarsha took it briefly, still wary. They were silent for a long time, neither quite sure where to take the conversation—or even if it was a good idea to continue it. But Tarsha was curious to know more about this young woman. "Did I hear you say you were being sent home?"

Ajin sighed. "By my father, who disapproves of me using my own judgment and doing what he would have done in my place had he been here. He begrudges me any independence that he hasn't specifically granted me. So when he arrived early this morning, he dismissed me from service and ordered me home. I left him with the army, camped on the north bank of the Mermidon, directly across from a Federation fleet of airships. It appears to be a standoff for now."

"You wanted him to let you stay." Tarsha made it a statement of fact.

The Skaar princess nodded. "He needs me to manage the army. I need to be leading those soldiers, not him. I grew up with them. We fought together in campaigns all across Eurodia. I weathered everything they did, shared their food and their talk and all the hard times as well as the good. They are like brothers to me."

"Except for this one." She pointed to the man Ajin had killed.

"Except for him. He was in the pay of the *pretender*—my father's new queen. She's been undermining me for years."

Tarsha was having trouble following all this but wanted to keep the other woman talking. She still hadn't heard any mention of Dar Leah, and she wanted to find out how they had come to know each other.

She decided to be direct. "How did you meet the Blade? And how did you come to save each other's lives? That shouldn't happen on opposite sides of a war."

There was a longer pause this time. "No, it shouldn't. It's complicated. I saw him first with a pair of Druids and some Troll guards they had brought with them. They confronted us in the Northlands and we killed them. But Darcon was still aboard the Druid airship when the fighting started, and he came down to the grasslands and charged in to rescue those he had been charged to protect. It was suicide, but I've never seen anything like it. He was magnificent— a warrior. He was unstoppable, even by us, and we stop everyone we face. But not him. He rescued one of the Druids and fled, although we pursued and caught them in the mountains and blew their vessel apart. That's how I came to save him. He was hanging from the cliffs when I found him. I was in a flit and he was trapped out in the open, and I could have killed him. But I kept remembering his bravery and his skill with a sword. It just seemed wrong to take his life like that." She shrugged. "Part of my code of honor as a soldier, I guess. So I left him hanging there. I can't explain it. I just knew it was the right thing to do."

"And then he saved you?"

"After we destroyed the Druids and Paranor was cast into limbo. He found me when I was alone and put his sword to my throat. But I could tell he didn't want to kill me, so I reminded him of the debt he owed me. He let me go. He must wonder still how I talked him into it."

"Or he talked himself into it."

Ajin smiled. "Probably so."

Tarsha watched the princess shift to a new position, wincing from the wound in her side. The Skaar princess bent down to look at the injury, and Tarsha moved over next to her. "I can see it better than you can," she offered.

Ajin hesitated, then nodded her permission. The wound was not as bad as all the blood suggested. Tarsha studied it closely and then rocked back on her heels, her eyes meeting Ajin's. "I could close that wound for you, if you want."

"You mean stitch it up?"

"Something like that. I could help with your legs, too. Do you want me to do that?"

Ajin hesitated before nodding. "All right. Just try not to make things any worse."

Tarsha bent forward and began to hum, calling up the wishsong magic, bringing it to her fingertips and folding it over and over like a compress. When she had it sufficiently strong, she used her voice to press it into the wound. Ajin gasped at the feelings it invoked, but held herself steady. Then Tarsha moved on to Ajin's legs, still humming as she ran her hands up and down each one, her touch cool and soothing, even through the fabric of her clothing. When she was finished, there was no sign left at all of the injury.

"That was the oddest, most wonderful thing I have ever seen," Ajin whispered in awe. She was looking down at where the wound had disappeared and touching the new skin gently. Then she stretched her legs, testing them for strength and flexibility. She glanced up in disbelief. "You have a rare gift, Tarsha Kaynin."

Tarsha shrugged. "That was the first time I ever tried using it that way."

"What?" The Skaar princess stiffened in shock.

"I thought I should be honest about it. But it worked, didn't it?"

Ajin was still staring when Dar Leah reappeared, his arms laden with firewood. He took in the scene before him and stopped where he was. "What's going on?" he asked, looking from one face to the other.

Nonchalantly, Ajin d'Amphere rose and walked over, peeling off the top layer of wood to relieve him of some of his burden. She caught his eye just before turning away.

"Magic," she said, winking.

"What are the terms of the bargain you wish me to enter into?" Drisker asked.

Grianne Ohmsford stood before him, a frail and crooked image etched on the night air, her flesh-and-blood body still somewhere deep inside the Forbidding. Yet the power that emanated from her ethereal spirit form was unmistakable. Drisker did not for a second doubt her claim that she ruled over those unfortunates imprisoned with her. He did not doubt that if she were standing there in her corporeal form, she would be a dangerous adversary with enough magic to undo him.

But for now, she was still a shade and lacked power in every aspect save one—the words she spoke. He knew she was capable of a great deal using her voice alone. Her persuasiveness, with her friends and enemies alike, was legendary. He was not foolish enough to think that whatever bargain she was about to present would be either entirely transparent or comprehensible. But he had been given a choice, and it was a choice he would have to make. Should he make it, as he understood it now—incomplete and not fully revealed—or should he walk away?

She looked at him with those crone's eyes in a way that told him she knew what he was thinking and was enjoying his discomfort. Not one to let the knife be twisted for too long, the Druid gave her a shrug that suggested, *Doesn't matter to me if you want to drag this out. I'm in no hurry. I have all night, and I know you well.*

She gave him a nod, almost as if she understood. Her voice, when she spoke, was little better than a hiss of fury and regret.

–I have been trapped within the Forbidding for too long. I do not pretend at innocence. I know what I am. But I was dragged from my refuge—betrayed by my mistress and undone by that Ohmsford boy—all to serve a cause in which I had no interest. My life was turned upside down and taken from me as if it did not matter. I can never return to it; there is no turning back the clock. I am at the end of my life, and I do not wish to die like this–

She gestured at her crooked, emaciated form, at her deeply lined face and her stick-thin fingers. She ran her hand through her gray, lifeless hair and hugged herself.

–This creature that stands before you? This is *not* who I was meant to be at the end of my days! I have atoned for my sins, my failings, and my mistakes. I was living in a place where I belonged. I was happy— content to be nothing more than a flicker of motion and color on the air. I want back what was taken from me. I want to die as I was meant to die—not as what some capricious fate has bequeathed me–

"And you want me to give you this?" Drisker shook his head. "I do not know how to make you who you were."

–Then you must find a way, mustn't you? For that is to be your end of our agreement, and you must keep it. This is your end of the bargain. Return me to the young woman I was just before I entered into the service of Mother Tanequil—to the flesh-and-blood form that belonged to me–

Drisker shook his head slowly. "I cannot promise this."

She cringed away from him, almost as if to lash out, then straightened so abruptly that she seemed to tower over him. –You *will* promise me if you want my help. And you *will* leave knowing that if you fail to keep your promise, you and those you love will die as a result. I do not threaten you, Druid. I simply prophesy the future I see for you–

"You could be lying."

–If I cannot see the future, how is it that I know so much about you already? Besides, can you really afford to send me away? Ask your conscience–

She was right, of course. She was all that had come to him on his summoning, and he needed his questions answered. But the price she asked was too high. He could not think how he could honor it, even with his magic, even as Ard Rhys reborn.

"What is it you will do for me—*exactly* do—if I agree to your bargain?"

–Answer all your questions. Give you the information you seek. Tell you how to stop the war between the Skaar and the Four Lands. Tell you how best to deal with Clizia Porse. Tell you which direction you must go and what you must do to achieve a healing of your beloved Four Lands. That is what I will give you–

"And what if I fail in my efforts to bring you back to your former self? What if that turns out to be more than I can do, magic or no?"

She gave him a scathing look from which he took an involuntary step back, recognition already surfacing.

–Then your life belongs to me and it is forfeit–

There it was, laid upon the table as dark as her heart. If he failed, he died. If she held up her end of the bargain and he did not, he was a dead man. That she could make this happen seemed questionable— a spirit with no power, her real self sealed away in the Forbidding. But he understood that merely by withholding crucial information or by having him take one small step in the wrong direction, she could bring him down.

But he needed to know how to save the Four Lands. He must know. If he walked away, he did so understanding that he must proceed blindly in his efforts. He did not think this was something he could do successfully. If he wanted the answer to his questions and the resolution the Four Lands and its peoples needed, he must be prepared to give up everything.

Even his life.

"Very well. We have a bargain."

The Ilse Witch revealed nothing. She did not move; the twisted expression on her aged face did not change. She simply stood there, looking at him. Had he spoken at all, or did he simply imagine it?

–This is what you must do–

Her ragged voice and poisonous words confirmed his worst fears, but at the same time opened the door to what he sought.

# II

CLIZIA PORSE HAD RUN OUT OF PATIENCE; IT WAS time to go down into the Skaar encampment. She had been nearby all day, sheltering in the forest, well back from where the Skaar carried on the business of preparing to wage war.

Several things were immediately clear. First, she would no longer be dealing with Ajin d'Amphere if she wanted anything from the Skaar. Now that her father had arrived, Ajin would no longer be in command. He would insist on making all the decisions from here forward, and his approach might be entirely different from his daughter's. Not to mention his thoughts about Clizia herself, once she told him who she was and what part she had played in Paranor's fall. Ajin might give her some help in making her case, but she would not count on that. Everything might have changed. It didn't matter. She needed to form a pact with the Skaar so she could quit worrying about them turning on her. It was bad enough that she had Drisker Arc hunting her. Bad as well that she had the Federation and the Elves with which to deal. The Skaar, at least, must be persuaded to let her be.

At first glance, this seemed impossible. Nothing at all worked in her favor when you considered what she would be asking of Cor d'Amphere. Nothing would suggest to him that she was anything but trouble. What she needed to do was to give the Skaar king a reason to *want* to ally himself and the Skaar to her.

She surprised herself with how quickly she found the reason she was searching for. It had been there all along, right in front of her. Events might have cheated her momentarily of the Keep and its magic and put her at risk from Drisker Arc's wrath. Her plans for the future might be momentarily derailed, but now she knew she would be able to put them back on track.

Still, she must not act in haste. If she wanted to see the king, she must reach him directly. If his soldiers intervened, she might never get a chance to speak to him at all. She could not allow that to happen.

Which meant she must go into the camp unseen and unchallenged and confront him alone.

So she waited patiently, organizing her thoughts, deciding how much she should tell him and how much she should keep hidden. She worked her way through the arguments she would present, ordering and honing the words, considering alternatives to all of it should he react differently than she expected.

She considered as well how she would kill him if he proved too difficult to persuade. A last resort, but whatever happened she needed to be sure she was the one who walked away from it.

Now that it was nightfall, there was no reason to delay meeting with Cor d'Amphere.

She made her way to the Skaar encampment, choosing her path carefully, the darkness surrounding her nearly complete. It took her a long time just to get safely through the forest and close enough to allow the watch and cooking fires to lend sufficient illumination to reveal the vague outlines of the terrain about her. Once she had gotten that far, she paused to take in an overview of the camp, searching for what she supposed would be the king's tent. As she expected, it wasn't hard to find. It was easily the biggest structure visible, surrounded by smaller tents arranged expressly to encircle it, all flying flags that she knew to be the standard of the Skaar.

It was full night by now, and there were only a handful of sentries up and about. The bulk of those were stationed between the camp and the Mermidon, warding against the Federation. Some few would be stationed at other points to prevent a surprise attack from the rear, but in this blackness it would be all but impossible for anything of that sort to take place.

No, she thought, there would be no attacks this night. Both sides would be hunkering down, most of them catching what sleep they could while they plotted their strategies. A perfect situation for what Clizia needed to do, and she did not hesitate to consider it any longer. Down through the camp she walked, a ghost in the darkness. Keeping safely away from the hazy figures she could pick out through the curtains of gloom and rain, she stayed within the shadows. Her progress was slow, but necessarily so. Whatever else happened, she did not want to alert anyone to her presence. Twice she used magic to turn a sentry's eyes in another direction, just long enough for her to pass unseen. Not once was she spotted. Not once was she challenged to identify herself.

The camp was mostly sleeping when she reached the king's tent. She stood back from it for long minutes and studied the two sentries who stood watch before the closed flaps of the entrance. She would have to bypass them, but without causing them harm. It would be far easier just to kill them and be done with it but difficult to justify to Cor d'Amphere later. Nor did she want anyone to know of her visit to the king if things did not go her way. If she was forced to dispose of him, she did not want anyone to be able to report that she was the last one seen going in and out of his quarters.

No, this required a more subtle approach.

Summoning her magic, she rendered herself a part of the night, a shadow without an identity, a faceless disembodied bit of movement as she walked toward the guards through the driving rain. When she was still twenty feet away—the men still unaware of her—she caused a harsh muttering to erupt and an image of someone approaching from between the surrounding tents, all of it furtive and threatening.

The sentries noticed at once and immediately drew swords and assumed a defensive stance.

"Who's there?" one called out. "Identify yourself!"

Clizia generated more signs of a threat—more movement amid rough muttering—still appearing to approach the king's tent. She held her position, waiting on the sentries, knowing they must act. And quick enough, they did. Weapons held ready, they moved away from the entrance to the tent to confront this mirage, calling out for the intruder to stand and be identified. Clizia gave them time to get clear of the tent flaps and then moved quickly behind them, banishing the illusions they were confronting as she slipped inside.

The tent had several chambers, and in the one farthest away a light was burning through the otherwise heavy darkness of the canvas interior. His back turned to her, the Skaar king sat bent over a table, making notes on a document. She took a moment to look around, wanting to be sure she had not missed seeing someone else who was present before deciding that Cor d'Amphere and she were alone.

Silently, she approached until she stood next to him. "My lord?" she said quietly.

He was so startled he jerked to his feet in shock, his expression more than a little unsettled and wild-eyed. But when he saw it was an old woman who had intruded, and that she carried no weapons and offered no apparent threat, the expression turned to one of irritation.

"Who let you in here?" he demanded.

"No one, my lord. I did not trouble the guards to announce me. I needed to be sure we would be left alone while we talked."

"Talked? Talked about what? Who are you?"

She glanced around, saw an unoccupied folding chair off to one side, and gestured toward it. "May I sit? My age doesn't permit me to stand for too long without moving."

The king gave her a long, probing look. He was a man of average size and weight, his age not immediately apparent from his appearance, his hair still dark and thick and his face handsome in a severe sort of way. There was about him an air of confidence and self-assurance that strengthened steadily as he grew more convinced she posed no threat.

The way he regarded her suggested that his curiosity had been aroused. "Sit, then. And say what you came to say."

She took a seat, and he resumed occupying his own. She was an accepted guest now inside his lodgings, his attention fully captured by the fact she had somehow gotten there without the guards stopping her, and he wanted to know more. She stretched her limbs and allowed herself a small smile of satisfaction. "Much better. My thanks."

"I'll ask it again. Who are you?"

"My name is Clizia Porse. I was a member of the Druid order that your advance force annihilated at Paranor. The last member, as it happens. I served as your daughter's eyes and ears inside the Keep until I was able to admit her Penetrator as a student. I was the one who provided the Skaar with a way to get inside the walls of the fortress without the Druids suspecting what was coming. Because of me, the Keep was taken and the Druids killed. I did this for a number of reasons, but what you should know is that I did it mostly as a means of arranging an alliance with the Skaar."

She paused, giving him a chance to absorb everything and respond if he chose. "An alliance?" he questioned.

"The Druid order was rotting from the inside out. It needed a cleansing, and I was happy to provide the Skaar with the opportunity to give it one. Your daughter understood the value of my services. She is a very astute young woman. She said you would wish to have possession of Paranor and its magic artifacts—not for your own use so much as to deny their use to others. The Druids were your greatest threat. Now you face opposition only from armies inferior to the Skaar, lacking your abilities and military skills. Your position as invader is considerably improved, and for that you owe me your thanks. But I do not come seeking thanks. I am here because I believe I can give you something more."

Cor d'Amphere smiled. "Considering that you and my daughter also cost me possession of Paranor and its magic and placed me in a position where a battle against a much larger army seems inevitable, I would suggest *you* owe *me* something, too. Something that is now lost to me. My daughter, by the way, has been dispatched back to Skaarsland, so you no longer have your champion in this matter. And the prospect of an alliance between us, Clizia Porse, does not seem all that attractive."

"I do not blame you for saying so." Clizia gave a nod of agreement, holding his gaze. *Ajin d'Amphere dismissed? What a fool this man is.* She smiled nevertheless. "Perhaps I can offer you a reason to change your mind, if you will hear me out."

The king shrugged, still smiling. "Here I sit, a captive audience. Make your case, if you can."

A challenge—something she understood and welcomed. "Let's step back. First of all, Paranor is not lost to you. It has been brought back out of concealment and sits right where it was for centuries. It can be yours again, if you can bring yourself to trust me to get it for you. But be warned. Only I have the means to gain the access that will allow you and your Skaar soldiers, in turn, to enter after me."

She did not bother telling him about Drisker Arc or his means of access, preferring to leave that for another time. For now, the king need only know that something he wanted was there for the taking if he would grant her permission to present it to him.

"What is it that allows you entry and no one else?" he asked.

"Ancient magic wards Paranor. A very powerful magic. This is what destroyed the Skaar who captured it the first time. There is a defender of the Keep, a living presence with no other purpose than to keep out all intruders in order to protect the Druids. But if those who seek entry are invited in by one of the Druids, then entry may be gained through subterfuge. That is what happened with your daughter and her Skaar soldiers. Once the Druids were slain, however, the Keep's magic struck out at those who had proven themselves false."

"And you, as the Druid responsible for inviting my daughter and her soldiers inside, could not prevent this?"

"My lord, I was unable to act quickly enough. At least one of the Druids summoned the magic before dying, causing it to emerge and attack the invaders. Once set free, there is no stopping it until the Keep is secured again. But understand something. The magic has withdrawn, and the Keep is yours for the taking. I can arrange it for you."

The Skaar king folded his hands together and laid them on the table, his eyes still fixed on her face. "And your price for doing this is an alliance with the Skaar? Why would I want that? Why would you?"

"Why wouldn't I? The Skaar are a force to be reckoned with, my lord. Even I recognize that much. Once you find a home in the Four Lands, you will dominate the other governments and tribes. I hope you might consider offering me a share of that power if I can prove myself worthy. And I can give you access to more than just Paranor. I can give you access to places and things you otherwise might never know about. An alliance between us makes perfect sense."

She paused. "Let me prove my value. Give me twenty-five of your soldiers to go back into Paranor and claim it for the Skaar. I promise you I can do this. I can clear the way for you, and you can make whatever use of the Keep you choose. And the likelihood of the other governments challenging you if you have control of Paranor will be considerably reduced."

He shook his head, frowning. "I still don't quite see what you gain from all this. How does giving Paranor to me help you?"

"Simple. It gives me power. If you are my ally, no one is going to interfere with my own plans. Look at me. My life is almost over. I just want to make use of what's left of it."

"But you would agree to stay out of my way and not do anything to threaten the Skaar if I left you alone?"

"Give me just what I asked for." She was more insistent now, more confident she could assert herself. "Twenty-five men, and I claim Paranor in your name. A simple test of my value, one that will provide you with a strong reason for us to form an alliance."

The king nodded slowly. "All right, I'll give you those men and grant you your chance to prove your worth. But I will need an extra day before you can have them. Tomorrow, I must meet in conference with the Prime Minister of the Federation to see if we might come to some sort of agreement that will end our standoff and allow both of us to go about our business. If that goes poorly, I might not be able to grant your request; all my soldiers might be needed here with me. Come back the day after tomorrow and ask me again. With any luck, your men will be waiting and you will be on your way back to Paranor."

Cor d'Amphere rose, indicating that Clizia's time was up and her visit was over. She rose with him, making sure he saw how shaky and frail she was, giving him a further demonstration of why he need not fear her.

It was always a good idea to let others underestimate you.

It was deep into the predawn hours when Darcon Leah kicked out the embers of the small fire they had used to warm themselves, scattering the burning brands and coals into puddles of rainwater and melted snow that hissed and steamed at the unwanted intrusion. By then the storm had diminished to a slow mix of sleet and drizzle, the winds had died away almost completely, and in the skies overhead the clouds had begun to break up sufficiently that glimpses of the moon and stars could be had. Telling Tarsha and Ajin that it was time for them to go—that they needed to get back to meet with Drisker after he returned from the Valley of Shale—he had set them on the path to where their own airship had been left.

Ajin was understandably reluctant to go with them. She was a member of the Skaar nation—their princess and leader of their advance force until being banished by her father—so she thought it better that she simply go her own way and said so. But Dar wouldn't hear of it.

"You're alone and on foot in country you know nothing about," he pointed out. "You are miles from anything even resembling civilization and would have to walk for days to find shelter. It doesn't matter that you are who you are. I wouldn't leave my worst enemy in these circumstances. I want you with us until we find a safer place than this one."

He made it almost an order, but stopped just short because he knew how she responded to being pushed. Instead he made it a plea to an equal. And he did see her as that, even if he had been the one to suggest the idea back at Paranor when he had held her at sword point. With Ajin, reason and deference were always better employed than threats or attempts at intimidation.

And Ajin, to his surprise, had simply shrugged and come along with no further argument. Her legs seemed strong enough now to allow her to make the trek; the damage they had sustained from being pinned had been healed by Tarsha's use of the wishsong. Ajin limped only a little when they started out, and even that was gone within a mile. She had no trouble keeping up with Tarsha and himself, although she held herself apart and silent for almost the entire way.

The sole exception came when they were perhaps a mile from the airship and Dar had fallen back to see how she was managing, leaving Tarsha to lead the way. He asked her if she was experiencing any difficulty walking, and she shook her head.

Then she said, just as he was about to move ahead again, "You might not believe this, but I knew it was you the moment I saw you appear with the girl."

"You might have *thought* it was me, but you couldn't be sure," he replied. "You couldn't see my face. You could barely make out anything in that storm."

"Doesn't matter what I could see. I just knew. I think it was because, since we first crossed paths all those weeks ago and I watched you fighting to save those Druids and then found you hanging on that cliff face, I sensed there was something special about you. Don't laugh at me. I knew we were going to meet again, and that it would happen soon. I knew fate would bring us back together."

He looked at her directly. "That's nonsense."

"Is it? Do you believe that? Are so many unplanned meetings between us in such a short time simply random?"

He made no response, shaking his head in a dismissive way and moving ahead again to join Tarsha. But inwardly he was wondering if there wasn't something to what she was saying. How many times had they unexpectedly encountered each other? How many times had this reoccurred under circumstances where it seemed at least strange? On this night, it seemed impossible that of all the likely rescuers she would find to extricate her from the wreckage of her airship, he would be the one. It gave him further pause when he remembered that his instincts had warned him something was wrong and brought him back out of the Valley of Shale and down into the foothills in time to spy her airship falling out of the sky.

The chances of this happening—more so than any of the other unexpected encounters—made him wonder. Even if he didn't think it was anything more than coincidence, and she was still an enemy of the Four Lands.

But he wouldn't tell her any of this. What was the point? She would believe what she chose, and he would leave her to it.

When they reached the airship, it was undamaged and still where they had left it, concealed in a mix of trees and boulders. Dar thought about going back into the valley to find the others, but decided against it when he realized he would have to take Ajin with him if he was to keep watch on her, and she might not have enough strength left for another forced march. Leaving Tarsha alone to watch her was too dangerous, even if he didn't think she intended to run.

And really, if she did, why should it make any difference to him? But somehow it did, and he had learned a long time ago that instincts meant something when they nudged your conscience and demanded attention.

So the three settled down inside the aircraft to wait for the others to return, wrapped in somewhat less damp heavy-weather cloaks and dry blankets salvaged from the storage bins, staring out at the diminishing banks of clouds and a wash of emerging stars that had turned the countryside silver. Ajin and Tarsha, sitting close together behind him, talked in low voices, and Dar could not hear what they were saying. But there was no mistaking that it was intimate and personal. In spite of the circumstances, there was something between them that hadn't been there earlier. A sharing of some sort. A closeness, maybe.

He wanted to tell Tarsha to be careful of the Skaar princess, but then decided it wasn't necessary. Tarsha knew that already. And he did not think Ajin would do anything to cause trouble after willingly accompanying them. She might choose to escape later, if she began to think of herself as a prisoner, but not until she felt it made good sense. For the moment, she would wait to see what happened. She would stay with Dar.

He felt a twinge of discomfort. He found himself questioning why he could embrace the idea.

It was two more hours before Drisker returned with Brecon
Elessedil and Tavo Kaynin in tow, all of them looking more than a
little weary and diminished. He might have been mistaken in his further assessment of the Druid, but it seemed to him there was a discernible uneasiness about Drisker that was troubling. He was lost in
thought, his attention somewhere else entirely as he arrived, barely
acknowledging them until he caught sight of Ajin.

"You've picked up a stray," he observed, giving Dar a questioning
look.

"Ajin d'Amphere, princess of the Skaar nation and leader of the
advance force come into the Four Lands," the Blade informed him,
and then added, "until recently."

Ajin stood, facing the Druid squarely but saying nothing.

"She said she was relieved of command and sent home yesterday
under apparently unpleasant circumstances. She promised to tell
us how all this happened." Dar gave the princess a deferential nod.
"Princess, if you intend to keep your word and do not find it a betrayal, this would be a good time to do so."

He spoke in a soft, nonthreatening way and made it seem more
an entreaty than an order. Ajin smiled in recognition of his deliberate consideration. There was something in the way she looked at him
in that moment that he would never forget. It reached beyond all
of his doubts and suspicions—everything he knew to be true about
how impossible it would be for them ever to form a friendship—and
instead made him feel something that could only be described as unexpected intimacy.

Then she began to tell her story, and the moment disappeared.

# 12

AT THE CLOSE OF AJIN'S RECITATION, THE ENTIRE company had curled up in the cramped passenger compartment of an aircraft entirely too small to provide space for all of them and slept for several hours. Drisker hadn't revealed anything at that point about what had happened at the Hadeshorn, and no one felt the need to know until after they'd had a chance to rest. Their closeness inside the airship cockpit produced a much-needed warmth that helped keep the cold at bay. Dar Leah fell asleep almost instantly, stretched out in the pilot seat with his head cradled in the crook of his arm, the others finding places elsewhere in the passenger and storage areas behind him.

At that point, he was alone.

But when he woke, he found Ajin d'Amphere curled up beside him, pressed close against his back, one arm draped possessively about his waist. Sometime during the morning, she had abandoned her former space and come forward to share his. He was surprised this hadn't woken him, that he hadn't sensed her fitting herself next to him. He lay there for a few moments in guilty pleasure, actually enjoying the warmth generated by her body pressed up against his, though still confused by his own willingness to accept it. It made him wonder again if there was something to her claim that they shared a special connection.

Then slowly he extricated himself and climbed out of the aircraft

to walk a short distance to a hilltop, where he could reflect on what
might be happening between himself and the Skaar princess.

Later, when the others were awake and had eaten, Drisker called
them together to discuss his experience at the Hadeshorn. But while
the others gathered quickly, Ajin hung back, clearly aware she was
not one of them and unsure of what to do.

The Druid beckoned her over when he recognized her reluctance.
"Princess," he said. "Come join us. There is no reason you should not
hear what I have to say. You might even find you have something to
offer—perhaps something you can do to help. Even banished, there
might still be chances for you to plead our cause to your father."

Ajin nodded silently and moved forward to position herself close
to Dar. He gave her a brief smile. She was obviously less sure of herself since her father had stripped her of her authority and dismissed
her from his service. He was still wondering what the man could have
been thinking.

Drisker turned to the others. "I was able to summon a Druid to
speak with me about what is needed to settle the conflict between
the Four Lands and the Skaar, and what can be done to blunt the
continuing threat of Clizia Porse. As I expected, I did not get a direct
answer. There was considerable back and forth, but in the end I was
able to determine the first step we need to take."

"Was it Allanon you spoke with?" Dar asked.

"No." The Druid glanced at him and looked away again. "What
matters is that there is someone we need to find in order to discover
more: a boy who calls himself Shea Ohmsford. Tarsha and I have
both met him before. At the time, we were searching for an assassin's
guild in the city of Varfleet. The boy was able to act as our guide. I
was told he was the key to discovering how to put things right in the
Four Lands."

"Will he tell us what that something is?" Brecon Elessedil asked,
the doubt in his voice apparent. "This boy?"

Drisker shook his head. "I'm not sure. The one who spoke to me
would say nothing more. But it was clear that we need to find Shea
Ohmsford."

"And you don't think this spirit's advice is a deception of some sort?" the Elven prince pressed. "It feels wrong to me."

"It feels *typical*," the Druid corrected. "According to the Druid Histories, this is how the shades of the dead communicate. But even when I first met him, I sensed something special about this boy. He was not the Shea Ohmsford of legend, it's true. He does not have the use of magic; he does not even know the history of his own name or understand its importance. But he is nonetheless the key to our success."

Tarsha Kaynin said nothing. No acknowledgment of Drisker's decision, no word of agreement with the Druid's obvious faith in the boy. And that made Dar wonder.

"So we are to fly to Varfleet?" he asked the Druid.

"I don't think we can depend on finding Shea where we left him a few weeks ago. I think we have to use the Elfstones to discover where he is now. We don't have time to go hunting blindly. We need to know his exact location before setting out again."

"One moment," Ajin d'Amphere said suddenly, and everyone turned. "What do you intend to do with me while you're off hunting for this boy?"

"That is something of a problem," the Druid admitted. "You will not be welcomed anywhere in the Four Lands should folks discover who you are." He paused. "Though I must admit, that seems unlikely. Of the few who know your true face, most are already in this group. But if you like, we could return you to your father."

The Skaar princess shook her head at once. "He would never accept me. Not at this point. And I am not going back to my homeland until the *pretender* who stole the position that rightfully belongs to my mother is stripped of her power. I did not survive the storm and her attempt on my life just to place myself once more within her reach. I would rather stay here, in the Four Lands, until I can decide what I need to do."

"Why don't we keep Ajin with us until we find Shea Ohmsford and then decide?" Tarsha said. "She is still recovering from her injuries, and I am not comfortable having her out of my sight just yet.

If we are watching her, she shouldn't cause us any trouble. She might even end up helping us, just as Drisker has suggested."

"I don't want to see her harmed," Brecon Elessedil agreed, "but I've seen enough of the princess to know she can cause a lot of trouble—even under our supervision. She is clever and manipulative. We might be better off turning her over to my father for safekeeping. Dar, you know her better than any of us. Wouldn't you agree?"

There was an extended silence as they all turned to look at the Blade. "I think she should go with us for now," he answered quietly.

Brecon gave him a look that appeared to question his sanity, but Dar ignored him, his eyes on Ajin as she gave him a slow nod of agreement. He didn't know whether to feel satisfied or dismayed by his decision to speak. He only knew it felt right.

Drisker Arc glanced from face to face and nodded. "Then it is settled. Elven prince, can you use the Seeking Stones to discover where Shea Ohmsford can be found?"

Brecon reluctantly pulled out the Elfstones. "I'll need a description," he said.

Tarsha gave one that was so complete and accurate that Drisker simply nodded his approval once she was finished. Brecon stepped away from the group and stood facing south.

"Watch closely for any image that appears so we can be certain I've found the right boy," he said quietly.

He closed his eyes and held out the stones in his fist.

As his concentration deepened, the seconds slipped away. Nothing happened for a very long time, suggesting that either the description Tarsha had provided was flawed or the boy was dead. But Brecon Elessedil never wavered in his efforts, and Dar had to assume the prince believed there was still a chance of succeeding. The Blade shifted his feet, waiting patiently with the others for what felt like an eternity.

Then blue light abruptly exploded from Brecon's fist, and the Elfstones came to life, engulfing his entire hand and forearm before shooting away into the distance. Not south toward Varfleet, but west toward the Elven homeland. It revealed its path with multiple glimpses of the countryside through which it traveled—across the length of the Dragon's Teeth and out onto the Streleheim and off toward the kingdom of the Elves, a slow turn south toward the grasslands of the Tirfing before reaching the Westland border and the spire of the Pykon, and then farther south and onward toward the Wilderun to a bustling village where airships of all shapes and sizes were being constructed. Within a mass of faces and bodies, some of them clearly Rovers, a boy's face appeared.

"You've found him!" Tarsha said at once.

Drisker nodded as the Elfstones settled on Shea Ohmsford's young face, brightened with new intensity, and then went dark.

"Now all we have to hope is that when we reach him, we will discover what we are looking for," he said and turned back for the airship, beckoning for the others to follow.

Far to the west in the Rover village of Aperex, Shea Ohmsford experienced the strange sensation of being watched. He was standing amid dozens of Rovers who had come down to help Rocan and his companions retrofit the giant transport they had used to ferry Annabelle to the relative safety and concealment of the Westland. Traveling to Varfleet was suddenly off the table; Rocan had made it clear that anywhere in the Southland was open to Federation eyes. No matter what sort of precautions they took to stay hidden, the risk of being seen or drawing attention from someone who would report it to Ketter Vause was just too great.

Aperex, on the other hand, was deep in country that was primarily controlled by the Elves, who had forbidden any sort of trespass from the Federation. Rovers populated this part of the world, and there would be time and seclusion enough to work on engineering the *Behemoth* so that she could serve as a permanent mobile platform for Annabelle.

Shea had been extremely upset when Rocan had revealed his plans for the future, still determined to return to Varfleet and resume his old life. He was especially troubled by the fact that Rocan refused to explain his change of mind other than to insist they would be safer in the Westland. But he added, too, that Shea's former life was likely gone, and his identity too well known by Commander Zakonis for him ever to feel safe in his home city again. Better that he come live with the Rovers and continue to serve as a helper to Rocan and Tindall.

Shea was nothing if not adaptable, and he was finally persuaded to agree after extracting a promise from the Rover that he would not be put at risk again as he had been in freeing the old man, and that if he changed his mind at any point, he was free to leave. This last promise carried with it a pointed reminder that Rocan believe their relationship was, in some mysterious way, vitally important.

"Your ancestors and mine found common ground," he kept insisting. "Fate has decreed that you and I must do the same."

In the end, the credits Rocan had promised were an undeniable lure, and traveling to a new part of the Four Lands was intriguing. But mostly it was Rocan's charm and the boy's curiosity about how things would turn out that tipped the scales. Shea was young and eager to experience things beyond what he already knew, and returning to Varfleet, in the end, felt like failure.

So here he was, deep in the Westland, close to the outlaw town of Grimpen Ward and the intimidating valley of the Wilderun—not exactly places he had ever thought to go—arrived only two days ago at a Rover shipbuilding village that had already captured his imagination. It was exciting to be in Aperex; you could feel the energy of its people. The inhabitants of the bustling community were at work from dawn to dusk, constructing and repairing the airships that Rocan claimed were the best in all of the Four Lands. Highly sought after, these vessels were carefully allocated to those whom the Rovers felt most comfortable aiding—mostly the people of the Borderlands and the Elves. Not to say that the much-disliked Federation was denied Rover-crafted ships altogether. Business was business, and commerce trumped dislikes and suspicions. It was just that the Rovers were stingy with their Southland production, and this angered the Federation government from time to time—sometimes to the point of making explicit threats.

But the Rovers were used to threats. They had been threatened all their lives, and a few more threats were not enough for them to change their ways. By settling into the deep Westland, in country no one else wanted, they had staked a claim to a homeland where they felt they belonged. Shea knew this both from stories he had heard and from what he had observed since he'd arrived. These Rovers were a proud people, skilled and knowledgeable, and they felt confident in their ability to stand up to anybody.

"We are welcome here, Shea," Rocan said when they arrived. "And we will be kept safe, so long as we obey the rule. Which is that we need to be open with those who shelter us about what we intend and why we intend it. Lying is a death sentence, and duplicity is likely to result in exile. Just be open with them and supportive of their efforts to help us. It shouldn't be hard for a boy of your talents."

And it wasn't. Shea pitched right in with whatever tasks he was asked to undertake. He swiftly became part of a crew working to improve the *Behemoth*.

"We need to be sure Annabelle won't fall out of the sky because her carrier lacks the safety precautions she might require," Rocan told him. "It was one thing to carry her safely from Arishaig. It would be another if we were continually traveling from place to place."

Tindall was more forthcoming. "Simple enough, young man. Our efforts might require outrunning and even outfighting enemy vessels. We don't anticipate this, but it remains a distinct possibility. Annabelle needs to be protected, no matter how far away from safety we choose to take her."

Shea was able to worm more out of him when he asked about what sort of trips they might have to take. Shrugging, the old man advised him that finding the proper weather conditions might require them to travel very long distances into very unfriendly country. Or even out over the ocean.

The boy still didn't think he was being told everything, but when had Rocan ever been completely forthcoming with him? A man like that told you what he thought you needed to know and nothing more. So Shea settled for the more general explanation and a fresh promise there would be no more stunts like the one that had nearly gotten him killed in Assidian Deep.

It was just after midday when an honor guard escorted Cor d'Amphere to Ketter Vause's tented quarters on the southern banks of the Mermidon for their prearranged meeting. Vause had taken great care to provide an assurance of safe conduct to the Skaar king, permitting him to arrive in his own vessel with his daughter and guards, and to land in an area secured solely for his personal use. He made certain also to guarantee that their conversations would be kept private.

In truth, he would have liked nothing better than to squash this troublesome monarch like a bug and throw his treacherous daughter into Assidian Deep for the rest of her miserable existence. But it would not do to forget that a Skaar advance force of less than a thousand, led by a woman who was little more than a girl, had annihilated a vastly superior Federation force not two weeks prior—with almost no difficulty and very few casualties of its own. The Skaar were dangerous, and underestimating them would be a mistake. Plus, he could not afford to forget that there were other enemies waiting to see how this conflict played out—enemies who would love to take advantage of a weakened Federation. Chief among them were the Elves, and Vause knew better than to think the Westland folk would come to their rescue if they thought it would better serve their interests to stand aside.

So there was much to be lost should haste and misjudgment overrule caution and common sense, and the Federation Prime Minister was not about to let that happen. But he did intend to discover exactly what the Skaar king wanted of the Federation, so that he could decide if negotiation might prevent a battle.

He was straightening his robes of office when an attendant appeared to announce the Skaar king's arrival, parting the tent flaps to allow the man to enter.

Ketter Vause surveyed the king and found himself completely underwhelmed. Cor d'Amphere was a very ordinary man in appearance, his impeccable uniform more imposing than the man himself. He wore a sour expression—one that was rife with disappointment and vaguely suggestive of something recovered from a rubbish heap. He wore no weapons, not even an ornamental blade, and looked around with an expression that suggested both confusion and uncertainty.

*It will be easy enough to deal with this man,* Vause thought.

The king's gaze shifted to Vause as he stopped while still six feet away. "Prime Minister," he said, but the way he spoke and kept his distance revealed that he was a much different man than he first appeared.

"Your Majesty," Vause responded, hiding his distaste and irritation at his mistake. "I am pleased to have you as my guest."

The other nodded as if this expression of appreciation was his due. He was already glancing around the Prime Minister's sumptuously appointed tent with an expression that suggested disdain.

"Your daughter isn't with you?" Vause continued.

"My daughter has returned home." Cor d'Amphere returned his gaze to Vause. "She no longer commands the Skaar army."

Vause could not yet be certain, but this might work in his favor. The daughter had already proved herself to be a dangerous adversary. He might be better off dealing with her father.

"Shall we sit?" he offered, gesturing to the chairs he had set out for them.

Cor d'Amphere shook his head. "I won't be that long. I think we can settle matters quickly enough. My needs are simple and non-negotiable. The Skaar require a new homeland. We have chosen yours. We have a history of taking what we want, and I assure you that sooner or later that will happen here. In the past, all of Eurodia fell to us. We do not seek to occupy the entirety of the Four Lands, but we do claim the Northland for our new home—everything north of the Mermidon River to the borders of the Dwarf country east and the Elf lands west. The Trolls will be allowed to remain in their homes in the lands farthest north, which will become our protectorate. Am I clear?"

Vause fought down the fury that surged through him at the casual manner in which the demands were presented—as if the matter were already settled and no room for discussion remained. But in truth, these demands were much less than the ones he had been expecting. He was only being asked to give up a large but rather useless section of land, not the heart of the Federation domain. He felt a twinge of relief.

Which, a moment later, disappeared when the Skaar king added, "Needless to say, we may require more room later, as our population grows. But that discussion can be saved for a more appropriate time."

A time, Vause realized instantly, that would undoubtedly arrive all too soon. The Skaar were a nation of conquerors who saw nothing wrong with taking what they wanted, believing themselves entitled. They would seem to settle for a reasonable piece of the country at first, then go on to consume everything.

"I think you need to understand something, Your Majesty," Vause said quietly. "What you ask for now is satisfactory. But anything further will not be tolerated by the Federation or any of the other governments of the Four Lands. If you can accept that, then we can make a bargain quickly and be done with it. If not, we are prepared to resist your forced occupation of the aforenamed lands and cast you out."

His temper had slipped, and he could hear it in his tone of voice. But if he backed down now, he would be setting a bad precedent. So he faced the other man squarely, thinking that if he took a deep breath and blew forcefully enough at this skinny blowhard, he would knock him right over. Thinking, too, that he could have him killed here and now, promises of safety notwithstanding, and might solve a whole raft of problems by doing so.

"Do you accept my offer?" Cor d'Amphere asked calmly, as if he hadn't heard a word the other had spoken. "Aside from your pointless speculations on the future?"

Vause decided to dispense with any of the pleasantries he had been prepared to engage in—an offer of food and drink, of a night's lodgings, of female companionship—and get the man out of his tent and back to the other side of the river without further delay.

"I will consider it and let you know," he said.

The Skaar king took a step forward, smiling. "No need for any delay, Prime Minister. Your decision is already made. I read it in your eyes. But be warned. It would be a mistake to underestimate me. You see me enter your quarters and dismiss me as you would an insect. You see me without my daughter, which gives you false confidence. You see me without my guards and think maybe I could be disposed of and the threat of the Skaar would disappear."

He took a step closer, and now Ketter Vause was having trouble holding his ground. Cor d'Amphere was alone, but so was he. His guards were outside. If the other drew a blade, help might not arrive in time to save his life.

"Do you think I truly came alone?" the Skaar king asked softly. "Have you forgotten what abilities we possess?"

To disappear entirely. To become invisible to other men for short periods of time. The Skaar king was suggesting he had brought guards no Federation soldier could see. He was suggesting that any efforts to protect against this had been in vain.

"You understand now the danger you are in. I see it in your eyes, Prime Minister."

Vause's mouth went dry.

"Three of my soldiers stand within a few feet of you. Should I command it, they would slay you where you stand; you would not have time even to cry out before you died." He paused to let that sink in. "Understand—we are superior to you and your soldiers in every way that matters. We have a history of winning battles that those we fought against were certain we could not win. So think long and hard about what happens next. You have three days."

He held the Prime Minister's gaze for a moment longer, then wheeled away without another word and disappeared through the tent flaps.

Ketter Vause stood where the other had left him and knew, as sure as it was daylight outside his tent, an endless night had very nearly fallen inside.

# 13

SHEA OHMSFORD WAS HELPING THE ROVERS FIT THE big iron plates that were being added as reinforcement for the *Behemoth*'s hull when Rocan's cousin, Sartren Longlet, appeared and said, "Rocan wants you on the Apron."

Shea stopped what he was doing and looked up. "What for?"

Sartren, his brown face broad and friendly, broke into a grin. "Well, now, young Shea. Those who sent me did not feel it necessary to reveal that information. An oversight, I am sure, since they normally make it a point to tell me everything surrounding any request so I can judge whether or not it is worth my time to carry it out."

"You could have shortened that answer by at least fifty words and still managed to make it funny." Shea took in the other's disapproving look and sighed. "All right, all right. I'm on my way."

He started off with a smile. The two had become fast friends, spending time trading outrageous stories at the dinner table and afterward around the watch fires while drinking their evening tankards of ale. Shea liked Sartren in spite of his tendency to ramble on. He liked all the Rovers of Aperex, especially those who claimed kinship to Rocan. Although it was undeniable their number seemed to grow large enough after even five days to make him wonder if anyone in the entire village was not related to his benefactor.

Rocan himself remained mostly absent, off with the village elders and headmen to discuss what had brought him home again and what sorts of trouble were brewing elsewhere in the Four Lands. Shea had no idea how much Rocan was revealing and how much he was holding back, but his stature among the Rovers was such that they did not hesitate to do all he asked for the *Behemoth* and Annabelle.

For the most part, Shea would have been content to stay where he was. Aperex was growing on him, quickly feeling like a place he could call home. The Rovers were a friendly, open people—despite the claims in the Borderlands that they were thieves and cutthroats who would steal the eyes from a dead man. They worked and played hard in equal measure, and they were loyal to their family and friends. In five short days, he had been able to determine that much, and it was more than he could say for those men and women he had known in the Southland.

To reach the Apron—a broad, flat stretch of level grassland at the eastern edge of the village that had been appointed to serve as a landing area for all airships come to Aperex to do business—he had to pass through the entire village. There was a second landing area farther back in the lee of a high bluff, reserved exclusively for usage by the villagers. Hangars and storage space had been carved into the face of the bluff at various points beneath a rugged rock shelf that served as protection and concealment both. This was where the *Behemoth* was being fitted out and where Annabelle was hidden from prying eyes.

Ahead, there was evidence of a crowd gathering. Curious to see what was happening, Shea made his way to the edge of the airfield and found all the attention centered on an airship that was settled close to the eastern edge, with a small group of new arrivals standing before it. One of them he recognized right away. It was the smart-mouthed girl from Varfleet who had given him so much trouble while he was trying to help the grandfather.

And there was the grandfather, as well, standing almost next to her, deep in conversation with Rocan.

"Grandfather!" he shouted excitedly. He rushed forward to stand before him. "I didn't think to meet up with you again so soon. Do you need a guide to get you through the village?"

He missed the sharp exchange of looks that passed between those assembled as the dark-robed man extended his hand in greeting. "Not this time. But it does seem we are destined to begin a new adventure, Shea Ohmsford."

Shea immediately released the other's hand. "Not I, Grandfather. I've found what I was looking for, and have no further need of adventures. Or credits, in case you were thinking of making an offer." He glanced at the girl. Tarsha? Was that her name? "But look. Here is my replacement—a fine young lady of impeccable virtue and the sharpest wits in all the Four Lands. Ready for anything, if I'm any judge. Look no further!"

The girl was scowling at him. When he smiled back, she rolled her eyes and gave a massive sigh of displeasure. "This isn't my idea!" she snapped. "I could have gone two lifetimes without encountering you again. An entire month with you is more than I can bear to think about."

"This is how you greet me?" Shea said, feigning shock. "After I have agreed to give you my place in whatever wild undertaking the grandfather has in mind? That's unkind!"

"Shea," Rocan Arneas broke in quickly. "Remember your manners. Drisker Arc is a *Druid*, and this young woman is his protégée."

Shea started to say something clever, then stopped as he realized there had been a decided edge to the Rover's voice. "Apologies, Grandfather."

Drisker Arc made a dismissive gesture. "My companions and I were sent to find you, Shea. Tarsha Kaynin you already know. Her brother, Tavo. Dar Leah. Brecon Elessedil."

He pointed them out one by one until he reached the most striking young woman Shea had ever seen—except perhaps for Seelah. But this young woman was not a changeling, and seemed somehow different from the rest of the company. He could not have said how he knew this, but he did.

She was standing slightly apart from the others, holding herself at rigid attention. As Drisker Arc hesitated, she stepped forward without waiting for the Druid to speak. "I am Ajin d'Amphere, princess of the Skaar nation."

Shea made a clumsy bow, responding automatically to the title, not wanting to make another misstep. He had no idea who she was and had never heard of the Skaar nation, but if she was a princess, she deserved some sort of respect. Straightening again, he glanced from one face to the next, finding the expression on each more than a little puzzling—save for Tarsha, who was glaring openly at him.

"Rocan," he said at last, turning to the other. "What's going on?"

"I believe any explanation will require a little time and should not be undertaken out here in the open. Why don't we all go up to the Commons and have something to eat while we talk? Our guests look tired and hungry, and we should not overtax them by standing around in the heat of the day." Rocan beckoned with an expansive wave of his arm. "Come with me. Food and drink await."

As they started off, trudging across the Apron toward the village, Shea fell into step beside Tarsha. "Go annoy someone else," she said irritably.

"Did you really come all the way here to find me?" he asked, ignoring her.

"Unfortunately, yes."

"How did you know where I was?"

She gave an exaggerated sigh. "A shade from the netherworld told Drisker it was necessary we do this if we wanted to accomplish our goals."

"A shade? A dead thing?"

She looked away. "Do you want to learn more about this?"

The boy nodded at once. "Of course I do."

"Then you'll have to wait with the rest of us. Apparently only the 'grandfather' knows, and up until now he's been keeping it to himself."

She picked up her pace and hurried ahead, leaving him thoroughly perplexed. Seconds later Rocan dropped back to walk with him, leaving Sartren to guide the others.

"Watch what you say when we get there."

Shea grimaced. Now what? "What do you mean?"

"The Druid is here for something more than a visit. I want to know what it is, and until I do I don't want you saying one word about Tindall and Annabelle. Not one. He'll ask you what you are doing here, but you make something up that doesn't involve the real reason. Understand?"

Without waiting for an answer, he moved away, hurrying to catch up with the others.

Shea lagged behind, perplexed and irritated and wondering what he was getting himself into this time.

Dispositions improved once they were inside the Commons and seated around a table laden with food and drink that had been prepared and served by members of the village. The Commons was a large chamber that served as a gathering place for feasts and meetings but was empty now, according them the privacy they needed for their discussion. Without preamble, Drisker Arc asked Shea to tell them how he had managed to get all the way from Varfleet to Aperex, and what sort of guide work he was finding among the Rovers. He asked in a relaxed, almost joking way, but Shea was already on guard about something—Drisker could tell. So although he spoke freely and at length, relating a questionable version of how he had met Rocan and been offered a job as his personal assistant, the boy was omitting something critical.

What surprised the Druid, as he sat listening, was how little of substance Shea Ohmsford had to say. Mostly it was devoid of anything but the sketchiest of details, and failed to adequately explain what had compelled him to leave the city he had lived in his entire life. Drisker was hoping for a fuller explanation, something that would point to whatever it was that made the boy so crucial that Grianne Ohmsford had insisted he must be found. Although he had kept her identity a secret from the others for reasons that had as much to do with his reluctance to let them know whom they were relying on as anything else, he nevertheless found himself convinced that she had not misled them. At this point, he could not afford to lose their support, and there was a real danger he would if they discovered the truth.

"And that's pretty much the whole of it," Shea finished up, sitting back and watching him.

*Watching to see if he convinced me,* the Druid thought.

"Now you must tell us why you have come all this way to see the boy," Rocan announced, jumping in to take control of the conversation. "Surely it was for more than a simple visit?"

"There is a war coming," Drisker replied, keeping his eyes on Shea. "You may have heard we have been invaded by a people called the Skaar, who come from the continent of Eurodia on the other side of the Tiderace. Their home is beset by an endless winter that has killed their crops and starved their people. There is apparently no indication that it will end anytime soon, so they began searching for a new home and discovered the Four Lands. Now they have established a foothold by destroying a couple of Troll tribes and a sizable Federation response force. All this was accomplished by an advance party of no more than a thousand."

"One moment," Rocan interrupted. "If the Skaar are invaders and Princess Ajin is a Skaar, what is she doing here? Shouldn't she be with her own people?"

Drisker shook his head. "She is not welcome there at present. Her own father, the king, dismissed her from his service. I am hoping she might at some point provide a bridge to speaking with him."

"Isn't that something of a reach?" Rocan persisted. He gave Ajin d'Amphere a shrug. "No offense meant, Princess."

She smiled. "None taken."

The Druid gave momentary thought to offering a further explanation and then shook his head. "For now, we are keeping her with us. The Skaar king is camped with his entire army on the north banks of the Mermidon just west of Varfleet. They are engaged in a standoff with a Federation army of equal or greater size camped to the south. A battle is almost certain unless something changes. As Druids, speaking with the shades of the dead is one way we discover how to change the future—in this case, preventing the Skaar from occupying the whole of the Four Lands. I was told to find Shea Ohmsford, if I wanted the solution."

"That's crazy!" the boy exclaimed. "How am I supposed to do anything about this war?"

"It may not be you who does anything personally," Drisker replied. "It may be something you will do or have done, someone you know or something you know, that will provide us with the direction we need. But it does all start and end with you."

He stopped there, realizing that saying more was pointless. He had not missed the flicker of surprise in the boy's eyes at his last comments. Shea Ohmsford was holding back. Something was preventing him from saying more.

"We can certainly ponder this," the Rover offered, rising from his chair just a bit too abruptly. "It might be that either Shea or I will stumble over what you are looking for."

*Shea or I,* Drisker noted. "I have an idea that might help, if you are willing to give us a few hours of your time. Would you be willing to guide us about the village, just so that we could see for ourselves if there might be anything here that could help us? I know it is an inconvenience . . ."

He let the thought hang. After a long few moments, Rocan nodded. "Why not? If it will help you in your efforts, the few hours you ask are a gift I am pleased to offer. Finish your lunch, and we can be off."

Drisker waited until they were all rising from their seats and moving outside the Commons once more before he pulled Tarsha aside. "Shea knows something. I want you to find out what it is."

She gave him a look. "We don't even like each other!"

"You don't need to. You just need to get him alone. Use the wishsong if you have to, but find out. Rocan is keeping him quiet, but once he is alone, he might be more willing to open up."

Tarsha made a dismissive gesture. "I doubt he will choose to reveal anything to me. But all right, I'll try to find out what he is hiding. What happens to Tavo while I'm doing this?"

"He comes with me. I've seen his interest in the airships. I don't think he will object to leaving you."

Shea Ohmsford was just approaching as Drisker moved away, and Tarsha reached out to grab his arm. "Do you have a minute?"

"Hey, no rough stuff, lady."

She scowled. "Do you have any idea how insufferable you are?"

He started to answer and then stopped, shrugging. "I'll give you that minute, if it will make you stop being so angry with me."

Tarsha gave him her sweetest smile. "Oh, I think it might go a long way toward improving my mood. Come on. You can show me around while we talk. I have a few questions for you."

Allowing the others to leave without them, Shea and Tarsha lingered behind and then set out in the opposite direction, with the boy leading the way. Neither spoke as they walked. Tarsha was absorbed by thoughts of how she might extract anything from Shea Ohmsford, and Shea was simply staying silent. After they had reached the north edge of the village, the boy veered off into a pretty tree-shaded park filled with flowers and birds that flitted from limb to limb in flashes of bright reds and blues.

"I thought you might like to see something as pretty as you are," he said, and this time there was not a shred of joking or teasing in the way he said it.

Tarsha stared at him to make sure, then added, "That was a very nice thing to say."

The boy shrugged. "You don't need me giving you a hard time. I can tell things have been difficult enough. Do you want to sit down?"

They sat on a bench at the center of the park, closer than Tarsha would have ordinarily allowed. She was already revising her approach, thinking that using threats or magic felt wrong. She might get what she wanted that way, but she didn't want to live with the knowledge that she might have caused harm to someone who didn't deserve it.

"So why are we out here?" he asked after a minute or so. "I know you're after something."

She nodded. "No one could ever accuse you of being dim. I was impressed by the way you handled things back in Varfleet, and how you helped Drisker. And me, as it happened. So thank you. I didn't say that before."

The boy shrugged. "He paid me well enough that thanks weren't necessary." He smiled. "But it's nice to hear the words. Now, what's going on?"

"Drisker was watching you during our meeting, and he knows you are hiding something. I'm supposed to find out what it is, even if I have to use magic against you. And I can, you know. I have a very strong magic, and I can probably use it to make you tell me everything I want to know. But I don't want to. I just want you to tell me."

"Maybe your magic wouldn't work with me. I'm pretty talented when it comes to resisting things. Maybe even magic. But say I risk it and tell you no. What happens then?"

She took a deep breath and exhaled slowly. "What you need to understand is that Drisker Arc is trying to save the Four Lands from an all-out war. If it starts, I'm not sure where it will stop—or even if stopping it is possible. But a Druid's connection with the dead is very strong, and when a shade tells you that this is what you must do, then it's what you must do. So coming here was not a whim. And your name being mentioned in particular means you have the answer we need. And an obligation to *everyone* in the Four Lands to provide it."

"Even at the cost of betraying a promise?"

Tarsha leaned close. "If a promise is given out of context, it lacks validity. You made a promise without knowing all the facts, didn't you? So now that you know them, you have to reassess the reason for that promise and the nature of the consequences if you keep it."

"Breaking it might not do anything to help you," he said, a note of stubbornness in his voice.

"Not breaking it might lose us the Four Lands." She leaned back again. "You have to decide, Shea. You have to make the choice and live with it. I told you what I know to be at stake. If what you reveal does not harm Rocan Arneas—and I am pretty certain it was he you made the promise to—then how much trouble can you be in?"

The boy looked away momentarily. "A whole lot more than you think. He is my benefactor. Without his help, I'd be back on the streets of Varfleet, struggling to make my way."

Tarsha gave it a moment before replying. "I think Drisker would help you, if that was how things worked out. But I also think that once Rocan understands why you did it, he will forgive you breaking your promise."

"Yeah, when pigs fly. Look, I like you and all, but I have to think about this."

"You might not have that kind of time. *We* might not—any of us. What else can I say to persuade you?"

He gave her a funny look. "Nothing. But there is something you can do."

"Name it."

"Kiss me."

"What?"

"Kiss me. Once, on the lips. Give me something I've been thinking about since we first met. Something to take with me when I get thrown out on the streets. And don't ask me to explain."

"I am not going to kiss you!"

Shea nodded. "I know. And now you know how I feel about breaking my promise. So you do something you don't want to do, and I'll do the same. Otherwise, we can just walk on back to the Commons and wait for the others to return."

Tarsha stared at him for long moments. "Why are you asking me to do this? You don't even like me."

"Yes, I do. Just because I tease you a bit doesn't mean I don't like you."

"But why a kiss?"

"Curiosity? I don't get many chances to kiss pretty girls."

"So I'm your lucky choice?"

He shrugged. "When opportunity knocks, you open the door. Come on. One kiss."

She stared at him some more, and then she nodded. "One kiss, that's it. Then you tell me everything."

"That's the agreement."

He leaned forward, waiting for her to do the same. She did so slowly, reducing the distance between them to inches. All she could seem to think about was how annoying this boy was and how little she wanted to do anything to please him. Kissing him seemed like a betrayal of her personal beliefs. He leaned forward a little more, very close now, his lips pursed. And then he stopped, a perplexed look on his face.

"We don't need to," he said. "I just wanted to see if you would do it."

Her response was instantaneous. Who did he think he was messing with? She seized the back of his neck and pulled his mouth tightly against hers, holding the kiss for several long seconds, letting him savor the feel of her lips.

Then she released him and moved back again. "A deal is a deal. Start talking."

# 14

IT WAS NEARING EVENING WHEN DRISKER ARC AND Shea Ohmsford appeared before Rocan Arneas and asked to speak to him in private. They had been talking for several hours, debating how to handle the boy's revelations about Tindall and Annabelle. Someone had to confront the Rover with what he had tried so hard to keep hidden, and convince him it was better that it was out in the open. Shea had promised Rocan he would say nothing, but he had known from the moment Tarsha told him about the danger of a war and the reason behind it that he was going to have to break that promise. It wasn't so much that he believed she could have wormed it out of him using her magic. It was more the sense of obligation he felt toward the people of the Four Lands that had persuaded him to take the leap.

But Rocan would never forgive him. Rocan would hate him forever. He would cast Shea out of the village and into the wilds without a second thought. The Rover was a firm believer in loyalty, and the boy had violated his trust in the most egregious way possible.

Tarsha assured him he was mistaken, that Rocan would understand his reasons and would not consider it grounds for casting him out. But Shea was certain she was wrong.

So now the Druid and the boy stood waiting on the Rover's reaction as he turned to face them. To the surprise of neither, Rocan read the truth in their eyes immediately. Ignoring Drisker and looking directly at Shea, he said in a calm and quiet voice, "I never thought you, of all people, would do something like this."

Drisker had done his best to persuade the boy not to come with him as he told Rocan what he knew must now happen—that Tindall must show them Annabelle, because there was no questioning that she was needed. If she could change the weather, then they must consider using her to discover if the winter that had engulfed the Skaar homeland for more than two years could be ended.

"It might be better if I went alone," he had argued. "You can speak to him later, after he has a chance to think things through and calm down."

But Shea shook his head. "I need to go. I'm the one who has to answer for this. I have to face up to what I did. I won't hide like a coward."

Now, hearing the hurt and anger reflected in Rocan's eyes, he wished he could reconsider. It was all he could do to meet the other's gaze as Rocan gave a small shake of his head. "Anyone but you."

His disappointment made clear, the Rover beckoned and took them back to the Commons and a space with a table and chairs at one end of the meeting hall where they could close themselves off and speak in private.

Drisker wasted no time. "Understand, Rocan," he began, "we don't know if it will work. But I have to think there is a good chance it will. The shade I spoke with at the Hadeshorn made it abundantly clear that following the thread that began with Shea would prevent the coming war between the Four Lands and the Skaar. If their weather can be improved and their lands made fertile once more, if crops and game can be brought back, then they have no need of our land."

*Well, maybe,* Shea thought. A lot of maybes, in fact. All sorts of things could fail to transpire, from Annabelle being able to alter the weather over an entire country to the Skaar agreeing to give up their claim to the Northland and go home again. Drisker knew this, of course, but he had nowhere else to turn and no other solution on which to rely. He needed this strange machine and its creator to prove themselves. If Rocan was intending to fly to other parts of the Four Lands to test Annabelle's capabilities anyway, then why not try her out in a way that might save thousands of lives and a future in which a war might rage for years?

Rocan clearly did not agree. "You are risking something that isn't yours to risk—something that Tindall and I have spent years creating. It cost me several fortunes and a good deal of effort to make Annabelle a reality. For Tindall, it's been his life's work. Now you want to step in and take all that away with no promise that anything good will come of it? Why should I even listen to this nonsense, let alone consider doing it?"

"Why is flying to Skaarsland any more risky than flying to faraway parts of the Four Lands?" Drisker persisted. "This is the perfect opportunity to test your machine—and in a situation where changing the weather might save an entire country and its people. What are you giving up to take the risk?"

"The chance to test her in the way I think best!" Rocan snapped. "Control over how she's tested. Everything that assures me no wrong decisions will be made. There's always someone like you, Druid. Always someone there to say, *Wait, now. I have a better use for her than you do. I have a better way to find out how she can be made to serve.* How many times have I heard that? Governments, politicians, leaders of men—that's always their excuse. They take what we have envisioned and created and claim it for themselves. That's what the Federation was trying to do when we slipped Annabelle out of Arishaig and came here. Now you want her for the Druid order! How is it any different?"

Shea took a quick breath. "I don't think that's what . . ."

"You shut up!" Rocan wheeled on him so fast the boy flinched in shock. "You don't say a word!"

"You blame him senselessly," Drisker cautioned, giving the Rover a hard look. "We would have discovered the truth anyway, but he had the foresight and courage to recognize that sharing it with us freely was the right thing to do. It is *you* who are looking at this all wrong,

Rover, and I sense a decided selfishness to it." His hand came up as Rocan started to object. "Wait. Grant me the courtesy of finishing. You are misreading the situation entirely. We don't want to steal your idea; we want to borrow it. Not for selfish reasons, but for a good cause. We don't want to tell you how to use Annabelle; we want you to do that. We want you to come with us. We want you and Tindall to be the ones who do the actual testing."

"Maybe all this is so and maybe it isn't!" Rocan snapped. "It still requires us to do something we had not planned on doing. Just the thought of traveling across the Tiderace in a cumbersome transport is troubling enough. What if there's a storm? What if we go down and the machine is lost? We could never build another in the time we have left—assuming any of us managed to survive."

"And what good will come of you not going? What if the war between the Skaar and the Federation flares up and engulfs all of us? What good is your machine to anyone then? What point is there in changing the weather if all of the people it's meant to help are dead?"

The two glared at each other for a long, silent moment. Then Drisker said, "If it makes you feel any better, I won't be coming with you."

Rocan's eyes narrowed. "Why not?"

"I have something else that needs doing here that is equally urgent. So you and your Rovers will be responsible for taking Tindall and Annabelle to Skaarsland. Yes, some of those who traveled with me will accompany you, but only to provide the help you will need. You would be traveling to a foreign region, and you and Tindall will need every protection to carry out your testing safely. And one among us knows exactly what to expect there."

The Rover nodded slowly. "The princess. She will know the country where you want us to travel."

"That, and a good deal more. It is her homeland. The Skaar are her people. She will have insights that will be helpful. Contacts, perhaps, that will prove friendly. Dar Leah and Brecon Elessedil will accompany you as well. Both have considerable magic to use for protection and guidance." He paused. "And Shea will accompany you."

"Absolutely not! He stays here."

Drisker Arc shook his head. "No, he must go. He is the talisman you will need, the catalyst for something important. I have been told of this, Rocan. You are angry now, but you must let go of that anger. Shea is loyal to you. He cares about what he has done, and he needs you to understand that. He did what he thought was right, but it was not done to hurt you and it was not done without consideration for your feelings."

Rocan looked over at the boy. A slow burn of anger and resentment was evident in his expression. "He betrayed me. Why should I take him with me now?"

Drisker shook his head. "It is not for me to answer. Let Shea speak for himself."

The boy hesitated, and when Rocan shrugged, he turned first to the Druid. "I don't know what I'm supposed to say. I don't know if I want to go. You presume I do, but I have a choice in this, too. I'm not just some pawn in your game."

He paused, taking a deep breath before he spoke again, this time turning to the Rover. "I know I broke my promise and gave your secret away. For that, I am truly sorry. I didn't want to tell what I knew, but I was not wrong to do so. There is more at stake than credits and time and dreams. There are people who will live or die depending on whether Annabelle can do what you think. That's what's important. More important than anything else."

"Your loyalty was to me, boy!"

Shea shook his head. "My loyalty is to all the people of the Four Lands. And my responsibility is to do what I think is right, no matter what."

Rocan nodded slowly. "You probably believe that. It sounds about right for someone your age. But that will change soon enough. Life will change it for you." He shifted his eyes to Drisker. "I will think on it. That's all I can give you. No promises; not about anything. I'll give you my answer in the morning."

He gave Shea a final, indecipherable look and walked from the room.

• • •

The Druid and the boy lingered for a few minutes after the Rover had departed, at first saying nothing, just sitting there. Shea was aware that Drisker was studying him, but he refused to meet that dark, probing gaze. Instead, he looked at the walls, the floor, the ceiling, and into space—anywhere but at those eyes. He wished he had never agreed to accompany Rocan Arneas. He wished he had done what he originally intended to do after escaping Assidian Deep and had just gone home to Varfleet. He wished none of this had ever happened.

Finally, without looking at the other, he asked, "Is it really necessary that I go with the others? This isn't some game you're playing, is it?"

The Druid shook his head. "No game playing. What happens with Annabelle and the Skaar is too crucial to the future of the Four Lands and her people. Your presence aboard the *Behemoth* is necessary."

"The shade told you this?" the boy asked quietly. "That I was supposed to go? How could it do that? It didn't tell you about Annabelle. You didn't even know where I was at that point. So how could it tell you where I was supposed to be during this journey to Skaarsland?"

*Sharp, as always,* Drisker thought. *Sharp as a tack.*

"It told me in ways I can't explain. Most of it is a kind of recognition of what is needed—almost a sixth sense. It has to do with what isn't said as much as what is. It has to do with feelings and instincts. I was given to know more than what I revealed to the others, Shea, some of it through words spoken, some of it not. I will trust you enough to tell you that. But that will have to be enough. Neither you nor they are ready to hear everything just yet. But yes—Darcon Leah, Brecon Elessedil, the princess, and yourself are the ones who must go. Tarsha and her brother must remain behind with me."

Shea thought about that for a moment and realized, once again, that there must be a reason for Drisker keeping the Kaynin siblings with him. But what did it matter to him why that sharp-tongued girl would be staying behind? His thoughts flashed back momentarily to the kiss she had given him. Soft, sweet, and lasting a little longer than was necessary. The memory lingered. But still, it was just a kiss.

"Come," the Druid said. "We need to tell the others what's transpired."

They rose and left the building, walking through the village to where the others had been given quarters for the night.

"I still don't see what purpose my presence will serve," the boy said.

"Sometimes our purpose cannot be known in advance of its coming. Sometimes we sense things rather than know them. We see the possibilities without understanding the specifics. It is so here. You will have to be patient, Shea Ohmsford. But when your purpose is revealed, you will have to decide how to act on it."

"If I should *choose* to act on it."

"If you should choose."

"I might not."

But Shea knew that choices were frequently made for us and that fate so often dictated the direction of our lives. He did not admit this, thinking he had said enough on the matter.

"Out of curiosity," the Druid said, "how did Tarsha persuade you to tell her about Annabelle and Tindall?"

The boy got a curious look on his face, and then looked away quickly. "I don't want to discuss it. She just did. That's all that matters."

After that, they stopped talking altogether.

That night, after she presumed the others were asleep, Tarsha left Ajin d'Amphere sleeping in the bed beside hers and went into the chamber Tavo occupied with Dar Leah and Brecon Elessedil. The Blade and the Elven prince were sound asleep, their breathing heavy and their snores regular; she did not think they would wake. So she sat beside her brother and watched him as he tossed beneath the covers, his expression changing as swiftly as light changes when clouds fly across the sun. Brightness into shadow and back again, over and over. Her brother was dreaming, and his dreams were disturbing him. Asleep, he looked so young to her; she could almost see the little boy in him, the brother whom she had adored and cared for until he became someone she didn't know.

When his eyes suddenly opened, it caught her by surprise. But she held his gaze and waited on him as he stared at her.

"What are you doing?" he asked finally—the first words he had spoken to her in years.

"Keeping you company. I wanted to be sure you were all right." She hesitated. "I want us to be friends again. To be brother and sister."

His voice broke. "What are you talking about? No one wants to be friends with someone like me. I know what I am. Look what I've done."

Tarsha almost started to cry, his words were so sad. He had gone through so much that he no longer felt deserving of friendship. She had to find a way to reach him.

She swallowed hard. "That's not so."

"It is. I've killed people. A lot of people. Including our parents. Especially our parents." He shook his head too hard, as if he was trying to shake out the memories. "Go back to sleep."

She stiffened her resolve. "I want to help you. I've *always* wanted to help you. You might not believe me, but everything I did—including leaving you behind, wrong as that turned out to be—was meant to help you. And nothing has changed that. Yes, it hurts deeply to know what you've done, but it wasn't your fault. It was the magic, using you. But maybe that can change."

"Nothing will change for me. Not ever." He rubbed at the collar Drisker had strapped about his neck, the movement almost reflexive. "Maybe you really do want to help, but you can't. No one can. Not even that Druid."

"He can do a lot of things, Tavo. His magic lets him help people in ways that would surprise you. And I can help you, too. I want to. I don't want to just let you go."

He stared at her in disbelief. "There is no help for me, don't you understand that? You can't bring those people back to life. You can't change the way I am by being nice to me. This collar is the only thing that keeps me under control. I hate my life!"

"This isn't you! This is Clizia Porse talking. I hate what she's done to you. Lying, manipulating, trying to make you her creature. *She's* the cause of your belief that no one can help you but her!"

He sat up abruptly, and she jerked back in sudden fear. "You don't understand. I know all this. The Druid helped me understand. He helped clear my head, helped take away her words. I hate her, too. I know she lied to me. She tried to use me, and then abandoned me. I'm rid of her, Tarsha, but that doesn't change what I am. And do you know what I am? I'm a slave. Even free of the old woman, I am still a prisoner to thoughts that control how I think and what I do. Thoughts that come and go, that want me to do bad things. Even knowing they are bad, I still want to do them. I try to control myself, but I can't. And I won't ever be able to."

Off to the side, Dar Leah opened one eye and stared at them for a long few moments before rolling over so he was facing away.

"I don't want to talk about this anymore," Tavo said. "Go back to bed. Tomorrow, the Druid will tell me again what I have to do to get better. He tells me every day. Mostly, he hopes I won't try to kill you again. I don't want to anymore, but that doesn't mean I won't change my mind. I have all these thoughts, and I can't tell which ones to listen to. That's who I am!"

She saw an emerging glimmer of something very dangerous in his eyes as he spoke, and it caused her to pull back. He saw her reaction, and his eyes closed quickly. "Get out of here. Now!"

He turned away from her and pulled the bedcovers over his head. Tarsha stayed where she was for a moment longer, then reluctantly rose and slipped out the door.

Ajin d'Amphere was waiting in the hallway for Tarsha to emerge, leaning up against the wall, arms folded across her chest. She was wearing a night shift lent to her by one of the Rover women—a garment that was so close to transparent, she might as well not have been wearing it at all. This did not trouble her. Propriety was annoying.

When the girl finally appeared, easing from the bedchamber and carefully closing the door behind her, Ajin said, in a teasing way, "Paying someone a late-night visit?"

She watched Tarsha startle, her young face darkening momentarily as she saw Ajin. "Aren't you supposed to be asleep, Princess?"

Ajin shrugged. "I was worried about you, wandering around by yourself. I didn't want you getting lost."

But the girl didn't take the bait. "I'm going to bed. Late-night visits aren't always such a good idea, as it turns out. But you can find that out for yourself, I imagine."

She went down the hall with her head up and her body rigid, and Ajin knew at once she had suffered some sort of setback but was trying to make the best of it. After she had disappeared into their shared room, Ajin remained where she was for a moment, puzzling it through. Tarsha had been visiting her brother, she realized. She had tried talking to him, and her brother had turned her away. Ajin probably wasn't supposed to know as much about this as she did, but there were those all too ready and willing to talk about this strange brother–sister relationship. She didn't know the whole story, but she knew Tavo had been Clizia's creature until Drisker had somehow freed him. She knew there was bad blood between them.

But none of this had to do with her. She was here for something else entirely.

She pushed off the wall and went into the sleeping chamber where Tarsha's brother and Brecon Elessedil were sleeping, but—more important—where Darcon Leah was sleeping, too. Other young women would have thought twice about entering a room of sleeping young men in the dead of night but not Ajin. She closed the door behind her, peered around in the near darkness, spied the Blade's long-limbed form sprawled on his bed, walked over, lifted up the covers, and climbed in next to him. As he stirred in recognition, she stretched herself out full-length and pressed up against him.

"I thought you might be lonely," she whispered in his ear.

Dar, his back turned to her as she fitted her body to his, glanced over his shoulder in shock. "Are you crazy? What are you doing here?"

"I just told you."

"You can't be here!"

*A furious whisper. My, my. Concerned for my virtue, no doubt.* "Well, since I already am, the point is moot. I thought it would be good to spend some time alone with you—or as alone as we are likely to be for a while."

"Ajin, you have to stop this. This whole business about somehow being fated to be together . . ."

She leaned in and put a finger to his lips to silence him. "I need you to understand something, Darcon Leah. I don't know where I belong anymore. I don't belong with the Skaar, unless I am willing to accept the house confinement assigned me by my father and the very real possibility of an assassination attempt by my stepmother following close behind. I don't belong with the Skaar army because I have been dismissed and sent home. I don't belong in the Four Lands—this isn't my home, and these aren't my people. But is Skaarsland my home anymore, when you come right down to it? Don't you see? I don't belong anywhere. I don't feel *right* anywhere."

She paused. "Except when I am with you. So maybe you would indulge me this once. Maybe you would consider letting me have my moment of freedom from fear and anxiety and anger. Maybe you would consent to share your space with me. How hard can that be?"

He turned slightly to stare at her. When they were face-to-face, she kissed him on the nose. "That's more like it."

"Ajin, I'm sorry about what's happened to you, but that doesn't change anything. I can't be found with you like this. We'll be in all sorts of trouble if that happens. Brecon could wake up at any moment. Tavo may already be awake."

She kissed him again, this time on the mouth. "Then maybe you had better be quiet and just let this happen."

"This? What's this?"

She took a deep breath and exhaled. "Just a few minutes where you put your arms around me and you hold me like you care about me, and I feel like I'm not going to break down like a little girl. Because I am close to doing so, no matter how I appear."

He stared at her. "You? Break down?"

She closed her eyes. "Please?"

She waited and was finally rewarded by the feel of his body shifting and his arms coming around her, pulling her close to him. She fitted herself against him and let her head rest on his shoulder. She felt herself drifting, contemplating the direction her life had taken, revisiting the choices she had made and the setbacks she had suffered, but remembering, too, the times shared with her soldiers and Kol—with all those she had grown up with to become who and what she was.

It was bittersweet, but lying there with the Blade, warm and secure and enclosed, she found it all bearable. Time slipped away and neither spoke. She fell asleep for a while, although she couldn't have said for how long.

When she woke, it was still dark and Dar Leah was sleeping. She studied his finely chiseled features and kissed his perfect lips, and knew she loved him in a way she had never thought herself capable of loving anyone.

She rose then, easing from his bed—from the warmth and strength of his body, from the comfort he had given her. She was reluctant to leave, but she knew it was time. He had given her what she had hoped. She had not been wrong to come to him.

As silent as the darkness that wrapped close about her, she left the room.

# 15

MORNING ARRIVED IN A BLAZE OF SUNSHINE that tried its best to disguise the winter chill in the air. There was no snow this far south, but it would be heavy north of the Streleheim and in the mountains. Even so, there was frost on the ground, and when Darcon Leah found Drisker alone outside their sleeping quarters, staring off to the east, the ground was glittering as if crystallized.

The Blade came up to stand beside him, and for a few moments neither spoke. Dar was lost in thought about what had happened last night, when Ajin came to his bed. He was conflicted about how it made him feel and what it meant for the future. That he had let her stay instead of sending her away was troubling enough; she already had all the encouragement she needed just from her own misguided beliefs in faith and serendipity. Now he had added fuel to the fire by succumbing to his compassion for her situation—alone, abandoned, bereft of people and home.

Nothing had really happened, of course. That would have been a huge mistake, and the Blade was not accustomed to making mistakes of that sort. They had simply shared space and warmth and a sense of closeness that he had come to believe, at the end, might give her both hope and comfort. He could not deny he found her both attractive and fascinating. He thought her every inch his equal as a fighter, and he shared her moral compass.

But she was still the enemy, still an invader from a foreign country, and still mistaken about the connection between them.

He was not going to talk to Drisker about all this, however.

"Are you still determined that taking this machine across the Tiderace to Skaarsland is the right course of action?" he asked, breaking the silence between them.

Drisker shrugged. "I wouldn't admit this to anyone else, but how sure can I be about anything at this point? I'm getting my information from one of the dead, so there is every reason to think I could be making a mistake. So no, I'm just making the best of the choices I have."

"Yet you're sending all of us off on this voyage—all but you and the Kaynin siblings. How wise is that? The assumption you're making is that taking the machine to Skaarsland will change everything. That the machine actually *can* change the weather. If we ignore for a moment the other possible obstacles—weather, time, enemy intervention, and a dozen other things that could sink this whole effort—if the machine fails to do what's needed, we've likely lost everything."

"Likely. So that's why we're leaving today to go back to the Hadeshorn and try to find out if we are on the right track." The Druid looked at him. "Did I forget to mention that?"

Dar gave him a look. "How long ago did you decide to do this?"

"Just this morning. I spoke with Rocan early. It seems he and Tindall were up half the night arguing about what to do. They were of two minds—the old man in favor of giving Annabelle the toughest test they could find, the Rover in favor of proceeding with more caution. Experience and stubbornness won out, so Rocan agreed to test the machine as we've asked. He was not too happy about it, but he calmed down a bit when I told him we would go back to the Hadeshorn for a second opinion on the matter. Just so we could all be sure that this was what the shade wanted us to do."

"Well, I don't mind telling you that I feel better about it. At least this way, we might be given some hint of whether or not we are on the right path." Dar paused. "But shouldn't you come with us on this journey? Wouldn't we be better off if we had your skills and experience to call on?"

The Druid looked at him for a long moment, then said, "Let's walk while we discuss this."

They set out into the Rover village. Aperex was just beginning to wake up. Doors were opening as the villagers went off to work, smoke was rising from the chimneys as fires were heated up, and voices were calling out from within cottages and outbuildings. Already, the deep glow of the forges that shaped the metals and composites from which the builders crafted their airships was growing stronger as the day's work got under way. In the distance, a small transport was just lifting off to fly to the northwest.

"The problem is, while I would like to come with you, I can't," Drisker said so softly, Dar almost missed hearing it. "My path and yours must diverge. I'm not sure for how long, but it may be for very long indeed. I am given another task, one that will keep me here in the Four Lands. Other schemes are in play, most of which will destroy any chance of resolving the difficulties the Races are facing. It is my part in this drama to stay behind either to find solutions or to keep the pot from boiling over. Clizia is at the heart of one or two of these, but there are other players, as well—some of whom you don't even know about."

"These are not problems you can leave behind long enough to settle on whether or not the weather machine will work?"

"No. We each have our role to play, and this one is mine. It means we will all have a hard struggle ahead of us. But at least we will all have companions and allies to stand with us."

The Blade made a dismissive sound. "I wouldn't put too much trust in any help you might get from the Kaynins. Tarsha, maybe. But she is linked too closely to her brother to be trusted if he goes rogue again. And he is insane, Drisker. For all that he seems ordinary enough now, he is one blink away from the madness that claimed him earlier."

Drisker nodded. "I know the dangers. I believe I know how to handle them, and Tarsha will help me. You must have faith in her. She is much stronger than she seems."

Dar kicked at the earth in frustration and said nothing. They walked to the edge of Aperex and stopped. For a few moments, they did not retrace their steps but merely stood there staring into the village.

"You know Clizia will try to get back into the Keep?" the Blade asked, glancing over to measure the other's reaction.

Drisker looked back with a smile. "I certainly hope so," he said.

"Just through this next stand of trees and up the hillside to the bluff," Clizia Porse advised the Skaar squad leader.

She didn't know his name and didn't care to. He and nineteen of his men had been lent to her the previous morning by Cor d'Amphere, who had promised twenty-five but had changed his mind when she had appeared at his tent flaps.

Twenty men was what he claimed he could spare, and in truth it was more than enough to do what was needed. So she let the slight pass and simply made sure the squad leader knew who was in charge and what was expected of him and his soldiers. She did this with the king standing next to her so there would be no question of her authority later.

"You are not to question my orders," she had said. "You are not to do anything I do not first tell you to do. You are to stay close to me and stay together. What we are attempting to do will not be dangerous if you obey these rules. Make sure you understand. Make certain you heed my warning."

So far, they had. The company had flown all day, arriving at the forests surrounding Paranor by early evening, landing safely away from the Keep so that their craft would not be at risk. She did not say so, but distancing the transport was also intended to keep anyone—or anything—that still lived within the Keep ignorant of their coming. She would not risk any of them by attempting to enter through any of the exterior gates. Instead, they would use the underground passageway with which she was most familiar, and to which she knew the codes to unlock the barriers that would confront them.

They slept near the ship that night and began their trek the following morning. As Paranor came into view, she heard small gasps and mutterings from among her followers, but she ignored them. Instead, she maneuvered them away from the bluff and through the forest until they had reached the tunnel entrance, where she brought them to an uncertain halt. She gave them a few moments longer to wonder what she was about before speaking.

"From here, we go underground. A tunnel that leads to the cellars of the Keep will be our point of entry. You cannot see it yet; it is carefully concealed with magic. But I will reveal it, and you will follow me down to the tunnel, which will then lead us into Paranor. There will be no talking or stopping until I say so. Remember my warnings about what not to do—and here, especially." She paused. "Are you ready?"

Most nodded. No one spoke. Clizia was pleased. The less they said, the better.

She gave them a demonstration of her magic, removing the concealment to the tunnel entry and releasing the locks. Once the tunnel was open, she used her magic again to fire up a line of permanent torches that lined the passageway, the brands lighting up one after the other until they disappeared from view. Summoning cold fire to the tips of her fingers—a final demonstration of what she was capable of doing—she led the way down into the darkness.

The walk was not overly long, and they completed their journey in less than twenty minutes. Once at the huge iron door that sealed the Keep, she paused again. So much depended on handling this the right way. The treasures stored within Paranor's vaults were priceless, and she didn't want any of these men to stumble into them by accident. So she would need to keep them with her and away from what mattered.

Her plan after that was simple enough. They would climb to the main floor of the tower, determine that all was as it should be, and then she would order them all to the outer walls to assume a watch—presumably to await the coming of Cor d'Amphere, but actually for something much more pressing.

She had no intention of sharing anything of real importance with the Skaar king, of course. She would have to admit him into the Keep in order to gain his support, but she did not have to reveal any of the magic it housed. A few odd baubles brought out as a tease, and the rest—she would claim—must have been pilfered away by the Druids before the Keep fell to his daughter.

But in truth, she would have used the hour or so she needed after placing her Skaar contingent at watch to come back down into the archives and retrieve and hide all the artifacts and talismans that might prove useful to her in the months and possibly years ahead. She would conceal that magic so thoroughly there would not be even the remotest possibility of anyone, save her, finding it. Drisker, after all, was still loose somewhere in the Four Lands, and he would be hunting for her. Eventually he would return here, if she failed to find and kill him first. But she did not want him retrieving the magic for his own uses any more than she wanted the Skaar king to possess it.

Of course, the possibility remained that Drisker had carried some portion of it out with him when he had escaped, but she could do nothing about that now. She simply had to hope he had been too eager to get away from his prison to risk going back in again.

She summoned her magic and released the locks on the iron door to the Keep one by one. When the last clicked free, the door swung open to admit her. With her Skaar soldiers staying close, she marched inside. To her relief, everything seemed exactly the same as when she had left it. Nor did a quick search with her magic reveal the presence of any other living creatures. The Keep, it seemed, belonged to her now.

Beckoning to those who followed, she climbed the stairs of the tower to the main floor; her senses pricked against any surprises Drisker might have left. She walked down the main hallway to the closest doors and outside. Another quick scan revealed no life out there, either.

She turned to the squad leader. "Place your men at intervals on all four outer walls where they can stand watch. If they see anyone or anything approaching, give warning. You are to come into the cellars to fetch me only if the need arises. Otherwise, I will be down there on the king's business and need to be left alone. Do you understand me? *Left alone.*"

The squad leader nodded and turned to his men, sending them to the walls to take up their positions. Without bothering to spare her even a glance, he followed after them. She watched as they climbed to the battlements and began to spread out, the squad leader calling out names and assigning stations.

After a few moments to be sure they were otherwise occupied, she went back inside.

Instantly she knew something was wrong.

The air inside the Keep had turned cold and misty, the latter reflecting a greenish color. From deep within the bowels of the building, a long sustained hissing sounded, gaining intensity with every passing second.

Clizia wheeled about, almost as if expecting to find what she feared was already waiting.

The Guardian of the Keep was awake.

*No!* She hissed audibly. *It can't be coming out now! It retreated back into the depths where it slept with the destruction of the Skaar invaders, and these minions are in my company and should be protected . . .*

But they were not protected, she realized. Any of them. They were being viewed as invaders. Somehow, in some way, Drisker had managed to convince the Keep or its Guardian that she was no longer a Druid.

It was impossible that he could have managed this, and yet there was no other explanation. Already, the mist was leaking through the windows and doors, from the trapdoors and vents that opened from the cellars. In minutes, it would spread everywhere throughout Paranor, overpowering those who did not belong, sentencing them to death.

And herself? Was she right about what Drisker had done? Would she be treated as an enemy, too?

She felt all too certain that she would be—that Drisker had connected with the Guardian in a way no other Druid ever had. What price he had paid for this, she could not imagine. But her efforts at gaining control of the Keep's magic and making it her own were over—along with any plans to occupy and control Paranor itself.

She glanced around hurriedly, assessing her situation. The mist was not yet in view in the corridors behind her. As a precaution, she quickly used her magic to disguise herself so that she would appear to be a part of the walls around her.

But out in the courtyard, the greenish mist was spreading. After crawling from the Keep's cellar's exterior vents, it had flooded the open spaces between the buildings and was climbing the outer walls at a slow, steady pace. Already it had blocked all the stairways leading down. The Skaar were turning around now, sensing that something was wrong, seeing how the greenish haze had flooded everything below them.

The squad leader rushed down the stairs, vaulting the mist that occupied the lower steps to land in a swirling lake of ichorous brume. Heedless of how its tendrils were wrapping about him, he staggered across the courtyard to the doors she stood behind, gasping and choking, his hands working spasmodically, his face gone bloodless.

She waited until he was right up against the door, his fingers fumbling at the handles to open them, before she threw the locking bolts.

The man screamed in fury, yanking on the doors, trying to force them open. It was a hopeless effort; she could see it, even if he couldn't. He was on his knees a moment later, the last of his strength draining away. His face pressed up against the glass panels, his eyes fixing on her. His body was disintegrating, melting like ice in the sun, his skin and blood first, his organs next, his bones last.

And then he was gone.

The rest of the Skaar were suffering the same fate, but she chose not to stick around to watch, and instead bolted for the stairs leading down. She was vaguely surprised to find that the Guardian had not yet closed about the interior of the tower, focused perhaps on the larger number of intruders that lined the wall. She glanced over her shoulder to find the mist seeping toward her from down the hallway, and she went down the stairs in a rush, her efforts little more than a frantic shuffle, which was the best she could manage. But it was enough to outdistance her otherwise unavoidable fate, and she gained the cellar door leading out, still open from when they entered.

Pulling it closed behind her, she secured the heavy locks anew and began to run once more.

It took her almost no time to reach the entrance leading in from the forest, although it felt like forever. She charged up the steps and secured the trapdoor anew before dropping in exhaustion to her hands and knees, panting like a horse run half to death.

On the walls, the Skaar were dying, their screams a terrible sound as the mist enclosed and devoured them. She could not stand to listen and yet could not help but do so. She waited them out, waited until all had faded away and the forest was silent once more.

A wave of despair washed through her, and tears of frustration filled her eyes. What was she going to tell Cor d'Amphere? How was she going to explain to him that everything she had promised was lost? There was no possibility now that the Skaar king would do anything to help her in her efforts to reform the Druid order. She would be lucky not to be put to death.

She was suddenly enraged beyond words. This was all Drisker Arc's doing, and she swore on everything she held sacred that she would see him pay for it!

Still seething, she dragged herself to her feet and stumbled away.

By midday of the same day, Drisker and those who had arrived with him—along with Rocan, Tindall, Shea Ohmsford, and a crew of Rovers—were flying east toward the Dragon's Teeth and the Hadeshorn in the *Behemoth*. It might have been easier to go in a small vessel with fewer travelers, but the Druid had decided this would be the wrong choice.

In the first place, he wanted a test run for the *Behemoth*, so that all of them could experience what it was like to fly her and to make certain that everything that should be operating was doing so in the proper fashion. While the Rover crew would be flying her and none of the others would be required to assist—in the absence of an emergency—it was still a good idea to get the feel of a vessel as large and complicated as this one while help was still close at hand. Because once they set out across the Tiderace, they would have only themselves to rely upon.

In addition, no matter what he learned at the Hadeshorn, either they would embrace the assurance of the shades that they were on the correct path, or they would abandon the effort and return to Aperex. But for Drisker, the latter was not an option. Whatever they were told, he was committed to them continuing on. Since that much was decided and there were no extraneous passengers or crew at this point, it made sense not to mention a return. The assumption he was instilling in his companions was that the shades would affirm what he had already indicated, and nothing in their current plans would change.

Of course there was still the problem of what would become of the Kaynin siblings and himself, who would not be going with the others after the *Behemoth* departed the Hadeshorn. Once left behind, they would have to find a new form of transportation. To solve that problem, Drisker had asked that a three-man flit be loaded aboard—ostensibly as an additional precaution, but in fact so that the three remaining behind could use it once the others were safely on their way to Skaarsland.

So the journey had assumed a finality that left little doubt in anyone's mind as to what the future held: The *Behemoth* and its passengers would be flying on from the Dragon's Teeth east to the Tiderace and eventually to Skaarsland, but without Drisker and the Kaynins. It was troubling to have made the decision beforehand, but the Druid had decided that this was how it must be. How this would all play out in the days ahead was difficult to tell, but at least there was an acceptance on the part of everyone that this was what was expected to happen.

Even so, Drisker was unsettled for other reasons.

He did not like removing himself from any chance of helping those traveling to Skaarsland, did not like that Ajin d'Amphere was the best they could do for a guide or interpreter or source of information. While she had been cooperative enough up until now, he knew they could not expect her to stay that way. As soon as she was back in her homeland, she might well revert to form and turn them over to her people.

He was worried enough about it that when they stopped that first night on the borders of the Tirfing, still well west of their destination, he pulled Darcon Leah aside. They were moored out in the open, as there was no shelter anywhere in sight of sufficient size to conceal their transport. The others were still eating, and the Druid had managed to catch the Blade's eye before rising and moving away to the bow of their craft.

Out of sight of the others, Drisker spoke. "I don't like it that I won't be with you, especially since you might have to rely on the Skaar princess at some point. How far do you think you can trust her?"

The Blade was quiet for a moment. "She's a complicated young woman, Drisker. She can be ruthless and devious and clever when it suits her, but she also lives by a strong moral code. Which is why I am still alive, as you know. In this case, I think she feels ill-used by her father. But her homeland is dangerous for her, too. Her stepmother wants her dead, and she is afraid that going home will allow it to happen. But by the same token, I think she agreed to go just so she could settle things with her stepmother once and for all."

"Which means what for the rest of you?"

Dar shook his head. "I'm not sure. But I intend to keep a close eye on her, and Brecon will do the same. He trusts her less than I do, but that's mostly because he's seen her with his father and saw how intent she seemed on bedding him. I think that was all just for show—just to gain his favor. Anyway, if she says she will do something, she will do it. So, at least in the early stages, she will be of some help."

Drisker nodded slowly. "Just promise me you will be careful. Watch her closely and do not give her the opportunity to undo the mission. I trust you most of all. Rocan is strong, but he swings with the winds of opportunity. His men will follow him. Be on your guard."

"Always," the Blade answered with a grin. "You'd best do the same. Especially where Tarsha's brother is concerned."

As he disappeared back to join the others, Drisker stayed where he was a moment longer. Tavo Kaynin. What were the chances anything good could come from him?

# 16

CLIZIA PORSE WAS NOT CERTAIN WHAT TO DO after leaving Paranor and the unfortunate Skaar who had gone with her to their doom. She retrieved the Skaar transport—which she had no trouble taking command of since she could bypass its alarms easily enough—but instead of lifting off, she chose to stay where she was. She was in little danger of being found by anyone—and certainly no one from the Skaar camp—so she had time to consider her options. Haste was almost always a mistake, and while she was still furious at Drisker Arc, she was aware that giving in to her emotions would gain her nothing. What was the old saying: *Don't get mad; get even*? Well, she had done that often enough in the past to understand that, in the long run, it was the far more satisfying result.

Still, the truth was dismaying. Drisker had known it was safe to leave Paranor unguarded, and she was no threat, because the Keep and its Guardian no longer saw her as a Druid. Trying to go back had been a huge mistake, and she should have seen this right from the beginning. But she had been so eager to blunt the impact of Drisker's return to the Four Lands and her embarrassing failure to destroy him that she had misjudged.

But was this an irretrievable loss? Could she not recover her status as a Druid and be readmitted to Paranor? And if so, what would it take?

She wondered if maybe the problem was the result not of her own actions in betraying the Keep but of Drisker's. If he was now acknowledged as a Druid once more, had the Keep decided to restore his status as Ard Rhys as well? Because someone had to hold that distinction if there was to be a Druid order, and it clearly wasn't her. So if Drisker had somehow been anointed, then he would have the right to choose who served in the order. And he would have made it clear that she wasn't to be one of them.

What would happen, though, if Drisker was killed and she was the last living Druid? It was possible she could then regain control over the Keep and become the new Ard Rhys. But killing Drisker, of course, was the only way to find out if she was right. And that would take time and luck and persistence—none of which were likely to arrive in a timely fashion. In the meantime, she was stuck with the problem of what to do about Cor d'Amphere. With Paranor at least temporarily lost to her, she needed another base of support and some faction of the Four Lands to recognize openly her claim as Ard Rhys—and, despite all that had transpired, the Skaar king still seemed her best option. Neither the Federation nor the Elves had any reason to want to aid her. Her contact with both during her tenure as a Druid had been minimal, so any approach to either government now with a claim that she had orchestrated the Keep's downfall and arranged for the destruction of the Druid order would be met with suspicion and doubt.

And, likely, open hostility.

No, the Skaar remained her best chance for an alliance, but she would have to find another way to convince them of this. What could she offer that was too valuable to spurn?

She sat there, brooding on it, until night had fallen. She carried the problem into sleep—and when she woke the next morning, she had found the answer she was searching for. Immediately, she climbed into the pilot box of the transport, powered up the diapson crystals, and flew south. It took her the rest of the day, passing through the Dragon's Teeth by way of the Kennon Pass before turning east to where the Skaar encampment waited. Because she was flying a Skaar vessel with Skaar insignia, she was not challenged as she returned to the landing area where the other airships were moored. Setting down, she exited her craft and demanded to be taken to Cor d'Amphere, already preparing herself for the confrontation she knew was coming.

Their meeting was every bit as bitter as she had expected. She was admitted to the Skaar king's presence quickly enough and then left alone with him. In a calm, reasoned voice, she gave him a highly modified and largely false version of the events that had transpired.

"I gained admittance to Paranor just as I promised I would. But one among our company disobeyed my instructions and caused a disruption that summoned the Guardian of the Keep before I could intervene. Almost instantly the magic destroyed your men. I'm sorry to say they never had a chance. When such a creature rises from the pit, there is no stopping it."

The king nodded slowly. "And now they are dead. All twenty."

He did not make it a question. He simply stated it as fact. There was a barely controlled rage evident in his voice, but Clizia did not react to it. She simply nodded.

"And you could save none of them," he continued.

She shook her head. In the silence of the moment, she was aware of the distant voices of Skaar soldiers and the familiar rustlings and hissings of cook fires as the camp prepared for dinner and nightfall. She could hear the scrape of weapons and the clash of armed men sparring. More distant still, she could hear the sound of an airship powering up and readying for liftoff, intending perhaps to make a run for supplies or to scout the Federation by moonlight. The night skies were clear enough, and flying would be pleasant if you could ignore the cold. Patches of snow still lay on the ground, not yet melted, and there was a fog forming over the Mermidon. Winter was settling in.

Cor d'Amphere broke into her reverie, clearing his throat. "Yet in spite of everything, you managed to escape without a scratch."

Ah, there it was. The accusation she knew she would have to face. But she was prepared for it. "I had an advantage your men did not. My magic enabled me to hide from the Guardian. But I was not the one who caused the death of your men. I was not the one who broke the rules. They should have listened to me more carefully."

An out-and-out lie, if you knew the whole of it, but this man did not. Yet his ignorance might not be enough to save her. Her life still hung in the balance, should his anger outweigh her words.

"My lord," she said quickly, giving him no chance to respond to her accusation. "I accept responsibility for losing your men, even though I was not the cause. But if you will hear me out, I think I can make amends."

The king smiled. It was not pleasant. "You cost me twenty men, you fail to gain for me possession of the Druid's Keep, and you all but admit that what my daughter has already lost once, you have now lost a second time. And still you ask for a chance to make amends? You are aware, as I recall, that I dismissed Ajin from the army and ordered her home for just such a failure? And I rather like my daughter; I have not forgotten the many successes she had before this solitary failure. You, however, I have no such feelings for."

"What if I were to show how I could be useful?" she asked. "What if I were to tell you that I could turn the tide of this impending battle between Federation and Skaar in your favor without you having to lose a single soldier? Would that buy me a reprieve?"

The king shrugged. "I have already reached an accommodation with the Federation. When I met with the Prime Minister, I gave him three days to grant the Skaar the land we already hold. This is the third day, and not six hours ago they sent a messenger to advise me that an accord had been reached. It only remains for us to work out the details. There will be no war. There will be no loss of life. I have nothing to fear from an impending battle. And there is nothing you can do to improve my situation."

This was a new wrinkle, but Clizia held her ground. "You are mistaken on several counts, my lord—especially if you think the Federation intends to bow to your demands. They are stalling, at best. If they make an agreement with you, I can promise they will not honor it—not while they still believe they are the dominant power. They, too, covet the land you now claim. And despite the fact that you cost them an entire army, the Federation is huge and can rely on grinding you down eventually. Yes, you have skills and some capability to alter your body mass, but you lack reinforcements and supplies—and their access to both is virtually limitless. No, you need something more if you are to be free of the threat they pose. This is what I am offering you, and I am the only one who can provide it."

He stared suspiciously at her. "You make bold claims, old woman. Why should I believe they would renege on their accord?"

"I am going to explain why, my lord. In detail. If, when I am finished, you find my logic impossible to embrace, then send me on my way or do whatever you think best. But first hear me out, and I think you will decide that you are right to trust me."

Slowly, painstakingly, she detailed what she had in mind, laying out her plans, giving him all the reasons she believed she could succeed. What she did not do was reveal any of her hidden intentions—those that would set her in position to re-create the Druid order and regain control over her own destiny.

She watched his face and his posture as she explained, and the further she got into it, the more he exhibited signs of both understanding and approval.

By the time she was done, he was hers.

Aboard the *Behemoth*, Drisker Arc was standing alone at the bow, looking out over the wintry landscape of the Callahorn as the airship continued across the grasslands toward the Mermidon River. He was not happy they had been forced to come this way, aware of the confrontation taking place between the Skaar and the Federation not all that many miles ahead of them. But to detour either north or south far enough to assure avoidance of all detection would cost them valuable time. And it was time he was afraid they did not have. The days were slipping away, and if the war was to be prevented, they needed to complete their visit to the Hadeshorn.

The bulk of their company would continue on to the Tiderace and cross to the Skaar homeland; that was settled in his mind. His own mission, in which he would be accompanied by Tarsha and her brother, was another matter entirely. The Ilse Witch had revealed much to him that he had kept hidden, in the manner of Druids everywhere. Still, it troubled him to keep such things from his companions—including the identity of his sinister helper, Grianne Ohmsford, who had somehow slipped the bonds of her imprisonment within the Forbidding to send him her image. It should not have been possible—but then he would have said the same about his ability to send an image of himself out of lost Paranor to reach Tarsha.

In any event, he had let them believe it was Allanon's shade that had advised him, and had not revealed the bargain he had made, which none of them would have condoned. But impending disaster required extraordinary measures, and a willingness to do what otherwise would be avoided.

At some point, of course, he was going to have to tell them the truth. But at least he would have this final meeting before deciding. He pondered on it until he had worn the subject thin, and then tucked it away for another time.

Ahead, the eastern sky was quickly darkening, flooded with clouds that allowed only glimpses of a moon sliding silently from behind their ruffled curtains—here one moment and disappeared the next. The air was very cold, and they had left the *Behemoth* dark, with the warming fires unlit, so as to avoid detection from those they must pass over on their way to the Valley of Shale.

Tarsha Kaynin appeared suddenly at his side, a silent presence. She stood next to him without speaking, her eyes directed forward, her young face intense. He waited for her to tell him what she had come to say, knowing she was there for a reason.

But in the end, when long minutes had passed, he lost patience. "Where is your brother, Tarsha? Is there some problem?"

The girl shook her head. "He is behaving as if he is a new person. What did you do to him, Drisker? Is he cured?"

The Druid turned to face her. "He is not cured. What I did was use magic to smooth over the rougher parts of his thinking to give him an overall sense of comfort and peace, but this will not last. At some point, the old demons will reassert themselves. He may have further visits from his darker half. His condition is permanent, but it can be tempered and controlled."

"So he is still a danger to himself and others?"

"Yes. But for now, he is otherwise engaged. I watched him in the pilot box taking instruction from the Rovers. He is fascinated by the airship and its workings. It might be that this will distract him for a time."

"But I will need to find a way to reach him in the meantime, won't I?" She looked momentarily lost. "I haven't had much luck with that so far."

Drisker nodded. "Give yourself time and space. Keep talking to him. Don't give up on trying to reach him. You will succeed, at some point. He has been lost for a long time, but he wants to be found. We will be traveling together after the others depart for Skaarsland, so we will both have opportunities to reach him. But your chances of doing so will be better."

She nodded slowly. "I wish I could believe that. But he tried to kill me. It's hard to stop thinking about that."

"He wasn't himself, remember. Clizia had poisoned his mind. She had asked him to kill me, but his rage over your perceived abandonment led him to target you first. The magic I used on him pushed those feelings deep down, so for now, at least, we have a sane mind and a willing spirit to work with."

"I hope that's enough."

He smiled. "We'll have to make it enough."

The *Behemoth* was swinging north now toward the Dragon's Teeth, bringing her closer to the peaks in order to stay as far away from the Skaar encampment as possible. Since the airship had the look of a transport, it might not attract the attention a warship almost certainly would. It was dark enough by now that they would probably not be seen at all, especially with the clouds as heavy as they were. The Rovers were skilled fliers and could keep this cumbersome monster low and close enough to the cliffs to minimize the possibility of detection.

"Are those the Skaar?" Tarsha asked him, noting the dim glow of watch fires in the distance.

"Those are my people," Ajin d'Amphere answered, coming up out of the darkness. "My father and my soldiers. How strange to see them like this."

"You could go back," Tarsha reminded her. "We could set down and let you off."

Whether they could or not was a question left unanswered; the princess quickly responded with a shake of her head. "No. I'm dismissed and my father will not let me return, airship crash or no. I will go back to Skaarsland with you, to face my mother and my people."

A long silence followed. "Will you confront your stepmother?" Tarsha asked finally.

The Skaar princess gave her a searching look. "I haven't decided yet. What I will do is guide you safely to my country and give you a chance to do what you intend with your machine. Other than that, I cannot say what I will do."

After that, no one said anything until she walked away.

On the ground, near the north edge of the Skaar encampment, Clizia chanced to glance skyward just as the moon was emerging from behind a cloud, and a massive shape was backlit against the dark wall of the mountains.

She slowed in spite of herself, peering up at the shape as it came into sufficient focus that she could tell it was a giant transport. Oddly configured, it appeared to be a hull with three masts and several giant buildings or statues or some such settled in place just behind and ahead of the mainmast. She squinted hard to make out what she was seeing, but before she could manage it, the moon disappeared once more, leaving her staring at the blackness of the clouded sky.

Still she stared, waiting for the moon to reveal it again.

*What was that?*

But when the moon appeared, it was gone, masked by other clouds.

Even so, she lingered a moment longer, wondering at the immense size and strange shape of the airship (for it most certainly was an airship that high up) before dismissing the matter and continuing on.

# 17

IN THE FEDERATION ENCAMPMENT ON THE SOUTH banks of the Mermidon River, Ketter Vause was up early, dressed and sitting at his worktable, when Belladrin entered. He had sent word for his aide while it was still dark, his anger and his impatience keeping him from sleep and driving him to act now, before any further time had lapsed. That he had been brought to this point by Cor d'Amphere was galling, but he resolved to have the other's head spiked above the gates of Arishaig before another month was out. He had bought the time he needed to accomplish this by agreeing to a cessation of all fighting while the two of them attempted to reach a truce. In the Skaar king's view, that meant the Federation must accept the terms he had offered. In Vause's view, it meant finding a way to put an end to the Skaar invasion once and for all.

He believed he had found such a way.

"This is very early," Belladrin said, yawning. Her hair was tousled and her fine features still heavy with sleep. "Even for you."

"I want you to draw up an agreement to be delivered to the Skaar king. I want it to approximate the one he has insisted upon, while not following it exactly. I want one or two things left out. I want it to sound gracious, even slightly subservient. Can you do that?"

She scowled. "You don't intend to give in to him, do you? He threatened you, Prime Minister. He treated you as if you were no one."

Vause stared at her. "How do you know this?"

She tightened her scowl. "I was just outside, listening."

"My, my. You're developing bad manners, young lady. Well, you need to understand something. Sometimes it is best to let an enemy think you weak and malleable. His daughter was more direct in her approach by openly challenging us, and was more likely to follow through on her threats. But this man, as bold as he seems, is less dangerous. He postures without taking time to accurately assess the situation. He doesn't realize that I was a commander in the Federation army before I was Prime Minister. He wrongly assumes he holds the upper hand because his people have the ability to disappear. We will make him pay for that."

Even as he said it, he remembered the fear he had felt in the other's presence, wondering if his guards stood invisibly close at hand. He remembered, too, his shame at having experienced such fear afterward.

"So you don't intend to accede to his demands?"

Vause shook his head slowly. "I intend to see him and every last one of his Skaar destroyed. To that end, I need him to think he has already defeated me. But I require time, as well, to prepare for what must be done."

She grinned. "That sounds more like the Prime Minister I know. I'm so glad you brought me with you."

He had brought her so he could train her, already finding her smart, efficient, and highly capable. Her command of strategy and her ability to reason were impressive. It put her head and shoulders above so many of his commanders and Coalition Council ministers, whose lack of wisdom rendered them seriously deficient. When he was tired of being Prime Minister, for whatever reason, perhaps Belladrin would be even more skilled than he was at carrying out his duties and, eventually, with enough time, be a logical choice to succeed him.

This was all in the future, but training her now was the key to everything that would follow.

"Draft that agreement, and when you are finished bring it back to me for review and we'll send it off. After that, I have another task for you. It will require that you make a journey into the Eastland with a contingent of soldiers and Federation commanders. You will be my personal representative, tasked with meeting and speaking to members of the Dwarves at the village of Crackenrood. Are you game?"

She pursed her lips. "I am. But why would you send me, when you could dispatch someone with more experience?"

"There may be those who question this decision—who question why one so young should be given such authority. But it is not their place to do so, and you must ignore them. To aid you with this, I intend to send someone to accompany you who will make certain you are not interfered with."

She was silent a moment, staring down at her boots. He waited impatiently, wondering if he had said the wrong thing or embarrassed her somehow. Talking with young women was not something he was accustomed to, and as much as he admired this one, he didn't want her around if they couldn't talk freely.

"I don't want to fail you," she said finally. "And I am afraid I will if you give me this mission."

He almost laughed—but that would have been a mistake he could never have fixed. Instead, he simply shook his head. "You underestimate yourself, Belladrin. You are indeed young and still learning, but your skills at recognizing what needs to be said or done and finding the right answers to problems are formidable already. I would go myself, but I need to stay close to the army while we wait out the results of our gambit with the Skaar. A delicate balance must be maintained."

"I want to believe you are right about me," she said.

But there was still uncertainty in her eyes. He wondered for a moment if he had misjudged her. But he did not think so and made the decision not to back down. He had believed her the best choice for this mission, and he saw no reason to let a few doubts persuade him he was wrong. And if he was wrong, it wouldn't be the first time. And it wouldn't be fatal.

"Then go to Crackenrood," he told her. "Carry the message I will give you. Present the argument I wish you to offer. Believe me when I tell you a seasoned negotiator is the wrong choice for what I intend. A fresh face is needed but not a callow mind. You are exactly the person I require. I have faith that you will not fail me. Put aside your doubts and carry through in the way you always have."

She took a deep breath, exhaled slowly, and nodded. "All right."

Ketter Vause smiled. "Well done. Now let's get to work."

Midnight had come and gone by the time Drisker Arc and his companions arrived at the foothills below the pass leading into the Valley of Shale. By then the cold of darkness had turned bitter, and all those aboard *Behemoth* were wrapped in heavy cloaks, their hoods pulled up for additional warmth. They would have liked to fire the deck burners to provide a little warmth, but the Druid forbade it. The risk of revealing their position to any enemies was too great. While no one was happy to hear this, all of them understood. They were in territory filled with people who would like nothing better than to get their hands on the *Behemoth* and her strange cargo.

Drisker took the time to warn Dar against letting any of the others wander away from the airship before setting out for the Hadeshorn. He took Tarsha with him—to her obvious surprise—because of something the Ilse Witch had told him during their previous meeting. Tarsha, she advised, was crucial to everything and needed to be present if he was to summon her again. He was to bring her down to the shores of the Hadeshorn, but she must not be allowed to speak. This was not a suggestion; it was a requirement. Although he had asked the reason, none had been provided. Tarsha was to be there with him; that was all he needed to know.

Because he had followed the instructions he had been given thus far with no attendant difficulties, he saw no reason to ignore them now. Tarsha was more than a little curious about the reason she had been asked to accompany him, but the Druid simply told her it was necessary and he would explain why later. The others wanted a reason, too—especially Tavo, who was suddenly suspicious of what the Druid was planning.

"You cannot leave me," Tavo whispered, coming up to Tarsha so that only she and the Druid could hear. "You cannot go!"

Tarsha took him by the shoulders—not yet sure enough of herself to try for a full-on embrace—so that he could look into her eyes as she promised to return by sunrise. She held him fast until he nodded and vowed to listen to Dar Leah in her absence. This was important, she told him. This was necessary.

*Good girl*, Drisker thought to himself. He was impressed by the compassion and intensity of her words, by the depth of truth that infused her promise and gave her brother the reassurance he was looking for.

They set out after that, Drisker leading the way up the slopes to where passage into the valley could be found. The skies were still cloudy and the light from moon and stars intermittent, but their path was clear enough for them to make the journey safely. It was slow going, though, the terrain rocky and uneven, preventing them from any attempt at hurrying. They had until an hour before dawn to reach the Hadeshorn and summon the shades of the dead, Drisker reminded himself, and there was more than enough time.

They walked in silence for a long distance while Drisker wrestled with whether or not to tell Tarsha whom they were going to meet. In the end, he decided not to. While she would know of Grianne Ohmsford and maybe something of her history, she had no personal knowledge of all the particulars, and likely did not know of Grianne's fate following the collapse and subsequent restoration of the Forbidding several centuries earlier. When it became apparent that he must tell her the truth, he would. But not until silence no longer remained an option.

"You did well with your brother," he told her finally as they neared the entrance to the pass. "You were persuasive but compassionate as well. He read your honesty in your voice."

She nodded, a small movement of the hood that covered her head. "I think I am closer to reaching him. And he seemed to want to believe me. He listened and did not argue. I think I have a chance of getting him back."

"He has a long way to go, Tarsha. Do not deceive yourself. But you are making a good start. And don't worry. The others will look out for him while you are gone."

A wind that had been absent until now blew across them with sudden force, ice-cold and stinging. They hunched down within their cloaks and picked up the pace to reach the shelter of the pass. Once there, they stumbled inside and paused to catch their breath. On the slopes behind them, loose snow was snatched away in windy swirls to form miniature tornadoes that soared skyward before breaking apart and scattering in bursts of white.

"The weather will be better where we're going," the Druid assured her.

He wondered anew why Grianne Ohmsford had felt it necessary to bring Tarsha to this meeting—why she had insisted that the girl's presence was so important. Something was at play here that he did not understand, and he worried that Tarsha was being placed at risk. Still, there was nothing for it but to continue on and hope for the best.

They set out anew, winding their way through the narrow pass, the shadow of the walls on either side blocking out all but the dimmest of moonlight when it chanced to surface from behind the clouds. Morning was still well off, so they held no expectations of help from sunlight. Hands stretched out to ward off unpleasant encounters with the rock corridor. Eyes shifting from the uneven ground on which they walked to the twists and turns in the darkened corridor ahead, they advanced cautiously. The deeper in they went, the stronger the sound of the wind, which seemed to be coming from all around. It grew into a howling, wailing cry that chilled them, even though both had some familiarity with it from their previous visit. The souls of the dead seemed to be calling them, and no summons of that sort was ever pleasant.

When they finally emerged, they found themselves in a place of windless silence, the valley a sprawl of glittering obsidian surrounding the greenish-tinged mirror of the Hadeshorn. Mist had crawled down from the higher elevations to layer large portions of the valley and the shores of the lake. There was no movement anywhere, no signs of life, and no indication that anything could even exist in this barren landscape. Drisker took them down a short way and then seated himself, beckoning to Tarsha to join him.

And there they would remain until the hour before dawn when they would go down to the Hadeshorn to summon the dead.

Time drifted away, and neither spoke. They sat together, staring off into the distance, thinking their separate thoughts. Their world was a silent tableau into which conversation would be an intrusion. But at least the bitter cold was substantially reduced, barely registering with either as they sat quietly, still wrapped in their cloaks but no longer shivering.

Drisker found himself thinking of his time in lost Paranor, fighting to discover what it would take to get free. The answer had been so simple and at the same time so daunting. He had given up his future—his life as he had wished to finish it out—in order to escape his captivity. The pain was less than it had been initially but still a nagging reminder of what he had lost.

*Enough,* he decided finally. *Enough of this bitter meditation.*

"Time to be off," he said to Tarsha. He rose quickly, adding, "A final warning. Do not speak when we are down there. Not a word. Understand?"

The girl nodded, and they began the slow walk down to the Hadeshorn's shores. They were careful how they placed their boots on the loose rock, gingerly searching out solid footing. Ahead, the mist that had crept down earlier in thin, ragged strips was growing more substantial, the strips joining to form larger blankets that threatened to swallow the entire valley. Drisker took note. It was almost as if it sought to bar his coming.

By the time they reached the shores of the Hadeshorn, the mist was a solid mass lying across the lake. It was roiling in a windless expanse as if stirred by an invisible hand. The lake lay placid and unmoving beneath it, but that would change quickly enough.

Leaving Tarsha to wait several yards behind him, Drisker began the summoning. Weaving his hands to form the symbols and uttering the words of magic that would enhance the path of the shades rising from the netherworld, he called them forth. The Hadeshorn announced their approach surging with heavy waves and wild spray—a churning cauldron of mass disruption that sounded deep booming coughs and belches. The blanket of mist hanging above the waters came alive with new fervor as the sounds increased and the lake boiled. Suddenly the whole of the Valley of Shale was a cacophony of sound and fury. Drisker shrank from it instinctively, forced to shield his eyes against the sting of the spray while standing firm against the heaving of the lake's angry waters.

Then the dead began to rise, their frail forms swimming skyward through the spray and the mist, seeking the freedom they so desperately desired and yet could never have. Drisker glanced back at Tarsha and found her down on one knee, her head lowered within her hood, clutching the folds of her cloak tightly about her slender form. She clearly felt besieged by what was happening, frightened of the power she was witnessing.

As well she should be. This maelstrom was unlike anything he had experienced here before, and he also felt a sudden lick of fear.

A deep hissing sounded, and a solitary figure emerged from the turmoil. A shade had separated itself from the others, wrapped in a black cloak and hood, gliding as if weightless upon the surface of the lake. Drisker peered at it through the brume and immediately realized that it was substantially bigger than Grianne Ohmsford.

He waited uncertainly for the shade to draw closer, but as soon as the face concealed within the shadows of the hood lifted into the pale light of moon and stars, he knew.

It was not Grianne Ohmsford who had come in response to his call.

It was Allanon.


Tarsha watched the dark shade's approach with trepidation. Drisker was a Druid and a big man physically, but the shade was bigger still. It crossed atop the surface of the lake before coming to a halt, and Tarsha felt grateful she had Drisker standing between them. When the shade pulled back its hood to reveal its face, Tarsha could see the immediate startle in the Druid's posture.

"Allanon," he whispered in shock.

Which was odd, since she had been assuming all along that it was Allanon to whom he had spoken earlier, and Allanon whom he had called back now. But she dismissed the matter as the shade began to speak in a deep, rough voice that seemed to promise retribution for countless wrongs.

–You might have been expecting someone else, but she is not coming. When I discovered she had broken through the Forbidding into the netherworld, I sent her back again and blocked her from further intrusions. She does not belong here. She has no right to use our pathways–

"And her warnings of what was needed to help the Four Lands? Was that all a lie?" Drisker demanded.

Again, Tarsha found herself surprised by the challenging way in which the Druid responded.

–Her warnings were real and her advice well considered. She has talents as a seer, ones not evident during her time in the Four Lands. Perhaps she developed them while imprisoned in the Forbidding–

Tarsha was further confused. *The Forbidding?*

"Then why are you here at all?" Drisker asked. "Have you further advice to offer? Have you insights to share before my company and I undertake our separate journeys?"

The shade considered, dark features tightening as if some ill thought had crossed his mind.

–What you have been told is all you need to know. You have chosen the right paths for you and your companions, and for the company that travels to Skaarsland. It is through these efforts that you will succeed or fail in your endeavors. No other avenues are open to you. But know this. Some avenues you seek to travel are already closed. Some others, old and new, will reveal themselves in ways you will not care to discover. Still, all those who dwell within the Four Lands face such vagaries and vicissitudes while they are alive. You are no different–

"Then tell me of these avenues. Show me what I might need to know, even if I cannot change it."

*I would never ask that,* Tarsha thought. *Not after what happened with Parlindru.*

But Drisker seemed to think it necessary. He did not change his stance or offer to retract it but simply stood waiting for the shade of Allanon to respond.

–You would do well not to ask such favors, Drisker Arc. To know the future is too painful. For it only shows you how little of your life is under your control–

"I would know anyway. It might give me some small measure of insight I will need later."

–Such insights will come too late to be of use. Nor do I have all that many. I think it best we leave the future to reveal itself as it chooses. Knowing it does not help. So to spare you, I will not answer–

Drisker hesitated then, as if considering. "Can you tell me why it was so important that I bring Tarsha Kaynin with me to this meeting?"

He gestured in her direction, and when Allanon's dark gaze fixed upon her, Tarsha wished she could crawl into the ground and pull the earth up over her head. Heavy weight she would never wish to carry pressed down on her as the shade spoke.

–It was not me who sought to view her; it was the one you were expecting. But since I stand now in her shoes, and I have the sight, as well, I can tell you. This girl will do what another seer once told her she is fated to do. She will make a decision that will change the world. She is here now so that I might judge this for myself–

*Three times you shall die . . .* Tarsha closed her eyes against the prophecy, against the rule of three and all that Parlindru had promised would come to pass. Against the future she would face. Against her certainty that there was nothing she could do to avoid it.

–You know what is needed, Drisker Arc. Do it. Do it while you and I bear witness to its consummation. Ordain her. Now–

Tarsha heard her companion give a deep sigh before walking to the edge of the Hadeshorn and leaning down to dip his fingers in the roiling waters. Waters she had heard were poisonous to all living human creatures. Then he returned to stand before her. "Kneel," he said.

She did so without objection, the power of his words enough to persuade her that she must. The Druid bent to her, and his dampened fingers touched her forehead. As they did so, he spoke in a whisper words she did not understand. She felt a chill run through her from the other's touch that left her shaking with cold.

When the fingers lifted away, the words were all spoken but her shaking persisted.

Allanon's gaze left her, and Tarsha felt its weight lift from her shoulders. Even so, she was left infused with a lingering sense of having brushed up against her own death.

The shade was speaking once more.

–Go now. Do what you have been given to do. Do what you know you must while the time remains–

He turned away and retreated across the lake to the wild reverie of the other shades before disappearing. The Hadeshorn erupted and spit with fresh fury, and the shades that remained were dragged back down into its depths until the waters had closed over them. The mists swirled and broke apart and were gone. Seconds later the winds quieted, and the deep silence of earlier returned. Drisker and Tarsha were left alone in the vacuum that remained, and above the eastern wall of the valley, the sunrise broke.

Drisker stood without moving for long moments before finally speaking. "We must return to the others. We must retrieve Tavo so the *Behemoth* can depart on her journey to Skaarsland and we can begin a journey of our own. Come."

"Wait!" she called out, stopping him as he was turning away. "What was all that about, dipping your fingers into the Hadeshorn and touching my forehead? Who was it you spoke to earlier? Did I hear the shade say something about being trapped in the Forbidding? What's going on?"

The Druid gave her a long, intense stare before again turning from her. "I'll tell you another time."

He started away, and Tarsha Kaynin had no choice but to follow.

# 18

LAKODAN WAS WORKING IN HIS SHOP, FASHIONING A new ax blade to replace his old, which was chipped and split so badly its edge had the look of a hacksaw blade. It was an older weapon, but one he had used in the wars against shore pirates along the Tiderace, and the Gnome raiders out of Strenk Reach, not five years earlier. It seemed he was always being called away to serve the Dwarf nation in one cause or other—missions he accepted willingly enough at first but which by now, as he entered his fifth decade, he found less palatable.

If it weren't for Battenhyle and their long friendship, he would probably have announced that he was done—a warrior still but a warrior retired. The Dwarves had younger men and women, some nearly as good at fighting, if not as experienced. Which was why he devoted time to teaching them what he knew. Young Tellick was the most promising, and Lakodan had trained him separately from the rest, recognizing his promise early and seeing in him the young man he had once been. Besides, he liked the boy, found him a match for his own wicked humor, and wanted him to become his greatest accomplishment as a teacher.

But fate and circumstance could change all that in an instant. Things were no longer as they once had been. The Dwarves were a beaten people these days, in thrall to the Federation machine. A *protectorate*—a word both offensive and ridiculous. They were all but slaves, forbidden from even the smallest deviation outside the terms drawn for them in their surrender twenty years earlier, when the armies out of Arishaig had crushed them and executed all their leaders. A lesser people would have degenerated into depression and hopelessness, but the Dwarves were proud and determined. A time would come when this would change, when they would again be a people with no restrictions.

Although, Lakodan admitted to himself in the privacy of his thoughts, he might not live to see it.

Because life was uncertain, a fighter of his stature learned early to take it one step at a time—each day, month, and year—without making the mistake of looking too far ahead. Life played tricks on you, and some of them were wicked. If this was not the case, then how did you explain why the only woman he had ever loved had left him for another man? And not just any other man, but a man so quiet and unassuming and bereft of any possibility of real accomplishment that he spent his days tending gardens and planting flowers? How did you live with the idea that a woman possessed of such wondrous beauty and warmth of personality had abandoned a warrior of his stature to live her life in relative seclusion, with no day-to-day changes that merited more than a moment's thought?

He realized he had stopped working, caught up in his memories, and he quickly returned to what he had been doing. Relinda had been special. No one else had come along to replace her, but he'd made peace some years back with the idea that he was not meant to have a wife and children. He would have to be content with who and what he was. He was famous, successful, and recognized everywhere within the Dwarf nation as a warrior without peer. His like, they said, would not soon come again.

Even so . . .

"Neighbor!" a familiar voice boomed out, and the burly figure of Battenhyle rounded the corner of his workshop, his bearded face a map of his own struggles. The big man was Crackenrood's titular chieftain, and a formidable warrior in his own right. He was also a good five years older than Lakodan and at least that many years wiser. Of all the heads of Dwarf villages in the Eastland—and that included Culhaven—there was no better man to be a leader of Dwarves, and no man more respected. That Battenhyle had been his friend since childhood was a happy coincidence. Both had been born and raised and made their homes in Crackenrood, and both had undertaken a lifelong effort to keep their village safe.

"Big Bat," Lakodan greeted him in turn, and the two Dwarves embraced warmly. "I see a storm cloud settled on your brow. A thunderhead, Old Bear. What news?"

The big man made a face. "Oh, nothing much. A visit from the usual dog scat that treks into our village every time we start to get too comfortable."

"So, the Federation?"

"A small pack of them. My scouts just reported that a transport has landed and moored on this side of the pass—under heavy guard, because you know what thieves we are—and its passengers are coming in on foot. Whelps, novices, and irritants, all of them."

"Numbers?"

"Maybe a dozen. It doesn't look like an armed confrontation. Something else, I think. Threats only, this time."

Lakodan shrugged. "Or maybe public recognition of your long and able service as village headman. The truth might have finally dawned on them. Anything's possible, they say." He paused. "So, you want an ax at your back when you speak to them?"

"I want a dozen. But mostly, I want the one I know I can trust."

"Come, now. They all love you. No one would fail Battenhyle, Vanquisher of the Bear of Bargoda. Who would dare?"

It was a standing joke. Once upon a time, Battenhyle had run up against a Koden in the mountains of Bargoda Bar. All alone and facing a two-ton animal with an uncertain disposition, he had done what any wise man would do: He had faced it down. Running was suicide; it would pursue, and it was much, much faster over short distances. Facing a Koden down confused it, or so the stories went. Battenhyle decided to go with the stories. He stood there without moving, dead in the path of the bear, with the monster staring right at him. It was down on all fours at first, but it quickly lost patience and rose on its hind legs to somewhere over fifteen feet tall, and roared with all the force it could muster.

Battenhyle had roared right back, the sound emerging as something between a roll of thunder and a shriek. The Koden, not knowing what to make of it, had decided that discretion was the better part of valor and turned aside. Battenhyle later admitted privately to Lakodan that, as soon as the bear was out of sight, he promptly threw up.

Whatever the case, it was one of those tales that caught fire and kept burning—a tale of courage and victory against a superior enemy, the kind of story men loved to tell over and over. Some doubted it, of course. Some doubted everything. Not so much Dwarves, but others who were unaware of the fact that Dwarves never lied. If they were found to have lied, they were seen to be without honor and cast out.

Battenhyle had heard his own story or references to it at least a thousand times too many, and he gave Lakodan a derogatory grunt. "Spare me, neighbor. Point is, I never know what these weasels will be wanting next, so I am left with no choice but to go out to meet them and find out. Going alone would be foolish. Going without my favorite ax would be beyond foolish."

Lakodan reached for his spare and shouldered it. "Number one is under repair, but I think number two will suffice for this adventure. Lead the way."

They departed Lakodan's workshop and ambled down from the heights and through the village, picking up a handful of others on the way. Word of the Federation visit had already spread, and some deemed a confrontation with men they didn't much care for a good way to pass the time. Their fighting days were limited of late, and many were anxious for a scrap of some sort. Having it with Southlanders was always preferable to mixing it up with anyone else. Especially given their long history of conflict—a conflict he and Battenhyle were all too familiar with.

Back when he and Battenhyle were much younger, they were hardworking and ambitious, skilled craftsmen in a community of lifelong friends. They were under the iron hand of the Federation even then, but the Southlanders seemed a distant, almost benevolent presence, their emissaries seldom even appearing in the village. Until an older, less tolerant Dwarf firebrand named Chisletkin had begun a campaign to throw off the Federation yoke. Men and women flocked to him, heeding his fiery rhetoric, fed up with being a forced protectorate with its taxes and conscripts and rules, and captivated by the thought of being free once more.

The matter might have faded away and been forgotten entirely if not for an organized attack by the rebels against a Federation command sent to find and punish the leaders of this infant rebellion. The Dwarves caught the Southlanders unprepared and killed them all. The result, which might have been anticipated if Chisletkin and his fellows had been thinking clearly, was the arrival shortly thereafter of a sizable army that crushed the rebellion with little effort. In the aftermath, they hauled the unfortunate Chisletkin to the nearest tree and hung him in front of his fellow survivors, then cut him into pieces and threw the remains into a pigpen.

Then they killed the rest of their prisoners, too.

Battenhyle had been part of this band for a time—a powerful young man able to stand against four or five opponents at once, much admired for his bravery and fighting skills. But on the day the rebels were slaughtered, he had been home so sick he had come close to dying himself. He escaped the fate of his fellow rebels, but that was not the end of it for either him or Lakodan. The Federation decided to make an example of Crackenrood, and all those other villagers they considered at least tacitly complicit. So they conscripted a hundred of Crackenrood's strongest young men—Battenhyle and Lakodan among them—and marched them under Federation command to the far eastern frontier, to root out and destroy a particularly troublesome band of Gnome raiders who had been preying on Southland shipping for the better part of a year. Over the course of the campaign—deemed a huge success by the Federation—more than half of those conscripted lost their lives. Lakodan and Batten-hyle, who had guarded each other assiduously, were among the lucky ones who made it home safe, but the experience had left scars.

"Odd they didn't send word they were coming," Lakodan observed as they passed out of the village and marched toward the Pass of Jade. Already they could see the Federation officials and soldiers approaching from downslope, wandering out of the trees like tiny animals in search of food.

"As if what the Federation does can ever be anything but odd." Battenhyle cocked an eyebrow. "I think they must all be born odd and never quite be able to escape their fate. Still, maybe they intend to surprise us."

"Oh, surely." Lakodan chuckled. "There's a tactic they are so adept at. That and treachery."

They eased up on their pace as they caught a glimpse of the young woman who walked in the midst of the Federation soldiers and officials. Lakodan took her to be somewhere south of twenty-five. This was a surprise. He could not remember the last time the Federation had sent anyone that young as part of a visiting delegation.

"Maybe they've run out of seasoned diplomats," Battenhyle muttered, thinking the same thing his friend was.

Lakodan frowned. "Perhaps this is meant to throw us off guard about what's coming."

"Uh-uh. Not throw us off. Soften us up."

"Sharpen your wits, Old Bear."

"Sharpen your own, neighbor."

As they stopped where they were—allowing the Federation party to come the rest of the way to them rather than the other way around—Lakodan noticed something else. The rangy, hawk-faced man at the young woman's side was well known to both Battenhyle and himself.

"Choten Benz," he murmured.

Battenhyle nodded but said nothing.

Lakodan made a quick count. The Federation party was thirteen strong. An unlucky number, but hopefully not for them.

The young woman started to step forward, but another man—an

older, hard-faced Federation officer bearing the insignia of a lieutenant commander—quickly moved in front of her. "I have seniority,
young lady," he announced. Looking as if he found the task altogether
too distasteful, he faced Battenhyle. "We are here to levy a conscription. The Federation requires a brigade of Dwarf conscripts from
your village to serve in the Federation army, starting immediately.
Call all your men and women over the age of sixteen and under the
age of forty together, to allow me to make my selection. Any refusal
to do as I have ordered will mean a . . . a . . ."

He trailed off, staring at the Dwarf. Battenhyle was shaking his big
shaggy head. It made a noticeable impact. His broad, expressive face
was covered in coarse black hair, and what wasn't was weathered by
sun and age and sat comfortably on a neck as thick as the speaker's
thigh, balanced atop a short but powerful body.

"Now, who are you, exactly?" Battenhyle asked companionably.

The lieutenant commander looked both irritated and confused.
"Lieutenant Commander Arturus Barta Fillian," he snapped.

"Well, then, Lieutenant Commander, my name is Battenhyle, and
this ugly fellow standing next to me is Lakodan. A single name tends
to be sufficient for Dwarves, so that's all you get." He grinned. "Now,
what is it you want?"

The lieutenant commander turned scarlet. "You heard me well
enough, so don't . . ."

"Excuse me, but your tone of voice is unnecessarily rude." Battenhyle suddenly looked dangerous. "I asked a reasonable question, and
it is up to you to give a reasonable answer."

The other man fumbled for a response. "You are required to . . ."

"No, that is a poor beginning. It sounds like a demand rather than
a request. Besides, we are not *required* to do anything." Battenhyle
took a step closer to the man. "As a courtesy, we will hear you out.
But then we must decide how we will respond to what you ask of us."

The lieutenant commander, clearly unfamiliar with how Dwarves
operated and feeling the butt of a joke he did not understand, lost it
completely. "You are a defeated people!" he screamed. "You have no
choice in what you do or do not do! You are nothing but—"

"Commander!" The voice carried such authority that it silenced him midsentence. The young woman stepped forward a second time. "Let's leave off, please. Other villages lie ahead, but this one is exempt. Have you forgotten?"

Fillian's jaw tightened. "I have no way of knowing if what you claim is—"

He did not finish this sentence, either. She cut him short by thrusting a document in his face. "Read this, then!" she snapped, "since your memory seems to be suffering. And do not presume to question me afterward. You know the extent of my authority, and you must appreciate the consequences of an unfavorable report should I be forced to give you one."

Lakodan was impressed. This was bold talk for a young woman to give a seasoned soldier. Still, young or not, she must carry some weight with the Federation hierarchy to be able to speak like this. He exchanged a quick glance with Battenhyle, who shrugged. None of their business, said the shrug.

The lieutenant commander finished reading the paper, then handed it back. "Very well. My men and I will return to the airship to wait for you. Meanwhile, you are on your own."

He wheeled away, beckoning to the others. "Follow me."

The rest of the party turned to follow—all but one. Fillian stared at him with annoyance. "You also, Benz."

"Actually," said the man both Lakodan and Battenhyle had identified earlier, "I am under orders to stay with Miss Belladrin and keep her safe. Those orders come directly from the Prime Minister and supersede your own, Lieutenant Commander."

Fillian hesitated only a moment before turning away. Not surprising, Lakodan noted to himself. Benz was not the sort of man you challenged without good reason. But he was also not a Federation man. Or hadn't been, until now. It made the Dwarf wonder.

The young woman stepped forward a second time, extending her hand. "Blessings on you, Elder Battenhyle," she said, offering him a traditional Dwarf greeting.

"And on you," the chieftain replied, engulfing her small hand in his own.

When he released it, she turned to Lakodan and extended her

hand to him, as well. No hesitation, no sign of fear—even alone and in the face of two huge, bearish Dwarves. This dark-haired young lady couldn't weigh more than a moor cat's newly born kitten, yet she was not the least bit afraid.

She turned back to Battenhyle. "My name is Belladrin Rish, and I have the honor to serve as personal assistant to Prime Minister Ketter Vause. I am here at his request, to speak to you of an urgent matter. Have I your permission to continue?"

Battenhyle nodded. "You do."

"Then first let me sort out the terms of my involvement with Lieutenant Commander Fillian's conscription. First of all, the conscription is real. He is charged with fulfilling it, and if he fails today he will be back at some point with enough Federation soldiers to complete it. A part of my purpose is to stop that from happening. While the Prime Minister normally does not interfere with the prerogatives of his army officers in carrying out their duties, he does sometimes make exceptions and allowances. This is one such time." She paused. "Are you familiar with the events taking place on the banks of the Mermidon River just west of Varfleet?"

Battenhyle exchanged a quick look with Lakodan. "Rumors, only. It is not Dwarf business."

"Please let me explain why you are wrong."

And she went on to do so in great detail—a thorough accounting of events over the past few weeks that included the arrival of the Skaar, their march south after decimating several Troll tribes who opposed them, their destruction of the Druid order and seizure of Paranor, and finally their further advance to the north banks of the Mermidon.

"They were opposed by a Federation force of more than five thousand soldiers, and they annihilated it in a single night," she finished.

Lakodan pursed his lips. "Well, that's impressive. How did they manage all this?"

"Apparently," she answered, "they can make themselves invisible when they choose—at least for short periods of time. It's difficult to fight what you cannot see, as those who opposed them were unfortunate enough to discover."

"Magic?" Battenhyle asked.

Belladrin shrugged. "No one seems to know for sure. What the Prime Minister does know is that the Skaar are a people intent on conquest. And at present, they have the Four Lands in sight."

Lakodan was certain there was more to this than what they were being told, but he held his tongue. In negotiations, you always kept something back to avoid looking desperate. Belladrin might be doing the same, or she might simply be telling them what she knew. Ketter Vause was a shrewd fox, and he would not hesitate to use others— even those he valued—to get what he wanted. That was how politicians held on to their power, wasn't it?

"Fascinating story," Battenhyle ventured. "What has any of it to do with us? We are not involved with these Skaar, and we have no wish to change that. Who would? Surely, Ketter Vause does not expect the Dwarves of Crackenrood to march forth to face these invaders on the Federation's behalf."

"As a matter of fact, he does not. But he does need your help. If you are willing to give it to him, I am authorized to spare Crackenrood from any further conscriptions for a period of ten years."

"Ten *years*?" Battenhyle repeated in disbelief.

"Ten years," she reaffirmed.

Lakodan was impressed. Ten years was a lifetime in terms of conscriptions.

"Can we sit down together somewhere while I explain?" Belladrin asked. "I'm very tired. We flew for two days straight to get here."

And Lakodan suddenly realized what it was that Ketter Vause and the Federation wanted from his village.

*So far, so good,* Belladrin was thinking as the three of them sat together in the Dwarf council lodge drinking cold ale and eating cheese and bread. She was both thirsty and hungry from the trip; there had been little time to do anything during the flight other than to prepare herself for what was needed once she arrived. The Prime Minister had introduced her to Choten Benz, and she found him scary and at the same time reassuring. He had been quick to tell her that whatever she needed he would do, and there was a look about him that suggested he was quite capable of following through.

Nor had she been overly worried about Lieutenant Commander Fillian, whom she recognized as a man who firmly believed men should always be in charge. Mistaking her for an inexperienced girl rather than a capable young woman was his first mistake. Trying to assert his dominance when they arrived was his second and last.

"You were about to explain why the Prime Minister is being so generous," Battenhyle prodded gently, his deep voice reverberating through the empty lodge.

She gave him her attention instantly. "I was. Recently, Cor d'Amphere, the king of the Skaar, met with Prime Minister Vause and presented a series of demands that he claimed would avoid any further battles. However genuine that offer might have been, the Prime Minister saw it as a deliberate sign that any refusal by the Federation would be met with force."

"That would not have sat well with him, I imagine," Lakodan ventured.

"He agreed to negotiate."

The Dwarf was taken aback. "But he didn't want that, did he?"

"No. What he wants is to defeat the Skaar and send them back to wherever they came from. Eurodia, I am told. Which brings me to why I am here."

"You want the Reveals," Lakodan said.

For a moment, she hesitated, clearly caught off guard. "Yes. The Prime Minister wants the Reveals. But he knows that he needs the Dwarves of Crackenrood to provide whatever fuels them and to operate them successfully."

"He can develop the mixture and train the men on his own," Battenhyle pointed out.

"Over time, yes. But he doesn't have that kind of time. He has perhaps thirty days. So he makes you the offer as a way to settle matters quickly."

Lakodan shook his head. "How does he even know the Reveals will work? They've never been fully tested. What if the Skaar are immune?"

The young woman shrugged. "He knows the risks. He intends to test them first, to be sure. Even if they don't work, he will honor the bargain he is making with you. Ten years, no conscriptions."

Both Dwarves were quiet for a long time, glancing at each other in silent contemplation. They had known each other all their lives; words weren't necessary in certain situations. Lakodan held up five fingers. Battenhyle nodded.

"Fifty," he said to Belladrin.

"What?"

"Fifty years, not ten, if we agree to help you."

"I would have to ask him . . ."

Battenhyle held up his hand to stop her. "No you won't."

"You are a very bright, capable woman," Lakodan explained. "Ketter Vause is a careful man. He would not have sent you to bargain on his behalf without full authority to act for him. You said yourself there is no time for delay. So he has already given you leeway to agree to what we ask, providing it is not entirely unreasonable. Fifty years is more than reasonable, given what it will save in Federation lives and prestige. Fifty years—with no conscription."

"After all, I want this prohibition to last at least for the remainder of my life," Battenhyle teased, then broke into laughter.

Belladrin grinned in spite of herself. "Which, in your case, might actually come to pass. Very well, we have an agreement."

"Ask the Prime Minister to write it up. No clever games, tell him. No tricky language. We're not stupid, but we do have short tempers. In the interests of saving time, we will bring the Reveals to you, but make sure that—when we arrive—you have the contract ready and waiting. If it is not as we agreed, we will depart again—taking the Reveals with us."

He rose to his feet, Lakodan with him. The meeting was over. Belladrin exhaled sharply. Things couldn't have gone better, discounting the number of years of non-conscription she had been forced to give up. But they had asked for nothing else, and she had been empowered to give them almost anything. How the Prime Minister knew of the Reveals was a mystery to her, but he was adamant he must have use of both them and the Dwarves who were trained to operate them.

She hadn't believed it was real at first—hadn't believed there was a machine that could discover hidden things so long as they were of material substance. It was a Dwarf invention, he had told her, initially used—ridiculously, perhaps—for painting walls.

But why couldn't it be used to uncover soldiers who could make themselves disappear as well? Why couldn't it be used to detect Skaar, who could vanish through either genetic manipulation or magic?

Ketter Vause was betting everything that it could.

And Ketter Vause, she knew, seldom made a bad bet.

# 19

Two days following Drisker's return from the Valley of Shale, and his departure with his young charges on their own journey, the *Behemoth* arrived at the eastern edge of the Four Lands. Ahead, the dark, choppy waters of the Tiderace appeared as a ragged sprawl that stretched to the horizon and beyond. The air smelled of the ocean—of fish and crustaceans, kelp and seagrasses. There was in the smell and sights and feel of the Tiderace an irresistible timelessness and promise that whispered of experiences and adventures. It was a siren song. In the manner of the creatures rumored since the dawn of time to lure men to their doom, it called to you. If you were disposed to heed such calls, if the sea was the answer to how you should spend your life, you responded. You put aside everything else—land, home, family, friends, and community—and you went to her. And you were welcomed into a cold unforgiving embrace that promised nothing more than a chance to experience a deeper closeness to the proximity of death.

To this, the *Behemoth* had come, to the first real test of what she could manage, of how much she could withstand. It would take two weeks to cross the Tiderace—a journey of wild expectations tempered by harsh truths—and she would have to weather whatever fate nature would throw her way. Once beyond the shores of the Four Lands, there would be no turning back. There would be no help save that which the men and women aboard her could provide. Landing on the ocean's surface would be possible but very dangerous. And if it was required, their vessel was all the comfort they would find.

All this crossed Darcon Leah's mind as he stood looking out from the bow of the *Behemoth,* well forward from the rest of those he traveled with, alone with his thoughts. Fears and doubts rose in waves, and he found a need to tamp them down quickly and firmly—to reassure himself that he and his companions were equal to the demands of the challenges ahead. To promise himself that they would overcome whatever obstacles they would encounter and succeed in what they had been sent to do.

The highlander shook his head at the prospect.

He could not help but wonder if Tindall's machine was up to it— or even if it could possibly do what the old man believed. It was such a mad, hopeless claim, and Dar was not one to believe in pipe dreams. To change the weather—to alter its intended course by taking forcibly from nature's hands the management of a quixotic and frequently unreadable aspect of life's inevitability—was more than troubling. In the abstract, it seemed a violation. In reality, it seemed to foretell dismal consequences.

If men were not meant to tamper with the mechanics of nature's workings, as so many beliefs and legends claimed, what sort of doom were they courting by attempting to do so here?

"You seem lost in thought, highlander," said a voice at his side.

He glanced over quickly, startled to discover that Rocan Arneas had come up beside him; in his reverie, he had not heard the man approach. Not so strange given the rush of the winds this near to the coast and the creaking and thumping of the *Behemoth*'s component pieces as it was buffeted.

But still . . .

"Just wondering what lies ahead," he replied.

"Time and tide and what they choose to offer. The foresight to see any of it before it happens is not given to mere men and women. It is a daunting prospect, but there's excitement to it, as well. A new continent, new lands and new peoples. New discoveries of all sorts . . ."

The Rover let his voice trail off and then laughed. "But this is a

Rover's life and has been for centuries untold. Travel the world, make her your home. It's like exploring a vast house with many rooms—so many rooms you know you will not see all of them in a single lifetime. But there is the challenge, isn't it? There is the promise of a life worth living."

Dar was not so sure, but he guessed it was in the blood of Rovers who, for the most part, rarely settled, even though some had taken root. As had those in Aperex who built vessels like the *Behemoth* and found in the results of that effort the life they were looking for. But the larger number of Rovers still preferred to travel, to move about the world and never stop anywhere for too long.

"Two weeks, then?" Dar asked. "The time remaining in our journey?"

Rocan shrugged. "As best I can make out from what little I already know, and from what the Skaar princess tells me of her journey here." He paused. "A fine young woman, that one. If I were ten years younger and still inclined to risk everything for love, such a dangerous beauty could tempt me. Wild and a bit headstrong, determined to be who she wants and never anything less. A fine bedmate for anyone. A fine wife and mother, too, one day."

"A *bit* headstrong?" Dar shook his head. "You have no idea."

Rocan laughed again. "Then you must enlighten me, highlander. I love a good story, and she looks to be one."

"One night, when I'm drunk and foolish enough, maybe."

"Oh, that will come, I think. And sooner rather than later."

They were silent for a moment. "So you believe this machine the old man has constructed can do what he claims?" Dar ventured finally. "Change the weather? Reorder nature? Because despite Drisker's belief in what the shades of the dead claim, I am having serious doubts."

"Well, you would be a fool not to, highlander." The other man shifted about to face him.

*Highlander,* he called him. Not Blade or any such ominous or tradition-laden title that would reference the Druids. Here, on this vessel, he was an equal and a fellow traveler. Well, fair enough. The Druids were history and best left that way.

"I have doubts, as well," Rocan continued. "But I have hopes, too. Expectations of what might be. Dreams, if you wish. And I have seen Annabelle at work. I have seen what she can do, and it is beyond anything I had ever thought possible. She shoulders her way carrying bags of possibilities and reveals them as truths. I have given myself over to embracing those truths. I would not have expended my time and credits otherwise. I would not be here, standing beside you."

"But even if it works, even if it *can* alter the weather—this everlasting winter freeze—how long can we expect any change she makes to last? How far-reaching will it turn out to be? Will it in any way change the course of the struggle we left behind, or the thinking of these Skaar? If Ajin d'Amphere is typical, then I am doubtful of the latter. And that's at the crux of what Drisker Arc is hoping to achieve. He wants the invasion reversed, and how many times in the course of your experience has that happened?"

Rocan shrugged. "What I believe is that sooner or later everything changes. Knowing that, I don't have any unreasonable expectations about what Annabelle can accomplish. What I hope is that whatever she manages to do will last long enough to make a difference."

Dar smiled. "Take what you're given and be thankful?"

"Something like that. In my world, it's pretty much the most you can expect." He glanced around. "I should get back to the pilot box. I worry those youngsters at the controls might have us going back the way we came. We'll talk more later, eh?"

Dar Leah nodded. "If we do, you'll probably convince me of your arguments about Annabelle. Why did the old man name her, anyway? She's just a machine."

Rocan started away, then turned back with a finger to his lips. "Sshhh. Don't tell him that. He thinks she's alive."

And he burst out laughing.

On the stern of the *Behemoth,* Shea Ohmsford was watching Tindall as he used a series of cloths to wipe down Annabelle's sea-dampened components, polishing her as one might a prized Sprint. The old man did this every day, mostly at the same time, and every day he took almost two hours doing it. He had started on their first day out of

Aperex, and Shea, lacking anything more interesting to occupy his time, had wandered over to join him. He had thought to stay only for a few minutes, but the intensity of Tindall's efforts and the mystery that surrounded Annabelle had captured his attention. Enough so that he had come back to watch again on the second day, and by then the two were talking.

At first, they had not spoken at all. Tindall had worked diligently on cleaning off the machine, barely glancing at the boy, while Shea had been content simply to watch. But by the second day, the old man had begun describing what various parts of Annabelle were intended to do—sometimes digressing into complicated explanations of how the science functioned, and how in the Old World she would not have been so much the oddity she was now. Science, he said, was once the primary mover and shaker of the world, and magic was thought to be impossible.

"In those days, centuries ago, the world was a different place, Shea." He used the boy's name casually, which was something of a surprise since Shea didn't think he even knew it. "It was through science that all the great inventions were brought to life. We had flying machines that could travel off this world entirely. We had machines that could transport you from one place to another in seconds. There were mechanical people. There were machines that could think and talk like you and I. It was a marvelous time, a wondrous time, and it should have lasted much, much longer, given how far we had progressed. But then it spun out of control, and wars, poisons, sickness, and irrevocable damage to our natural resources put an end to it."

"The Great Wars," Shea said.

Tindall nodded. "A cataclysmic destruction of everything we knew. Science was virtually obliterated—all the knowledge, the books, and the records first, then the scientists themselves. All gone. It was all we could manage as a species just to survive. Machines weathered, rusted, fell apart, and were gone. The knowledge of how to build them disappeared—in part, at least, because those who had survived wanted nothing to do with science anymore. It was throwing out the good along with the bad, but people were wary—and some were militant. So a machine like Annabelle became a fairy tale and an impossibility. Magic replaced science as a means for progress, and the world changed—as worlds will do when disaster befalls them."

"Yet you knew how to build machines?" the boy asked.

Tindall chuckled. "I knew how to *read* about how to build machines, and I was lucky enough to find books and records that had not been destroyed. So I began the process of inventing anew. It was so fascinating to re-create things once believed lost! And I have barely scratched the surface of what is possible. I am a poor beginner trying to take the place of the really great minds that preceded me. And Annabelle . . ." He paused to run a hand lovingly across a long stretch of her smooth metal-and-composite surface. "Annabelle is my greatest achievement."

So the conversation had begun, and now, on the beginning of the fourth day into their long journey, they were meeting again. Tindall was cleaning the dampness of the sea-soaked air off Annabelle, all the while speaking of earlier times and the sciences of the Old World, while Shea sat watching and listening and now and then asking his questions. A bond was growing between the old man and the boy, until both were so at ease with each other it seemed their new relationship had just been waiting to surface.

On this day, Tindall was working harder to clean Annabelle than before, because there had been rough weather during the night that had left the machine coated in salt. Although canvas wrappings protected her, nothing could keep that salt water and air from getting in. Left so coated, Annabelle would begin to rust and corrode. Parts of her machinery would become clogged or damaged, and if that happened, it was possible she would fail to function as intended.

Shea sauntered over from the aft decking where he had been watching Ajin drilling with a sword, and waited until the old man glanced over.

"Do you know what happened to Seelah?" the boy asked.

Tindall paused what he was doing. "Why do you ask?"

"Because I haven't seen her since we boarded the *Behemoth*. I wondered if maybe Rocan had left her behind."

"I don't think the choice would be his." Tindall gave Shea a look. "But would you be troubled if he had?"

"I might. Yes, in fact. She's saved us more than once. We might need saving again."

Tindall nodded. "Point taken. Well, you can stop worrying. She's aboard. She's just keeping out of sight, the way she usually does. She doesn't like airships anyway. She's a ground animal. Flying is something she could live without."

"So she's in hiding?"

"If you haven't seen her, then it seems likely, doesn't it? Now, that's enough questions, young man. I have things to do that don't involve giving out answers."

He turned back to Annabelle, wiping down her smooth metallic surfaces. "Can you tell me something about how she works?" Shea asked.

Tindall harrumphed. "Seelah or Annabelle?"

"Your machine, of course. Tell me how it functions. Can you?"

He had been working up to this for days, wanting to know the answer, but was afraid of rushing the question and making it seem as if he did not believe she could do what the old man claimed. So he had held back from asking, impatient to know but wary of choosing his time. But now that they were well under way into the unknown, his patience had failed entirely.

Tindall gave him a look—one that lingered, as if he was measuring Shea's purpose in asking. Then he shrugged. "Hard to explain the specifics. It's all in scientific terms with which you are not familiar, and trying to explain them clearly would take more time than I have left on this earth. But in simple terms, Annabelle takes elements and remakes them, then puts them into the air, which causes a reaction. Different configurations of those elements produce different results. The trick is in finding which elements create which reactions. So if you have a drought, you need one set of elements reconfigured to create rain. Once, these elements were called particles, and the particles were broken down into even smaller bits and called by different names. The machines that did all this were amazing creations, and they accomplished things I can only dream about. But Annabelle is a simpler form of such machines, a less complex creation."

"But she can make changes in the weather, like you say? You just have to let her know what those changes need to be?"

The old man nodded. "Theoretically, yes. But I've only tested her in one or two different ways. What we plan to do in Skaarsland is a new usage entirely, and I cannot know for certain if she will respond to the challenge. Not until we get there and put her to the test. But I think she will succeed. I have faith in her."

What he had went well beyond faith, the boy thought. It was more an obsession. Or addiction, maybe. Tindall was bound to Annabelle in a way that would have been disturbing if the boy had not become so close to him and found him so reasonable to talk to. Odd, that no one else had made the effort. Rocan alone seemed to share Tindall's passion, but the Rover lacked the scientific understanding of Annabelle that the old man had accrued. He lacked the experience of having worked for years to create her, learning about her anew virtually every day.

Shea was in the same boat, but he wasn't so much interested in the specifics of how Annabelle worked as he was in what it meant to be so committed to her. All those years spent in trying to realize a dream. All those years of inventing things—some great, some small, some successes, some failures—but all of it leading to the building of this one machine. What did that require? What sort of mindset did you need to make a single dream a reality? He had witnessed such single-mindedness in only one other type of individual—the men engaged in the politics of war, who sought to build empires and claim power. And they were all self-serving and ego-driven. Such men always claimed they were acting for the benefit of others, but at the end of the day they were mostly acting for themselves.

Tindall, he had decided early on, was of a different sort entirely.

"Would you teach me a little of the science that makes Annabelle work?" he asked impulsively. Then added hastily, "I wouldn't want to take up too much of your time. Just a little, maybe?"

The old man stopped his cleaning and looked over. A smile crossed his pinched lips. "I would be pleased to do that. Let's begin today, as soon as I am finished."

The smile lingered as he went back to work.

Farther aft, right up against the stern railing of the *Behemoth*, Ajin d'Amphere was going through a series of training exercises, both with and without weapons. She did this every day as a way to keep strong and to occupy her time usefully—a habit she had acquired early in her life and adhered to obsessively since. It derived from her understanding of the fact that being the king's daughter—back when she had decided that marrying herself to the Skaar army was a way to gain her father's approval—would still not result in anyone showing her any special consideration. If she wasn't as quick and strong and prepared as every other soldier, she would quickly lose what initial respect she was accorded. She had to be not just as accomplished as her compatriots but better. So more training, harder effort, deeper concentration, and extensive study became a part of her life.

As she grew, she surpassed the other soldiers quickly in proficiency and knowledge, but kept their respect and earned their friendship by always putting them before herself. That she was a princess ceased to matter. Whatever she did in those years, she always approached it as if she were a low-ranking soldier still trying to prove her worth.

So here, on the *Behemoth,* exiled from her fellow soldiers by her father, she knew better than to abandon her daily regimen out of self-pity or despair. Her current situation was only temporary. She would be back in favor quick enough.

But until then she had to remember one very crucial fact of her new life. She was in danger, and she would remain in danger every single day until she was removed from the predatory reach of the *pretender,* her scheming and hateful stepmother. No effort would the *pretender* spare to dispose of her once and for all. It was largely because of the false queen's efforts to undermine her in her father's eyes that she was being sent home in the first place. Her father might think his duplicitous wife would not dare to harm his daughter without his permission, but accidents were known to happen, and if no fault could be found, how could the *pretender* be blamed?

So she worked her way through stretches and lifts—isometrics passed down from generation to generation by her ancestors since the time of the Great Wars, and her own self-designed exercises that tested quickness and accuracy. Once that was done, she went on to weapons practice. Starting with throwing knives and stars, then on to swords, both long and short. Rocan Arneas, who had taken a fancy to her almost immediately, had supplied the weapons. She was used to men who coveted her, and she could read their intentions almost before they did. But the Rover was a good man, if a typical opportunist and manipulator in the way of so many men. She did not think he would attempt to breach her boundaries, which she had made clear to him right from the beginning, even if he hoped she might at some point bend a few for him. His affection for her was open and genuine, and she did not sense any hidden dark intentions that he might one day choose to visit on her.

In fact, he reminded her more than a little of Darcon Leah—though the attraction she felt for the highlander eclipsed the possibility of any attraction she could imagine having for another man.

At this point in time at least, she amended with a smile. You never wanted to close the door on matters of the heart.

So she was working hard with her long sword, feinting and lunging, blocking and parrying and working high and low with cuts and slashes, when she realized she was being watched.

When she turned to see who it was, she found the Blade staring at her.

"I would be more than a little uneasy if I was someone you were angry with," he said. "You aren't, are you? Angry with me?"

She smiled her reply. "Do I seem like someone who is angry with you?"

"I think I should take nothing for granted where you are concerned. You are . . . unpredictable."

She lowered her sword. "Not where you are concerned. I think I've bared myself completely to you—well, in all but the literal sense. Not that you've responded yet in the way I would like. But you will. My opinion of what's between us has not changed."

"Nor mine. Too bad we aren't of a single mind." He paused. "Since

I still hold your favor, would you care to spar a bit with me? Not with blades, of course, but with staffs. I can bring us a couple."

She nodded slowly. "A physical confrontation but only in jest? Nothing of magic from you? Just a straight-up test of agility and strength?"

"And no disappearing from you," he added quickly.

She gave a firm nod. "Agreed."

"Wait here."

He disappeared for a few minutes, leaving her to ponder yet again her unmistakable attraction to him. All that passion and wanting she had revealed to him, and still he failed to respond. He had been sweet and tender enough the night she had crawled into his bed, eager for his embrace. And embrace her he had, but only as a friend would and nothing more. She treasured her memories of that night, and at the same time felt bereft that it had not come to more.

He returned, a pair of six-foot lengths of oak in hand. Where he had found them, she couldn't imagine. They must belong to the Rovers, who she knew did some training of their own aboard ship.

"I promise to go easy on you," he said teasingly.

"And I on you," she replied. "Once I have you pinned to the deck and disarmed."

"Such a lady."

They began circling each other, each in a semi-crouch, staffs held at port arms, ready to strike.

"You seem awfully confident," the highlander said.

"With good reason," she answered.

A rush and a feint, and he almost broke through her defensive block. But she sidestepped quickly and went back into her crouch. Darcon turned slowly to follow her, watching and waiting, relaxed in his more upright stance. His movements were so smooth, she thought, so graceful.

*Don't think about him! Don't open yourself to him!*

She went at him immediately, a rush that became a drop-back feint. Blows were exchanged in a clash of wood against wood—quick strikes that rang out sharply but did nothing to disarm or damage either opponent.

She watched him back away, searching for an opening. He had taken her measure, and his attack would be for real this time. She knew he favored an upward swing from the right, his side of preference for an opening gambit—one that would land a blow to her forearm and loosen her grip on the staff. Then he would break past her defenses and have her.

Well, he would try anyway.

*Let him come.*

Come he did, a sideways spin that brought him right up against her so quickly she did not have time to back away. But it also exposed his right hand. Before he could strike her arm, she slammed her staff against his hand with numbing force. She heard him grunt, saw his fingers loosen, and struck at his staff in an uppercut that wrenched it away. It spun across the decking to drop with a clatter, and he stood disarmed before her.

He straightened, bowed. "Well done, Princess. You are a worthy opponent. I concede. Care to try again?"

She did, of course, and nodded at once. She was enjoying this interaction. It was not the one she imagined she would enjoy the most but patience. She gestured to his staff, and he moved over to pick it up. Again, they faced each other, weapons held ready.

A few of the Rovers had heard the sounds of their exercise and had come to watch. They said nothing as they gathered—no calls of encouragement, no taking of sides—but Ajin could see the excitement dancing in their eyes. They loved a good fight, even when it wasn't theirs and only pride was at stake. She saw them whisper, exchange a nudge or three, place a few bets, and settle eagerly in expectation.

Dar Leah and she resumed their dance, circling, feinting, setting and resetting themselves, watching for an opening. Neither was in any hurry this time; it was more of a waiting game than a rush to engage. Catching the other off guard was less likely now that they had been given a chance to measure and judge each other. Both made tentative attacks, testing the other's response, but neither attempted to carry through.

Soon, though, Ajin warned herself. Very soon now.

When he came at her with clear intention—a strike that would bring her down quickly and surely—she was ready for it. She met him head-on, blocking him with momentary strength and position and then sliding past him with agility and swiftness. She was congratulating herself as she whirled to face his riposte when she found him already on top of her, his staff inside her own, twisting. He had guessed what she would do and found a way to turn it against her. A sharp twist of his staff and her own was gone. A swipe down against her boots and she was on her back, the wind knocked out of her.

She lay where she was for a moment, catching her breath. Then she began to laugh. A hearty, approving, congratulatory sound that brought him up short. The Rovers who were watching looked at one another, perplexed by her reaction.

They were still whispering among themselves when the high-lander reached down to help her to her feet. As he lifted her up, she seized his arm and pulled him against her.

To his credit, he did not resist her. "What are you doing?" he whispered.

"Marking my territory. I want to make it clear to everyone that you and I are together."

"But we aren't!"

"Yes, we are." Her voice was a seductive whisper. "You just haven't been paying attention."

He stared at her in disbelief. He was still staring when she released her grip on his arm and shoved him away from her, bending at the waist to present him with a swift bow of concession. "One round apiece, Darcon Leah," she said in a voice everyone could hear. "Perfectly matched, you and I. Let's try again soon."

And to a scattering of hoots and hollers and shouts from those watching, she turned and walked away.

# 20

IMMEDIATELY FOLLOWING THE DEPARTURE OF THEIR companions aboard the *Behemoth,* Drisker had ushered Tarsha and Tavo Kaynin to the modified Sprint so they could get under way. The day was not conducive to flying, the cloud cover low and heavy and thick enough that their surroundings seemed to shape-shift, causing their sense of direction to become uncertain. But the Druid was determined to reach their appointed destination that day—and before nightfall, if possible.

That destination being, he informed the siblings when Tarsha asked, the Druid's Keep.

"Why would we go back there?" Tarsha asked at once. "I thought we were trying to find Clizia Porse."

"We are," the Druid assured her. "But in order to do that we are going to need some help. We don't have the Elfstones anymore to reveal where she is, so we have to track her another way. She won't be easy to locate from out here. If we return to Paranor, we can use the scrye bowl."

Neither Tarsha nor Tavo had any idea what that was, so he took a few minutes to explain it to them. Standing next to the Sprint, the mist shrouding everything around them and leaving them isolated from the rest of the world, they listened intently.

"The scrye bowl is a Druid magic, and there is only the one. It has the capability of detecting magic used anywhere in the Four Lands. Its waters replicate the disturbances such usages cause to the elements, pinpointing the locations and measuring the strengths of the magic employed. It will tell us enough that we can at least make an educated guess if it's Clizia who is using it, since there are no other Druids or powerful magic users left. I think she will not be able to avoid invoking magic sooner or later, if only to hide her movements. It might take us time and effort to monitor the scrye, but we have no other options to choose from unless we simply go hunting for her blindly. And that would be not only a waste of time but also dangerous. We might be looking for her, but she will be looking for us, as well. She knows I will be coming after her, and that I will probably have others with me. She would like nothing better than to trap us all, and if we are not well-enough prepared, she is likely to succeed."

"But won't it be dangerous going back into Paranor?" Tarsha pressed. "I thought you wanted nothing more to do with it."

"Well, I didn't say that exactly. I said it was too soon to go back inside right away after finally getting out. But that's in the past. It won't be pleasant—I was trapped there for too long to want to return this quickly, I admit—but I don't see that I have a choice. We need a starting point to begin our hunt."

Tavo, who had said nothing at all until now, cleared his throat. "I don't ever want to see that witch again, but I know I will probably have to. Couldn't we just wait on her? Won't she just come back at some point to finish what she started? She seemed pretty intent on finding a way to get rid of you when she tried using me for the job. Why don't we just let her come to us and do what we have to then?"

Drisker watched him closely as he argued. The young man spoke calmly and without any trace of anger. There was no hint that he still saw himself as Clizia's creature. This was good news.

"A reasonable approach under other circumstances," he responded, "but we lack the time to employ it. We need her found and incapacitated quickly if we are to prevent a war with the Skaar."

"How do you know this?" Tarsha asked. "You seem very certain."

Drisker exhaled sharply as he looked off into the mist. "I don't know why I bother trying to keep anything from you, Tarsha. You are entirely too quick to recognize it. Yes, I am certain of what I am telling you. The shade I spoke to made it clear that to save the Four Lands, two things needed to happen. The *Behemoth* and its passengers—and especially its cargo—must reach Skaarsland, and we must find Clizia. I received no further explanation as to what should happen afterward. It's maddening, I agree. But because I was instructed not to go with the others, when my good sense says I should, I have to assume that staying behind is extremely important."

"So you have no idea why Clizia is so important?" Tarsha pressed.

"Look at what she's done so far!" Tavo snapped, irritation in his voice. "Look what she did to the Druids! Look what she almost did to us! Isn't that reason enough to assume she is?"

"You're right," Tarsha agreed quickly. "She's too dangerous to be allowed to run around loose."

"She wants to restore the Druid order with herself as Ard Rhys," Drisker pointed out. "That's bad enough. But to accomplish this, she must have a plan that involves finding support from the Federation and the Elves. Or possibly from the Skaar. So she'll try to do that first. Come, we have to go."

They boarded the Sprint, strapped themselves in, and were off. Drisker took the controls, while the siblings seated themselves behind him, side by side. Not so very long ago, Drisker thought, glancing back, that wouldn't have been possible. But now whatever bad feelings Tavo had harbored toward his sister had been commuted.

With his eyes directed forward in order to find their way through the heavy mist, he was aware nevertheless of their voices behind him. They were talking in calm tones, their exchange devoid of any hint of unpleasantness.

He found himself smiling. It was something of a miracle. And maybe, too, a new beginning.

They flew through the rest of the day, stopping only once to set down and eat a hasty lunch before resuming their flight. They passed through the Kennon Pass at midafternoon and were setting down inside Paranor's walls on the airship landing pad by sunset.

The sunset's deep-purple and scarlet fires barely penetrated the clouds and mist to the west, breaking through in vivid streaks that appeared jagged and angry. There was a surreal feel in the air as they climbed out of the Sprint, a sense of being in another time and place, another world. Elevated as they were by the promontory on which Paranor rested, and by the Keep's towering buildings themselves, they felt as if they stood inside the clouds. The mist was so heavy that, from where they stood two stories up, they could only make out glimpses of the grounds below. Everything was hushed by the swirl of white brume, and in the dimming light it felt to Drisker as if he might have somehow been returned to the limbo world from which he had just escaped.

This unpleasant feeling persisted, and he found he had to fight hard to convince himself his worst fears had not somehow been realized and that Clizia Porse had not found a way to send all three of them out of the Four Lands forever. The silence about them was absolute, suggesting a complete lack of life—which was not at odds with what he presumed to be the reality of the situation. No Druids remained but himself; all save Clizia had been killed in the Skaar attack weeks earlier. How many days ago had that been? He could not recall. He had lost track of time since his return, a carryover from his imprisonment when each day blended into each night, and the passing of time lacked any frame of reference.

Anxious to put this memory out of his mind, he beckoned the other two to join him, and they entered the Keep. Once inside, they descended to ground level and walked out from the main building into the courtyard facing the west gates. It wasn't the way to the cold room and the scrye waters, but he had something else to attend to first. He had caught a glimpse of something troubling as they landed, and he wanted to make sure he wasn't mistaken about it.

He wasn't.

They encountered the first body not a dozen yards from the gates—or rather, what was left of the body. More than half of it had been turned to ashes, and what remained was savaged. He heard Tarsha gasp and told both siblings to remain where they were. Advancing, he bent for a closer look, and then walked on to find more dead, some of them hanging off the battlements, some sprawled on the ground. Skaar soldiers, he knew, since he was able to identify bits of clothing and pieces of weapons.

And he knew at once that his assumption about what Clizia might do once he was gone had not been wrong.

He walked back to join his charges. "The dead are Skaar. Clizia did exactly what I was afraid she might do. She tried to reenter Paranor. She managed to recruit a complement of men and women from the Skaar army to come with her to reclaim it. Because she was a Druid, she assumed she would be welcomed back and those who accompanied her would be allowed to enter as her guests, but she assumed wrong. During my transformation from outcast to Ard Rhys, I made sure that she would be recognized as the Keep's betrayer and would no longer be seen as a Druid. The Guardian knew this, as well."

"So it killed them?" Tarsha asked. "It reemerged at their intrusion and killed them all?"

"All but Clizia. There is no evidence that she was among the dead, and I would have been able to tell if she was."

Tavo looked from one to the other. "Who is this Guardian you are talking about?"

It took a bit of doing for Drisker to explain, but he patiently did so, stopping to elucidate when Tavo looked confused, embellishing when it seemed necessary. He needed Tarsha's brother to feel he was a part of their effort. If he failed to feel that he was an equal, there was a real danger that the old Tavo might emerge, threatening all the progress he had made and undermining everything Tarsha was trying to do to keep him stable. So far, they had made remarkable progress. But it was dangerous to assume the struggle was over.

"Come back inside," he finished. "We should be reading the scrye waters rather than standing around contemplating Clizia's foolishness."

He took them back to the main building and up several flights of stairs to the hallway that led to the cold room. When they were inside the room with the door closed to preserve the requisite temperature, he took several long minutes to study the surface of the waters, using

gestures and whispered words to conjure responses. Tarsha stood behind him, watching closely, while Tavo wandered off to examine the
drawings and books shelved to one side.

When Drisker finally stepped away from the scrye bowl, he shook
his head. "Nothing. At least, nothing in the past few days. The last
readings are of the Guardian's response to Clizia's attempts to reclaim
the Keep, and the emergence of the shades of the dead in response
to my summons at the Hadeshorn. We will need to be patient a little
while longer."

"How much longer?" Tavo asked.

"It's impossible to know. One of us needs to keep watch on the waters in case something happens—starting now. Tavo, will you agree
to stand guard first while Tarsha rests and I do a quick search of the
Keep to make sure everything is still in order?"

Tavo nodded eagerly, as Drisker had thought he might. Even
though a constant vigil was not needed, it was another way of giving
him responsibility and showing him that he was an accepted member
of their little company. "Just wait until the waters are disturbed and
remember where the disturbance occurred. You will see that a map of
the Four Lands has been inked on the bottom of the bowl to give you
a reference point. I will be back within a couple of hours and your
sister will be sleeping right next door in the watch room."

"I want to go with you," Tarsha said at once. "I'm not sleepy, and I
want to see the Keep."

Drisker hesitated and glanced momentarily at Tavo. "All right," he
agreed after a moment. "You can come."

"Just don't leave me here alone for too long," her brother mum-
bled, mostly to himself.

The girl went to him and folded him in her arms. "Never again,
Tavo. Never again. My word of honor."

He nodded into her shoulder but said nothing.

Tarsha trailed after Drisker as he prowled the hallways and rooms of
the Druid's Keep, from the floor where the cold room was located to
the cellars that lay deep beneath the building. They moved quickly,

Drisker seldom slowing to do more than glance around. When she asked him how he could know if everything was as it should be, he told her he was only checking for recent intrusions. He found little evidence save on the main floor and in the cellars by the escape tunnel. He was assuming these were all places Clizia had passed through after gaining entrance into Paranor, and that she had not had time to get much of anywhere else before the Guardian emerged.

They were walking in silence as they retraced their steps to return to the cold room when Tarsha said, "That was Allanon you spoke to at the Hadeshorn, wasn't it?"

Drisker nodded. "His shade."

She grimaced. "He was terrifying."

"He was so in life, as well. Everyone feared him. Even those he was trying to help. Even the first Shea Ohmsford, whom he helped guide on the boy's search for the Sword of Shannara."

"What did he tell you about me?"

"Nothing much."

"But something. Tell me."

Drisker stopped and turned to face her. "What makes you think it was anything worth repeating?"

She did not back down; she wanted an answer. "You asked me to come with you. You told me it was necessary because the shade had insisted on my presence."

"He did want you there, it's true. He wanted to take your measure—to assess you in the way the dead do. He wanted to see if you were up to what he believes lies ahead. He would not speak of it, but he knows you possess the magic of the wishsong. That would be reason enough for him to worry, but I think it was something more. I sensed he believed you had an important role yet to come."

"But why would it matter if he saw me at all, if he knows so much of what is hidden from us?"

"Maybe he didn't know this."

"And he could find the answer by just looking at me?"

Drisker turned away and started walking again. "Good question. I don't know the answer. As you know, he had his look, he made a

vague statement about your importance and the extent of the challenges that you might face, and that was it."

For a moment, she didn't say anything. She just kept walking beside him, head down, eyes staring at the floor.

"It troubles you," the Druid said quietly.

She nodded. "Wouldn't it trouble you?"

"Not so much. I know the dead talk of things we cannot know but
of which they have some knowledge. They like to tease us with their
insights, play games to make us guess at what they are, yet will never
divulge them."

Tarsha nodded absently. "What about the way you placed your
fingers in the Hadeshorn and then touched them to my forehead.
What happened there? Why did you do that?"

Her companion hesitated. "I think we should leave that for later."

She took hold of his arm and pulled him to a stop. "That was what
you told me while we were at the Hadeshorn. I've waited long enough.
I have a right to know. I think you should tell me now."

He shook his head. "Not yet. Be patient."

Tarsha masked a surge of anger as they climbed the stairs to the
next floor and continued on. "What do you think about Tavo?" she
asked, forcing herself to change the subject. "How well do you think
he is doing?"

Drisker smiled. "Well enough. We have to keep working with him,
letting him know he is not in danger from us, giving him fresh reasons to keep his demons at bay. He doesn't appear to hear the voices
anymore, which is very good. Nor does he seem to see you as his
enemy, either, which is even better."

"I think he sees me as his sister again. I've talked with him over
the past week about how much we share and how close we once were.
I think he wants that back. I haven't talked about our parents and
what happened with our uncle, or with any of the others he killed. I
don't really know how to start that conversation. It would probably be
better if it began with him rather than me."

The Druid shrugged. "I think you have to use your own good
judgment about that, Tarsha. I don't know that there is any right or

wrong time for it. But when you talk about such things, you have to feel as comfortable with it as you can. You have to make a solid connection with Tavo if the conversation is to accomplish anything. At some point, he has to come to terms with what he has done. He has to know that you forgive him, and that he has to forgive himself. There is no redemption for such terrible acts, but there can be understanding. He was not in his right mind then, and he had at least some provocation for everything he did. And at the end of the day, you can never go back—you can only go forward. You can make a better life for yourself only when you put the past behind you."

"As much as anyone can ever put it behind them when it has shaped all they are and do."

"Each situation is different. Tavo is on the extreme edge of sanity and will require a great deal of effort and time. Maybe he will never find peace. Not entirely. But maybe he can find a balance."

They walked on together in silence, and Tarsha found herself wondering what more she would do to make this happen.

In the cold room, Tavo was sitting on a bench, hunched forward as he paged through a book of maps of the Four Lands. There were so many places to go, so many he had never been. He had spent years locked away from everything—first in his parents' home, and then in his uncle's shed. The memories of the latter stirred angrily for a few seconds before he chased them off, put the book aside, and walked over to the scrye waters. He peered down into their depths, down into the darkness where the map of the Four Lands was lying in wait. He stared at it a moment. Had something moved just now?

No, he decided. The waters were placid, their surface a reflective shimmer of his face and shoulder as he leaned close. Nothing was happening. Just as nothing had happened since the Druid and his sister had departed the room.

He felt a fresh twinge of concern. Tarsha had said she was coming back, but she had said that before when he had been given to his uncle. By the time she had gotten around to coming, it was too late. The damage had been done. His body had been defiled and his mind twisted into knots. He knew she had good reasons for why she had failed him—after all, she had explained it to him endlessly. She was prevented from going to him by their parents, and then thought he didn't want to see her after the one time she had actually managed to find him. Hadn't he told her to go away? Of course he had, but it was the rage and shame and horror of his situation that had made him do it. Shouldn't she have recognized this? Shouldn't she have tried again after seeing how bad it was?

The questions chased themselves around and around in his mind like trapped ferrets, though there was nothing playful about them. About any of it. He closed his eyes and tried to think of everything good she had told him about what he meant to her—about how important he was to her, about their relationship as brother and sister. But things were shifting inside him once again, more rapidly now since they had decided to come to Paranor. He could almost hear the old witch whispering to him, cajoling in words he did not understand but knew to be warnings. He could see her face clearly in his mind. He could see her smiling.

He shoved away from the scrye bowl and went back to the bench, picking up the book of maps and paging through it once more. He took his time, letting his thoughts settle, envisioning some of the places on the map he thought he might like to visit. He tried to imagine what they might be like. Arishaig—that wondrous capital city of the Federation, that legendary site of so many famous battles. Sprawling and vast, filled with hundreds of thousands of people, all of them victims, like himself, of their own lives. What tales they could tell him! Wouldn't it be good if they could share them? Might not that help him to find peace?

*There is no peace for you, Tavo.*

Words, whispered by a familiar voice. He startled in fear.

*Why do you pretend that things are as they should be when you know they are not?*

Fluken.

"Go away. I don't need you anymore. You aren't even real."

His protestation was sharp, filled with a keen understanding of what it meant to listen to his old friend. His fake friend. His friend, who had abandoned him.

*Oh, I'm not real, am I? All those times we had together didn't happen? All that advice I gave to help you find your way through the lies of those who betrayed you didn't matter?*

Tavo buried his head in his hands, the book of maps falling to the floor. "Leave me alone!"

*You don't mean that. You listened to the Druid's advice. You succumbed to his magic wiles. Yet he does nothing for you.*

"You're the one who does nothing for me! What have you ever done? You wanted me to kill people. You wanted me to hurt them and destroy them. You are a monster!"

*Not so, little boy. I think we know who the real monster is. So why don't you admit it? Why don't you see yourself as you really are and stop all this pretending?*

"No, no, no!"

He was yelling the words as Tarsha and Drisker Arc walked through the doorway. They stopped instantly, staring at him. Fluken disappeared, his voice silenced. The room was deathly silent.

"It was Fluken," he blurted out, tears leaking from his eyes.

Tarsha rushed to him, knelt to embrace him, and held him close. "It's all right, Tavo. I'm here, just as I promised." She paused. "Who is Fluken?"

"No one. A voice, that's all. Trying to trick me."

"You don't need to listen to Fluken. Or any other voices. You don't need to be afraid anymore. I'm here, and I won't leave you."

He nodded into her shoulder. He believed her. He believed what she was telling him.

And yet, at the same time, he didn't.

# 21

CLIZIA PORSE WAITED THREE MORE DAYS TO ACT on the agreement she had made with Cor d'Amphere. It wasn't that she wasn't prepared to carry it out or didn't know how to implement it. She had known that immediately after departing Paranor, leaving behind her dead Skaar companions. It was a trade he was making, after all. She had cost him twenty soldiers and likely all chance of getting inside the Druid's Keep anytime soon, but what she was promising now was something of much greater value.

She was promising that his two greatest enemies—the Federation and the Elves—would abandon any efforts to attack him once she had done as she promised.

This was a bold guarantee to make, and one few others would even consider. But Clizia was made of tougher stuff than most, and once she set her mind to something, it took an awful lot for her to change it.

What she needed to be sure of was exactly how many people she would have to kill in order to be sure her promise was maintained. Because if she failed again, the possibility of any support from the Skaar nation was finished. Another failure would ensure that her dreams of rebuilding the Druid order with herself as Ard Rhys were over and done with, and any reason for her to think her life had any meaning was nothing more than a sham.

So she took the time she needed, requisitioned a Skaar fast flier called a Blister that was something on the order of a Sprint, and set out at sunrise of the third day for Arborlon. It was a calculated risk. Common sense would suggest she would be better off starting with the Federation and Ketter Vause, but that would likely prove a more difficult undertaking. If she neutralized the Elves first, it would free her from any threat they might offer and at the same time give Vause something to think about. That had a certain value. Frightened men tended to make mistakes. It was her belief that when it came time to visit him, he would make a big one. The only thing she had to determine was the form it would take.

She did not like leaving Drisker free to search for her, especially with those with whom he had now allied himself. Dar Leah was bad enough; he was smart and intuitive and his blade was a weapon of real power. And that Elven prince had the use of the Blue Elfstones that might help to track her down. But it was the two very dangerous siblings that troubled her most. The girl was the real concern. The wishsong provided her with a weapon against which little could prevail. And her brother, of course, was insane—and insanity and magic mixed together were an explosive concoction. If they found her, she would have a difficult time escaping them again. She would likely have a difficult time even surviving the encounter.

So she must not let them find her. They might think they would locate her in the Skaar camp, but they would never consider she might be going to Arborlon. Eventually, they would discover what she had planned, but by the time they did she would be finished with what she had come to do and on her way elsewhere.

Even then, they might not immediately comprehend her intentions. But if they did, it would be too late. By then, she would have gone on to complete her plans and set the stage for what chaos would follow. They would come hunting for her, but they would not find her in time.

And then there would be no stopping her.

By then, she would be the one doing the hunting.

She flew through the day and got as far as the eastern edge of the Streleheim before setting down to have dinner and get some sleep.

She might have tried flying straight through, but that would have taken too much out of her and she needed to be fresh on her arrival. She nested inside the Blister, hunkered down in blankets to ward off the chill, protected by alarms that would warn of any approach to her craft. She stared up at the stars for a time, embittered by her failures and losses, but buoyed by a certainty that, this time, she would turn things around. The Skaar could be manipulated. Their king was a vain, ambitious man—an easier mark than his smart, calculating daughter—and he could be made to serve her interests once she got him to believe that she was the answer to all of his problems. She wondered a bit at the rapidity of Ajin's fall. She had seemed so much in command of things, so favored by her father. But monarchs were capricious, and perhaps Ajin had been caught off guard.

Something Clizia would not let happen, she promised herself as she drifted off to sleep.

She resumed her journey at sunrise and arrived in Arborlon by midafternoon on the fourth day. She left her craft at the public airfield, and wrapped in her black cloak and cowl, an old woman of no consequence and little interest, she disappeared into the bowels of the Elven city.

Crais Aquina was working in his leather shop on aprons and body padding for the metalworkers down at the armor factory when the door opened and the old woman walked in. He felt a twinge of fear and a certainty: This was the time he had been dreading since he had entered into the arrangement with her twenty years earlier. He was no longer a young man, and was now a husband and father. He would gladly take back what he had agreed to those twenty years ago now if it were possible.

The old woman closed the door and locked it behind her, turning the sign that said OPEN to CLOSED. She gave him a sharp look. "Surprised?"

He nodded wordlessly. A tall, lean man slipping toward paunchy, he scratched his thinning head of hair. "Is something wrong?"

She shuffled over to stand before his workbench. Her hunched form was so much smaller than his own sturdy presence, but her aura of dark possibility overshadowed their physical disparity. He knew what she was capable of. Even if he had been layered in armor and armed with deadly weapons, he would have felt small and vulnerable in her presence.

Their arrangement of twenty years before had been straightforward. She wished to have a spy in the Elven camp, and he wished to have credits enough to live better than he could on a leatherworker's wages. He was never asked to do anything dangerous. He simply spied on the Elven hierarchy to acquire useful information, then passed it on to her. His value lay in his ability to get inside the walls of the palace and courts, and he was able to do this because he was the boot maker of choice for almost all the members of the royal family and the Elven High Council. His work was exceptional; he could measure, fit, and craft boots like no other cobbler. So his access to the palace and government buildings was pretty much unrestricted. He was, in his own words, as familiar as the furniture.

More to the point, no one thought anything about talking in front of him, and seldom gave consideration to what he might overhear. This was not a dictatorship, and the Elves were not a paranoid people. They lived their lives openly and without restrictions on speech, thought, or actions beyond what their personal moral codes required of them.

So it was easy enough then for Aquina to provide Clizia Porse with the things she asked of him. And for the most part, with no regrets.

But now he was no longer in need of the credits she gave him, no longer struggling with his life. He was successful and he was happy—if you discounted what had become for him an odious arrangement with a demon witch.

"I have something I wish of you," she said to him now. "Something I want you to do. It won't be difficult. You won't even have to leave your shop. And afterward, I will release you from any further obligation to me."

The leathermaker stared in disbelief. He had never expected this, not in his wildest dreams.

He gave her a low, sweeping bow of gratitude. "Thank you, my lady. I have been honored to serve you. You have always been most gracious to me. Tell me what it is I can do."

"I want you to draw me a map of the royal quarters."

"A map?" He was confused.

"A floor plan—a complete one—of all sections, floors, and rooms within the palace. And I want them labeled, so that I can know exactly the designated use for each space. Am I being clear enough?"

"Yes, of course," he said quickly. "If you could give me just a day or so, I think I can . . ."

"I can give you until tonight, at closing. That's three hours, and plenty of time to do as I have asked. You know the palace; you visit there frequently. Close the shop. Devote the remainder of your day to the task I have set you. When I return, I expect you to be finished." She paused. "You will be finished, Aquina, won't you?"

"Well, yes, of course, but I . . . I just have . . ." He caught himself before he could equivocate any further. "I will have it ready."

"Good," she said, and she turned away from him and went out the door.

Crais Aquina closed his shop and spent the remainder of his afternoon drawing up the floor plans she had asked for. He meticulously detailed each room and hallway, indicating doors and windows, careful not to overlook spaces that were dedicated to storage and service equipment, mindful of the sizes and shapes of each, trying his level best not to miss anything. All the while he replayed in his mind her declaration that, after today, she would ask nothing more of him and he would be free. This bright promise helped speed him through his task and focus on its completion, so that by the time she opened the shop door once again—just at closing time, as she had promised—he was ready.

She entered and locked the door behind her. "Finished?"

"All complete, just as you asked," he assured her.

He handed over the drawings, watching impatiently as she perused each. She took her time, studying them carefully. A couple of times she asked him questions, sometimes demanding a more complete explanation, confirming dimensions, and making sure all the windows and doors were accurately indicated.

Finally she nodded, rolled up the sheets into a cylinder, and slipped them into her robes.

"Well done, Crais Aquina," she said. "You have served me long and well, and for that I will always be grateful. But a bargain is a bargain. It is time for us to part ways."

She held out her hand for him to kiss. But as he bent forward to do so, she placed her fingers against the side of his face and scratched him. He felt a sudden pain ratchet through him and stumbled back in shock. He brought his own hand up to feel the damage, but it was negligible; there was barely any blood. Yet the pain blossomed quickly and became almost excruciating.

"Why did you . . . do that?" he gasped.

He was having trouble forming words, and he felt the entire side of his face go numb. He took a step forward, but his legs gave out and he fell to his knees.

Clizia Porse bent close. "Just relax and let it happen," she whispered. "You have barely a minute before it is over. I promised I would release you from your service, and I have done so. But I can't leave you alive to reveal what you know of our acquaintance."

Aquina was gasping, finding it increasingly hard to breathe. He tried to object, to question, to demand—but no words would come. She was already turning away from him, moving toward the door. When she reached it, she looked back one final time.

"It will seem that you died of a heart attack—which is not too far from the truth. But take heart. Your family will do quite well without you, thanks to our business arrangement. Goodbye, Aquina. You do have my thanks."

Then she was through the door and gone, and Crais Aquina was left lying on the floor of his shop, breathing his last.

Once she was outside and moving away, Clizia Porse gave no further thought to Aquina. For her, his death was simply a necessity—and a perfectly acceptable one. Men like Aquina were venal and corrupt by nature, or they wouldn't sell out their country and their people for credits and the expectation of favors. That he had thought she was really going to release him from her control demonstrated the depth of his ignorance.

She walked through the city toward the palace grounds, found a bench in a shady park about five hundred yards away in a place where she wouldn't be seen by anyone who didn't approach her directly, and settled down to wait. She had debated eating before deciding she would be better off completing the coming night's work on an empty stomach. But she needed it to be darker outside first, so there was nothing for it but to wait in a place where she was unlikely to be noticed.

She dozed for a time, waking at one point to find a small boy looking at her. Studying her, really, as if she were an interesting insect. When her eyes opened and she stared back, he turned and ran. *Foolish child,* she thought sleepily, *you never run from people. You never give them reason to think you are vulnerable. You stand up to them. You back them down.* She would never have harmed him; there was no reason to do so. She didn't waste her time on doing things that didn't serve a purpose.

She closed her eyes again and napped anew.

When next she woke it was full dark, the sun long disappeared below the horizon, the sky clear and filled with stars and the lights of the city shining in bright bursts all around her. She sat within a collection of shadows thrown across her by the sheltering trees. She rose only long enough to walk around and loosen up her ancient joints and withered muscles so they would be ready to do what was required of them, then returned to her seat.

She waited until after midnight before deciding the time was right.

From the park, she walked to the palace and made her way along its perimeter, wrapped in her robe and ignoring the Home Guards, who in turn ignored her. She took her time, moving to the entrance at the southern end of the compound. She paused in the darkness afforded by a heavy layer of shadows and studied the surrounding area. Two members of the Home Guard were visible, but she knew there would be others patrolling the grounds and perhaps even hidden in the shadows. She considered her options, measured her chances, and made a decision.

Using her magic, she caused her corporeal form to alter so that it blended further into the darkness and effectively disappeared. It was a talent she had perfected, although she could only maintain the illusion for short periods of time. But a short time was all she would need if things went according to plan.

She moved out of the shadows and made her way across the grounds toward the palace. She kept to a slow but steady pace so as not to disrupt the magic cloaking her, holding herself steady as she walked, shifting her gaze repeatedly to keep watch for patrolling Home Guards. But all she saw were the ones at the south entrance, none of whom even glanced her way. By the time she had reached the floor-to-ceiling glass doors that led to a reception waiting room, she was convinced she had done so undetected.

Holding the magic in place a moment longer, she unsealed the locks on the doors, eased them open, and stepped inside. No alarms sounded. None were thought necessary with the Home Guard on watch. She released the cloaking to reveal her presence—the strain of keeping it in place was beginning to wear on her—then closed and relocked the doors. She stood where she was for long minutes, listening for the sounds of an approach. There were none. She had escaped all notice.

She pulled the drawings Aquina had prepared for her from beneath her cloak and studied them carefully. She was at the right place to reach her destination, though still several rooms and who-knew-how-many guards away. It would become more difficult from here.

She smiled to herself. "Difficult" was a relative assessment. She was prepared; her plan was in place and she was confident she could carry it out.

Waiting just long enough to tuck the drawings away again, she opened the door to the hallway and peeked out. There was no sign of anyone near. She used her magic to disappear once more—although this time the strain on her was considerably more intense—and started down the hallway. She counted doors as she went, stopping when she reached a corner of the hall to have a quick look at what waited.

Three members of the Home Guard stood twenty yards and three doorways ahead—two on the right before a broad set of double doors and one opposite them at the wall. Everything was quiet, and no one else appeared to be about. Still invisible to those ahead, she rounded the corner and started toward them. The magic continued to protect her and they did not look her way. When she was within a few yards, she took out the Stiehl and held it ready.

She advanced on the pair of sentries to her right, and with two swift strokes of the Stiehl laid them out, dead before they fell. The other guard stood watching, stunned and confused by what had happened, and before he could call out or otherwise act, Clizia silenced him, as well.

Immediately she opened the door to the king's sleeping chambers and dragged the men through. No one appeared to interrupt her, and within moments she was inside the room with the dead men, and had shut out the hallway behind her.

Deep, slow breaths calmed her as she listened. Silence. She stood in an anteroom full of couches and chairs and a desk littered with papers. Shelves of books lined two of the walls, and maps of various sections of the Four Lands were pinned to a third. The last wall, the one that held the double doors to the bedroom, was decorated with pictures of the royal family. Clizia released the magic that hid her and became visible once more. A man about to die should see the face of his killer before he expired.

The staff slept in rooms to either side, so she knew she had to act quickly and silently to avoid waking them. But this whole business would be over long before anyone even suspected what was happening.

She walked to the closed doors opposite the entry and stood listening. She could hear the heavy breathing of the king inside. This was his sleeping chamber, and she knew there might be members of his staff who slept on mats beside him in order to be at his immediate call should the need for help arise. But if such unfortunates were present, they would provide Gerrendren Elessedil with company on his journey to the netherworld.

She eased the door open and peeked inside. The king lay on his back in the middle of his huge bed, the covers pulled up to his neck, his arms tucked inside. She scanned the floor quickly. There was no one else present. The king was sleeping alone.

She did not worry about the queen. The pair had not occupied the same bed for some time, according to information passed on to her by the late Aquina. Her appearances in this part of the palace were infrequent and usually confined to daylight hours. She kept her own quarters in another part of the building, and rumor had it that she had preferred it that way for many years now.

Clizia still held the Stiehl ready as she eased over to the king's bedside. His sleep was deep and untroubled, and he would die swiftly and peacefully enough. It was a better fate than he probably deserved, but what he deserved was irrelevant. She simply wanted him dead. And she wanted his death to bring disruption and uncertainty to the Elven monarchy, sidetracking any effort on the part of the Elves to interfere with the impending battle between the Skaar and the Federation.

Because this was how she had promised Cor d'Amphere she would help him solidify his foothold in the Four Lands. This is what she guaranteed him would keep the Elves from interfering in something that was essentially none of their business.

Well, it was half of what she had promised anyway. The other half would have to wait a few days more.

She took a deep breath and exhaled slowly to relax her aging muscles.

Then she cut off the king's head with a single stroke of the Stiehl.

# 22

IT WAS BY COINCIDENCE THAT DRISKER WAS IN THE cold room with both Tarsha and Tavo when the scrye waters began to boil with unexpected fury, sometime well after midnight of their fifth day at Paranor.

Tarsha had the watch, and Tavo had chosen to sit with her—strangely unwilling to leave her side since that first day, almost as if he was afraid of what might happen if he did. Tarsha, to her credit, encouraged his presence and spent the time talking with him about how much she had missed and worried over him, and how much better things were going to be from now on. Tavo had limited himself to whispers and small gestures in response, most of which the Druid could not understand, but which seemed to make the young man calmer and more comfortable. Drisker knew better than to interfere with these exchanges. No one was better suited to the job of keeping Tavo from his demons than his sister, and so far she seemed to be having some success.

When the waters erupted—an almost volcanic reaction to magic of considerable strength—all three were on their feet and standing over the bowl in seconds. The scrye basin's reaction to whatever magic had been employed was dramatic and sustained. And according to the map of the Four Lands inscribed on the inner surface of the bowl, it was occurring somewhere in the vicinity of Arborlon—which was a surprise.

"What is it?" Tarsha asked at once. "What sort of magic was used?"

He shook his head. "We can't know that. Not yet anyway. Whatever its nature, it was sizable. That close to Arborlon would suggest it was a form of Elven magic." He passed his hand over the place where the roiling of the waters still continued. "But it doesn't feel like that. It registers as something darker."

"It's her," Tavo said at once. "The old woman. The witch. I know it—I can feel it!"

*Clizia.* Drisker thought it possible. He didn't think there was any way Tavo could know this, but then there were things about the boy that were still very much a mystery. And his accusation made sense. Other than Drisker and his charges, Clizia Porse was the only person capable of wielding such power. But what was she doing in Arborlon? He felt a sudden dread. If this was indeed her doing, she had done something very bad indeed.

And at almost the same instant that he thought this, he remembered the Stiehl.

She still possessed it, after all. She had retrieved it after Tavo's failed attack on his sister, as Drisker was subduing Tarsha's brother. The weapon that could cut through anything, the blade capable of penetrating stone and killing whatever it was used against.

Yes, any use of the Stiehl would register such a violent reaction in the waters of the scrye bowl.

"Gather up your things," he ordered at once. "Tavo might be right. If this really is Clizia Porse, we need to act quickly. We're going to Arborlon to find out what's happened."

So they collected their meager possessions, boarded the modified Sprint, and departed the Keep. It would have helped, Drisker knew, if he could have used the scrye orb to connect to Clizia and attempt to verify where she was and what she was doing. But he believed she was too smart to allow the connection when it would be so clear what he was trying to do. All she was interested in doing now was destroying him.

They flew through that night and all the following day, the Druid unwilling to stop even to eat and sleep. Instead, he remained at the controls, taking his food and drink while flying, allowing the Kaynin siblings to grab what snatches of sleep they could find in their seats. It was considerably less comfortable than stopping, but Drisker felt certain that acting quickly was too important to allow concerns over comfort to delay them.

By then, he even felt certain he knew what had happened.

Exhaustion finally drove him to rest, so it wasn't until midday on the third day that they reached Arborlon and set down on the public airfield. Leaving Tarsha and Tavo to keep watch over their airship and cautioning them not to leave it for any reason, he set out into the city.

Clizia Porse, in the meanwhile, was on her way back to the Skaar encampment to pay a visit to Cor d'Amphere. She was not making the trip as fast as Drisker and his companions, finding herself unexpectedly drained of strength from her use of the Stiehl—a side effect she had not anticipated. She had not found the effort required to wield the blade's magic particularly demanding. But immediately after, on her way to the airfield and her vessel, she had been swamped by an immense sense of weakness, accompanied by dizziness and shivering—almost as if she had contracted an illness. Unwilling to risk a long flight while so debilitated, she had flown to a secure location on the far side of the Pass of Rhenn and, after landing, had instantly fallen asleep just after daybreak.

When she woke again, she was feeling better—her strength returned, the dizziness and shivering gone—but she had lost an entire day. Dawn was just breaking on the horizon, the birds beginning their morning chorus. She took a moment to think through what had happened and concluded that the power expended through use of the Stiehl demanded much more of the user than she would have expected. She had never used the blade before, and so had no firsthand experience with how she would react to it. But she knew now that any further use would take a great deal out of her, and she must be prepared to escape at once and find a safe place in which to recover. It was an annoyance she could have done without, but she did not see a way to avoid it.

Setting out once more, sufficiently rested to be sure she could complete her flight without suffering any sort of collapse, she continued on. But her energy was still low, and it was three mornings later before she reached the site on the north shore of the Mermidon where the Skaar remained encamped. By the time she landed, she was feeling sleepy again. As she climbed out of her craft, she was already aware of the need for further rest before continuing.

But first Cor d'Amphere needed to know what she had accomplished.

Drisker, she had to assume, would already be tracking her. She could not afford a lapse of concentration in her efforts to avoid him. He would be coming for her, and he would continue coming for her until she was dead. Or at least until she wished she was dead. It was not that she hadn't anticipated any of this or that she had failed to foresee the toll it would take on her. It had more to do with timing. She didn't want to confront him until she was ready, and she was not yet ready. She needed to set the time and arrange the conditions, and she could not afford to be caught off guard in the meantime.

Amid the Skaar, she could enjoy some measure of safety. It was highly unlikely the Druid would expect to find her here.

When she was escorted by sentries to the king's tent, he was in a meeting with his unit commanders and so did not notice her when she entered. But a whispered message drew his attention. Immediately, he glanced up, excused himself from the meeting, and beckoned her to a rear chamber of his quarters where they could speak in private.

As soon as they were alone, the canvas entry sealed, he said, "Did you do it?"

She nodded. "I did. Gerrendren Elessedil is dead."

"And this will prevent the Elves from acting against us? You're sure?"

He was anxious, even worried, and she did not miss this in his tone. "I am as certain as I can be. They have no way of knowing who killed their king, so they will look first to the obvious, and choose their mortal enemy, the Federation. Then there is the question of who will be the new king. There are four sons. The firstborn should ascend by rule of law, but he is weak and is not likely to be looked upon favorably. The second would be preferable, but then the first must abdicate if he is to lay claim. Time and effort will be required to settle the matter, and until it is resolved, the Elves will not want to be distracted by the war between the Skaar and the Federation."

"But what if you're wrong, old woman? Is there no possibility?"

She wanted to shake him—or at least permit herself to sneer openly at his lack of confidence. This king would have been better off if he had kept his daughter close at hand. She, at least, had a backbone.

"I am not wrong. But you are wrong to question me."

"I am the one risking everything, witch, not you. You've already shown you cannot be trusted to correctly evaluate the situations you create. I am giving you this final chance because you begged it of me, but you still have to prove yourself."

She was stung by his words and tempted to kill him on the spot. Who was he to question her? Who was this posturing king, this interloper from another land entirely, to challenge *her* given word?

She saw him flinch at the look she gave him, and it pleased her.

"If I complete both tasks I promised, will you then be satisfied?" she hissed. "Or should I simply leave you to deal with matters on your own? Decide now."

She had no idea if they were actually alone. There was every possibility that his guards stood right behind her, invisible and lethal in their intent, ready to strike her down. She did not sense anyone, but the possibility was there. And a signal from him would spell her doom. She had risked exposing herself like this because a face-to-face meeting was necessary if she was to keep his trust. But Cor d'Amphere was not an entirely rational ruler, and his need to be obeyed defined who and what he was. She found herself longing for the girl again—for Ajin—who was lethal as well, but always rational and carefully attuned to every discussion in which she was engaged.

"If you are still my benefactor, I will need you to confirm it. And I will need you to help me with a few small details."

She held herself in place, facing him unafraid. She was an old woman, just as he had so disparagingly called her. If this was to be her end, best that he get on with it.

He seemed to hesitate, perhaps deciding how much she meant to him, balancing the risk to which he was exposing himself by trusting her further. She had killed Gerrendren Elessedil, and that had proved she could do part of what she had promised.

But the look on his face seemed to indicate he was not entirely sure about her ability to carry out the second and more difficult part.

Finally, he nodded. "We should not quarrel at this point. I have given my promise, and I do not intend to take it back. You still have my trust, and you have only to do what you have said you would to keep it. I leave it to you to decide how it will be done and ask only that you do not delay. The Federation army masses on the south banks of the Mermidon, and eventually they will come for us. Tell me what you need in order to finish this."

She held his gaze for a long moment, her hard, ancient eyes reflecting a world of uncertainty and dark promise as she did so, and then she nodded back. "Some time to rest, so that I may recover from the magic used in killing the Elven king. Then I will complete what I have started."

She paused. "Give me this and a few other things, and I promise you that you will see the Prime Minister of the Federation dead within a week."

Later that same day, on the south side of the Mermidon, with Clizia abed on the north shore and deep in slumber in an effort to regain her strength, Lakodan and Battenhyle and a Dwarf contingent of fifteen from the village of Crackenrood arrived at the perimeter of the Federation camp and were hailed by sentries to discover their purpose.

"We are here at the request of Ketter Vause, summoned by his personal assistant, young Belladrin." The Dwarf Chieftain gave the Southlanders a mild look in response to their more threatening glares, almost as if he found them amusing. "So I suggest you carry word to them. Either that, or turn us around and send us on our way. It's been a long journey and a rough one. Make up your mind and let us get on with it."

The sentries glanced past the Dwarves to the strange pieces of equipment that sat loaded in a pair of large wagons, barely visible beneath the canvas coverings strapped atop them. Clearly, they had no idea what they were looking at and were uncertain about whether to allow this odd band to enter the camp.

"Belladrin Rish?" one of them asked finally.

"The very same," Battenhyle answered. "Can you fetch her for me? She can affirm what I've told you."

It was decided that this was the safest course of action, as Battenhyle had assumed it would be. When in doubt, soldiers always looked for a way to shove the decision making further up the chain of command. So it was this time, as well, and after a hurried conference the sentry set off for the interior of the Federation encampment, leaving the Dwarves and his fellow soldiers to sort things out as best they could.

The Dwarves, accustomed to allowing matters to proceed at their own pace and seldom inclined to insert themselves into situations where life and limb were not at risk, sat down where they were, clustered in small groups beside their wagons. Battenhyle and Lakodan sat alone, placing themselves directly in front of their own men and women to face the Federation sentries, who stood about in awkward silence, apparently not sure what else they should be doing.

"Tell me again," Lakodan said quietly to his friend, "how these dunderheads managed to reduce us to a conquered people?"

"Superior weapons and numbers," Battenhyle replied, stretching his thick legs to ease the muscles.

"Ah, yes. I remember now. At least I don't have to live with the knowledge that it had anything to do with superior intelligence."

"Oh, maybe here and there among their numbers there were one or two who momentarily exhibited such a gift. But overall?" He shook his head. "Not a chance."

"I should tell you I am finding it hard to believe we are doing this."

Battenhyle grunted. "You've told me so already, at least a dozen times. You know the answer. We do it for our village. For our friends and neighbors. For a promise of years of peace and quiet and no intrusions by Federation soldiers seeking to levy conscriptions against us."

Lakodan nodded. "A worthy cause, admittedly. But I still hesitate to believe these people will keep such a promise."

"We were promised it in writing."

"As if that was ever enough to hold Federation feet to the fire."

"Best we can do." Battenhyle grinned. "I'll provide them with a gentle reminder before we go too much further along this path."

"The young woman seemed honest enough. Belladrin."

"That she did. But we need to see how she reacts to Ketter Vause and he to her when the matter is out in the open. That may give us a better idea of how things really stand."

They were quiet then, sitting in the fading sunshine, taking pulls from aleskins to quench their thirst against the unusual heat of the day. Technically, it was winter, and it was only a day or so ago that snow was on the ground and the chill in the air was bitter. But now and then stray bits of summer drifted in before reluctantly giving way to the demands of the unfinished season. Such days were usually seen as a promise of better times ahead, and Lakodan was inclined to view them that way now. It was always better, after all, to look upon gifts with favor rather than suspicion.

After perhaps thirty minutes, the sentry returned with Belladrin and Choten Benz in tow. The former gave them a welcoming wave while still some distance away—a clear indication of how pleased she was at finding them here. Her companion, inscrutable as always, made no such overture, but simply kept pace with her.

The young woman came up to Battenhyle and offered the traditional Dwarf greeting. She then extended the same courtesy to Lakodan. "Your presence is much appreciated. The Prime Minister is anxious for you to demonstrate the Reveals and begin the process of removing these Skaar invaders from our lands."

"Yes, well." Battenhyle paused, scratching his bushy beard. "Before we begin the task we have agreed to, we first need that signed contract. I think it might be a good idea for us to meet with the Prime Minister. It would be wise if all of us were clearly agreed as to the terms of our bargain."

"He sent me to bring you to him," she said at once. "Commander

Benz will see your companions and your equipment to a campsite reserved especially for you."

*Commander* Benz? Lakodan took time enough to give the man a questioning look and received a small lifting of one eyebrow in reply.

"Come with me," Belladrin invited.

Leaving their fellow Dwarves and the carts with the Reveals behind, Lakodan and Battenhyle followed Belladrin Rish deep into the center of the Federation camp, glancing around with no small amazement at its size. There were easily a hundred thousand men and women gathered here, and in the distance they could see dozens of masts from warships moored farther back near the bluffs. Lakodan experienced a sense of claustrophobia as he took it all in, the feeling so strong he found himself wishing he could turn around and go back the way he had come. If anything went wrong at this meeting, he didn't much care for their chances of getting out in one piece.

After what seemed like a very long time, they reached a complex of connected tents that bore the pennant insignias of the Prime Minister. Guards warded every possible entrance. But Belladrin barely slowed, merely acknowledging the guards, who stepped aside for her and her companions with little more than a nod.

In moments they were inside an entry chamber where yet more guards waited. Belladrin ignored them as well and instead turned to a scribe working at a small table to one side, leaning down to speak to him. He nodded in reply and beckoned the Dwarves toward an interior set of flaps, which were intricately embroidered with dragons and castles and tightly drawn.

Again, Belladrin paid no attention but simply brushed on through, holding the flaps open and waiting for the Dwarves to follow her in.

Here, in a second antechamber, an officer of the guard was waiting to relieve them of all their weapons. Lakodan exchanged a glance with Battenhyle, who just shrugged. *What did you expect?* he was indicating. Lakodan sighed and nodded. They gave over everything in view, but both kept the daggers that were hidden in the lining of their leather jerkins. Smiling broadly, Belladrin led them through to the unexpected surprise that waited beyond.

Upon entering this new chamber, Lakodan felt immediately out of his element. The plush interior was draped with silks and tapestries, carpeted with soft rugs, and overhung with bright panels of webbed fabric cut into the tent's topmost reaches to allow broad swatches of light to stream through. Brightly colored couches and chairs occupied most of the open space before them, although an ancient wooden desk was present, as well, its polished surface piled high with maps and papers on which were written columns of figures. Ketter Vause sat reading through several such sheets but looked up upon their entry and rose at once to his feet.

"Blessings on you, Elders," he said in greeting—the same sign of respect that Belladrin had offered. He gave a small bow and extended his hands to each of them in turn.

"You honor us, Prime Minister," Battenhyle replied with a brief bow. "I feel as if I am in the palace of a king."

Ketter Vause gave him a wry smile, "Yes, it is all a bit much."

He gestured for his guests to sit on one of the couches, and then took a seat of his own on a chair situated across from them. "A true indulgence, and something of an embarrassment. But apparently protocol dictates that the Prime Minister must set himself apart from common soldiers and camp personnel to clearly demonstrate his stature as leader. I would do away with all of it, if I could." He gave Battenhyle a wink. "I imagine you suffer through something of the same sort in Dwarf camps of war?"

Lakodan had to work very hard to keep from laughing aloud. But Battenhyle, ever the diplomat, simply nodded his agreement.

"They would be greatly appreciative of such comforts, I believe," Belladrin interrupted smoothly. "But what they seek for now is simple confirmation. Would you be kind enough to personally reaffirm for them the terms of the agreement they are entering, as you understand them? They are anxious to get on with business."

Ketter Vause nodded. Quickly and efficiently, he outlined the terms exactly as they and Belladrin had agreed to them, covering all of the additional changes Battenhyle had insisted on.

"Here is the agreement in writing," he finished, passing a document over to Battenhyle to read. "You need not sign it. Your word is good enough for me. Everyone knows Dwarves do not lie. If they say they are going to do something, they do it. I am the same. I keep my word. But read it anyway. Just to be sure."

They sat together quietly then, all four seated across from one another, as Battenhyle read through the pages of material, and when he was finished he nodded his approval. "Still, signatures would remove the doubts of others who might quibble," he said to Vause with a smile.

"Indeed. Signatures it is, then."

All four signed. One copy was handed to the Dwarves, the other kept by Vause. "Now, then," said the Prime Minister. "A toast to our combined efforts to put an end to this invader who threatens to enslave us all. Belladrin, would you?"

She rose and retrieved glasses and a pitcher of ale from a nearby table, giving a glass to each and carefully pouring out measures of the thick amber liquid.

"I would have chosen something richer still, but I know that ale is the customary drink of the Dwarf people and would honor you by offering what you are accustomed to." He raised his glass. "To your presence in our camp and your services to come."

They drank the ale, the Dwarves wasting no time at all in slaking their thirst, then Vause rose. "Commander?" he called through the closed flaps of his quarters. A heavyset fellow with grizzled gray hair and hard blue eyes appeared at once. "Escort our guests to their new quarters, please. And treat them well."

As Lakodan followed Battenhyle and the Federation commander outside, he found himself wondering. All this felt a little too good to be true. A lifetime of experiencing the treachery and ruthless behavior of the Federation made it impossible for him to relax his guard.

Well, there it was, wasn't it? In spite of all the assurances and camaraderie, he still wasn't quite ready to trust Ketter Vause.

Drisker Arc did not return from his journey into Arborlon until almost midnight. By then, Tavo had fallen asleep inside their airship and Tarsha was pacing the ground surrounding it, increasingly worried about what had happened. She felt a surge of relief when the Druid appeared, his black-cloaked form materializing out of the darkness and silence in the old, familiar way. By then, the airfield was virtually empty save for the watchmen the field manager employed to protect the vessels against thieves and vandals. All three on duty had passed her at least twice by then, and she was thinking they would soon be on a first-name basis.

But petty gripes and small irritations disappeared the moment she saw the expression on Drisker's face, and she ran up to him at once. "What's happened?"

"Gerrendren Elessedil is dead, killed in his sleep by an assassin." The Druid lowered himself to the ground and sat cross-legged on the grass, waiting for her to join him. "The common opinion is that whoever killed him was from the Federation, but we know better, don't we?"

"Clizia Porse?"

He nodded. "She used the Stiehl. The cuts—so smooth and clean and deep that great force would have been necessary otherwise . . . Only one blade could achieve that. I spoke with the queen. She is recovering now, but was in shock when her husband was discovered two days ago. Mostly, she was concerned for the safety of Brecon, but I was able to assure her he was in no danger from the king's assassin."

"You told her it was Clizia?"

"I told her not to allow the High Council or her sons—especially whichever becomes the new king—to wrongly attach the blame to the Federation. Unless there is an alliance I don't know about, this seems more likely to have been instigated by the Skaar. After all, Ajin d'Amphere secured Clizia as a Skaar ally early on so that she could gain entry to Paranor. It seems reasonable to assume that her father continues to make use of Clizia—or she him—in this new arrangement."

Tarsha stared at him. "I don't understand. Why would she do this? What does she gain by killing the Elven king? He isn't allied with either the Skaar or the Federation, is he?"

"Not presently. But I think this has more to do with the future. She moves people around like chessmen, and she takes them off the board when they pose a threat. So if she seeks to ally still with the Skaar, it is best to remove those who might present a threat to them.

And Gerrendren Elessedil commanded the second most powerful army in the Four Lands and had use of a modicum of magic, too."

"So what do we do now?"

"We keep searching for Clizia until we find her. Then we try to persuade the Skaar and the Federation to settle their differences."

Tarsha almost laughed at the seeming impossibility of it all. "How do we do that? And how are we ever going to find her?"

"I was thinking about it on my way back from the city. I could try using the scrye orb to summon her, but I don't want to reveal that we are onto her just yet. But the logical conclusion to me is that she is trying to aid the Skaar in their efforts to establish a foothold in the Four Lands by giving any potential antagonists something else to occupy their time and effort. Realistically, she has only the Elves and the Federation to worry about. If she can draw their attention away from the Skaar, she has a better chance of making her own plans for a new Druid order to take root."

"Isn't that a bit of a stretch? How many things have to fall into place for that to happen?"

Drisker shook his head. "I agree, it seems an impossibility. But she doesn't have much else to work with. She needs the support of at least one power, and the Skaar offer her the best chance. Neither the Federation nor the Elves will have anything to do with her. Besides, she is slow and methodical, and she always takes the long view. For her, the passing of a few more decades would not be a problem. She has lived a long time and undoubtedly plans to live a lot longer. She will play this game until she gets what she wants or is stopped. She's already proved that."

Tarsha was mulling it over. "So she killed the Elven king to give the Elves something to do besides worry about the Skaar—and maybe to give them the impression that the killing was done on Federation orders." She paused and looked at him. "But that suggests that she might want to do the same thing with the Federation."

Drisker nodded slowly. "She might use the Stiehl next on Ketter Vause." He climbed to his feet. "And we have to hurry if we want to stop it from happening."

# 23

CLIZIA PORSE HAD INTENDED TO SLEEP ONLY through the remainder of the day and into the next morning before setting out again, but her need for rest and healing proved much more extensive. So when she woke at last, almost two days were gone, and she was deep into the second full day after her arrival at the camp of the Skaar and her meeting with Cor d'Amphere. At first, she didn't realize how much time had passed, and when she did she was worried for the first time about her health.

Using the Stiehl had required so much more of her than she would have expected. As old as she was, as many years as she had lived, she had always been quick to recover after engaging in magic. But not this time. The years were catching up with her, perhaps, and it could be that her ability to employ magic needed more consideration. She was not pleased to think of herself as growing old, but then she had known these days would come eventually. It was why the Druid sleep was so necessary for those who overextended themselves. Magic required a price, and a part of that price was always a loss of strength and a shortening of life.

So she accepted her lot with a mix of bitterness and resignation, but still acknowledged it as fact and moved along. She had much to do in the hours ahead, and her next undertaking would require the same loss of energy and need for rest afterward as the last. Once she had used the Stiehl on Ketter Vause, she would again have to find shelter and concealment while she recovered her strength, or Drisker Arc and his allies would find her and put an end to all her plans. She harbored no illusions about this. The Druid was hunting her, and he would not stop. He was likely already aware that she had killed Gerrendren Elessedil. And if he knew that, then she had to suppose he had concluded the rest and knew she would now go after the Federation Prime Minister.

And she had to expect that he would try to stop her.

Again, she found herself wishing that he had not escaped Paranor and the Guardian of the Keep but had died there as she'd intended he should. Things would be so much simpler if he had. But it was in the nature of life that even the best-laid plans should go awry, so she refused to waste time dwelling on it. Her only choice was to keep moving forward, to work that much harder at achieving the goals she had set for herself.

She dressed, ate a little of the food she was offered at the cook tent, and wandered through the Skaar camp to walk off the lingering effects of a sleep that had stiffened too many muscles. Even in daylight—for it was now midafternoon—she was a dark presence as she passed, wrapped in her hooded black cloak, head bent, ancient hands clasping the folds of her garments as if they provided a second skin. No one deigned to speak to her, and she made no effort to speak to anyone in turn. Hers was a solitary existence even in the most crowded and bustling of spaces, and that was the way she preferred it.

Sometimes, she missed the company of her fellow Druids, even though so many of them had been weak and foolish. At least they had shared some small part of her understanding of magic's vast possibilities and scope. So many distrusted magic and yearned to see it banished forever. So many believed it a black art and anathema to ordinary lives. Small minds and limited understanding fed such fears, but she was one of the fortunate ones upon whom the gift of magic had been bestowed. And she possessed the determination to see that gift honored and empowered by her personal vision for what constituted a better world.

She had no regrets; she had no wish to take back a single day of her long life. Why would you ever regret that which had raised you head and shoulders above your fellow human beings? Why would you ever wish to be less than what you were? To do so would be a denial of everything you had ever done and everything you were. It marked you as weak and foolish, and she would never think of herself that way.

After a long, meandering walk, she returned to her tent to pre-pare for the night ahead. She was, in fact, ready now. She wore the clothes she would need and carried the Stiehl hidden within them. She had arranged for her aircraft to be readied for her departure. She had studied maps provided by the Skaar king that detailed the layout of the Federation camp. She knew where she would find Ketter Vause and what it would require to get to him once she had arrived.

There was little else needed save for the sun to set and the night to provide her with the cover she required to reach her quarry unseen. That and her magic would be sufficient to put her close enough to the Federation Prime Minister to make an end of him. By this time to-morrow, she would be back in the Skaar camp and asleep once more, the deed done and her cherished dreams of the future one step closer.

By the time night finally arrived, she was beyond impatient to set out. She saw no point in announcing her departure to Cor d'Amphere or anyone else in the Skaar camp—these invaders meant less than nothing to her and were little more than pawns—so she took her leave as swiftly and silently as she could manage. The airfield manager did not question her as she moved to the small aircraft she had been given. If anything, he seemed grateful that she kept her distance. So much of her success depended on people's desire to avoid her. Some would have been broken by the knowledge that their presence was abhorrent, but Clizia Porse reveled in the power this granted her.

She powered up her airship and lifted off, wheeling west to fol-low the Mermidon for the better part of twenty miles before crossing over to the southern bank and continuing southeast. Her route would eventually place her in a position to come into the Federation camp from behind. Not that there wouldn't be as many sentries there as anywhere else, but those on the rear lines were less likely to be vigilant. Besides, a small craft with a single flier would barely catch their attention and seem to offer no real threat.

As time passed and her flight continued, she found herself musing on the bargain she had entered into with Cor d'Amphere. What he required was a serious distraction to draw the attention of both the Elves and the Southlanders. If both were too busy to give time and thought to engaging in a battle with an enemy that wasn't actually providing any immediate threat, then the chances for the Skaar to seize their desired territory unopposed were substantially improved.

In the case of the Elves, that goal was already achieved. It would be weeks before the Westlanders determined who was to blame for the death of their king—if that was even possible—and longer still before a new king could be agreed upon. Until then, their High Council was unlikely to find much support for mounting an attack on the invading Skaar.

That left the Federation—admittedly the more pressing problem—but Clizia had been clear that once Ketter Vause was gone, it would find itself in a position similar to that of the Elves. The effort to determine who was responsible for Vause's death would be difficult. Any choice for a new Prime Minister would take time and extensive negotiations on the part of the members of the Coalition Council. The army might stay encamped on the Mermidon while this was taking place, but no one would be willing to suggest attacking the Skaar when matters were so unsettled.

That would give Cor d'Amphere the time to persuade both potential adversaries to permit the Skaar to establish a foothold in the Four Lands. The most successful sorts of invasions, after all, were relatively peaceable ones. First the invader gained a foothold. Then it settled in as a neighbor, intending no harm. Then it began to work at destabilizing the established powers. And finally, it eliminated them, one by one.

It would happen that way here, too, she believed. Once Ketter Vause was dead, there was no reason why it shouldn't.

She flew farther south of the Federation camp and turned back again. When she was still a mile away from their perimeter lines and well out of sight of any sentries who might be keeping watch, she landed her airship in a patch of heavy forest.

She shut down the parse tubes and thrusters, locked the controls, and climbed out. A few moments of using her magic to conduct a careful search of her surroundings revealed there was no one else about. She was safely alone.

Her robes wrapped tightly about her scarecrow frame for warmth against the night chill, she began walking north.

Kol'Dre had been getting through the recent weeks with more than a little difficulty. Separated from Ajin, forced to stay behind when every fiber of his being screamed at him to go after her—and burdened with having to now serve as an adjutant to Cor d'Amphere, his king and Ajin's father but also a man for whom he had little regard—was almost too much to bear. He had gotten through it by staying busy as best he could, carrying out the orders he was given, and spending his free time in the company of common soldiers with whom he was more comfortable than the officers who were of equal rank.

None of it, however, gave him much satisfaction or relief.

He was worried for Ajin, and not without reason. Sending her home was an ill-conceived notion at best. The queen, Ajin's step-mother, bore her enough animosity that there was no doubt at all in the Penetrator's mind that she would try to have the princess killed. Ajin knew this, and she was smart and strong-minded, but the queen was equally determined. And that was what Ajin was facing until her father came home to set things right.

He kept hoping there was something he could do to help her, but thus far he had failed to come up with anything useful. Everything he could devise involved rushing to her aid and either setting up a line of defense or spiriting her away. He was trapped by his circumstances, and it was maddening.

In the midst of his agony, he received a report from the scouts on the forward lines that forced him to drop everything and hasten at once to speak with the king.

He found Cor d'Amphere reworking his lines of communication

with home, arranging for a regular run of ultra-fast aquaswifts and couriers, both human and avian. The birds were called falconlets, and they were a variety of falcon, only much smaller, better suited for long flights and better equipped to make them. Kol'Dre had not yet been returned to favor in the king's eyes, given the Penetrator's close personal relationship with Ajin and his clear involvement in whatever it was she had been doing here, so the initial look the king gave him on his approach was anything but welcoming.

"What is it?" he said, his words clipped, his tone of voice flat.

"Majesty." Kol gave him a respectful bow. "Our sentries have sighted unusual activity in the Federation camp. Something is clearly happening."

It was the middle of the night, so any activity taking place at this hour was troubling. But the king was dismissive. "Send one of our scouts to find out what it is." He hesitated. "Better yet, go yourself. Penetrating enemy territory is what you do best, isn't it?"

Kol'Dre could have argued the point but chose not to. If he were ever to be returned to favor, it would come from exceeding expectations.

So he went back to his tent and changed his clothes, choosing a plain black tunic and pants. Then he walked down to the airfield in the darkness, picking his way through sleeping men and scattered stacks of equipment and supplies to find the manager and request a flit. He was given his pick of the airships available and chose one he knew to be quieter when it was in flight—not so powerful as some but agile and tested. Also, more important, one that lacked a recognizable identity and could just as easily have been crafted by the Federation as by the Skaar. Thanking the man, he boarded his craft and soared out of the camp and straight down to the Mermidon. The night sky was clouded over sufficiently that there was no sign of moon or stars, and even ambient light was almost nonexistent. He crossed the river swiftly, angling away from the Federation camp and then swinging back again when he drew nearer to the far bank. Making no effort to hide his coming, he found their airfield and settled down on the western edge of the field.

A sentry approached within moments, as Kol'Dre knew one would. The Penetrator began speaking first.

"No time for that," he said breathlessly, speaking fluently in the Southland dialect he had long since mastered. "I have an urgent report I must make to the Prime Minister. Can you maintain watch over my vessel until I return?"

"Yes, sir," the other man answered at once, offering a hasty salute, immediately assuming from Kol's confident tone that he was a superior officer. "Will you be long?"

Kol'Dre shook his head. "Just long enough to deliver my message. Something is happening across the river, and I have to make certain what it is."

"Yes, sir!" The sentry provided immediate assurance of his cooperation. "Your airship will be ready when you are."

"Very good, soldier. I won't forget this."

Off he went without a backward glance, another shadow lost in the darkness, working his way through the camp with its tents and weapons racks and sleeping men to where the activity noted by the Skaar sentries had been seen. When he got to within fifty yards, he slowed to consider what he was seeing.

There *was* considerable activity ahead, down toward the Mermidon but behind the foremost fortifications. Several platforms were being constructed—broad wooden layers of planks closely fitted and ringed by low walls constructed of stakes with sharpened ends. Each structure sat eight to ten feet above ground level and had wooden stairs so that it could be mounted from the rear through a break in the walls. The three platforms, spaced perhaps fifty to sixty feet apart, were in various stages of completion, with one being substantially finished and the other two somewhere in the halfway range.

Kol'Dre stared. What were these platforms supposed to accomplish? They were too small to provide space for more than a dozen soldiers, so they didn't seem designed to provide elevated fighting stations. Their appearance suggested they were more likely there as mounts for some sort of fighting weapon—flash rip cannons or slingbacks. But why hadn't they been placed closer to the forward fortifications and why were they raised if they were intended to serve as platforms for launchers?

*These are for something else entirely,* he thought.

He walked out of the shadows and down to where the work was being done, fully aware of the risk he was running. If he was caught, he would be executed. But none of that mattered. Sometimes you took the path that was offered, risk or no.

He chose a soldier standing off to one side who looked to be overseeing the work and sauntered up to him. "How far along are we?" he asked. Sometimes if you acted like you knew a thing, people just accepted that you did.

The soldier shrugged, answering without any concern for Kol's identity. "We're about halfway done. Should be finished by daylight." He turned, suddenly concerned. "Are you one of the inspectors?"

Kol'Dre nodded. "Just trying to determine what still needs doing. We have to know how soon we can proceed."

The man nodded, more attentive now. "Have you seen these things work? The ones we're putting up on the platforms?"

Kol shook his head. So he had guessed right. "Not me. Guess they're pretty effective, though."

"Well, if what they say is true, the enemy can disappear right in front of you. Being able to stop that from happening, taking away their ability to hide themselves—it will make all the difference."

The Penetrator had to work hard at not looking shocked, but inside his stomach was clenching. "So they think they can do that? I hadn't heard any details."

"I'm told the stuff that machine puts out, whatever it is, will reveal them just as clear as could be. No escape from that."

Kol'Dre was already looking to cut this conversation short. He'd found out what he wanted and needed to get back with the information. "Let's hope for the best. I've got to move along now. Still got more to do before the night is out. Good talking with you."

"Wait!" The soldier grabbed his arm, and Kol froze, fear surging through him, one hand moving to his concealed blade. "Tell the materials men we need more planking. We're running out."

Kol'Dre let his breath release in a slow, silent exhale. "I'll do that."

He turned and hurried away, back toward where he imagined the materials site was located, trying to look like he was doing what the other man had asked of him. The fear had diminished, but he was sweating anyway. That had been entirely too close. Another man, more alert, might have found him out. He had risked too much.

But it had been worth it.

When he reached the edges of the camp, he kept going. He had to get word back to the king. If the Skaar were to be deprived of their ability to conceal themselves and left open to those Federation flash rips, they would be cut to pieces. And would the Southlanders actually attack them once these platforms were in place and these mysterious weapons were installed? He needed to know more, but there wasn't time to find out, and the risk of attempting to do anything else at present was entirely too great.

The airfield opened up ahead of him, and he crossed to his vessel, waved farewell to the sentry, and climbed aboard. In seconds he was airborne, his mind spinning as he fought to assemble the arguments he would need to make to Cor d'Amphere, to persuade him of the danger they were in.

Because he already knew the king was not likely to want to believe a word of it.

It was several hours after midnight, and the bulk of the army was asleep. Only those on watch or engaged in building the platforms were still awake. It was not at all certain when the Federation would attack their neighbors across the river, but the general consensus was that it would be soon. The Skaar already thought them weak and incapable of withstanding a sustained attack. The Federation needed to be able to demonstrate that it possessed the ability to repel these invaders. An attack would provide it with a chance to expose the Skaar's vulnerability and perhaps rout their entire army. But it also carried its risks. Any failure on the part of the Reveals to perform as expected would probably doom the Federation. If they were to suffer a defeat here, it was hard to imagine what else they could do. The Reveals were their last, best hope.

Clizia Porse, picking her way through the trees at the perimeter of the Federation camp, knew nothing of the Reveals. Had she known, she might have felt a bit more urgency about reaching Ketter Vause—although it would have been difficult to ratchet up her sense of urgency any higher. The anticipation of disposing of the Prime Minister and what that would entail roiled within her. This would change everything, once it was done. This would give her back everything she had lost and show her a clear path to what she coveted.

She reached the southern perimeter of the Federation camp, then stopped to catch her breath and take stock of what lay ahead. Information gathered by Skaar scouts during overflights told her where she would find the Prime Minister's quarters. His complex of tents was difficult to miss, but there would still be uncertainty as to where he could be found inside this maze. And there would be guards and plenty of them. She would have her chance, but it would only last for a few short minutes. She would have to move swiftly and silently. No alarm could be allowed to sound.

When she had rested a bit—she still found herself surprisingly weak—she rose and cast a concealment spell to hide herself from view. She knew she could only maintain the spell a short time, so she could not suffer interruptions or delays. The darkness and the relative quiet of the camp helped, but this remained a dangerous undertaking.

She walked from the trees, an invisible presence as she entered the camp. Sentries and then a few stray soldiers engaged in various tasks passed her by, but none saw her. She was into the midst of the tents and close to her destination, moving smoothly and silently, driven by adrenaline and a burning need to accomplish her intended task. She felt oddly stronger the farther into the camp she went, her anticipation a sharp-edged and controlling prod.

Ahead, the sprawl of tents that served as the Prime Minister's quarters came into view. She never hesitated, choosing the main entrance over an attempt to cut through the fabric with a blade. Guards stood at watch but did not see her. No one could see her. She was invisible. She was death's silent wind come to gather a victim.

At the tent flaps, she threw off a bit of sound to distract the guards long enough for her to push her way through the opening, barely disturbing the canvas barrier. The chamber just inside was empty of everything but a pair of desks and a few chairs. She moved on to the next chamber, this time slowing at the covered entry to peek through. A pair of guards stood watch. If she tried to enter, they would see the movement of the flaps as she brushed them aside. She called to them instead, throwing her voice and giving it a masculine sound. "Guards! Come out here!"

They came at once, parting the flaps and stopping just beyond to look around the empty space. By then, she was past them and into the Prime Minister's overly large and sumptuously indulgent sleeping chamber. She sneered in spite of herself. *All this opulence will not be enough to save you, Ketter Vause.*

She slipped the Stiehl from its hiding place within her cloak and moved toward his bed. She could see the outline of his sleeping form through the gloom. She could just make out the shape of his head on the pillow.

A sudden movement to one side caught her attention and brought her up short. Something pushed at her, and her concealment was ripped away. She stood helpless and enraged as a sudden wash of light revealed her.

"Well met, Clizia," Drisker Arc said.

# 24

D RISKER ARC FELT A SURGE OF SATISFACTION AT
seeing Clizia stripped of her concealment and brought
to bay at last. The look on her face told him everything
he needed to know. Shock and rage were all stark in her expression as
she stood before him, the deadly Stiehl held loosely at her side.

He saw the blade begin to lift and let the blue fire he had been
holding back blossom at the tips of his fingers. "Don't," he said quietly.

She glanced at the empty bed, which in the wash of light he had
summoned revealed the outline of a sleeping man but in fact was
nothing more than bedding rolled and positioned to suggest one.

She lowered her weapon once more. "This small setback won't
stop it from happening, Drisker," she said. "You think you have me,
but you still have a lot to learn. I am not some neophyte necromancer
who can be taken and held captive, and you know it. You waste time
needlessly."

Drisker smiled. "Oh, I don't know about that. You seem very
much a prisoner to me. Once you're safely locked away, a whole raft
of unfortunate possibilities will be ended. As will your ability to disrupt events in the Four Lands. I should, by all rights, kill you here
and now. But I think I'd rather see you locked away for whatever life
you have left. Encased in iron, maybe? A whole suit of it? Your magic

is of the Faerie kind, isn't it, Clizia? However you managed to infuse yourself, it has all the earmarks of the Fae. I think maybe this time you are finished."

She looked around the tent chamber. "So Ketter Vause is safely tucked away somewhere close by? No, don't bother answering. It is not my concern, now. How about your little friends, your siblings of song? Lost them along the way, have you?"

"They're no longer your concern, either. Better worry about yourself. Why don't you put down the Stiehl?"

She gave him a look. "Why don't you come take it from me?"

They faced each other across the tent chamber, eyes locked, expressions fixed and hard. "You don't want me to do that," Drisker said finally.

Clizia said nothing, did nothing, and gave nothing away. She might not even be there at all, given how still she was. She looked as if maybe she were nothing more than an empty image . . .

He caught himself. *No!*

He swiftly sent his magic flying into her with enough force to disable her, but instead she simply exploded and was gone.

She *was* an empty image! He had been tricked! She had slipped away, using her magic to disappear!

He wheeled around just in time to see the tent flaps ripple as she stepped through them. Shaking loose from his disbelief, he gave chase, determined she would not escape. He charged across the room, flung the tent flaps aside . . .

And slammed straight into what felt like a wall, careering away in a wild tangle of arms and legs to sprawl on the tent floor.

Clizia gave a satisfied glance back to where the invisible wall had momentarily floored Drisker Arc. It had taken her only seconds to create it, a momentary barrier that by now would have already disappeared. Not so smug now, was he? She would never be taken prisoner by a magic wielder of lesser ability. Drisker might think of himself as Ard Rhys, but he was still just a failed Druid who had walked away from his duties and was now scrambling to get his authority back. A name was only a name, and a title only a title. If you couldn't back up what it demanded, you were nothing.

She hastened through the antechamber and to the outer tent flaps, drawing on her concealment once more. Invisible, she passed through the main entry. The guards who stood on either side did not even note the rippling of the fabric, their gazes directed toward what might be approaching rather than what was behind, and she slipped past without paying them further heed. She had failed tonight, but there would be another time. She just needed to give the matter a little more thought and come up with a different approach. Drisker Arc was proving to be a bigger thorn in her side than she would have thought possible. Perhaps he was the one she needed to eliminate first. It wasn't as if she couldn't manage it. She could set a trap and finish him. It should be easy enough. Now that he had lost her, he would almost certainly come after her again.

The night remained dark, the sky clouded over; small patches of brightness from the campfires between the tents provided the only light. She slowed momentarily, wondering if there wasn't some sort of mischief or disruption she could cause the Federation before leaving.

It was then she saw Tavo Kaynin.

Tavo had been drawn away from his sister by a sense of Clizia's presence that he couldn't account for but did not question. His extended, wild use of the wishsong had left him with residual effects that he could not explain. One of them was the ability to sense the proximity of other magic. He had kept this from Drisker Arc, afraid of what it would mean and how the other would react. But then there were lots of things he had kept to himself, even given the Druid's efforts to help him.

The Kaynin siblings had been left to keep watch over the sleeping Ketter Vause while Drisker baited the hook to catch Clizia. In part, they were to provide a last line of defense should something go wrong, but mostly Tavo knew it was simply to keep them away should the worst happen. Drisker was particularly protective of Tarsha, something that Tavo appreciated. After all, she was his sister and he loved her *(no, no, no—don't question it!)*, having realized through long conversations and much consideration afterward how deeply he had deceived himself. Obviously, the Druid was her mentor and should feel close to her. Tavo believed Drisker Arc cared about him, as well, and that was a welcome reassurance. Everything the Druid had done to help him recover from the madness caused by his use of the wishsong demonstrated the depth of that caring.

Although the voices had returned, and the voices told him otherwise.

*He doesn't care for you; he's only pretending.*

*He plays you for a fool. He uses you for his own purposes.*

*How could anyone ever care for you? Think of what you've done!*

He had been able to keep the voices at bay until recently, brushing them aside as lies and ravings, remembering the lessons the Druid had taught him about how to banish them whenever they surfaced. He had managed decently thus far. He had even managed to keep Fluken from returning. Mostly.

Now he was standing outside the Federation Prime Minister's tent, watching and waiting for what he knew was coming. For her. For the witch, Clizia Porse, back to cause more trouble. He saw the tent flaps when they parted and no one appeared, saw her invisible form as a soft shimmer in the darkness moments later and knew her at once. Another side effect—to be able to spy out those who thought themselves concealed. Whatever Drisker had thought to do to hold her, it had failed. She had broken free or sensed a trap, and now she was fleeing. No one could see her, no one knew she was there—no one save him. He was all that stood between her and freedom.

He watched her come, not yet aware of him, making her way with slow, careful steps.

Suddenly she stopped, seeing him standing there, perhaps sensing that he could see her in spite of the magic she had used to hide herself. She stared at him for a moment, perhaps deciding what she should do, and then slowly she approached. As she did, her concealment dropped away, the magic abandoned, and she was fully revealed. Old, bent, and exuding a predatory look, she was intimidating in a way that would have sent a sane man running for his life.

But Tavo Kaynin was not entirely sane, and he was not afraid.

"Tavo!" Clizia Porse greeted him as if she were happy to see him again, one withered arm lifting in greeting. "Have you decided to leave those who deceived you and return to me?"

He stiffened in a way that suggested she not come any closer. "Return to you? You deceived me! You used me to try to kill Drisker Arc. Then you left me."

Clizia stopped short and gave him a long look, then shrugged. "You should be smarter than this, Tavo. I fled with the intention of finding you again, and now I have. If they have told you something else, they have lied. I warned you they would do so. I warned you that if you listened to their lies, they would make you into something you were never meant to be. Your sister? Remember what you told me? You hated her. How many times did you say so? You hated her enough that you wanted to kill her. She abandoned you and she—"

"Stop it!" he screamed. Heads turned. A few Federation soldiers came to a stop and stared at them. "You tricked me!" he howled in fury. "You used drugs to make me do what you wanted. You pretended to be my friend, but I know the truth now. You were never my friend and you never cared about me! I know what you are!"

She shook her head. "And this is what you tell me after I took you in, treated your injuries, cared for you, and gave you back your life. I offered you so much—everything you asked—but you threw it all away on a few false words from a failed Druid. Look at you. What is wrong with you? Something clearly is. I can see it on your face. Don't you feel it?"

In truth, he did. Something *was* wrong with him. Something had always been wrong with him, and he knew it. But knowing what it was and what to do about it had eluded him for years. Until the coming of the Druid.

"You can't change yourself overnight," Clizia continued, her words soft and persuasive. "You can't be someone you aren't. You can sense it, can't you? That certainty that things aren't right yet—that things might never be right. You have to accept this truth, which is the reality of your life. You are who you were born to be, faults and all, and by now it is much too late to change. You've killed so many people, Tavo, and you've hurt so many more. Stop lying to yourself!"

He flinched, the words cutting to the bone. He *was* lying to himself. He *was* pretending at being someone other than who he was. Her words were true; he could feel them impressing themselves on his mind.

"I'm going to stop you from leaving," he announced abruptly, shaking off the feelings of inevitability, clinging to his original intentions. "You have to stay here until the Druid comes."

She laughed at him. Openly. Laughed! "Oh, Tavo, you can't hold me! What will you do? Use your magic on me? Hurt me? Add my life to the collection of lives you have taken already? No, Tavo. You won't do that. You won't do anything but stand just where you are."

He knew in that instant she was right. The Druid had bound the collar around his neck—the collar that prevented him from using his magic. He was helpless as a baby before her.

She was already moving, walking past him and giving him no consideration at all. She did not look at him. He did not exist for her—he could feel it. He stared at her helplessly as she moved away, then looked down at his boots so as not to have to watch her go. He wanted to stop her, but the Druid's binding had prevented him. The very man who claimed he was an equal in this endeavor had blocked the magic that could maybe have helped.

Behind her, the tent flaps to the Prime Minister's quarters flew open and Drisker Arc stumbled into view. He took in what was happening and flung out his arm as if to stop her, but Tavo realized that the act was something more. A tiny bit of light flew from his fingers and spun through the air almost too fast to follow before landing on Clizia's robes and sinking from view into the fabric.

Then she was gone, and Drisker collapsed to his knees.

In the aftermath of Clizia's escape, Tavo shuffled reluctantly up to Drisker Arc and stood looking down at him. Drisker felt weak and disoriented, and there was blood on his cheek and a deep bruise on his forehead just below the hairline. For a moment, under Tavo's baleful glare, he felt a lick of fear.

"I was going to stop her," Tavo said, his voice flat and dead. "I sensed she was coming and I knew what I should do. But this binding—your binding"—he gestured angrily at his neck—"prevented me. I couldn't do anything!"

Drisker levered himself slowly to his feet, looped one arm about Tavo's hunched shoulders, and leaned close, head bent wearily. "I am proud of you, Tavo. I might have blocked your magic, but your desire was to use it for good—and that alone shows how far you have come. And you mustn't blame yourself. It wasn't you who failed. It was me. I was the one responsible for taking her prisoner. I had her, and I let her escape. You have to let me accept the blame for this. It was never yours to shoulder."

He felt Tavo's shoulders shudder under his arm, and suddenly Tarsha was there as well, reaching out to take her brother in her arms. "Are you all right, Tavo? Are you hurt? What's happened? Was it the witch?"

It was Drisker who answered her. "Tavo thinks it was his fault she escaped. She challenged him to stop her from leaving, and he couldn't, because of my binding. But his instincts were correct. Tell him, Tarsha. Make him understand."

Drisker released Tavo and moved off, leaving Tarsha whispering to her brother in urgent tones, explaining how his impulses had been correct. But like Tavo, Drisker fought back the bitter self-recrimination he was feeling for letting Clizia outsmart him. He knew she was slippery. He knew she was clever. But he hadn't acted quickly enough to counter either. And he had bound up the magic of another who could have helped him.

Now he would have to go after her.

Movement and voices brought him around as Ketter Vause approached. "Where is she?" he demanded, red-faced and sweating. There was real fear in his eyes. "Did you let her go?"

Drisker had come to him one night earlier and advised him of the danger he was in. Skeptical at first, he had finally allowed himself to be persuaded to let Drisker take his place in his sleeping quarters to intercept Clizia. Knowing she could harm him in spite of all his precautions and his guards was enough to convince him he needed the Druid's protection.

But now that he realized he hadn't gotten it, he was furious.

"You said you would trap her and put an end to this!" he screamed. "You promised! Now she's escaped and she can come back and kill me! I trusted you for no good reason!"

"You trusted me because you had no other choice," Drisker said quietly, ignoring the other's anger. "Yes, she escaped me. But I intend to go after her. In the meantime, find someone capable of protecting you in case she does come back." He paused. "You should go home to Arishaig and the safety of your own quarters, at least for now. Give me a few days, and I will see what I can do."

"A few days?" Vause asked incredulously. "Why bother?"

He turned and stalked away, and Drisker watched him go. He didn't blame him for his anger, but his irrational response to the continued danger was foolish. Staying out here on the banks of the Mermidon wasn't smart. He was doing this strictly because he didn't want to appear weak to the Skaar. The Druid shook his head. He had never been able to come to terms with what it was that drove men to seek power and then protect it so jealously.

In any case, Clizia wouldn't escape him again. His last act on stumbling from the tent after nearly knocking himself senseless had been to tag her with a bit of magic. Embedded in her black cloak, it would bring her back to him as surely as a hook and reel would snag a fish. She might be gone for the moment, but she was not safely away.

He waited for Tarsha to finish talking with her brother, staring off into the darkness, watching the guards disperse and Ketter Vause return to his tent, listening as the tumult of the moment lessened and faded, and the familiar noises of the camp reemerged in whispers and small scrapes and clinks. In the distance, he could hear the sound of tools at work, and he wondered what the Federation might be building at this time of night.

Impulsively, he made a crucial decision.

When Tarsha and her brother rose to their feet again and embraced, he walked back and stood before Tavo. The young man could not look at him.

Drisker lifted the other's chin so they were eye-to-eye. "You have done everything any of us could ask of you, Tavo Kaynin. You have proven yourself to both your sister and myself. You no longer need this."

And he reached up and released the inhibitor from Tavo's neck and tucked it away inside his robes.

# 25

KETTER VAUSE WAS WELL KNOWN AS A MAN OF IN-
finite patience—slow to anger, deliberate in his thinking, nonjudgmental, and willing to take the time to
weigh the advisability of his actions carefully. But he knew even Belladrin could tell he had reached the breaking point. He had glimpsed
her watching his angry encounter with the Druid, Drisker Arc, and
then his retreat into his tent, his posture and gestures making it all
too clear how far he had been driven.

Belladrin had always held him in high regard, but she was also
smart enough to know that more than one career had been cut
short through foolish attempts to act precipitously. Deciding that
he needed to reassure her of his self-control if he expected her
to continue to have confidence in him, he summoned her to his
tent.

He was seated at his desk, bent over a series of maps, but when she
entered he looked up immediately, dismissing his messenger, who
had been trailing behind, with a wave of his hand. He did not miss
the hint of reluctance in her posture as she stood before him. "Belladrin," he greeted her warmly. "Please sit."

He gestured to the most comfortable chair and watched her arrange herself. He could not have said exactly why he felt it so important that he have her support, but it was there, an undeniable urge.

Perhaps it was because she was so eager to be his student and he so pleased to be her mentor.

"I am a patient man," he said in a tone of voice that suggested he was again a figure of supreme competence. "But this . . . this deliberate effort to disrupt any chance of an accord between the Federation and the Skaar is too much! An attempt was made on my life tonight, and while the attempt was thwarted this time, there is nothing to say it will not reoccur. I can abide most things, but I cannot abide this. Not when the perpetrator is an invader in my own country."

She did not have to ask for details. He had advised her earlier of the arrangements he had made with the Druid to protect his life.

"Was the assassin captured?" she asked.

"No. She was an old woman, and still she managed to slip past the Druid and his companions. Such blatant failure is unforgivable. I have dismissed the Druid from my service."

Discovering that even a single Druid was still alive had come as something of a shock. That he had come to deliver a warning and offered to help had seemed at first an astonishing piece of luck. But Ketter Vause hated the Druids, and it wasn't enough that this one had saved his life. He had wanted the assassin caught and executed. As this had not happened, he saw no point in tolerating the Druid's presence further.

"What can I do to help?" Belladrin asked quickly, the concern on her face apparent.

"Inform my commanders that I want them here at dawn tomorrow. I intend to mobilize the army and attack the Skaar. There is no further reason to think there will be any kind of peaceful settlement. There is no further reason to delay. We have the Reveals the Dwarves brought us. This should tip the balance in our favor. We will draw the Skaar out of their fortifications, we will smash their army, and we will send whatever remains of them back to wherever they came from."

Belladrin hesitated. "Preparing the army for battle will take time. We cannot be ready for another few days. And do you know how much time it will take the Dwarves to prepare their machines?"

Vause smiled. "You are always quick to see the flaws in any plan, Belladrin. I admire that more than I can say. But this time you misjudge me. The plan of battle I intend to implement will have several phases, and the first will be a quick strike that will draw the Skaar out and bring them to us. A force needed to accomplish that can be assembled and dispatched much more easily than the entire army. So that part of the plan will be implemented as quickly as possible."

He paused. "As for the Dwarves, I have decided that perhaps they are not the ones best suited to man their machines in the coming battle. As soon as you have summoned my commanders, you will go to their Elders and tell them I have decided to use Federation soldiers to operate the Reveals, and they are to provide the necessary instruction. They are to teach us everything they know about operating the machinery. Should they refuse to do this or fail to instruct our soldiers adequately, I will have to consider revoking the conscription agreement for their village."

Belladrin gave him a long look, as if weighing her response carefully. "Perhaps you are right to use Federation soldiers," she agreed. "Their loyalty and commitment would be less in doubt."

He leaned toward her. "You are an intelligent lady, Belladrin. I admire that. The Dwarves are simply a means to an end. I trust you to do what is needed. Convince them that I mean to send them home again once the battle is won. You have a way with words, so choose them well. Go now."

She gave him a short bow of acknowledgment and backed away. He watched her go. She knew what was expected of her. She might even suspect that he was lying about his intentions. He would have the Dwarves killed no matter what happened. He had never intended anything else. As he said, they were a means to an end and nothing more.

Politicians could be ruthless and brutal when it was needed. She was smart enough to understand this. They had to be in order to stand up to the machinations and deceptions that surrounded them. But she needed to continue to see him as a man of significant achievement and strong leadership. She needed to see him as someone she would continue to be eager to follow.

As he watched her walk from the tent to summon his Federation commanders, he was already thinking ahead to what he would say to them when they were assembled.

Wondering how much of it would be the truth.

• • •

It was right before dawn when Belladrin Rish appeared at the door of the building in which Battenhyle and Lakodan were being housed. Both were already up and moving about; daybreak was their normal time to rise and begin work—a habit they could not break even when there was no work to be done and no particular reason to be awake. Neither was expecting her, but both were glad that she was there because it signaled the possibility that something was finally going to happen.

Once the door was open, she walked right in. "I won't pretend I am here with good news," she said before either could speak. "I have been given a message and told to deliver it. So here I am, in spite of my reluctance. The Prime Minister has decided he will have his own men operate the Reveals, and not the Dwarves. He needs your men to instruct them on how this should be done. This is not a request; it is a command. If you resist him, he will consider revoking the agreement he made with you. I know him well enough by now to believe that he means it. He intends to engage the Skaar, and he is afraid of doing so without the Reveals. So he needs your help, and he will have it one way or the other. Will you do as he asks?"

Lakodan made a snorting noise and turned away. Battenhyle stepped closer to her and placed a big hand on her shoulder. "And if we agree to this, how do we know that he will keep his word?"

"You don't," she answered. "But I will see you freed anyway, even if I have to do it myself. My time with Ketter Vause is drawing to a close. I want you back home, safe and sound. I want my conscience cleared of what I have inadvertently done. Do you believe me?"

The big man nodded. "I do. But tell the Prime Minister that we insist on a further condition. Lakodan and I will be the ones who offer the instruction. We know the machines better than our comrades. Best we do the teaching if they are to work correctly."

She nodded, grim-faced. "I will give him your message and urge him to agree." She paused. "It is a small gesture. But if I ever see you again once you are gone from here, I want to be able to look you in the face and not feel ashamed."

Battenhyle shrugged. "We are none of us responsible for the conduct of others. Sooner or later, we are all placed in uncomfortable situations not of our making."

Lakodan glanced over. "I spoke roughly to you. I apologize. If you find a way to persuade the Prime Minister to keep his bargain, I will forgive you everything. I hope you will do the same for me."

Belladrin smiled broadly and turned away. As she went out the door and left the Dwarves behind her, she was already feeling much better about the chances of success for the plans she was making.

It was four hours after dawn of the following morning that the early strike force, assembled on orders from Ketter Vause, lifted off in formation from behind Federation lines and flew north toward the Mermidon. The sky was a brilliant blue, deep and mesmerizing, its vast expanse filled with artistic clouds. Some were delicate paintbrush strokes ending in swirls and gradually decreasing ellipses; some were fluff balls tied together by slender threads; others seemed like outlines of cities faintly recalled from memories of childhood. None were large enough to blot out the sun or dim its bright glow.

Deciding on how and where to place his attack force so that this bright, inviting sun would best aid the Federation and most inconvenience the Skaar was essential. Approaching the enemy camp from the east would put the rising sun behind the attackers and more or less directly in the faces of the defenders. An even bigger advantage might have been gained if Vause had been willing to attack later in the afternoon when he could take advantage of the sunset and come in from the west. But he did not want to risk extending the battle into darkness; he wanted the matter concluded before then. If all went according to plan, the Federation strike would last less than thirty minutes, and his airships would be back across the Mermidon and landed anew by midday.

That he was being unduly optimistic never occurred to him.

The complement of airships that he had requisitioned included three fully armed warships, each with a dozen flash rip cannons and numerous rail slings; six escort gunships bearing explosive devices that could be dropped from above on fortifications and soldiers; a handful of single-man flits for smaller targets; and a pair of slightly larger two-man scouts for reconnaissance. Flags of the Federation government fluttered from the mastheads, and pennants identifying each airship division and their individual squads hung from the yard-arms. The airships all flew their light sheaths, drawing down the sun's power, allowing the diapson crystals contained within parse tubes to convert it to energy so the ponderous vessels could fly.

Ketter Vause had taken control right at the start, reminding one and all of his long-standing position as a commander in the Federation army before his ascendency to Prime Minister. Naturally, he would go with them; he knew they would expect no less. He chose one of the larger vessels as his flagship—quick to assure the commander normally in charge of the craft that he was not there to usurp his authority but only to provide the necessary details as to what the strike force was expected to do. Perhaps the commander believed this; perhaps he knew better. Frankly, Vause didn't care. The Prime Minister was tired of watching his commanders make mistakes, and he was determined it would not happen this time. His ship would lead the way, and the others would follow. Using signal flags, which would be clearly visible in full daylight, he would select the targets and the vessels responsible for destroying each, and he would see to it that his orders were carried out.

Off into this glorious day the attack fleet sailed, flying west for a time, then turning north to cross the Mermidon and begin a descent toward the Skaar fortifications. Ketter Vause, standing amidships on the decking of his chosen command vessel, had transformed into the soldier he had once been. He did not wear the Prime Minister's robes but the jacket, pants, and boots of a commander of the Federation army—epaulets, decorations, and all. Proudly visible to all who worked the airship from topmast to scuppers, and bow to stern, he gave his soldiers the leader they needed, standing there, fully exposed, knowing they could not help but be encouraged. They would take heart at the sight of him and do their duty as a consequence.

He was not entirely delusional but certainly misguided in his assumption of how those who served him would respond. But then he was not entirely aware of what he was getting into, either.

His plan was straightforward enough. This would be a strike against the Skaar on the order of the one the ill-fated Commander Dresch had launched a month earlier but with very different results. This time, the Skaar would be caught off guard, and the result would be massive destruction and loss of life. A retaliatory action was to be guarded against, but if attempted it was destined to fail. The Skaar would be forced to use what remained of their airships, after having been hammered from all sides by superior numbers. If they chose to land, they would have to rush Federation lines that were ready and waiting for them. If they attempted to disguise their numbers and their positions by disappearing, the Reveals would be employed. The Skaar would be coated with a sticky substance that would expose them utterly and result in their annihilation.

In theory, it sounded reasonable. But it had been many years since Ketter Vause had served in the military, and he had never been directly involved in any real action. His skills lay in planning and assessment. Time had eroded his abilities, however, and in the heat of anger and urgency he forgot an important detail.

Signalmen stood to either side of him, ready to raise the flags designated to indicate the attack targets and those elements of the task force responsible for destroying them. This should have been done earlier, but Vause wanted to orchestrate the attack personally, implementing every detail with finely tuned precision.

Which ignored more than a few realities when it came to implementing combat tactics on a scale this size.

As the fleet closed on its target, coming in from the east, Vause gave the order to raise the flags, and the warships separated—the Federation flagship heading for the center of the camp and Cor d'Amphere's quarters, the second warship flying toward the airfield where the Skaar airships were moored, and the third warship swooping down to skim the length of the forward fortifications and their defenders. Two gunships and a scattering of flits accompanied each, and the scouts split off on search-and-destroy missions of their own.

Imagine their surprise when they found Cor d'Amphere's tented quarters and virtually all of the smaller tents surrounding it empty and lifeless. The airfield was likewise empty of aircraft of any sort. Only scarecrows formed of wood and straw and wire manned the fortifications that lined the north bank of the Mermidon River.

But none of this was visible at first—not until after the separate attacks were under way, the flash rip cannons and rail slings raining down fire and jagged metal, the explosives canisters jettisoned over the railings of the warships to tumble earthward and erupt in huge craters. The failure of even a single soldier to appear in the aftermath gave proof to a disbelief that quickly became a certainty.

No one was there.

The Skaar camp had been abandoned, and the Skaar army—along with its airships, weapons, and equipment—had vanished.

# 26

THE ONE IMPORTANT DETAIL KETTER VAUSE HAD failed to pay sufficient attention to was that when military tactics were employed, matters seldom went the way they were anticipated to go. If anything, the expected course of a battle tended to change all too quickly. He had assumed that his preparations were more than adequate for what was needed. The attack, after all, was a preliminary engagement, intended to draw the Skaar out from behind their fortifications and across to where the Federation could effectively use the Reveals and their superior numbers and weaponry to put an end to the invaders. This would have worked perfectly if the Skaar had simply stayed put and let it happen.

But from the very beginning of their engagements with the Federation, the Skaar had always been one step ahead. They had managed this through superior skills and experience, and the one small detail to which the Prime Minister had failed to pay sufficient attention.

The Skaar could be standing right next to you, invisible as the air you breathed, and you would never know it.

Oh, he had given it enough thought when it came to a direct engagement—to a battle in which revealing the Skaar to his Federation soldiers was of paramount importance. But he failed to give it sufficient consideration when he was making his plans to engage the Skaar in battle so that his new weaponry could be used to destroy them. He had failed to consider that the Skaar might already know about the weaponry and his plans for using it, and work around it.

Belladrin Rish was sitting at the Prime Minister's desk, organizing and preparing to deliver his marching orders to those left behind at the Federation camp—which was almost the entire complement of the army. The crews and soldiers who had departed two hours earlier for the north bank represented a relatively small portion of those who had been brought up from Arishaig for the confrontation with the Skaar. Most were engaged in ordinary pursuits while they waited for the Prime Minister and their fellows to return.

Belladrin was so preoccupied with her own work that at first she barely heard the sudden tumult that surfaced beyond her tent walls. But when it grew stronger, she rose and went out to see what was happening. A jumble of shouts and cries rose to greet her, a clear indication of things gone wrong.

A pair of beleaguered-looking commanders stumbled forward, a dozen soldiers trailing in their wake. "We need to get word to the Prime Minister!" one blurted out. "We're under attack!"

She calmed him down enough to discover that those who had witnessed their arrival saw what they believed to be the entire Skaar invasion force landing not more than a mile to the south—thousands upon thousands of soldiers ready to descend on the Federation camp.

"Have our soldiers been deployed?" she demanded, trying to ignore the frantic looks and voices.

They had, and new defensive lines were being assembled to stop the advance. But Vause had taken most of the top leadership across the river with him, and what commanders remained were more used to taking orders than giving them. Plus, there was a rumor spreading through the Federation ranks that the Skaar army was an unstoppable juggernaut and its soldiers something more than human. The Federation defensive lines would be smashed, the camp overrun, and everyone put to the sword.

She gave it a moment's thought, the irony of the situation not lost to her. Here she was, a person with no leadership experience, no military background, and nothing more than common sense—a spokesman for the Prime Minister at best—and she was the one they were consulting. She forced down an urge to laugh, her circumstances so much more complicated than any of them knew

She had a decision to make, and for once did not know how to make it.

As if by magic, Choten Benz appeared at her elbow. "Belladrin?" he said quietly, drawing her attention. "We have to move the Reveals from the riverbank to the rear of the camp, where they might be more useful. They're the only effective weapons we have."

*And he's asking my permission. Well, there you have it.* She nodded immediately. "Yes. Order it done."

Benz turned to the officers and the men clustered about them and gave the order. Not wanting to take the matter any further, and secretly relieved to have something specific to do, the commanders set out with several dozen of their men to collect the Reveals. Belladrin watched them go, conflicted on several fronts. Was there enough time to manage the situation? Could she turn this around, or were they facing disaster?

She couldn't be sure.

By now the entire camp was mobilizing for battle, but Belladrin harbored no illusions. Federation soldiers were well trained and experienced, but all the experience and training in the world would not save them if the Reveals did not reach their defenses before the battle began. Instead, the Skaar would disappear, one after the other, right in front of the defenders, and begin killing them.

She made a quick decision. "We need to summon the Federation soldiers who have been trained to operate the Reveals!" she shouted.

"What we need," Choten Benz replied, stepping right in front of her and seizing her by the shoulders, "is the Dwarves. Those Federation soldiers aren't the ones best able to operate those weapons in a situation like this!"

He was right. Efficient use of the Reveals was crucial to the army's chances for survival, and while Battenhyle and Lakodan may have provided instruction to the Federation soldiers chosen to operate the weapons, there was no substitute for the real thing.

"Let's go get them," she agreed and raced off to find the Dwarves with her taciturn companion right behind her.

Even before the banging on the doors of their quarters began, the Dwarves were aware that something was wrong. The sounds of frantic activity, coupled with a rising cacophony of shouts and cries, were deafening. The sudden appearance of Belladrin and Choten Benz only confirmed their suspicions.

"We are under attack," Belladrin announced without even the most perfunctory of greetings. "The Skaar have crossed the river and come up behind us. They are preparing to strike from the rear, and there are thousands of them—perhaps their entire army. The Prime Minister is off on his own expedition, so I am taking it upon myself to put you back in charge of the Reveals. Without them, we cannot keep the invaders from disappearing during the attack. I need you and your men to agree to man your weapons and use them to save us all."

"Taking it upon yourself?" Lakodan repeated in disbelief. He started to grin. "Ketter Vause will skin you alive!"

"He won't have anyone *left* to skin if we don't have reliable operators for the Reveals," Choten Benz said quickly. "How well prepared do you think those Federation soldiers you instructed might be? Can you promise they will be able to keep those Reveals functioning in a battle of this magnitude?"

"No," Battenhyle said at once. "There wasn't enough time for the level of instruction needed. It should be Dwarves doing the work."

"Then Dwarves it will be," Belladrin declared. "If you stand with us in this struggle, I will see to it that everything I promised to do earlier gets done."

"Well, the odds don't sound all that promising." Lakodan rolled his shoulders, and his compact, muscular body seemed to swell within his clothing. "But no one lives forever." He glanced at Battenhyle. "And it's a fine morning for a fight, isn't it, Old Bear? I think we should stick around."

It was a casually given, recklessly made commitment, both inspiring and mad. There were perhaps twenty-five Dwarves, and they would be the focus of the Federation attack the moment the enemy discovered what the Reveals could do. But you made the best of things in situations as extreme as this one if that was the only choice you had.

"Commander Benz and I will take you to the others," Belladrin offered quickly. "The Reveals are already being brought up."

They left the stockade and proceeded to where the other Dwarves were being housed. From there, they all moved as quickly as possible to the rear of the camp and the focal point of the impending attack. They were joined by plenty of others on the way. Soldiers were scrambling to join their units, their efforts frantic and their shouts wild and urgent. Flash rip cannons were being hauled from the riverfront to the newly established southern perimeter, massive iron mouths gaping skyward. However shocked they might be by the unexpected appearance of the invaders to their rear, the Federation army was not giving in to panic or despair. If anything, they seemed less a panicked mob and more a determined, angry collective. Shirtless, hatless, in some cases shoeless, they nevertheless carried their weapons and yelled encouragement to their fellows as they went.

*We might actually survive this,* Lakodan thought.

Unless, of course, some bullheaded senior commander had countered Benz's orders and kept the Reveals facing across the river, emboldened by a self-imposed superior feeling that he should not have to listen to a young woman with no experience or training. Such men existed and always seemed to surface at the wrong moment. He knew well enough that, without those Reveals, the Federation would be overrun and cut to pieces. Still, there was nothing to do but to assume the weapons would be ready and waiting when they arrived.

There were two types of Reveals. The stationary Reveal resembled an ancient cannon—an artifact conjured up from times even before the Great Wars. Its broad iron barrel rested atop a pair of heavy wooden wheels that allowed for it to be moved about and positioned as needed. One end of the barrel was slightly flared and covered with a wide-mesh screen that capped the opening and diffused the liquid mixture the weapon emitted upon being fired. The other end was a mass of attached containers with feeds looped to several large wooden barrels grouped within an enclosure of thick iron sidewalls that rested atop a platform attached at the rear of the weapon. Pumps powered by parse tubes of fully charged diapson crystals fed the contents of the barrels into the containers attached to form the mixture.

It was the composition of the mixture that made all the difference.

The Reveal was not a true weapon. It did not fire projectiles or cause harm to whatever it was fired upon. Its name said all you needed to know about its function. When charged and ignited, the barrel emitted a wide spray of the mixture formed by the contents of the barrels up to almost a hundred yards. Because the spray tended to break down the farther it traveled, it was most effective at half that distance. And it was quite by accident that this particular usage was discovered. The machine's original purpose was for spraying composite or paint much more quickly than workers could manage by hand. The nature of the mixture was calibrated to the intended use. For instance, composite required a heavier mixture than paint.

This meant that the operators of the Reveal had to be trained in how to form the necessary mixture. The barrels on the rear platform contained a variety of extracts for base materials, thinners, and thickeners. Using the proper amounts for whatever was required was a very exact science. If you failed to create the proper balance, the Reveals would produce an ineffective mix or, even worse, clog the feeds.

It was a new science, and only the Dwarves of Crackenrood were well versed in its usage. In part, this was because those few who had heard about it thought it of little importance. They might have felt differently if they had known it could do more than initially intended, but using it to reveal concealed or camouflaged objects was a very recent discovery. Even use of the name *Reveal* was only just beginning to catch on, and then only in the Dwarf community.

The portable Reveal was not invented until after the stationary Reveal had been in use for months. It was built by a Dwarf who had been instrumental in the creation of the original and, after thinking on it for a time, came up with a new design. Working alone in his shed, he crafted a handheld version with a tank that strapped to the back. This mobility made the device more diversely functional and therefore the operator's work much easier.

Had nothing further happened, that might have been the end of the matter. But two months later, a Gnome raiding party invaded Crackenrood's remote west end, descending on the outlying homes at night intending to steal away women and children to sell as slaves. The Dwarf, half asleep and unable to lay hands on his battle-ax, grabbed the closest potential weapon he could find, which was his new handheld invention. Strapping it on, still fully loaded with paint from the previous day's work, he went out to join his neighbors and sent clouds of sprayed paint onto the attackers in an effort to blind them.

The result was something of a surprise. Not only were his targets indeed blinded, when not quick enough to shield their eyes, but also Gnomes he had not been able to spy in the darkness of a moonless, clouded sky were coated by the container's luminescent paint and clearly revealed to the Dwarf defenders. In the end, the raiders were driven off and the Dwarves were made aware of an important new use for the soon-to-be-renamed Reveal.

But the residents of Crackenrood kept the secret of this new use to themselves—secret even from the other Dwarf villages—as they began a series of experiments seeking to make their new weapon operate more efficiently. So even its very existence had been carefully guarded since then, and it was something of a surprise that Ketter Vause had found out. Still, the Prime Minister's spies were everywhere, and like so many secrets this one had been leaked or bargained away.

And now both Reveals were about to be tested in a way neither had been tested before. Lakodan thought about what was at stake and what would be expected of the Dwarves and found it daunting. But before any testing could be undertaken and any measure of the Reveals' success measured, the battle would be under way.

On this day, fate favored the bold, and they found the station-

ary Reveals in place, heavily barricaded and still fastened to their elevated platforms. How the Captain of the Guard and his men had
managed this feat was anyone's guess, but it brought a smile to the
Dwarf's lips. With Battenhyle urging them on, they divided into
three groups—some set to loading and priming their massive weapons and others to attaching the barrels that held the spray mixture
that would be used against their enemies once the attack began. With
help from Choten Benz, they drafted soldiers to act as runners for
fresh supplies, including the ingredients for refreshing the mix, additional diapson crystals, spare hoses and barrels, and water wagons
with pumps to protect the vulnerable parts of the Reveals and their
fortifications from the fire the Skaar would almost certainly try to use
to destroy them.

It was all done in a flurry of wild activity, but it was done. Even
before the Skaar legions came into view, the defenders were ready
and waiting. They had chosen a gap formed by steep hills and heavy
timber to either side—a natural passageway that the Skaar army must
attempt to pass through. Here, the bulk of the defenders and all the
stationary Reveals had been positioned. The Dwarves, including
those bearing mobile units strapped to their backs, were divided into
three groups. The largest group remained with the stationary Reveals.
The smaller two split up to accompany the units of Federation soldiers that fanned out to either side of the gap, climbing to the apex of
the forested ridgelines where they would await flanking attacks that
would almost certainly be launched.

In addition, the warships and smaller fighting craft that had remained behind after the departure of the Prime Minister's fleet were
sent aloft, fanned out across and slightly behind the Federation defenses to engage any Skaar airships that might attempt a breakthrough
from above. In spite of the drain on the fleet from the unfortunate
preemptory attack, the Federation still outnumbered the Skaar—and
still possessed superior firepower. If the Skaar could be stopped from
vanishing at will, they would have a hard time securing a victory even
over this diminished Federation army.

At least that was what the commanders told their soldiers, assuring them that their weapons, experience, and courage would be enough.

Lakodan wasn't so sure, but a shared glance with Battenhyle was all he permitted himself. He was still trying to get used to the idea that he was actually going to fight alongside the very men and women who had been his lifelong enemies. It was a difficult reality to accept.

So he didn't try. He simply celebrated that—for the moment at least—he and his companions had been given a chance at gaining a reprieve from the hated conscriptions that had made virtual slaves of their people for decades. There was nothing for it but to employ their extensive and formidable fighting skills and experience, and hope for the best.

As the Skaar airships hove into view and their soldiers on the ground marched out of the brightness of the midday sun—which was now at their backs and directly in the eyes of the defenders—the Dwarf warrior realized he had lost sight of Belladrin in the confusion of preparing for battle.

Now, as he looked for her, she was nowhere to be found.

The Skaar army approached the defensive lines of the Federation at a steady walk, swordsmen leading, spearmen in the second ranks, slingers and bowmen last—everyone proceeding at the same pace, steady and unhurried. They approached as a single unit until they were within a hundred yards, and then split into three commands, the centermost striding directly for the defensive lines, the other two peeling off to begin climbing the forested hills in the already antici-pated flanking movement. Rather than attacking stripped of every-thing but boots and weapons, as they had been reported to favor, they wore hooded cloaks tied about their necks and thrown back over their shoulders.

The day was unseasonably warm and the wind almost nonexis-tent. And the cloaks seemed almost counterproductive to any effi-cient use of their fighting skills. Lakodan, far to the right and high up on the ridgeline, with one of the portable Reveals strapped to his back, felt a twinge of uncertainty. He looked for Battenhyle, but his friend was down in the center of the defenders with another portable Reveal. Ajost, bearing the third and last portable Reveal off to his left, caught his eye and pointed to the advancing Skaar, a questioning look on his broad face. He had noticed the cloaks and was wondering the same thing. Lakodan's uneasiness grew stronger.

Then the drums started, their heavy booming a deep, steady rhythm that reverberated with such power the ground shook and the leaves on the trees shivered. Weapons raised, the Skaar continued to advance, still marching in lockstep, all of them visible, none yet attempting to vanish. But they would do so, Lakodan told himself. It was what they always did.

Except this time, they didn't. By the time they were within fifty yards, not a single Skaar soldier had disappeared.

Still they came on as if they believed themselves indestructible—as if they believed themselves impervious to anything the defenders might do to stop them. Lakodan was still trying to figure out what was happening when the front line of the advance launched their initial attack. From behind the bristling array of swords and spears that led the way, slings and bows dispatched a barrage of stones and arrows into the defenders, who were positioned along the center of the defensive line—still waiting for the enemy to disappear so the Dwarves could begin using the Reveals. The suddenness of the attack was shocking, but the response was immediate as Federation flash rips began spraying fire into the front ranks of the Skaar.

Down went the entire forefront of the attackers, catching fire as they were struck, igniting like straw dolls—because, Lakodan realized with sudden recognition, that's what they were. The front ranks were dummies fastened to one another by sticks and held upright by living soldiers at the ends of each rank—puppets moving enough like men to fool the defenders from a distance.

And now, in the face of the catastrophe that the Dwarf warrior could see unfolding, the Skaar began to disappear. Not in ones and twos or even tens and twenties, but all at once. Shock at this turn of events further froze the defenders, giving the Skaar just enough time to rush the hastily assembled fortifications and reappear.

By now Battenhyle had also realized how they had been tricked and roared to his companions to use the Reveals. The Dwarves began to spray the seemingly empty space behind those already engaged in the fighting, spreading a wide swath across the plains to expose those Skaar who thought to hide themselves. After a few minutes, cloaked figures began reappearing, coated in spray. But almost immediately they threw off the cloaks in which they had wrapped themselves to be shielded from the mixture and disappeared again, all while still charging the defenders.

Before there was time to adjust the Reveals to launch a fresh fusillade, the Skaar were climbing over the barricades and descending on the Reveals. Dwarves and Federation soldiers alike battled fiercely to throw them back, but by now the advantage had swung in favor of the Skaar. The defenders were forced from the walls, and the stationary Reveals were smashed apart. Flash rips kept the attackers from overrunning the Federation lines entirely, but defenders were dying everywhere. Many of the Dwarves were gone as well, killed when the stationary Reveals fell. On the left and right flanks and at the defensive center, Lakodan, Ajost, and Battenhyle, all carrying portable Reveals, fought on, continuing to expose the enemy but being forced back even as they did so. Chaos dominated, and the heavy layer of swirling black smoke that rose from the burning straw men engulfed the entire battlefield in a thick haze, further adding to the confusion.

On both flanks, additional attacks were under way. The Skaar came at the Federation defenders in waves, weaving through the trees while wrapped in their heavy cloaks, absorbing the mix spewed by the mobile Reveals when they had to, using trunks to hide themselves where they could. Working to get close enough to break through the defensive lines, they used feints and sudden rushes to draw fire away from one another, disappearing and reappearing like ghosts.

But the Federation soldiers fought on valiantly, allowing the Dwarves to use the portable Reveals in short bursts, then triggering their flash rips to bring down the exposed enemy soldiers. The struggle surged back and forth, all of it within a confusing maze of trees and brush obscured by ascending smoke from the battlefield below. It was the same on the left flank, although the Federation defense there appeared to be having more success after choosing to break up into groups of half a dozen, to allow the members in each group to better defend one another while holding their ground. Lakodan saw this and yelled to the commander leading their beleaguered band of fighters, only to see him collapse an instant later with an arrow through his chest.

Overhead, airships from the two armies warred with each other, the battlefield too obscured by smoke and ash to allow either to do much damage to the soldiers below. A few went down, none of them warships, and it seemed as if the fighting taking place in the sky overhead was entirely removed from what was happening on the ground.

Fate's pendulum might have swung in favor of either army at this point, the attacks and retreats on both sides ebbing and flowing equally, the dying and wounded diminishing in equal numbers for both. But then a broad-shouldered figure at the very center of the lower battlefield surged to the forefront of the fighting, a huge two-edged ax gripped in both hands, and drove right into the heart of the Skaar ranks. Lakodan knew him instantly. Spears and swords cut and slashed at Battenhyle but to no discernible effect. Federation soldiers shouted their battle cries and rallied to join him, the entire complement throwing themselves recklessly at the enemy.

It was a defining moment. The Skaar recovered from the rush and held their ground once again for long minutes before attacking anew. This time it was the Federation that was pushed back, and for a moment it looked as if the defensive line would be broken. Then the Federation rallied again, Battenhyle at their head, and threw back the Skaar once again. Slowly but surely the mobile Reveals were negating the ability of the invaders to disappear. Efforts to bring down the remaining bearers had failed, for Lakodan and Ajost were surrounded by Federation soldiers determined to protect them.

Finally, the enemy drums began to beat once more, but with a different tempo this time, and the Skaar started a slow withdrawal. When the Skaar had pulled back to beyond a hundred yards, they began to disappear again, one by one. It was a slow, deliberate process, a kind of taunt to demonstrate their superior abilities. In a slow fading, they abandoned the battlefield until no more remained.

Federation soldiers and Dwarves stood side by side and waited, suspicious still, eyes fixed on the grasslands where the Skaar had last been seen. The Dwarves bearing the Reveals expended a few further bursts of the coating mixture, broad sweeps of clinging liquid sprayed all across the open expanse to expose any of the enemy who might have chosen to linger.

But none were visible.

For this day, at least, the Federation had prevailed.

# 27

FLYING ABOVE THE CHOPPY WATERS OF THE TIDE-race, miles from any shore and almost two weeks from its point of departure, the *Behemoth* was still plowing through air currents and clouds, working its way toward its destination. For Shea Ohmsford, that destination seemed as distant now as it had when they set out—a phantom as elusive as the wraiths that were said to roam the Wilderun, and just as likely to disappear. He was used to being patient, but he was also a boy who possessed an impulsive nature, and he was growing steadily more eager to speed things along.

In an effort to lessen the pressure of that urge, he began spending more and more time with the old man, listening to him explain the workings of his wondrous machine, absorbing everything he was told, making it his business to become as educated as he could about what Annabelle could do and how she was supposed to work. It was arduous at times, Tindall's explanations so confusing that he became lost. But each time he simply admitted his failure and asked to be told again. Tindall, a born teacher, was so entranced by Shea's interest that he never once complained or argued but simply did as he was asked. In the boy, he had found the perfect student, and he was not about to discourage that.

The effort was taxing on both of them, however, for the old man grew easily tired these days, the travel wearing on him both physically and emotionally. Still, he seemed to enjoy the effort and perhaps the distraction of not having to worry about how Annabelle would perform once they reached Skaarsland, and so he pressed on.

On the other side of this give-and-take, it was difficult for Shea to get his head around the whole idea of a machine being able to change the weather, much as he wanted to believe it was possible. Believing required too many assumptions that contradicted everything he knew about weather and climate and the way they impacted the world. Not to mention how every effort made by Mankind over the ages to control the weather was said to have ended in disaster, usually costing the lives of those who dared to challenge nature's rules. So the best he could manage was to take a wait-and-see attitude, keeping an open mind even as his doubts and misgivings threatened to stifle his optimism.

When he wasn't spending his time with Tindall, learning the intricacies of Annabelle or hanging about Rocan on the fringes while the other regaled his friends with stories of his wild adventures, he could usually be found in the pilot box learning how to fly the *Behemoth*. His teacher—when Rocan wasn't about—was usually the Rover's cousin Sartren, who didn't seem to mind the boy asking questions. He explained the complexities of flying a craft this huge, distinguishing them from what was required to fly a warship, frequently letting Shea take the controls to handle the craft on his own. He kept close watch while the boy did this, of course, but Shea was so excited at being given a chance at flying the big airship that Rocan's cousin was happy to offer him the opportunity.

Not once during all this time was there any sign of Seelah. Shea looked for her constantly, even going so far as to rise in the dark and wander the decks in the hope of encountering her. At one point, he asked Rocan outright where she could be found, but the Rover simply smiled and shrugged. Seelah could only be seen when she wished to be seen, and for now she preferred to remain hidden.

So the days drifted away—some more quickly than others, some dragging like an anchor chained to everyone's patience. But the weather stayed friendly and offered no obstacles, and according to Ajin d'Amphere's frequent calculations—she somehow had a means for reading where they were in relation to Skaarsland—they were making good time.

Then, just before completion of the second week since departing the shores of the Four Lands, a storm caught up with them. It blew out of the northwest, its coming signaled by a bank of dark clouds that seemed to pile on one another like rocks in an avalanche the closer they got to the airship. Then the storm found a tailwind to speed it along, and soon it was barreling down on them with frightening swiftness and increasing size.

After repeated attempts to outrun and outmaneuver it, Rocan finally gave in to the inevitability, had the sails hauled down until only the mainsail remained aloft, and ordered the *Behemoth* to come about and turn into the storm. It was huge by then, blotting out the sky and horizon, slowly gobbling up everything as it swept over them, until there was almost no light left and the toxic mix of clouds, rain, and wind was everywhere.

Crew and passengers alike were ordered to secure themselves with safety lines anchored to iron rings screwed into the heaviest support timbers. Most did so immediately. Tindall was allowed to anchor himself to the platform on which Annabelle had been fastened, but a member of the Rover crew was assigned to stay with him. Shea was placed inside the pilot box with Sartren. He looked for the others and found Brecon Elessedil near the bow and facing into the wind, blond hair streaming out behind him like a ragged pennant.

Of Dar Leah or Ajin d'Amphere, there was no sign.

Arneas Rocan was the last to fasten his safety line, and then only after making sure that everyone else was securely attached to something sturdy.

"Now you're going to see a real storm," he informed the boy as he joined him in the pilot box. "These sorts of blows can be so fierce they take down masts and shred sails." He laughed as if he could imagine nothing more entertaining. "We're in for it now!"

As if to emphasize his words, the wind accelerated into a howl of such mind-numbing proportions it became impossible to hear someone standing right next to you unless they were shouting in your ear. Although the mainsail was still flying, it was already beginning to fray along the edges, and Shea was certain it would not last out the storm. He watched the clouds scudding across the sky in huge, roiling banks to form an almost impenetrable blackness that swiftly closed about the *Behemoth*. Although Shea couldn't hear what Rocan was shouting to Sartren, he could guess based on the latter's renewed efforts to keep the airship pointed into the wind. But the *Behemoth* was a massive, cumbersome beast, and her response was ponderous and slow. Sartren was losing the battle to keep her in line until Rocan joined him, the two of them wrestling with the steering in a desperate fight to deny a hurricane-force wind that sought to wrench their control away.

A crash sounded from behind, and Shea turned to see that the aft mast had lost her main yardarm, which was lying on the rear deck. A pair of spars, smaller and higher up, shattered as the wind buffeted the rigging relentlessly. Forward, casks of water had broken loose and were rolling about the decks. One cask gained sufficient momentum from the rocking of the airship that it slammed into the railing with enough force to burst through and disappear over the side.

Shea was crouched down within the pilot box, pressed against its protective walls, his hands over his ears in an attempt to shut out the howl of the storm. It was a futile effort. The wind was a scream of rage and madness, its volume so overpowering that it was almost deafening. Rain lashed the crew and passengers with stinging force and hammered the wooden decks and hull with a staccato drumming that suggested it might somehow manage to bore right through the timbers. On all sides the clouds were overwhelming the ship, swallowing them as if an ocean of darkness that intended to drag them down.

The *Behemoth* was a twenty-ton airship, but she rocked and shook within the maw of the storm as if a cork set upon churning rapids. Everyone save the pilots, who were forced to remain standing while they worked to control the huge vessel, was hunched over and pressed up against whatever support they could find, fighting to keep from being torn loose from their anchors, eyes shut and hands pressed hard against their ears.

So it was a shock when Shea felt Rocan's hands grip his shoulder and pull him to his feet.

"We're losing altitude!" Even though he was bending close, the Rover was practically screaming. "Something is wrong with the parse tubes aft! I have to take a look!"

"Can't we use Annabelle to help change the weather?" Shea asked impulsively, shouting back at him.

"Not in the middle of a storm like this!" He clapped one hand on the boy's shoulder. "Lend a hand here until I get back!"

He shoved the boy toward Sartren and the heavy wheel he was struggling to hold steady, and then deftly slipped his tether. Hauling the unfastened end coiled about one arm, he vaulted the walls of the pilot box without bothering to open the door, scrambled across the open decking to the aft port railing, and hooked himself up anew. Down the railing he crept, clinging to whatever support he could find, the wind and rain whipping at him. After a short distance, he stopped moving and peered over. Apparently finding what he wanted, he went over the side without a moment's hesitation and was gone.

The boy held his breath. The tethering rope pulled taut, which indicated that Rocan was still attached. But it was swinging wildly with the violent lurching of the airship, and it didn't seem as if it would take much to wrench its fastenings loose and send the Rover plunging to his death. Even while he was fighting the wheel with Sartren, Shea kept looking over his shoulder, fearing the worst.

But eventually Rocan reappeared, pulling himself back up and dropping exhausted on the deck, where he lay prone and unmoving for several long minutes. The boy started to go to him, but Sartren grabbed his shoulder and pulled him back, shaking his head.

The minutes dragged by.

Finally Rocan stirred, dragged himself to his feet, unclipped the tether, and lurched back across the deck to the pilot box.

"Something crimped the exhaust on the upper parse tube . . .

likely one of those spars . . . so the power was . . . cut off and the tube exploded." He was gasping for breath, his words yanked away by the wind the moment they were spoken. "We lost all the crystals . . . and the explosion put a hole in the hull . . . maybe ten feet below the railing. We have to get it repaired."

"Not until we make landfall!" Sartren shouted back. "Sit down, will you? Before you fall down!"

The Rover hooked himself up to a fresh line, glanced at the expression on Shea's face, and grinned. "What? You thought you'd lost me? To a storm? Not likely, my young friend. Storms and I, we have an understanding!"

"Must have something to do with insanity!" Sartren waved impatiently. "Shea and I are fighting a losing battle here. We need someone else to take this on for a bit!"

Rocan was up at once, off his tether and scrambling over the decking to summon help.

"Crazy, that one," his cousin said, almost too softly to be heard. "Just like this storm. Can't tell which way he might blow next."

But Shea's thoughts were elsewhere. To have Rocan call him "friend" again—after he had worried that their friendship was beyond repair because of what he had revealed about Annabelle to Drisker—was heartening. It was worth all the worry and uncertainty he had weathered just to hear that one word.

Other Rovers appeared to take control of the wheel, giving Shea and Sartren a chance to rest. But there was little rest to be had as the storm raged on for several hours more, driving the *Behemoth* where it chose and likely, Shea thought, far off course. But he was too exhausted to contemplate how far, and eventually he fell asleep.

When he woke again, the storm's power was diminishing as its leading edge finally moved on, leaving them only the tail end. The sky was brightening and the rainfall diminishing, and the crew were beginning to untether themselves in order to resume their duties. Even sitting propped up as he was at the rear of the pilot box, Shea could feel the *Behemoth* lurching unevenly while she struggled to maintain altitude and power. It was apparent she was experiencing a problem.

Rocan, appearing out of nowhere, knelt next to him. "How are you holding up?"

Shea nodded. "The ship doesn't feel right."

"You can tell that, can you? Sartren's lessons must be doing you some good. We've lost parse tubes and diapson crystals on both sides of the ship, but more port than starboard. We've put up sails again, but there's only so much solar power you can draw down when you're working with half the number of crystals required to absorb it. So we need to make repairs, and we have to set down to do so. We're searching for land that will allow it."

"How long do we have?"

"Hard to tell. I don't know exactly where we are."

"No," the boy interrupted, his face serious. "How long until we can't stay aloft?"

Rocan started to answer and then stopped himself. "Okay, young Shea. You deserve the truth. You're all grown up; you're one of us now. So, best guess? Maybe a couple more hours. Then it's down to the waters of the Tiderace and a very slow sail until we can get the ship repaired and back under way."

Brecon Elessedil appeared in time to hear these last few words. "How far off course are we?"

Rocan shrugged. "The princess says we've been blown a long way south. Hundreds of miles, maybe. I wish I knew. She seems pretty certain, though."

The Elven prince's features tightened. "We can find out more than that. Come with me. Where is our princess prognosticator?"

Together, the three of them walked to the stern railing, where Ajin d'Amphere was deep in conversation with Dar Leah. Shea still didn't know where they had been during the storm, but he noticed that the two were spending more time together than they had at the start of their voyage.

"Ajin!" Brecon called, bringing them both about. "Rocan tells me we're way off course, but you don't know how far. What if I were to help you with that? Can you describe a few defining features of your city or your homeland?"

"The Elfstones?" Dar asked at once. "Can they measure distance as well as direction?"

Shea wasn't exactly sure what the Blade was talking about, but he was excited the moment he saw Brecon produce the Elfstones and hold them out in his palm. They were a deep cerulean in color and as bright and depthless as a cloudless autumn sky.

When Brecon looked questioningly at Ajin, she began describing geographic features of her homeland and iconic buildings and architectural features of her city. The images were clear and precise, even in Shea's mind. Skaarsland was a place he knew virtually nothing about and had never visited, but a clear picture began to form in his mind of a great city in a wild and formidable land.

"That's enough," Brecon said finally.

He turned to look north, his hand outstretched with the Elfstones gripped firmly in his fist, his eyes closing as he disappeared somewhere inside himself. Shea exchanged an unexpected glance with Rocan, who gave a small shrug of confusion and shook his head. The princess also seemed confused, looking from one face to another. Only Dar Leah was excited, clearly anticipating whatever was supposed to happen.

Long seconds passed before anything did.

Then a brilliant streamer of blue light exploded out of the Elven prince's hand and shot away into the distance, covering what appeared to be miles and miles of open water, an endless expanse that came and went without the horizon yielding anything new. The distance covered, however, never seemed to change the end point of the light, which remained fixed and unmoving—as if the watchers were being drawn toward something rather than standing unmoving on the decks of the *Behemoth*.

Finally, landfall arrived, and a short farther distance brought them to a walled, tower-studded city of white stone so brilliant it seemed to be a reflection of the sun. There it stalled, the image of the city brightening further for a moment, and then everything disappeared.

Brecon Elessedil lowered his arm and looked at Ajin. "Is that your home?"

Ajin nodded in disbelief. "How did you do that?"

"Never mind that," Rocan interrupted. "Can you do it again? Only this time to find us land close by where we can set down?"

"Wait! How far do the Stones tell us we have to go before we reach Skaarsland?" Dar Leah wanted to know.

A flurry of sharp exchanges ensued, everyone trying to talk over everyone else until finally the Elven prince shouted them down. "One question at a time, please!"

Everyone went silent, and he continued. "Dar, we are miles from where we need to go. Rocan, the Elfstones only work when you have a clear image of what it is you are looking for. A general vision of land won't take us anywhere. And Princess, you just witnessed a bit of Elven magic. The Elfstones are a part of my people's legacy from a much older time, and these particular Elfstones allow us to search out what we can't see so that we may find it."

He might have said more, but at just that moment a shout went up from one of the Rovers who was stationed on lookout port side forward. "Land! Land ahead!"

"About time," Rocan muttered, and all of them scattered forward to see for themselves what had been discovered.

Below and off to the starboard side of the airship, still several miles ahead, a broad-based, mountainous island appeared through a screen of mist and low-hanging clouds. Swatches of green forest appeared on the slopes of foothills fronting a trio of towering peaks that were flattened off instead of pointed, their shapes indicating they were volcanic formations. Thin strips of sandy beach glimmered white here and there where the island met the ocean, suggesting a tropical climate and vegetation.

But something was a little off. Shea, standing with the others, stared at the island as they drew steadily nearer, trying to decide what it was. Finally, when they were within a few hundred yards, he figured it out.

There were no birds flying anywhere, high or low. Not a one. Nor was there any sign at all of small animals. Nothing running or crawling on the beaches, nothing darting in and out of the forests, nothing on the trunks or limbs of the trees—nothing anywhere.

"Where is everything?" he said softly.

But no one heard him.

The day had not been a good one up until now, and it was already closing in on midafternoon when the call was given. But spirits rose considerably at the thought of being able to step off their craft and walk on solid ground again, even if for only a short time. Repairs to a lost parse tube and a hole in the side of their vessel did not of themselves demand a lot of time, but certain materials might well be needed, and the complexity of setting diapson crystals to draw down maximum power through the light radian draws was a different matter.

Darcon Leah decided to have a look around. Because Rocan had informed them they were likely to be on the island for a day or so, there was good reason for the Blade to make sure they would be safe from any predators or other dangers. He also saw it as a chance to go off by himself for a bit, to contemplate the troubling nature of his situation.

He had not wanted to come on this voyage in the first place. He had done so because Drisker Arc had requested it, and he had always believed that when the Druid asked something of him, he should try to comply. This was because he greatly respected the other man, but also because he fully understood the importance of what they were attempting. He was not sure he believed it was in any way possible, or that Tindall was anything more than another inventor of a failed machine. But Drisker seemed convinced that the attempt was necessary, and that meant traveling to Skaarsland.

With Ajin.

Which was the real source of the problem.

Traveling anywhere with the Skaar princess presented more than a few challenges. She was a key member of an invasion force that meant to establish a new home in the Four Lands by whatever means necessary. That by itself made her presence troubling. But because of the series of encounters the two of them had undergone, she no longer saw herself as his enemy—even when he made it clear to her that he was somewhat ambivalent about how he saw her. She was only there because he had found her entangled in the wreckage of her aircraft on the slopes of the Dragon's Teeth and had chosen not to let her die. It was Drisker who had decided she might prove useful when they reached Skaarsland, and so had insisted she come with them.

All of which reinforced her belief that she and Dar were destined for each other. So what he saw as a coincidence, she saw as proof of a fate that was drawing them ever closer. And now, in spite of his previous conviction that any further connection between them was doomed, he was beginning to wonder.

Such equivocation was not helped by the frequency with which she was creeping in to sleep with him at night. While all she did was cuddle up against him and all he did was hold himself rigid, he was beginning to find the arrangement pleasant.

Her unexpected appearance, coming up suddenly from behind him now, was startling. "Darcon! Hold up a moment. I'm coming with you."

She rushed to catch him as he turned, and then fell into step beside him. He shook his head in dismay. "Ajin . . ."

"Not glad to see me? I thought you might like some company. Besides, I've nothing to do back there but sit around. Here, I might be of some use. I've done a fair amount of exploring in strange lands."

He shook his head. "I can manage well enough on my own."

"That's a given. But an extra pair of eyes—especially when they're experienced eyes—doesn't hurt."

"I suppose not."

She gave him a long, steady look. "You were thinking about me, weren't you? Just now, before I got here."

It was an inexplicably correct guess, but coming so randomly it caught him completely off guard. *Don't look at her,* he warned himself, already feeling a smile trying to break through his mask of indifference.

"Don't bother trying to deny it," she continued, her confidence galling. "I can feel it in the way you refuse to look at me. You're trying too hard."

*Can she actually read my mind? Shades, what an unsettling possibility.* He forced himself to glance over, working hard to keep his expression neutral. "You can't tell anything just by looking at me."

Her smile was dazzling, and he turned away quickly as she laughed. "Have it your way. You're being stubborn, but don't tell me you don't feel it. The attraction is there, and it's strong. You and I, Darcon Leah, are meant to be together. And sooner or later we will be."

"We're not meant to be together, Princess."

"It didn't feel that way last night. Not a bit of it."

"Nothing happened. You just slept next to me."

"You weren't paying close enough attention if you believe that. There are all sorts of ways to be together, you know. Are you that new to all this? I thought you were partnered with that Druid who was killed."

He wheeled on her angrily. "Don't talk about Zia! Not another word."

She held up her hands defensively and took a step back, her eyes locked on his. The look on her face made him want to apologize for his abruptness, but instead he just shoved the matter aside and turned away.

They started walking again, neither speaking. They were entering a shallow valley that was rugged and heavily forested. Slopes and ravines slowed their progress, and mountains rose not too far in the distance. So far, they had seen no animals or birds, just the thick vegetation. Dar was beginning to wonder if anything at all lived here, or if the island was entirely devoid of life.

Overhead, the sun was inching toward the horizon, on its way to setting. The shadows about them were lengthening, and the whole of the forest they were passing through was growing darker.

"We're in the Nambizi," Ajin said suddenly.

"What?" He stopped and turned to her. "How do you know? Do you recognize this island?"

"Islands. There are nine of them. I know them from the stories told by Skaar explorers. I wasn't sure before, but I am sure now. That's where we are."

Dar glanced around. "What do you know about this particular island? Is it dangerous? What lives here?"

She held up her hands. "Settle down. I don't know much more than what I've just told you. Nine islands, off the coast of Nambia. That's about it. If I ever knew anything else, I've forgotten it. Except for one thing. We are a couple hundred miles south of where we should be."

"A couple *hundred*?"

"Give or take. What difference does it make? The point is, we're way off course."

"What difference?" he muttered, walking over to a fallen tree and seating himself. "Think about it. Shades!"

She came over to sit down beside him. "I know it's disappointing, but at least we're still able to get there. The repairs won't take that long. Will they?"

He shook his head, staring off into the distance.

"So we just need to complete repairs on the airship and keep going. That storm was a freak of nature—much stronger than we usually see in this part of the world. Things should improve once we fly out again."

He nodded glumly. "Maybe." He glanced over. "You're awfully cheerful about all this. Why is that?"

She hunched her shoulders and smiled. "I'm with you. And I get to be with you for a while longer. That makes me happy."

"Ajin . . ."

"Do me a favor, Dar Leah," she interrupted quickly. "Just let me believe what I want. Let me believe you will come around to my way of thinking. Let me believe the stars will align. Between my dismissal from the Skaar army and my father's loss of trust in me, I've had all the disappointments I can take just now. Don't add to them."

He studied her a moment and made a quick assessment. "All right."

"Just until things get a little better."

He nodded again, hesitated, and gave her a smile. "See? I'm being cheerful."

She laughed, and then she leaned in suddenly and kissed him on the lips. "I like you so much better this way."

He surprised himself by kissing her back. When he broke the kiss, she grabbed the front of his tunic and pulled him back, deepening the kiss.

*Well, now you've started something,* he thought. *And you were firmly against this very thing just five minutes ago.* But he allowed the kiss to continue anyway. She was leaning into him now; he could feel her upper body pressing against his as the kiss stretched on. *What in the world is wrong with you?*

Suddenly she stopped and froze. By then his eyes were closed, but he could feel her go stiff and draw back. His eyes snapped open, but she reached up quickly to hold his head still. "Don't move."

*Don't move.* Words you never wanted to hear. "What's wrong?" he asked, keeping his voice low and even.

"Stand up. Slowly. Don't do anything else. Just keep looking at me and follow my lead."

Her brilliant-blue eyes were shadowed by a starkness he found impossible to describe, the light emanating from them so cold and hard-edged that it suggested winter had found a new home. He stood slowly, letting her guide him as he did so, allowing her to use her strength to keep him completely under her control.

"Walk toward me," she whispered. She began backing away from him, pulling him after her. "That's it. One step at a time. Slowly, slowly."

It was all he could do to keep from looking over his shoulder to see what was there, but he managed it. Ajin held on to him firmly as they inched toward a patch of shadows provided by a stand of huge conifers.

"Just a little farther now, just a little . . ."

A massive roar broke the silence—a throated rumble of such power that the ground and the tree limbs all shook from it.

"Run!" she cried, turning at once and racing away.

Dar was quick to follow, sprinting after her as if his life depended on it.

And risking a quick look behind him, he saw that it did.

# 28

WHAT IS THAT THING?

That was Darcon Leah's first thought as he caught a glimpse of the monster thundering toward them. His second was an instant, absolute certainty they were not going to outrun it.

Inexplicably fast for something that size, it was bearing down on them with such speed there was no possibility it wouldn't catch them before they were out of the valley. For while they were forced to struggle across the rutted terrain—gullies and ruts, ridges and undergrowth, fallen trees and mud holes at every step—the beast chasing them simply ran through, over, or across these obstacles as if they didn't matter. And why should they, given that their pursuer was the biggest living creature the Blade had ever seen? Bigger, even, than anything he had ever heard described.

"Faster!" Ajin screamed.

The beast was impossibly huge—at least twenty feet high and almost as wide—a juggernaut with a mottled gray-and-black hide, loose folds layered about the neck and haunches to a thickness of almost a foot. Four short, powerful legs the size of tree stumps propelled a barrel-shaped body that rippled with muscle. Its head was a direct extension of its body, giving it the appearance of a battering ram. Its tiny ears jutted from just behind small, piggish eyes, but it was the eight-foot horn growing out of the forward portion of its immense snout and curving upward like a ship's prow that suggested the amount of damage it could inflict.

If it did not trample them to death first.

It had to weigh an unfathomable amount, yet it carried that weight as if it were negligible. Everything about it was like a nightmare brought to life, but there was no mistaking the reality as it thundered closer, its earth-shaking footfalls smashing everything in its path. Its small, squinting eyes were fixed on them, yet it didn't seem to Dar that those almost minuscule orbs were capable of distinguishing them from any other creature. Whatever it was, it was simply responding to instinct. It saw them as prey or intruders, and in either case they were something to be destroyed.

Then, abruptly, Dar went down, tripped by a hidden root or protrusion of some sort. Ajin turned back to help him, but he was on his feet again before she could reach him, and they were fleeing once more. The beast, however, never slowed, and it was almost on top of them. They were running full-out, but the Blade could tell that it wasn't enough. They were close to the entrance to the valley, but no matter how hard he tried to make himself believe otherwise, they were not going to outrun it.

Having accepted the inevitable, he yelled over to Ajin, "Keep running!"

Then he wheeled back to face the beast, pulling free the Sword of Leah. With both hands gripping what must have seemed like a toothpick to the monster bearing down on him, he gave the battle cry that had served his family for more than a thousand years. "Leah, Leah!"

The juggernaut thundered closer, unimpressed.

He caught a flicker of movement on his right. Ajin was there, sword gripped in both hands, refusing to take the small chance for escape he had offered. He was not surprised. He had never really expected her to abandon him, but he felt a surge of affection upon witnessing the proof of it. She was Ajin d'Amphere, and she would rather die than run.

But then with no more than twenty yards separating them, the charging beast rumbled suddenly to a halt, snorting and grumbling as it swung its massive head from side to side. In the ensuing silence, Dar heard a shrill whistle echo through the trees and off the slopes of the valley. It sounded and died away, then sounded again. The beast nodded twice—as if in response, as if the whistle was meant for it—and then turned away and began eating, pulling up huge tufts of grasses and small plants. Dar could hear the sound of its teeth as it masticated the greenery, paying them no attention at all.

The Blade was still catching his breath when Ajin grabbed his arm and pointed into the trees.

High up in a huge, gnarled old tree, a tiny figure stood silhouetted against the horizon. Garbed in loose-fitting clothes that rippled with a breeze Dar could not feel from where he stood, the figure seemed too small and inadequate to control a creature of this size.

Ajin leaned in, her grip tightening. "It's a boy. It's just a boy."

Dar, whose eyes still could not determine the truth of this, nodded anyway. Ajin's vision was better than his own. He stood with her for long seconds as the boy looked down on them. Then one arm rose and pointed toward the entrance to the valley. When they didn't immediately respond, the arm lifted again in a sharp jerking motion, repeating the previous motion with emphasis. The message was clear. *Go! Leave now! Back the way you came!*

The monster was peacefully chewing the grasses nearby, but it was still too close for comfort.

"Let's get away from here," he whispered, and they began backing away in the direction indicated, eyes on the beast. It showed no interest in them now, continuing to eat. When Dar glanced back to the tree where he had seen the boy watching them, he was gone. In a matter of a few minutes they were passing out of the valley and into less rugged terrain that led back through forested slopes and down to the beach where the *Behemoth* was moored.

Rocan Arneas sat silently as the Blade and the Skaar princess related their wild tale about an impossibly large beast and its boy companion, wondering if perhaps the two had experienced a shared hallucination. A creature the size of the one they were describing simply did not exist. How would it have gotten to this ocean island? How could it sustain itself? How could it be controlled—as this one apparently was—by a mere boy? There were so many absences of logic in their story that he could hardly count them.

"Well, I find it hard to believe," he ventured, when they had finished.

"I told you he would say that," Ajin d'Amphere announced with clear satisfaction the minute the words were out of his mouth.

Dar Leah shrugged. "You can believe us or not, Rocan, but this is what we saw and that is what happened. The question you have to decide, as nominal leader of this expedition, is how much attention are you going to pay to what we've told you?"

The Rover hesitated. "Do you think this beast might decide to come out here? Clearly it feels compelled to protect the valley, but do you think it might attack us?"

The Blade shook his head. "It didn't show any interest in us after the boy gestured for us to go. I think the valley is its home, and he was warning us away. Beyond that, it didn't care about us."

Rocan nodded. "I'll put a watch on the valley entrance, so we'll have some warning if it turns out you are wrong. And let's keep this among the three of us for now. No sense in saying anything to the others. They don't need the distraction. Now tell me the rest of what you found."

While they were doing so, the Rover was thinking that they should move quickly to complete whatever repairs the *Behemoth* required and make a speedy departure. Maybe what he was hearing was an exaggeration. But he believed they had seen something, and anything even remotely close to the size of the beast they had described was to be avoided.

He felt a chill go up his neck as he pictured the creature the two had described ramming into the *Behemoth* and Annabelle in the mistaken belief she was a threat . . .

When their conversation was over, he sent men south along the beach to see what lay in that direction. The beach north ended at a headland so huge that it effectively blocked any passage by land. He didn't think any threat would come by sea, either. The waves surrounding the headland were huge and the possibility of riptides strong. He spent a few minutes cursing their luck in encountering the storm that had forced them so far off course, and then went back to supervising the work being done on their transport.

The remainder of the day passed swiftly, and by nightfall repairs were pretty much complete. The hull was patched up, the damaged parse tubes on the port aft side replaced along with their diapson crystals, a fresh aft mast fashioned from a hardwood trunk cut down not far away and hauled back through the woods by means of ropes and pulleys and strong men to where it could be hoisted at sunrise and set in place. The rest of the damage did not affect their ability to fly, so at that point they would be ready to set out anew.

They sat around a cooking fire afterward, preparing dinner and talking, watching the darkness settle in and the stars come out. Rocan found himself glancing toward the valley time and again, seeking any sign of movement. He had placed a guard beyond the perimeter of the camp and close to the entrance as a precaution, but somehow that didn't reassure him much. The silence beyond the firelight, where the members of the company talked in quiet voices, was deep and unbroken. He walked to the edge of the light several times and looked out into the darkness. He would have thought there would be night sounds of some sort, but he heard nothing.

When the others began rolling up in their blankets and drifting off, he sat up, listening. He knew he would not get much in the way of sleep this night.

Another who could not sleep was Shea Ohmsford. He had overheard everything Rocan, Dar, and Ajin had said about the boy and the creature in the valley. He was intrigued by the idea of another boy here in this remote, faraway place—especially one who could control such a monster. It was hard to explain, but in imagining what his life must be like he felt an immediate connection to this boy. The boy would be doing the best he could with limited resources. He would be self-reliant. He would have learned the survival skills he needed, and would by now feel comfortable living in this wilderness. It didn't feel all that different from his own life—though the skills themselves would not be the same. It felt like they were kindred spirits, even without knowing each other.

Finally, with sleep evading him and curiosity nudging him along, he rose and crept from the camp for the valley entrance.

He didn't have a plan, really. He didn't know what he was going to do once he got that far. Going into the valley seemed foolish, but he hadn't ruled it out entirely. Mostly, he just wanted to get close enough to satisfy his curiosity and maybe learn something about this boy.

He bypassed the guard without effort—one of those very survival skills he had perfected in Varfleet. Once closer to the moonlit gap between the hills and ridgelines sheltering the valley, he slowed to a walk and then finally stopped, staring ahead. His eyesight had adjusted to the darkness, and he found that with the light of moon and stars he could see as well as if it were day. He stood where he was for a time, watching for anything that moved but seeing nothing. He did not feel threatened. He did not feel his safety was at risk.

He took a deep breath. He had come this far. No reason that he couldn't go a little bit farther

So he did.

He climbed the slope leading up to the valley entrance, keeping to the shadows so his profile would not be visible to the guard, edging his way along the side of the entrance where the moon and stars would not reveal him. He was wary as he went, listening to the silence, straining to hear even the smallest sound. But he was not afraid. He could not have said why, but he wasn't. Everything seemed so peaceful that he could not imagine he was in any sort of danger.

Later, when he was back in camp, he would wonder what he had been thinking.

He had always relied on his instincts and they had never let him down, so he was more than a little shocked to suddenly find himself face-to-face with the other boy. How Shea had failed to detect his presence before getting this close to him was a mystery. But it had the effect of startling Shea sufficiently that, for a moment, he was speechless.

The two of them stood facing each other, taking each other's measure. What Shea noticed right away was that the boy was holding a short spear by its haft—in an unthreatening and obviously comfortable position—with the longest, sharpest blade he had ever seen. The boy was very dark-skinned, with his black hair woven into short braids and his face painted in parallel lines of white stripes. He wore loose-fitting robes cut short about the legs and arms and bound at the waist. Rings decorated his fingers and ears, and a necklace formed of black stones that glistened in the starlight hung about his neck.

Shea wore ordinary seaman's garb and looked far less exotic by comparison. A long knife was sheathed at his waist, and he was careful to avoid touching it.

"What's your name?" he asked finally.

The other boy shook his head. Then he replied in a language Shea had never heard.

They stared at each other some more. Finally Shea pointed to himself and said, "Shea."

He repeated the word twice more, and then he pointed to the boy and looked questioningly back at him.

"Borshawk," the boy said finally, touching his chest.

Shea smiled and nodded, then tried to speak to him again. But as neither knew the other's language, communication was limited. Shea tried to think of something more to say, then finally mimicked the creature Dar and Ajin had described, dropping down on all fours and making a sudden rush to one side. Borshawk nodded and pointed into the valley and then back at himself.

Then he gestured back the way Shea had come and made a brushing movement with both hands. Leave, he was saying. When Shea hesitated, he pointed again, and this time his expression was more insistent. Shea held up both hands in a warding gesture and took a step back, nodding. The anger disappeared from the other's face.

Shea started to go, then turned back again. He held out his hand to Borshawk and said, "Friends, you and me."

The other boy stared at him. Again, Shea pointed first to himself and then to Borshawk and said, "Friends." He held out his hand once more.

Borshawk nodded, took the hand in his own, and held on firmly. "Friends," he repeated.

And then he turned back toward the valley and was gone, leaving Shea to ponder what it all might mean.


Shea had returned to his bed and fallen asleep while mulling over his encounter with Borshawk and wondering whom he should tell when the raiders attacked. Early-morning light was still only a faint strip along the eastern horizon, and the Rovers and their passengers were just climbing out of their blankets, yawning and blinking to come awake, when the warning shout went up from Rocan Arneas, who had been up most of the night and was scanning the skies for signs that would indicate what sort of weather was coming.

His warning was followed almost instantly by a flurry of wild cries and piercing shrieks that broke the silence into a million little memories.

Everyone was moving instantly, snatching up their weapons and charging toward the *Behemoth* to form a protective ring. Some few Rovers scrambled aboard to take up positions at the flash rips while the rest backed up against the hull of the great transport, taking advantage of the night shadows that still lingered.

No one had even gotten a close look at the attackers yet, including Rocan, who was the only one among them who had seen the movement in the near darkness and realized what was happening. It was pandemonium for a few minutes as everyone tried to make sense of the flitting shadows overhead that were sweeping down in sudden plunges.

Arrows, darts, and spears flew toward the defenders, most burying themselves in the ground or in the wood hull and decking of the airship, but a few finding their targets. And for the first time, the defenders got a good look at who was coming at them. The raiders numbered no more than a dozen and were dressed in ragged dark garb decorated with brightly colored scarves and bands that reminded the Rovers of their own attire in days now gone. Smallish, almost feature-less men, they were flying huge winged birds that looked to be more a species of bat than anything else. Hunched down aboard their rides, gripping crude leather harnesses with one hand or in some cases simply keeping their seats using the pressure of their knees and legs, they shot arrows or slung missiles with fierce disregard for their own safety.

A couple of the Rovers had gotten to the flash rips by now, which they turned on the raiders. But the attackers seemed able to antici-pate what the Rovers intended before they could act, and their bat creatures angled and swooped with sharp changes of direction, easily avoiding the charges that lanced skyward.

Shea Ohmsford had joined Darcon Leah and Ajin d'Amphere to crouch in the protective shadow of the *Behemoth*'s bow. Efforts to find either Rocan or Brecon Elessedil—or even to identify those close at hand—had failed. Still, he thought he had caught a glimpse of Seelah, leaping through the rigging from mast to mast before swinging down again, seemingly searching for someone. Rocan? He couldn't be sure. He couldn't be sure where *anyone* else was standing by then. He had only his knife with which to defend himself, and did not consider doing anything other than trying to keep safe. He got a few quick but clear glimpses of the attackers, and he was relieved to discover that although their skin was dark, they otherwise looked nothing like Borshawk—either in body or facial structure or in the clothing they wore. They were not decorated with face paint or jewelry. Nor did they seem particularly skilled at their chosen profession, relying mostly on the speed and quickness of their mounts to carry them safely through. It was an odd sort of attack, one that seemed to lack a clear purpose beyond causing havoc among the defenders. The raid-ers appeared to view them more as intruders to be driven from the island than as a source of material possessions.

Whatever they were thinking, they kept pressing their attack, and finally one of the spears found its mark and a Rover collapsed, the shaft driven all the way through him. A cry went up from a handful of the other defenders, and they renewed their efforts with such determination that finally a flash rip charge caught one of the bats in midturn. And with its rider still clinging to it and yelling defiantly, it crashed into the ocean.

The attack appeared to have reached a stalemate when Dar Leah suddenly leapt up, yelling to Ajin as he did, and without another word the two raced away.

It was an impulsive decision, taking Ajin with him instead of Brecon. But the Elven prince was nowhere in sight, and Dar did not feel he could wait any longer to act. If they were to put a stop to this attack, they needed to get up in the air and fight back. The *Behemoth* carried a pair of two-man gunships on the order of modified Sprints. Each required a pilot to fly it and a gunner to employ the flash rip mounted on a swivel at the stern. Ajin would not have been his first choice— maybe not even a choice at all—should almost anyone else have been near enough to summon. But he couldn't operate the Sprint alone, and Ajin was a seasoned fighter with good flying skills. Sometimes, you had to settle for what you could find.

As they clambered up the side of the transport using rope ladders, she shouted, "I'll fly! I don't know enough to use those flash rips."

He shouted back his agreement, and when they reached the closest vessel, they unhooded her, removed the tie-downs, and climbed in. In seconds Ajin had the Sprint powered up and they were lifting off. Dar, crouched at the rear of the little craft, had uncovered the flash rip and charged the diapson crystals, swinging the barrel around toward the fighting. Yelling back and forth at each other to be heard above the wind, they flew directly into the center of the attackers.

This might not have been the best decision, given that they were instantly besieged on all sides by diving bat creatures and their dark riders. Arrows and darts flew past them, a few striking their craft, and Ajin was forced into evasive action. Dar was jerked from side to side by these maneuvers, but he was safely strapped in, so it was only his aim that was thrown off. Ajin took their Sprint straight up to get above the attackers, then swung wide and came down on them at a steady enough descent that Dar was able to strike effectively. Two of the fliers went down, and as if deciding this was enough the rest of them swung away from the camp and flew north, breaking off the attack.

Ajin, impetuous as always, started to follow.

"Ajin, no!" Dar screamed from the rear of their little craft.

"Let's find out where they're going!" she shouted back.

"It doesn't matter!"

"You don't know that. Let's chase them a bit!"

"No!"

She glanced back. "When someone attacks you and then runs away, you go after them! Hang on."

While he struggled to release his restraining straps to stop her forcibly, she powered up the diapson crystals further and closed the distance between themselves and the fleeing raiders. But now they were past the headland that blocked the beaches south and pushing steadily up the north coastline. From their viewpoint in the air, they could see the rugged twists and turns of rocky headlands connected by steep cliffs with waterfalls tumbling down to the Tiderace from heavily forested mountains. There was no sign of life, but a million creatures could hide beneath foliage that thick.

Then they saw the ships, a small fleet of them, moored in a bay just ahead. They were single-mast sloops that clearly lacked the ability to fly. No light sheaths, just ordinary sails; no sign of parse tubes or radian draws. The technology employed by these raiders was primitive, at best. If not for the bat fliers, Ajin and Dar would have had nothing to fear. But as it was, the attackers swung back around now, realizing they were not going to escape without a fight.

"Use the flash rip!" Ajin shouted back at him as she climbed to launch a fresh attack.

And just like that, the power cut out.

It was possible the diapson crystals were drained. Or that one of the many missiles launched by the raiders had damaged the parse tubes. But whatever the case, the thrusters failed and the Sprint began to fall.

*We're dead,* Dar thought at once. *We can't survive a fall from this height.*

But Ajin was still working the controls, trying to reignite the crystals, to draw some last vestige of power from their store. For long seconds, she could find nothing. Then, suddenly, the starboard parse tubes began to hum, and the little craft righted itself.

"Got it!" she shouted gleefully.

But they were still descending, and the power store she had managed to access was not enough for any evasive maneuvers. All she could do was keep the Sprint from falling too fast, the loss of the port crystals forcing them to spiral steadily inland toward the jungle.

The raiders gave chase, but their mounts were not fast enough to keep up, and when they realized their pursuers had lost control of the airship, they pulled up and wheeled slowly back toward their sloops.

Glancing over their shoulders, they watched as the airship plummeted into the heavy foliage below and disappeared.

# 29

KOL'DRE RECEIVED THE SUMMONS FROM COR d'Amphere a week following the battle with the advance force from the Federation. He had been mostly at loose ends since then, trying to keep busy and not grow too impatient with the king's failure to act against Ketter Vause. When Kol had brought him the news of the Reveals and their potentially destructive impact on the Skaar, the king had acted decisively and without deliberating. Admittedly, it was at Kol's urging and using a plan of attack that the Penetrator had designed, but at least he had acted. The battle had not proved a decisive victory for either side, even though the Skaar had lost far fewer soldiers. But Kol was willing to call it a clear win nevertheless and was in full expectation of following up on it swiftly.

Cor d'Amphere, on the other hand, was less ready to plunge back in. The Reveals were still an effective weapon against the Skaar, and they could not depend on the trick of the cloaks to work a second time. Besides, as the king explained to Kol—which in itself was unexpected, given their relationship since Ajin's dismissal—the Federation's opportunities to bring up additional supplies, equipment, and manpower exceeded anything the Skaar could manage this far away from home. It was entirely too risky to enter into a war in which an exchange of lives was the only end result, no matter the provocation.

Kol'Dre almost said something at that point that would have gotten him sent home at once, if not worse. He almost said Ajin would never have let that stop her and would have beaten down the enemy through sheer force of confidence and willpower. But he held back because the king was talking to him again, which meant he had a chance to regain his position within the royal hierarchy and become once more a trusted aide and adviser. If that happened, he would have a better opportunity of not only influencing the king's thinking but also getting back to Ajin.

So he simply deferred to Cor d'Amphere's choice to sit and wait. The king clearly expected an offer of truce from Ketter Vause now that his sneak attack had failed. But whatever else the Prime Minister of the Federation could be called—and the king had already shared a dozen possibilities with Kol'Dre—he could not be called foolish. He had attacked the Skaar because Cor d'Amphere had tried to have him killed and had failed. Yes, Ketter Vause was alive and well, Cor informed him but also humbled. With the passing of every day, his doubts about his future would grow, knowing he must find a way to settle matters with the Skaar before he could return to Arishaig.

Thus, Cor d'Amphere reasoned, Vause would soon ask for a meeting. And a new opportunity to settle this matter without further loss of life might be found.

Kol was not certain the king's reasoning was sound, but he had no voice in the matter. He must sit and wait, biding his time like everyone else while still keeping his scouts and sentries alert and active against another surprise attack. It was unlikely one would come for a while, but sooner or later something would happen to stir things up further.

Once or twice, he thought to go back into the Federation camp, as he had before, just to see if anything more could be discovered. But to do that without permission from the king would undo everything he had accomplished in the interim, and he could not persuade himself to risk it.

Mostly, he thought of Ajin. She would be back in Skaarsland by now, back in their home city, facing trials of her own. She would be confronting her stepmother without Kol there to protect her. It didn't matter what her father thought; it didn't matter that he was king. His new queen was brash and confident of her position. She perceived Ajin as a threat, and she would find a way to remove her.

He thought about this constantly, riddled with guilt that he could do nothing to stop it from happening. It was all well and good to argue there was nothing he *could* do—that he had been ordered to stay behind to serve his king. Ajin was the woman he loved, hopelessly and endlessly. Ajin was his obsession, and his entire adult life had been spent dreaming of the day when she would be his.

Now, he feared, that could never happen. Before, it had seemed at least a faint possibility. Now, not even that was left to him. He told himself he should just go to the king and ask for her hand—even if there were no chance that his plea would be granted. But still he did nothing, and his inability to act ate at him with such a voracious appetite that he was in danger of doing something foolish. Yet his fear of losing all influence over the king persuaded him to continue on his present course of discretion.

But now the king had summoned him and he would have another chance to make his case for being sent back to Skaarsland, where he could be with Ajin. He was practicing what he would say in his head as he walked to the king's tent. The camp had been moved just before the Federation's failed sneak attack and was now situated farther downstream and deeper into the forests that bordered the northern banks. As a further precaution, they had removed the entire fleet save for two small flits, which could be quickly dispatched to summon help if needed. But for the moment, the orders were to hide and wait.

Kol'Dre was through with all of it, though. Today, whatever the king asked of him, he would respond with a clear and unequivocal demand that he be sent home to Ajin.

He reached the tent, announced his presence to the guards, and waited for the summons to enter. It came almost immediately, and he went through the flaps and into the lantern-lit interior where the king stood waiting.

"Kol'Dre," the king greeted him, an unexpected warmth in his voice, his hand outstretched. Kol took it in his and received a small squeeze in response. "You must be bored beyond words."

Kol nodded, wondering what was going on. "I prefer activity to idleness."

The king chuckled. "Who among us doesn't?"

They released hands, and the king beckoned his Penetrator to one of the chairs that sat beside his desk, taking the other for himself. All formality had apparently been abandoned.

"I want to find a way to put this business with the Federation behind me. I know I should attack them and be done with it, which is what Ajin would do if she were here, but I am not as ready as she is to embrace a more . . . impulsive lifestyle. She would jump off a cliff without hesitating, but I would have to think about it. I do miss her, though. She was always the strongest and the bravest of us. Had she not disobeyed me so blatantly, I would have kept her here with me."

He sighed, and Kol waited expectantly. Something was about to happen, he realized.

"I am going to ask a favor of you, and if you agree to provide it, I will grant you a favor in return. Of course, I could simply order you to do what is needed, but that isn't how I believe things should be handled in this situation. I am firmly convinced that nothing will change between the Skaar and the Federation until Ketter Vause is dead. So I want you to employ those formidable skills of yours and kill him."

Kol'Dre nodded slowly. "He will be expecting us to attempt something like that. If the Druid is still keeping watch over the Prime Minister . . ."

The king raised his hand quickly and brushed aside the rest of what Kol intended to say. "The Druid is gone, pursuing Clizia Porse, and there is no indication he will be returning anytime soon. So the Prime Minister is vulnerable once more, and it is up to you to succeed where Clizia failed. Can you do so?"

Kol hesitated. "Probably. But it won't be easy. Ketter Vause will have taken precautions. And if I am caught . . ."

"Yes, I am fully aware of the consequences. But you won't be caught. You've never been caught." He paused. "Would you like to know what the favor is that I will do for you in return?"

*This is a trap,* Kol thought instantly. But he kept his expression neutral. "Of course."

Cor d'Amphere smiled. "I will give you Ajin."

"What do you mean?"

"I will send you back to Ajin, and her hand will be yours."

Of all the things he could have been offered, this was the last one Kol would have guessed. For a moment, he was speechless.

"You do want this, don't you?" the king persisted.

"Of course. She is my closest friend, and we have been constant companions on every expedition since—"

"Just admit it," the king interrupted smoothly. "She is the woman you wish to marry." He smiled. "You must think me totally blind to believe I do not see how you look at her. How protective of her you are. I am her father, Kol'Dre. I see it all. I know what you desire, and I am offering it to you."

"Why would you do this?" Kol asked, abandoning any pretense. "You are the king, and she is your firstborn. I am far beneath her station. I could never be permitted to marry her; she has already made that clear enough."

Cor d'Amphere laughed. "Oh, I know. I know my daughter. She is proud and strong-minded, and she would never let personal relationships interfere with her ambitions. She chooses partners without caring about them and then casts them aside. I hear the rumors. But I have good reason to think it would be different with you. You are already close to her. You have her confidence and her respect. A good beginning to any relationship, in my estimation. If she is given a chance to consider the idea more closely, I think she will choose to marry you in spite of any misgivings. Once, I would never have considered such a thing. You are indeed beneath her in social status and prospects, but you are her equal in many ways. You are clever and intelligent. What you would bring to the relationship is a steadiness, and a voice she would listen to—a voice to help curb her impetuous behavior."

He shook his head. "Besides, I am tired of trying to manage her. I need someone else to take on this burden. She is my favorite child and my only daughter. She will succeed me as ruler of Skaarsland one day, but she never will be queen if she isn't forced to take a more rational approach to life. And I think you are the best chance for making that happen."

"She might see it differently."

"She might. But let's consider how we might get past that. You will kill Ketter Vause and rid me of him once and for all. Then you will return to Skaarsland to tell my daughter that I have chosen you for her husband. If she accepts, explain to her that she will be returned to my favor and to her former position in the army. She will also be openly named my successor and the next ruler of the Skaar nation. She will find that hard to resist. And I am sure you know what this would mean for your own fortune."

Kol caught his breath. The offer was astonishing. It was as if everything he had ever wanted was lying within reach. "I don't know what to say."

"Good. Now hear me out. If Ajin refuses your offer—my offer, essentially—she will be confined to Skaarsland until my return, and for however long it takes her to change her mind. Remind her that I am her king, and whatever I decide is not up for debate."

Kol nodded slowly. "She is stubborn."

"I am stubborn, too. So you must find a way to make her realize that I intend for this to happen and will suffer no refusal. She will have you in spite of her recalcitrant nature, and her life will be the one she has always dreamed of. As will yours."

It was a clever trade-off, and a wickedly enticing bargain. In order for Kol to get what he wanted, he must persuade Ajin it was what she wanted, too. Or at least what she must decide she wanted. How much it would change their relationship, he wasn't sure. But his need for her was impossible to deny.

"I will do what you ask of me," he said quietly.

Cor d'Amphere's smile was slow and appreciative. "Then do so tonight."

• • •

Not much preparation was necessary. Kol could cross the river and come at the Federation camp from behind. He would carry his weapons and little else. He already knew the layout of the camp and the location of the Prime Minister's quarters. He need only vanish long enough to gain entrance and then kill the man as he slept. He had done this dozens of times over the years. His skills as a Penetrator were unequaled, and his reward for succeeding would be the fulfillment of a lifetime's dream. Ajin would be his, and together they would eventually rule Skaarsland and see their new home in the Four Lands firmly established. Cor d'Amphere might even install her as his temporary regent, governing in his place while he returned to his new wife in Skaarsland, where preparations would be made for the migration of their people. Or perhaps he would ask Ajin and himself to arrange the migration while he remained behind . . .

His mind spun with the possibilities, a host of changes looming somewhere not far ahead. Ajin would resist the bargain her father had made for her, but Kol was persuasive, and she knew how he felt about her. She knew, as well, what sort of person he was and what sort of husband he would be. And by marrying him, she, too, could gain what she desired—a return to the army, and eventually the throne itself.

Excitement coursed through him, a rush of exhilaration and hope fueling his determination. That the king should offer him this opportunity was only slightly troubling. Necessity was the mother of invention, and the king would want his troublesome daughter brought under some sort of control before he restored her to favor. So what better way than to wed her to her closest friend and give her the assurance of his blessing and a path to the throne?

His thoughts of the future were jumbled and twisted around his plans for this night, and he knew this wasn't a good thing. He would need his full concentration for the job ahead. Nothing of what the king promised would follow if he was not successful. So he bottled up his thoughts about Ajin and the future and focused on getting through the rest of the day without letting his thoughts drift away again.

He was only partially successful. But he excused his lapses by reminding himself that he would be fully engaged when the time arrived.

He slept for the remainder of the day, rose to eat dinner at night-fall, and was aboard a Skaar flit and winging across the Mermidon ten miles south by the time the sun was setting. He was in no hurry to reach his destination. He had already decided to wait until at least two hours after midnight before going after Ketter Vause. He wanted not only the Prime Minister and his guards but also the bulk of the camp to be asleep when he made his strike. He would be swift, silent, and thorough before retreating the way he had come. By this time tomorrow, he would be looking forward to the return trip to Skaarsland.

And to making Ajin his.

Ketter Vause was finishing up plans for further action against the Skaar, which he would discuss with his commanders on the morrow. He was of two minds about this. On the one hand, it would be incredibly satisfying to attack the invaders again, this time making sure where their camp was situated and how many Skaar were occupying it. On the other hand, a truce would avoid another battle and put everything on hold while he sorted out the best way to come to another arrangement.

What he didn't want was another debacle like the last should he choose to attack, so he needed a plan to prevent this from happening. Nor did he want to lose any advantage he might have gained by stopping the Skaar at the Mermidon, should he choose to offer a truce. Perhaps the Skaar king would reject the truce out of hand, but Vause didn't think so. They knew now that their vaunted ability to vanish could be negated by the Reveals, and the Federation smiths, acting under the supervision of the Dwarves, were hard at work building new machines. If another battle took place, the Skaar would be facing at least a dozen additional Reveals and men newly trained to operate them. With regard to the latter, the Dwarves were at work teaching a select band of Federation soldiers the skills required. It was something of a miracle that the Dwarves hadn't bolted after being thrown into such a deadly battle, but Belladrin had spoken with the survivors at length when the battle was finished and persuaded them to remain.

So with Vause's assurance that he would abide by his agreement to terminate the conscriptions for fifty years, Belladrin had given Battenhyle, Lakodan, and their companions complete autonomy over the work being done on the Reveals. So far, things had gone well, and there had been no complaints.

Vause looked up from his musings to find her watching him. "Do you require something of me?" she asked at once.

He shook his head. "Just appreciating all the help and good advice you've given me."

"Perhaps you should give a little thought to your own situation. You are still the target of a possible assassination attempt, and Drisker Arc is no longer here to watch over you."

Vause made a rude noise and slammed his hand on his desk, his temper slipping. "He never watched over me in the first place! If he had, that witch wouldn't have escaped. I trusted him to protect me, and he couldn't manage it."

"He did stop her from harming you. She would have killed you otherwise."

"That was only half the job! He was supposed to prevent her from *ever* harming me! Now I have to worry about her coming back to try again."

She gave him a sympathetic look. "Whatever else happens, I will do what I can to keep you safe. I intend to sleep in the other room until this matter is concluded. No one will be able to get to you without coming through me."

He was shocked by her offer. To put herself in such danger took a fair bit of courage. "I can't allow it."

"You can't stop it," she replied calmly. "It doesn't appear to me that your guards were all that successful in protecting you. You might have better luck with me. Besides, what does it hurt? Think of how much better it will make me feel, to be of some use to you in this matter. I value you and my position as your personal assistant too highly to allow anything to happen to either. I will sleep on a mat off to one side in the shadows, where I cannot be seen. Because I am a light sleeper, I will hear anyone attempting to enter."

Vause rose, walked around his desk, and took her gently by the shoulders. "If it makes you feel better to sleep close by, I would be most pleased to have you do so. Having you close means a great deal to me."

He realized as he spoke the words that he might have gone too far, that his professing his attraction to her might cause her discomfort—even cause her to leave his service entirely. But she merely smiled and said, "You have done more for me than I could ever have expected, and you will always be my friend."

Releasing his grip on her shoulders with a fond pat, he went back to work on his agenda for tomorrow's meeting.

Kol'Dre waited until well after midnight before attempting his attack on Ketter Vause. He had arrived much earlier, five miles from his destination, concealed his flit in heavy undergrowth, and hiked to less than two hundred yards of the camp perimeter to wait for nightfall. When it was dark enough, he breached the watch lines and crept to within shouting distance of the army. All of this went smoothly enough, and he was not once in any danger of being discovered. He had dozed on and off afterward for the time that remained, his thoughts drifting frequently to Ajin and how she would react to the idea of being married to him.

He did not fool himself. She would fight the idea at first. She might even think it a big mistake. But she was a practical woman, and she would come to understand what was to be gained by choosing to accept her father's terms. She would be worried about her mother and want to see her protected. She would be aware of her own danger if she were to be confined for too long in Skaarsland with her stepmother so close at hand and so eager to see her eliminated. She would know it was best to do the smart, practical thing and accept Kol as her husband.

Then it would be up to him to make sure she never regretted it.

The moon and stars provided a clear indicator of the time he had to complete his work as he started forward, choosing to make directly for the Prime Minister's tent. He had invoked his ability to disappear, but he stayed in the shadows anyway, avoiding any contact with passersby. There were few to be found at this hour, and most were concentrating on getting to wherever they were going and paying scant attention to anything around them.

So the path to Ketter Vause was completed easily enough.

But at the main entry, he hesitated, debating. It would be quicker to cut an opening into the rear of the tent and enter that way. Cutting through canvas was noisy, though, and a rent in the fabric might be noticed before he could finish with Vause. So he used a different approach and distracted the two sentries by drawing them away from the tent opening just long enough to allow him to slip in behind them before they moved back at their stations.

Once inside, he took out his killing blade, the one he favored most—long and thin and razor-sharp—and waited for his eyes to adjust. An aide dozed in his seat at a desk to one side, paperwork scattered before him. Behind him, tent flaps concealed another chamber, likely an anteroom to the Prime Minister's bedchamber. There would be guards there, as well. Remaining invisible—a necessary precaution—he eased the flaps aside for a quick peek and spied a pair of guards standing watch on the far side of the room. They were standing close together in front of the flaps leading to the Prime Minister's sleeping chamber, whispering to each other. Good enough. He slipped swiftly inside and started forward.

And almost immediately he stopped. A figure lay stretched out on a sleeping mat to one side, barely visible in the shadows. In his eagerness to reach Vause, he had almost missed this. A closer look revealed a young woman. As he started moving again, she lifted her head and looked directly at him. He froze, knowing her reaction was automatic, her response to a sense of something being there. But she couldn't possibly see him; no one could. He had shifted into his Skaar invisibility mode. So he waited while she stared in his direction a moment longer and then lay down again, closing her eyes and returning to sleep.

A trickle of sweat ran down Kol'Dre's back. That had been much too close. For a moment, he could have sworn the woman had seen him, but the guards right in front of him had done nothing to suggest he was visible. He gave it another few moments, and then slipped behind them and through the curtains to the bedchamber beyond.

Ketter Vause lay asleep on the far side of the chamber, snoring softly. Kol'Dre dropped his Skaar concealment and crossed slowly to the bedside. This was all too easy. He took a long minute to study the sleeping man, his hands at his sides, his blade held ready. Already, he was picturing himself with Ajin, the two of them bound together by marriage and life.

He leaned forward carefully, placed his hand over the sleeping man's mouth, and drove his blade through the other's ear and into his brain. The Prime Minister's eyes flew open in shock, but his momentary struggles were weak, and in seconds his eyes dimmed and his body went limp.

Kol'Dre kept his hand firmly in place over the other's mouth a few seconds longer, just to be sure, then released him and stepped back. A quick look around revealed the chamber was still empty. No one had been alerted; no one had come to investigate.

He exhaled slowly. The matter was over and done with. He wiped his blade on the bedcovers and sheathed it. Ketter Vause was no more.

He was halfway back across the room and on his way to making an escape when a fist slammed into his chest. He grunted in response, the unexpected blow telling him everything he needed to know. Already he could feel the cold steel of a knife driven deep between his ribs and into his heart. He could feel the blade moving about inside him almost experimentally. Kol fought to break free, but his ability to function was gone. It was as if, in a moment's time, his strength had been sapped, and now his life was draining away with it.

*Ajin,* he thought in despair.

He would never see her again.

A figure materialized in front of him, and the shock of seeing the face of the young woman who had been sleeping in the anteroom was even greater than the realization that he was dying.

"Cor d'Amphere thanks you greatly for your service and bids me tell you it is no longer required," whispered Belladrin Rish.

They were the last words he heard before he died.

# 30

TEN DAYS EARLIER, WHEN CLIZIA PORSE WALKED past Tavo Kaynin and beyond the firelight of the Federation camp, she did so knowing she would not be immediately followed. She left Drisker and his young companions in such a state of disarray that it would take them some time to pull themselves together before they came after her. But she was not foolish enough to think they would not attempt pursuit, so once in the shadows she picked up her pace.

She was caught off guard at finding Drisker hiding in the Prime Minister's quarters, but she had turned the tables on him quickly and then faced down the brother before his sister could come to his aid. Still conflicted, that boy, but he had given her a clear path to an escape, which was all she needed. Her plans for doing away with Ketter Vause were shattered, along with any reasonable chance of getting to him later on. From now on, they would be looking after him closely, and extra precautions would certainly be taken to catch her out.

She had been lucky this time, and she knew it. But she could not count on that sort of luck again. Next time, it might turn out to be an entirely different story.

She hiked back to where she had left her small airship, glancing back every now and then to cast with her magic for any sign of pursuit.

But she detected nothing and decided that even though the Druid and his companions would eventually give chase, they wouldn't do so immediately. What they would do was give her time enough to get clear and begin to feel safe, and then pounce on her like hungry cats.

Because they wouldn't have any trouble tracking her, would they? Not with that bit of magic Drisker had flung into her cloak at the end of her confrontation with Tavo to make sure he could find her later.

*Well, let him come.*

She was rethinking all of it—everything she had planned and done, everything she had thought to accomplish or still might. Having done so, she decided she *wanted* him to find her. Drisker would never give up searching for her, so the obvious solution was to give him a clear path and then dispatch him. What was a little more problematic was how she might accomplish this. She might be a match for the wishsong siblings, but Drisker was another matter entirely. He was her equal in magic, her verbal disparagement of him notwithstanding. So however she chose to eliminate him had better be something he wouldn't see coming.

She reached her airship, climbed aboard, powered up, and flew off. She did not bother with attempting to return to the Skaar encampment. That part of her life was over. Cor d'Amphere would want nothing to do with her now that she had failed him once again. All her previous successes would count for naught, her elimination of Gerrendren Elessedil, an act that had left the Elves leaderless and uncertain of what to do about it, and her successful efforts to help his daughter and the advance force gain access to Paranor and the Druids, which had resulted in the almost complete annihilation of the latter.

No, the Skaar king would only remember that she had failed him here, and that the Prime Minister of the Federation was still alive.

Yet she did not feel defeated. She had not lost all hope of rebuilding the Druid order with herself as Ard Rhys. All that was still within reach, once she rid herself of Drisker Arc. When that was accomplished, she could find a way to deal with the Elves and the Federation and all the others who might try to oppose her. Whatever happened after that, she was more than a match for it.

But how was she to eliminate Drisker?

She experienced a momentary regret at having to leave the last of her possessions behind, but none of them mattered enough to risk a return. She had the Stiehl and the scrye orb, and those were the treasures that mattered. She had the use of her skills and experience, which were more than sufficient to protect her. The rest could easily be replaced. What she needed to settle on at this point was a destination.

And a trap from which Drisker Arc could not escape.

As she flew west—a direction she chose at random—she mulled over her choices. She knew the history of the Druid order better than anyone, having read the Druid Histories and attendant papers over the years. She had studied them thoroughly, and within their pages were the answers to anything she might want to know. She just needed to pull out the one solution that was foolproof.

And quickly enough, she knew what it was.

She continued flying west, the night providing her with a comforting shroud of darkness, the stars and moon bright and glowing overhead, the earth below a vague tapestry on which the lines of her future would soon be drawn. She needed to sleep, but she wanted to fly a bit farther first—out over the sweep of the Callahorn before turning south onto the Tirfing. She wanted to think about her plan. She needed to consider it from all possible angles and measure its chances for success.

She did so undisturbed, and by the time she landed her craft and curled up in a blanket to sleep, she was reassured that she had found what she was looking for.

The following morning, she set out once more. By this time, she had changed her mind about the marker. When she reached her destination, she would remove it from her clothing and grind it into dust. Then there would be nothing left for Drisker to rely on. She need not worry about him after that—at least, not until she was ready for him. When the time was right, she would simply summon him using the scrye orb.

When she had crossed the Tirfing and passed into the Westland, she continued on, flying north of the Pykon and the Wilderun toward the towering wall of the Rock Spur. She was following the westernmost branch of the Mermidon by now, using it as a guide to bring her to what she sought.

The sky ahead darkened with the storm clouds that perpetually hung across the Rock Spur, a clear warning of the dangers that could be found in those mountains. Already, it was beginning to rain, and once it started it would get much worse. She increased her speed, worried not about getting wet but about winds that could hurtle her small craft into the cliffs and leave her corpse dangling in the rocks for the vultures.

And then she caught sight of it.

There, on the left bank of the Mermidon, high in the mountains where it had been built centuries ago by Elves as a fortress to stand against all invaders, was Cleeg Hold. A vast outer wall closed about the keep and outbuildings, rising more than two hundred feet, jutting out of the rocks like a cancer that nature had been unable to stop from growing, there in the bleakness and dark. It was abandoned now and had been for hundreds of years. But neither time nor weather had done much to reduce it, and the structure looked as formidable as ever. Although only vermin and carrion birds made their home within, Cleeg hold was exactly right for what Clizia Porse had planned.

*This time, Drisker Arc, you won't find it so easy to walk away from the snare I shall set for you.*

Once she had landed, the first thing she did was to remove the tracker attached to her robes, grind it into dust, and cast the remnants into the Mermidon.

The next morning, Clizia began the work of constructing her trap at a narrow juncture of a maze of corridors on the northern side of the keep where the light was weakest, the stone slippery and treacherous, and the winds a relentless howling that filled the air with sounds that defied description. She found a room suitable for habitation on the other side of Cleeg Hold, one with a bed that was still in reasonably good shape and a fireplace that worked perfectly. She used bedding from her aircraft to make herself a hidden nest, and hunkered down to work.

The plan she had devised required a room or closed space where the Druid could be trapped. It required that she negate his unusually strong magic with sufficient stone and iron and earth that it would take considerable time to break free—time she wouldn't allow him. Finally, it would require a potion so powerful that no one had used it in centuries and thought it lost forever.

But nothing was lost to her, she mused. She had not spent her time at Paranor in idle speculation. Reading the Druid Histories had revealed many things, and few besides herself had bothered to delve deep enough to uncover as much as she had. The potion she required was described in detail, one of those forbidden forms of magic that had been used only once before a prohibition had been placed on it.

*The potion was called liquid night, and it was used on Grianne Ohmsford to send her into the Forbidding.*

Her age-twisted mouth managed a self-congratulatory smile. It would be the final piece of the trap she was setting for Drisker Arc, and when she had mixed it she would summon the Druid, and he would come for her and seal his own fate.

But first she must construct a confinement that would hold Drisker prisoner while the liquid did its work. The magic she would employ for this was called a triagenel. It, too, had been used only once before, and once again was meant to be used against Grianne Ohmsford. A renegade Druid named Shadea a'Ru, who had sought to replace the unpopular Grianne as Ard Rhys, had constructed it with the help of other Druid renegades wedded to her cause, but her efforts had failed. A triagenel required three magic wielders to construct it and consisted of webbing that would collapse about the intended victim the moment he or she entered the space over which it was hung. Once it was dropped, the victim was immobilized until freed.

Which would not be necessary in Drisker's case, since the liquid night was sending him to a place from which he would never be able to return.

Clizia did not have other magic wielders to aid her in this effort, however, which meant her construction of the triagenel would necessarily be flawed. It might not work exactly as she intended, but because she was the equal of any three other magic wielders, a close approximation would do. If she didn't get it entirely right, it wouldn't matter. All she wanted was to prevent Drisker from leaving the space in which she was intending to trap him for a few precious minutes.

It took her four days to complete the triagenel. When it was done, she rested a day, and on the sixth day she began work using a mix of ingredients and magic to brew the liquid night.

Drisker and his young companions had begun their search for Clizia almost immediately. Leaving the Federation camp and an irate Ketter Vause behind, they had retrieved their aircraft and set out. Using the tracker the Druid had embedded in her robes, they flew west in the direction it indicated Clizia was fleeing, but it soon became apparent that, after being up almost the entire night, they needed to stop and rest. So they landed their modified two-man on the eastern border of the Streleheim, rolled into their bedrolls, and slept into early morning. When they woke, they ate breakfast in silence—the Kaynin siblings intimidated by the Druid's dour expression and his seeming reluctance even to look at them—before setting off once more.

On the third day of their pursuit, the tracking device ceased to function. It happened all at once, its signal a clear guide one minute and gone entirely the next.

Drisker gave a deep sigh. "She found it," he told the other two, and they did not need to ask what he was referring to.

So now he was faced with an impossible dilemma. Did they continue their hunt and hope to locate her by chance? Or did they return to Paranor and keep watch on the scrye waters, hoping an ill-advised usage of her magic would give her away? Neither was a very appealing choice. But they had no other way of finding her without the help of the Blue Elfstones, and those were in the possession of Brecon Elessedil and on their way to Skaarsland.

By now, the Druid and his young companions were flying into the Westland north of the Wilderun, and it was a long trip back to

Paranor, which in turn was a long way from where Clizia appeared to be going. Perhaps it was better to continue on, stopping every now and then to ask if she had been seen. They had been so close to capturing her that Drisker hated the idea of turning around, even with the odds against them. So for the moment, he just kept flying west.

Midday came and went, although they stopped for a quick meal. By nightfall, they had seen no sign of Clizia, and it had been more than eight hours since the tracker had failed. At that point, Drisker gave Tarsha and Tavo a choice about what they would do. They could either keep searching or turn back. His own mind was made up—he would continue, even if they decided not to. The siblings heard him out, and both immediately announced they would stay with him.

The next six days were more of the same, endless hours of flying in all directions, searching the sky and landscape for something that would reveal her whereabouts, speculating as they went on what she might do next. Tavo believed she would circle back and try to finish what she had started with Ketter Vause. Tarsha was worried that Clizia might have decided to go back to Emberen to try to get her hands on Drisker's books of magic.

But Drisker had a strong suspicion by now that his continued efforts to thwart Clizia's plans had reached the point where ridding herself of him had become a priority. So long as he lived, she would face the same constant harassment. So long as he lived, there would always be a chance that he would catch up to her again.

On the seventh day, just after dawn—when they were deep into the Westland and close to the Rock Spur—the scrye orb Drisker carried still grew bright and warm against his body. When he pulled it out, there was Clizia Porse.

"Would you like to put an end to this?" she asked.

He could barely hear her above the sound of the wind rushing past him. They were back aboard their aircraft, flying along the edge of the mountains south.

"What do you want, Clizia?"

Her smile was hard and bitter. "You dead. The same thing you want for me. I'm sick of running from you. Let's settle this."

"Where are you?"

She told him the name of the abandoned fortress and its approximate location. She could have stopped with the name. He knew exactly where Cleeg Hold could be found. This was a trap, almost certainly. But it was also their best chance of getting their hands on her and settling matters, once and for all.

"I'm coming," he told her and shoved the orb back in his robes.

He glanced over at his two companions. Tarsha shook her head. "She's planning something."

He nodded and smiled. "Then we must plan something, as well."

Clizia Porse returned her scrye orb to her pocket. Everything was in place. She had constructed the triagenel and brewed a tiny batch of liquid night. She had conceived of a plan for luring Drisker to where she would spring her trap. Earlier, even before dawn, she had dampened the fire in her sleeping chamber so nothing of her presence on the leeward side of the keep could be detected, packed up her Sprint, and left it out in the open so that it could easily be seen. She retraced for the twentieth time the steps she would take to lead Drisker to the fate she intended for him and moved to the edge of the landing space where her Sprint was anchored. Standing back in the shadows where she could watch an aircraft approach from any of three directions without being seen, she put her back to a rock wall and waited.

The wait was short. Drisker must not have been far away because his aircraft appeared within the hour. Winging down from out of a darkened sky that foretold a storm's approach, the modified two-man slowed as it neared and settled next to hers. He might have chosen another landing site, but the rugged slopes of the mountain allowed for nothing better, and there was no reason to hide his coming since she already knew what he intended.

She waited until the three passengers had disembarked and were looking around before launching an attack. She struck out in a wide sweep, so that it would appear she was seeking to bring down all three, but it was the brother she was after. They were prepared, their defenses up, their magic in place against any attack, and so they were able to protect themselves. But Tavo took the brunt of her dark magic's force and was thrown backward against the side of the airship. She paused just long enough to watch Tarsha run to her brother, leaving Drisker to respond. The Druid did so instantly, a streak of blue fire hammering into the wall against which she crouched. Even though it was well off the mark, she cried out as if it hurt before fleeing back inside the fortress.

From there, she retreated at a steady pace, hearing Drisker's movements as he charged after her, determined this time to bring her to bay, his reckless insistence easy to read from the urgency of his footsteps. Three times they exchanged blows, their magic lancing through the gloom and careering off the fortress walls, sending shards of rock flying. But mostly they ran, Clizia able to keep her distance from him even though she was slower because Drisker could not risk running headlong into an attack that might be waiting around each blind corner.

They called back and forth to each other, Clizia taunting him for his ineffectiveness, Drisker replying with promises of what would happen if she did not give herself over to him. As if she had summoned him here for that, she thought darkly. As if she would ever concede to him under any circumstances.

Finally she arrived at the location of the trap she had constructed and paused beneath the almost completed triagenel. Hands shaking with expectation and eagerness, she connected the last of the strands of the triagenel netting that would be activated instantly by his body heat, then retreated a few steps to put herself out of reach. Hearing his approach, she dropped to one knee, bent her head, and began gasping as if fighting for breath. As if run to ground. As if finished.

Drisker appeared, huge and black in his robes, slowing as he neared the trap. "Clizia," he hissed on seeing her. "Surrender to me."

He could see her dilapidated condition and noted the rents and stains in her damaged robes. She waited, unmoving.

"Clizia!" he shouted.

"Never!" she screamed back at him.

He started for her, his hands alive with the blue light of his Druid magic. "It's over, Clizia."

"For you, it is," she whispered, reaching into her robes, her fingers closing about the vial of liquid night.

She tossed the vial at his feet so that it shattered against the stone flooring. Instantly, a dark mist rose, enveloping the Druid. Throwing herself clear as he started to thrash, she let his body heat trigger the triagenel, which fell down on top of him. Two quick bursts of magic—one behind him and one just ahead—instantly formed walls that sealed him into the killing zone. Scrambling quickly backward, she watched Drisker Arc and the entire chamber vanish.

After, she climbed back to her feet and stood watching for long minutes. Nothing reappeared. Drisker was gone. This time, unlike the last, there would be no returning from where she had sent him.

Because the passageway ahead was blocked, she continued on the way she had been going, intent on returning to her airship and leaving this place.

But first she would settle the fates of the Kaynin siblings.

# 31

W HEN CLIZIA EMERGED FROM THE DEPTHS OF Cleeg Hold, the storm was in full force. The skies were filled with black, roiling clouds lanced through with streaks of lightning and exploding with thunder, and rain was sheeting down. In the mountains of Rock Spur, the brilliance of the lightning and the booming of the thunder reflected and reverberated off rock walls and through gaps in the peaks with a ferocity reminiscent of battles fought with magic in earlier times, among the Faerie people. She hunched back into the shadows from which she had emerged as fat rain pellets hammered down, shrinking from the wet sting of their blows against her skin.

She was on the opposite side of the passageway into which she had fled with Drisker, and she stood now on an elevated stone ledge overlooking the landing site and the two aircraft that occupied it. Streamers of mist rolled over the clearing and the two figures crouched within their haze. Tarsha had lifted Tavo into a sitting position so that he was leaning against her. Her head was bent close to his, invisible within the cowl of her cloak, but Clizia could tell that she was speaking to him. Neither was aware of her presence. Both were helpless before her.

She gave a moment's thought to convincing them to join her.

Drisker was gone, and he wasn't coming back. Would they not be better off being with her, partnering to form a new Druid order? What else was left to them? If they rebuffed her, where would they go? No other opportunity awaited them—no chance for a better life than what she could offer. If they could put aside the lies they had been told about her and their own fears, she could do so much for them. She could teach them how to use their magic and how . . .

She broke off her musing. No. She knew it was too late for any of that. She knew they would never trust her again, and the girl would never forgive what she had done to Drisker Arc.

Better to end it here.

She stepped from hiding and took a quick look around. A worn and ancient stone stairway led down from her ledge to the landing space the siblings now occupied. She would have easy access to them. *Strike quickly, before they are aware of me, and I will gain the upper hand.*

She summoned magic to her fingertips and formed a fiery ball. Measuring the distance required, she sent it spiraling into Tarsha Kaynin with all the force she could muster. The girl raised her head, perhaps sensing the danger she was in, just as the magic struck her such a terrible blow that it lifted her right off her feet and threw her twenty feet away and over the cliffside, where she dropped from view.

Clizia walked to the edge of her rocky platform and looked down at Tavo Kaynin, who was staring at her in shock. He turned away, searching for his sister. With strength that came from some deep reserve Clizia did not know it was possible to possess, he climbed to his feet and, with a scream that cut through the sounds of the storm surrounding them, activated the wishsong. The force of his magic slammed into her, throwing her backward to sprawl in a shallow skein of cold dampness. She lay stunned a moment, and then shifted out of herself to form a dozen images that rose to face him.

Tavo never hesitated. One by one, he began to destroy them, vaporizing them with the wishsong. But by the time four were gone, Clizia, still untouched, had formed a diamond-hard disk of razor-sharp magic. From a kneeling position, she cast it. He might have been able to block it, had he been thinking clearly. But caught up in his rage and grief, he failed to do so. The spinning blade nearly cut him in half, and he collapsed in a heap, screaming with pain.

Clizia took her time leaving her platform and walking down to where he writhed. The way was slick with rain, and it would not do to slip and fall at this point. When she was standing over him, the boy in such pain he was not even aware of her, she bent down and said, "You should have stayed with me, Tavo."

Then she took the Stiehl from her robes and cut his throat.

When his struggles had ceased, she walked over to the edge of the cliff and peered down at the jumble of rocks, undergrowth, and the rushing waters of the Mermidon several hundred feet below. There was no sign of Tarsha Kaynin. She searched for the girl carefully, making sure she wasn't mistaken, needing to know that Tarsha had gone to join her brother in the netherworld.

When she was satisfied there was nothing to be found, she straightened and turned back toward the black-damp walls of Cleeg Hold. One more thing remained to be done, and then she could leave.

She walked back inside and went down the tunnel to the place where she had trapped and banished Drisker. The hallway was empty, the magic she had employed gone—the triagenel, the liquid night, the walls at either end of the space in which the Druid had been enclosed, all of it gone.

Because a banishing to the Forbidding required an exchange, what had come out to replace Drisker Arc would be waiting.

She found it lurking back in the shadows on the other side of the killing ground, deep in the darkness of the tunnel. She called softly to it. "Come out, my pet. Come meet your mistress. Come, now."

Her words were soft and cajoling, pitched to encourage obedience. Movement caused the shadows to shiver, and a figure began to take shape. The nightmare that appeared in response to the magic she had used to dispose of Drisker drifted into view on all fours, its loathsome face grinning in a mass of razor-sharp teeth.

"There you are," she purred, the pleasure in her voice evident. And the Jachyra gave a long, high-pitched whine in acknowledgment.

**Terry Brooks** is the *New York Times* bestselling author of more than thirty books, including the Dark Legacy of Shannara adventures *Wards of Faerie* and *Bloodfire Quest*; the Legends of Shannara novels *Bearers of the Black Staff* and *The Measure of the Magic*; the Genesis of Shannara trilogy: *Armageddon's Children*, *The Elves of Cintra* and *The Gypsy Morph*; and *The Sword of Shannara*. The author was a practising attorney for many years but now writes full time. He lives with his wife, Judine, in the Pacific Northwest.

Find out more about Terry Brooks and other Orbit authors by registering for the free monthly newsletter at www.orbitbooks.net.

ABOUT THE TYPE

This book was set in Minion, a 1990 Adobe Originals typeface by Robert Slimbach (b. 1956). Minion is inspired by classical, old-style typefaces of the late Renaissance, a period of elegant, beautiful, and highly readable type designs. Created primarily for text setting, Minion combines the aesthetic and functional qualities that make text type highly readable with the versatility of digital technology.

ARTWORK BY R